WILD

GOOSE

MOON

WILD

GOOSE

MOON

A Story of Love, Death, God, Sex and 1968

by
Ben Shepperd

iUniverse, Inc.
New York   Bloomington

Copyright © 2009 by Ben Shepperd

Cover Art by Jane Cornish Smith

All rights reserved. No part of this book may be used or reproduced by any means, graphic, electronic, or mechanical, including photocopying, recording, taping or by any information storage retrieval system without the written permission of the publisher except in the case of brief quotations embodied in critical articles and reviews.

This is a work of fiction. All of the characters, names, incidents, organizations, and dialogue in this novel are either the products of the author's imagination or are used fictitiously.

iUniverse books may be ordered through booksellers or by contacting:

iUniverse
1663 Liberty Drive
Bloomington, IN 47403
www.iuniverse.com
1-800-Authors (1-800-288-4677)

Because of the dynamic nature of the Internet, any Web addresses or links contained in this book may have changed since publication and may no longer be valid. The views expressed in this work are solely those of the author and do not necessarily reflect the views of the publisher, and the publisher hereby disclaims any responsibility for them.

ISBN: 978-0-595-52359-7 (sc)
ISBN: 978-0-595-51932-3 (dj)
ISBN: 978-0-595-62417-1 (ebook)

Printed in the United States of America

iUniverse rev. date: 05/07/2010

To my beloved wife Beth

Acknowledgments

Appreciation for contributions to this project must begin and end with my wonderful wife Beth. Her unwavering support as coach and cheerleader and her invaluable assistance as editor and adviser inspired and motivated me all the way along the journey of this work.

Additionally, friends who submitted to interviews for source material or who provided information include Eddie Leibman, Dr. Chester Studdard and Taylor Armstrong. While some of their input wound up "on the cutting room floor", their support and enthusiasm for the project was greatly appreciated. Also helpful were Whitney Shepperd, Joe Guy, Suzanne Griffin, June Johnson, Blake McCartney, Sharon Penfold and Susan Hasten, among the early readers who endured the original "really long" version and still provided encouragement. Thanks also go to Karen Marshall, who was "present at the creation" with encouragement plus word processing support.

The beautiful cover art created by Dallas artist Jane Cornish Smith put in place the last piece of the puzzle in bringing this work to fruition. From my extraneous mumblings and scribbles Jane brought forth a unique and striking cover of which I am so proud.

A special nod and attribution go to Philip Wuntch, as film critic first of the *SMU Campus* newspaper and later at the *Dallas Morning News*. Several of the movie references in the novel came from my recollections of his entertaining and insightful reviews.

And props go to the folks at iUniverse for their stewardship of my submission. Phil Whitmarsh, my first contact and since moved on, and Cara Neal, my last in the publishing process, were always helpful, encouraging and thoroughly knowledgeable, and the editorial evaluation crew was spot on with its recommendations.

My thanks to all of you.

Finally, this work started its long path on a legal pad at a table in Southern Methodist University's Bridwell Library. The cool, quiet peace of Bridwell's reading rooms has since been among my favorite settings for work on the novel. Also at SMU, research in the aforementioned newspapers in Fondren Library's archives was a great help.

But it all comes back to my muse, Beth. Oh, and did I mention her patience?

Ben Shepperd

Prologue

Late April 1968

A powerful storm passed south of Dallas early in the afternoon, and, although it brought no rain to the dry grounds of Wesleyan Southern University, it left the air thick and steamy. Walking up campus toward Old Wesley Hall, Tom Windham pushed his shirt up under his armpits to absorb the perspiration. He realized it was past time to get out of his jeans and into shorts, but his rural roots continued to dictate that wearing shorts to class was inappropriate. He walked carefully on the sidewalk, which had been tilted at odd angles by the roots of the aging live oaks that dated to WSU's birth. He glanced up occasionally at the dark green covering provided by the thick foliage of the trees, appreciating its relief from the heat and the glare of the afternoon. In an open segment of the sidewalk between two live oaks he slowed and looked up into the hazy blue sky connecting the distant roar that he heard with an airplane far above him. But as he followed its contrail, he stumped his toe on a sidewalk outcropping and caught himself. Straddling a crack in the sidewalk, he hesitated and looked down at his Weejuns to check for scuffing before continuing toward Old Wesley.

Upon entering the basement doors Tom was met by the familiar musty aroma and hospital green walls of the campus's original building. He ducked into Room B110 and found his regular desk by the basement windows, which were high off the floor. As his second semester at "Wazoo" sloughed languidly toward summer vacation, Tom turned toward the windows and started to plan his weekend. After calling roll his professor, a small, skittish woman with thin, cropped yellowing grey hair, picked up her lecture on random testing where she had left off Wednesday.

Sociology being his last class this Friday afternoon, he daydreamed out the window of his options and requirements of the weekend. He ticked through his mental listing of old and new movies on around town, discarding most, considering a second or third or more viewing of others. Staring down the barrel of Finals, he thought briefly about starting to review "Man and His World", Biology Principles of Accounting, or Sociology - his non-History courses with which he feared he might have trouble maintaining a "B". He grinned knowingly at the slim chance of his actually studying any of those, though, until Dead Week.

Catching references to margins of error, statistical sampling and test populations, his attention drifted in and out of the lecture. Finally, the 2:50 bell rang and the class cleared. Tom walked back to his dorm room at McCartney Hall working up a smelly sweat from the steamy humidity. Giving in to an acquired weakness and in spite of the heat, he called Wildcat Pizza to deliver a small "Kitchen Sink". He timed its delivery for the completion of the shower he knew he needed.

Soon after his return from the bathroom, a rap on the door signaled the pizza's arrival. He opened the hot box on his desk, sat by the open window looking down on the Men's Quad, and flipped on KLIF to the Lemon Pipers flailing away at "Green Tambourine". As he ate and observed the activity below, Tom recalled a recent evening when he had sat in the dark at the same window contemplating God, the universe, and his position relative to each. As he smiled wryly at the relative ease with which he now contemplated nothing more serious than his ability to single-mouthedly devour a ten-inch pizza, a news bulletin interrupted "Heard It Through the Grapevine". His immediate fear was bad war news or an assassination. The tentativeness in the newscaster's voice betrayed the freshness of the copy:

"We have an unconfirmed report that a Global Airlines jet has crashed near Butler Mills. The plane apparently departed from Houston's Hobby Airport on a flight to ... Dallas' Love Field. We have no information ..."

Tom sat motionless in his underwear in his chair next to the breezeless open window. He chewed in slow motion for a few seconds and then swallowed with difficulty as the phone rang.

"... as to the number of passengers or crew aboard. Nor is there any word of survivors. We will be back ..."

On the third ring Tom rose slowly from his chair. His legs were weak, and a hard cold fear was spreading through his chest and into his throat.

"... to you with further information as soon as it is available."

He picked up the receiver. When first he tried to speak, he choked. Coughing and clearing his throat, he said, "Hello."

"Tom?" The voice was familiar and full of concern.

"Yes," he answered numbly.

"This is Ward Brannigan, Tom. Have you been listening to the radio?"

"Yes."

There was a momentary silence. Finally, Ward said, "Tom, maybe you should come out here."

Chapter 1

Four Months Earlier

As he focused on her across Fat City's smoke-and-dust-fogged dance floor, Tom's mouth opened slightly and he stood frozen in place. Multi-colored streamers hung from the *Happy New Year* sign swagged above the bandstand, and with Rhode Kill beating out an ear-splitting "Judy in Disguise", bobbing and swaying high school- and college-age dancers pulsated in a blur of motion between them. Clair Kennerly was deep in conversation with a girlfriend. As Tom stared, though, he saw her demeanor change. She had been smiling, talking, and observing the action on the dance floor. First he saw her focus shift - drawing in as if in thought. Then she closed her eyes slowly. And as slowly as she had closed them, she opened them while turning her head toward the opposite wall - toward Tom. She looked directly at him, the smile gone from her face. There was no surprise or excitement in her eyes, but there was an unmasked depth to them. She did not return his stare so much as she drew him into hers. For his part Tom made no pretense of trying to deny the sincerity and the power in her eyes, which he remembered as crystalline blue. The awkwardness that he had felt - first in being caught staring at her and then in being so helplessly ensnared by her gaze - fell away. He allowed himself the unadulterated moment of honesty and of reverie that their eye contact afforded them. Neither moved. Neither smiled. Tom finally nodded slightly. She did not respond.

Suddenly, the club's strobe lights were activated in time with the band's hard beat. As the light jerked their faces from black to ghostly white, they continued to stare. Finally, Tom saw Clair's mouth frozen open for a split second, and he knew she had said his name. At that moment he heard her molasses-rich drawl in his mind as she said, "Tom", and somehow made two silken syllables of it - her voice rising slightly on the second, suggesting both acknowledgment and anticipation. The connection across the room was so pure, so complete that he could clearly call up the fragrance of her hair, her skin - as if his face were again buried in the softness of her neck. The memory of the joy and pleasure lasted for but a moment before being pushed aside by the pain of their last time together.

The delicate squeeze on his arm caused him to jerk and to spill several drops from the drink he held. His awareness widened to the music, to the dancers and to Meredith suddenly at his side.

With her dark brown hair flipped up at the shoulder, and with eyes of ebony, chiseled cheekbones, and a smooth, olive complexion, she looked older than her nineteen years and more exotic than she was. With his hazel green eyes looking out from a ruddy, rounded face along with his fine, thick, gel-dried short brown hair, Tom looked less than his almost twenty years and every bit as immature as he was.

"What are you staring at?" Meredith asked with a smile.

Tom whipped his head toward her and with unguarded guilt, replied, "No one ... uh, nothing. Here ... here's your drink."

"Thanks," she said, turning to scan the crowd on the dance floor into which Tom had been looking. Tom, too, turned toward the opposite wall in search of the eyes that had captured him moments earlier. He saw only Clair's thick blonde hair tumbling to the middle of her back. Scanning down, he saw her familiar full hips and her legs - made for the miniskirt she wore. As she faced the wall with head bowed, her friend stood beside her wearing a concerned expression.

Tom turned to Meredith and said, "I've got to –"

The slap on the back almost took his air, and he wheeled quickly. Rob Carver greeted him with a toothy grin and a beer-breathed, "Howdy!"

Glenda Bell, a short plump blonde, was wrapped around Rob. She yelled, "Hey, Tom," above the din.

Tom smiled and turned to Meredith, whose expression asked, 'who are these people?' "Rob! Glenda!" Tom yelled. "Meet Meredith Blaine. She's from here in Springfield - a freshman at The College. Meredith, this is Rob Carver and Glenda Bell - old 'Noofer' High buddies of mine. Rob goes to The University and Glenda's at Baylor."

As greetings were exchanged, the two couples moved in closer and ducked their heads together to hear one another. "So Tom," Rob began, "how are you liking W-S-U so far? Little more happening there than at Stover County J-C, huh?"

Tom recognized the beginning of the standard and obligatory "Joe College" conversation. He had heard variations on it countless times the prior semester, his first at Wesleyan Southern University since transferring there after a year at his county junior college. Rob dominated the ensuing discussion as he related fraternity party hijinks, beer bus trips to football games, uninhibited antics of inebriated co-eds, and pledge class hazings. Tom could tell that Glenda, who had attended Stover with him for a year, was still taken with Rob's line just as she had been off and on through high school. He understood that Glenda shared with him the subtle, unspoken inferiority of having attended a junior college her first year. Tom observed Meredith's reaction to Rob's braggadocio as being amused but detached. Hers was a different college experience at Springfield College, a small private liberal arts school.

Finally Rob came to the inevitable 'who did you pledge?' question.

"I'm a G-D –" Tom caught his language in deference to Meredith. "I'm an independent." As soon as the words left his lips, he knew he owed Rob, who had given away a barely perceptible face drop, and Glenda an explanation. "Yeah, I've been coming home to see Meredith every two or three weeks, so I didn't see any reason to pledge. Hey, miss the parties on the weekends," he offered with his best world-wise grin, "and be around all week for the work. Uhn-uhn. Not for me." His explanation seemed sufficient for all present, but as insurance he added, "Anyway, I may go through Rush next fall."

The conversation continued along its natural course with Glenda and Meredith comparing notes about Glenda's high school friends at Springfield and Meredith's at Baylor, and Rob and Tom also discussed their old chums. Tom was the only 1966 New Fredonia graduate at

WSU, but a number of their classmates were now at The University of Texas. The only obvious omission from Rob's spiel was that of his sexual exploits. With Rob's burly blond good looks and considering his formidable record of conquests in high school, Tom knew that the fifteen thousand-plus co-eds at UT had not gone unserviced. But he realized that the omission was in deference to Glenda and that it resulted from Rob's desire to add one more exploit to his list - to start the New Year with a bang.

As they conversed, Tom raised his head periodically and searched without success the opposite wall, the dance floor, and the trickle of departing revelers at the door. Tom was experiencing the gnawing anxiety of an opportunity lost. He stopped short of excusing himself to go look for her because he knew he had no acceptable reason. The risky choice of doing it without an acceptable reason was in combat with the status quo. But as the foursome's conversation wound down, Tom glanced up and saw Clair as she was turning her gaze away from him and moving toward the exit. For that split second, with her standing in the glow of the track lights, Tom saw the high, wide cheekbones, the tapering chin, the small, sensuous mouth… and the eyes. He saw the pain and the passion in them, and the tide turned against the status quo.

Interrupting, he blurted out, "Meredith," before switching to a hurried nonchalance. "Y'all, excuse me. I just saw someone I need to talk to. I'll be right back."

As Meredith said, "Okay, but –" he plunged into the crowd and moved toward the exit. He gave a glance to the short line at the door having their hands stamped for re-entry and bypassed it. He walked outside only to be greeted by a wintry blast through his sweat-dampened shirt. The wind cut through the East Texas night as if it had come straight and unimpeded from Canada. Crossing his arms and shrinking his shoulders in against the cold, he looked quickly left and right. Across the parking lot he saw her as she closed the passenger door of a white Camaro. He watched as she leaned back into the headrest before dropping her face forward into her hands. The Camaro pulled away, and Clair did not see Tom as he stood still in the dark until the taillights were out of sight. His chin began to quiver and his legs and shoulders to shake. He told himself it was from the cold.

Chapter 2

Tom awoke in the semi-darkness of the Boys Room, which he had shared with his brother Mark. The room was large and square; comprising the south rear wing of the house, it had windows on three sides. The light from a backyard gas lamp reflected dully off the varnished knotty pine paneling. The two corner built-in bookcases were still filled mostly with Mark's books - *Hardy Boys, Tom Swift, Chip Hilton, Lee's Lieutenants, Battles and Leaders of the Civil War*, a smattering of novels on Africa including Robert Ruark's, and on the top shelf: Hemingway, Salinger, Dostoevsky. In Tom's absence his parents had turned half of the Boys Room into a TV room. Two easy chairs rose near the foot of his bed and stared at a large boxy color television against the opposite wall.

He tiptoed across the cold floor to the Boys Bathroom and showered. Toweling off he could hear the voices of his parents in the breakfast room. The aroma of bacon frying made him rush through shaving and dressing. He donned his standard attire of light blue button-down oxford cloth shirt, blue jeans, navy wool socks, and well-worn oxblood Weejuns. Entering the breakfast room he was greeted warmly by his parents, both of whom were smoking Winstons and drinking black coffee. He looked first at his mother's eyes. The relief that he felt at seeing that she had not been crying was instantaneous and liberating. 'Maybe this whole day will go well,' he thought.

Nancy Windham was the source of Tom's rounded features and dark brown hair as well as his short, stocky frame. Her brown eyes were sad, the eyelids perpetually puffy. Her genuine smile, which she gave Tom this morning, was warm and pretty. Her skin was pale and lined, and, along with the grey streaks that had appeared when she quit dyeing her shoulder-length hair, it made her look her fifty years.

Johnny Windham was a small, handsome man of fifty-three. He wore his salt-and-pepper hair wet and combed straight back from his prominent widow's peak as he had from boyhood when the style was called a "Rat". His finely honed facial features and pinkish complexion along with small sparkling blue eyes suggested he would age well.

"'Morning, Son," Johnny said. "Where'd you and Meredith end up last night?"

"After Paco's we went to Fat City. What about y'all?"

Tom circled the breakfast table and kissed his mother on the forehead as his dad gave him a brief discourse on the winners, the losers, the surprises, and the food at the '84' party they had attended. Nancy filled in the gaps in Johnny's anecdotes, laughed along with him, and even mentioned a couple of personal highlights of the evening. Tom was encouraged and happy to feel the pleasantness at the table.

After breakfast Johnny dressed to go feed the cattle at the farm and to do some light fix-up work on the barn. He promised to be back in time for a late lunch and the start of the Cotton Bowl game between Texas A&M and Alabama. Tom and his mother did not begrudge him this time on his holiday. They understood Johnny's passion for his sixty-acre showplace five miles south of town, and they honored his unalienable right to piddle around out there to his heart's content. Tom had been pleased to learn over the holidays that his mother had started going to the farm with him again.

Tom sat with his mother looking out the glass doors into the expansive backyard dominated by towering, barren pecan trees. "Tom," she began gently and without shifting her view from the backyard, "it's a new year." She smiled as he looked toward her and nodded. "And I want it to be a better year for all of us."

"I do, too, Mom."

"I'm so sorry I'm the way I am," she said, the smile vanishing. "Sometimes I just can't control myself. I'm sorry."

"It's okay, Mom. I know you can't help it." Tom lied. It was not okay, and he most often thought that she could help it - that anyone should be able to control oneself better than she did. But though he had heard the same promises and resolutions before, only to have them disappear amid shrieking, tearful fits of anger, grief, and self-pity, directed principally at his father, Tom was willing every time - every morning after - to hope that a real change had occurred. This time was no different. He hated feeling the resentment toward her that her out-of-control behavior caused. He loved his mother, and he knew she loved him, but he felt at his core that she had ruined his father's life, his brother's life and her own life. Tom, at nineteen, held out a subconscious determination that she would not ruin his.

Tom also loved his father - and liked him as a friend. But Johnny had introduced two complications to his mother's problems for which Tom resented him and which resulted in a diminution of Tom's respect for his father. Johnny had been drinking for a number of years. It mellowed him out, eased his mind, and made him sleepy. He could handle it. Alcohol had become a problem for the Windhams when two years earlier Nancy had started drinking heavily. It took her deeper into her depressed moods, and it took her farther out of control of her screaming fits. And it had taken her occasionally into hand-to-hand combat with Johnny. When he stood aside and considered it, especially now with the opportunity afforded him by the one-hundred-twenty-mile distance separating Dallas from New Fredonia and by multi-week stints at WSU, he felt that one of the reasons she had taken to the bottle was what he considered a perverse notion that becoming his father's drinking partner would bring the two of them closer together. And Tom saw her need to get closer to Johnny as an offshoot of the second complication that his father had introduced - also about two years earlier. It was the specter of infidelity. Nancy's evidence was circumstantial, and the only time the subject was raised in front of Tom was when she was at her most out-of-control and, therefore, least able to rationally substantiate her charges. Johnny, of course, denied them. Though Tom and his father never spoke of it directly, both knew that the specter had resulted in a lessening of Tom's respect for his father. And Tom understood that while Johnny had almost numbed himself to Nancy's darkest moments, it was this loss of position with his son that hurt him most deeply. Because they loved each other, though, and because each still desperately wanted the other's friendship, there was an unspoken understanding that they would try to spend time together and do things together whenever possible.

Tom had always been more like his father in temperament - quiet, optimistic, a seeker after peace, romance and life's small joys. Tom felt that these attributes were natural to his father. In himself, though, he left open the possibility that they were at least partially acquired as a defense - and sometimes a hiding place - from the strife that his mother was able at any moment to visit upon their family life. But also remembered were Mark's independence, obstinance and willingness to go at it with his mother day after day. The lesson was not lost on Tom that Mark's chronic state of conflict with his mother must have been a significant - if not the most significant - source of his destruction.

In the mood in which he found his mother this morning, though, Tom could not resist the opportunity to plant more seeds of optimism and hope. "Mom, with me off at school now - and eventually getting out, getting a job, getting married - well, you know, it's just going to be you and Dad here most of the time. And in a few years I'll give you some grandkids to run around underfoot. Mom, you'll be a great grandmother -"

"Great-grandmother?" she cracked quickly. "Well, I've got to be a grandmother first," she laughed, and added, "and I'm in no hurry for that."

Tom took joy from this reminder of his mother's humor, and he allowed himself to hope.

Chapter 3

Early January

Through Tom's childhood in the 1950's, New Fredonia had been a hometown of backyards without fences, of streets without curbing, and of children and dogs roaming safe and free. National and international events, movements, and modes of thought had wafted over and around the town, but had changed it little – for bad or for good. Driving toward downtown 'Noofer', as its name had been conflated over the years, Tom reveled in the familiar veneer of his early years.

    After crossing the railroad track that separated the town's residential west side from its business east, he drove onto the softly jostling brick streets of New Fredonia's busy square, the outer lining of which was the economic heart of the city. The town's two Georgian-columned banks faced one another across the square, as did the display windows of its dry goods stores. The square and its feeder streets also housed variety stores, fountained pharmacies, jewelers, barbershops, cleaners, attorneys, and a panoply of other services. The grocer on the square took daily telephone orders and made deliveries to the housewives of New Fredonia in time for their maids to prepare the day's main meal - lunch - for many of the households of the town. At the center of all this was the aging three-story late-Victorian style Stover County Courthouse. But truly anchoring the square and on its west side was the Swan Cafe. There over steaming cups of black coffee and amid layered clouds of cigarette smoke at any time between nine and eleven of a weekday morning and between two and four after lunch, the men who owned and operated New Fredonia could be found - commemorating its past, discussing its present, and deciding its future. Through his youth when Tom had had occasion to seek out his father during the workday, he had learned early that the greater likelihood was to find him at the Swan than at his title office.

Driving a block past the square to the town's red light, Tom turned north to accomplish the ritual of "circling the Dairy Queen". Since obtaining his license, and in compliance with traditions dating well back into the early Fifties and passed down from high school class to class, circling the DQ to see and be seen was as natural an act for Tom as slipping on stretched-out Weejuns. And even now, as a collegian, a visit to New Fredonia still entailed several daily circuits to see if any of his friends from high school - either those who had gone on to college and were out on Semester Break like himself or those who had stayed in town and were either at Stover County J.C. or had gone straight to work - were there to visit with or to wave at. There was also the current batch of high school kids to impress by the simple act of being what he was - a college man home for the holidays circling the DQ. For them Tom reserved a droopy-eyed neck-jerk of a nod, which something inside him told him was "cool".

After two weeks of mostly waves and nods and of few visits with any of the small circle of close friends from his high school days, Tom took a loop of the DQ before returning to the square to meet his father at the Swan following Johnny's Saturday half-day's work. As Tom's holiday began to wind down, father and son had shared signals to do something together. Over lunch they planned a Sunday outing for Tom's last weekend.

* * *

Tom Windham loved auto racing - especially sports car and Grand Prix racing. His love of the sport was rooted in his introduction as a fifteen-year-old high school sophomore to the world of sports cars. That introduction had been provided by Jonathan Meador, a junior, in his 1961 Austin-Healey Sprite. With headlights placed in fixed raised pods on the hood instead of on the fenders, that original model was lovingly nicknamed the "Bug-eyed Sprite". Unremittingly impractical, irrepressibly cute, and British-quaint, the tiny car provided the coziest of cockpits, the bumpiest of rides, and a tight cornering capability that suggested the steering wheel was on a one-to-one ratio with the front wheels. It had toggle switches, a pushbutton starter, sliding detachable Plexiglas side windows, and an exhaust note as it wound out that Tom found irresistible.

A mutual friend had brought Tom and Jonathan together, and while they had found a number of other common grounds for friendship, both understood that the Sprite had opened to Tom a new interest area to which he was inexplicably, but undeniably, drawn. The progression from there to an appreciation of other sports cars and then to the magazines that road-tested them and ultimately to the racing of them was also quite natural. While Jonathan had an aptitude for and an interest in the inner workings of the cars themselves, Tom's interest grew to include the human drama of this elemental sport as well as the color and aesthetic appeal of the events. Not the least bit mechanically minded, Tom avoided the technical side of the sport. From a standpoint of appreciating human achievement, the fact that the Lotus 49's engine was an integral load-bearing part of the chassis off which the car's rear suspension was hung was fascinating to him. The mechanics of how that was accomplished, however, Tom found boring – and incomprehensible.

An additional source of Tom's infatuation with racing was his 1965 reading and re-reading of *All But My Life*, Ken Purdy's biography of Stirling Moss. The book's irreverent views of life, racing, and racers touched a cord in Tom. And Purdy achieved a few moments in the book where he conveyed to Tom the beauty and the drama of auto racing - especially Grand Prix racing - in a way that hooked Tom then and forever.

Aware of Tom's lack of mechanical aptitude or interest, his parents had been little concerned that he would pursue a career as a professional racing driver; therefore, with that threat removed they felt no reluctance in encouraging his observer's interest in racing. His father had taken Tom and Jonathan to the Polar Prix at Green Valley outside of Fort Worth three years earlier. The speed, the color, the sounds, and even the smells had filled Tom with an unquenchable and enduring love of the sport. It also showed him the high of "being there" - as opposed to getting words and pictures sometime later. And it was his parents' indulgence along with the luck of having a cousin in the military stationed in Paris that had landed Tom at the Twenty-Four Hours of Le Mans - the mother church of endurance sports car races - in the summer of 1965. Also, during his first semester at WSU Tom had flown to Mexico City to see Jimmy Clark, his Formula One racing hero, win his twenty-fourth Grand Prix in a wire-to-wire runaway. But, while East Texas offered no such exotic racing fare, Tom did know where he could experience the excitement of automotive competition, the nose-burning smells of rubber and fuel, and the ear-splitting sound of high-revving racing engines.

Thus it was that Tom offered an unusual suggestion when his father had asked if they could do something together on the weekend. Sunday afternoon found them motoring through the dormant rolling meadowlands south of Springfield toward the White Chapel drag strip. Though drag racing occupied the bottom rung in Tom's racing caste system, he had admitted to himself that the color, the sound, the crowds, and, occasionally, the feel of the real thing - though not the overall excitement - was there.

For his father "the event *with Tom*" was much more important than "the event". Though he could not help but have picked up some information about racing and racers over the prior four years, he preferred to be a *tabula rasa* in outings with his son - willing to draw out of Tom and be imprinted by those things about the sport that Tom found most interesting or noteworthy. Therefore, a drag was as good as a regional was as good as a national was as good as a Grand Prix for the elder Windham's purposes. He purely enjoyed being with his son and giving him his head to talk about anything that interested him. It never became too obscure or esoteric for him, as long as it was important to Tom. Approaching the entrance to the track, his father asked excitedly, "So, what are we going to see today?"

"A lot of color, a lot of tire smoke, and a *lot* of noise. Believe me," Tom emphasized, "you'll be able to *see* the noise. This may not be my kind of racing, but it ought to be a lot of fun to watch."

And it was. And between the cover-their-ears screams of the racing machines as they wound out, father and son found time to swap stories, often automobile-related, but from different worlds. Johnny told Tom how during his high school days he and his friends would tear down and rebuild the motors of their Model T's every Saturday morning. Tom related racing tales, and he got Johnny to elaborate on other stories from his father's youth. The afternoon was one of laughter and peanuts, ear-splitting roars and Dr. Peppers, racing oil fumes and sunshine. Common ground was fought for and won.

* * *

"Tom, your face is as red as a lobster!" his mother exclaimed as Tom and Johnny, back from the drags, entered the breakfast room with the early winter twilight closing in on the backyard.

"Or at least half of it is!" Aunt Nela added as she noted the effect of their having sat in the south stands for most of the afternoon. The women looked at Johnny for similar signs, but his year-round devotion to farm and yard work gave him perpetual color.

"I guess I'll just have to stand out in the yard facing the house all afternoon tomorrow to even it up," Tom replied, reflexively waving his way through the wreaths of cigarette smoke generated by an afternoon of smoking, coffee-drinking, and gossiping. For Nancy and Nela this daily visit, rotating between their respective breakfast rooms three blocks apart, provided - outside of their children - the highlights of their lives. Since neither dared smoke in public and either would have died of embarrassment if they thought anyone in town knew - though everyone in town did, but knew not to say - they confined their smoking to one another's houses and to trips out of town.

These sisters-in-law, by virtue of Nela's marriage to Nancy's older brother Bowman Carter, were closer than blood kin, and Tom loved his Aunt Nela for a number of reasons. It mattered a great deal to him that she was always unselfish and caring to a fault, and he knew she was always on his side. But more than that, her presence in his house or his mother's at her house had a sedative effect on Nancy. Tom never knew whether or how much Aunt Nela knew about his mother's problems, but he did know that she found relief from them in Nela's company. Thus he always greeted her presence, at a minimum, with relief and appreciation. The sincere affection she demonstrated toward him was a bonus.

As Johnny excused himself to change clothes before making a late run to feed the cattle, Tom accepted his mother's invitation to join them - even though he knew his presence would shut down the flow of information and innuendo as it had when he used to join them as a child after school. "You can go ahead and talk if you'd like. Please don't stop on my account," he teased.

"What do you mean?" his mother asked.

"Oh, I just know you're going to cut out all the juicy stuff as soon as I sit down."

"Why, Tom," Nela protested. "You make us sound like a couple of old gossips."

"No, no. I think you're both still very young!"

"Aghhh, well," his mother scoffed, while holding back a smile. "I am shocked to think that you would –"

"We just like to talk things over. Enjoy each other's company," Nela said in her hoarse, tobacco-scratched voice. "You have certainly never heard us say anything about anyone –"

"Howdy, ladies and gent," Bowman Carter boomed as he entered. Pink-faced, balding, and rotund, Bowman's appearance made Tom remember thinking as a child - having seen the effect on a Saturday morning cartoon show - that if his uncle stuffed his thumb in his mouth and blew, he would inflate like a balloon and sail away. Bowman worked for his parents at their truck stop/cafe/car wash north of town on U.S. 199 where the management had successfully kept their collective fingers crossed through the Fifties and Sixties against the threat of a north-south interstate running through East Texas up from Houston. Overshadowed in business by Tom's domineering grandparents, Bowman had spent his life finding vent for his creativity in hobbies and in supporting civic causes. The latter was now concentrated on his perennial chairmanship of *Harvest*, Stover County's autumnal fair.

While Bowman had assumed most of the day-to-day managerial duties at the truck stop as his parents battled their way through their seventies and their reluctant slide into semi-retirement, Nela worked the café's cash register on a part-time basis. Her basic sweetness was of such renown up and down 199 that drivers were known to time their stops specifically to reach New Fredonia during her shifts.

Nancy asked the obligatory, "How are Mother and Daddy?"

Lowering his head, Bowman replied, "Unchanged ... and unrepentant." Turning to Tom, he asked, "What are you still doing here?"

"What do you mean?" Tom replied defensively.

"Why aren't you back in school? The kids have been back now nigh onto a week."

"Why, he's a college man now," Nela stated. "He had his finals before Christmas, and he's off till next week."

"Well, then why aren't you working?" Bowman bellowed irascibly.

Fearing a reference to his uninspired stint clerking at the truck stop one summer during high school, Tom replied, "I didn't have time to work during the holidays."

"Sure you did," Bowman continued.

"Leave the boy alone and let him enjoy his Break," Nancy said half-seriously.

"Yes, it's a new year," Nela added. "Let him enjoy himself."

Picking up the thread from his wife, Bowman asked, "Well then, tell us your New Year's resolutions, college man."

Glad to change the subject, Tom thought for only a second and replied, "I resolve to quit being a teenager in February. I've been one almost all the way through the Sixties. I've been one for over a third of my life –"

"Well, that's kind of an automatic," Bowman said. "Anything else?"

"Let's see. I guess this is the year I'm going to have to pick a major."

"So, what's it between?"

"It's down to Business and History."

"History?" Bowman snorted. "Sounds good. Stick with it. I'm going to need a new assistant manager in about two or three years." As Bowman was waved off by Nancy and Nela, he winked at Tom while asking, "What about you, light o' my life? What do you resolve to do in '68?"

Nela squared her jaw and answered, "I plan to be a better Christian."

"How much better can you get?" Bowman asked.

"Aghhh." She again patted the air at him. "And I'm going to try to be a better wife and mother."

"Noble aspirations," he adjudged. "Boring ... but noble."

"What about you, Uncle Bowman?" Tom asked.

"Well, like Marie Antoinette said, 'I plan to keep my head when all those about me are losing theirs'."

As Johnny walked through in his khaki work clothes and Wellington boots, Bowman stopped him saying, "Whoa. You can't leave without giving us your New Year's resolutions."

Johnny smiled and quickly replied, "Oh, I guess I resolve to fill up 1968, and when it's full, head on into 1969." When he said it, Tom looked at his mother while the room was looking at Johnny. Her smile gave Tom hope that in her open, sober moments she still loved his father.

"You want to go out and help me feed those blamed cows, Son?"

"Sure," Tom replied, glad to leave the nicotine den for the fresh, crisp air out in the country.

On the way to the farm their conversation had recapped another disastrous season of Texas Longhorn football. After feeding the small herd of white-faced Herefords, though, their homebound talk, framed by the violet hues of twilight, turned to politics.

"Who do you think the Republicans are going to run?" Tom asked.

"Well, if they want any chance of beating Johnson, it'll have to be Nixon. Rockefeller'd be just as bad as Johnson."

"But would you vote for Rockefeller over Johnson?"

"I wouldn't vote for Johnson if my life depended on it. I remember when ol' Landslide Lyndon stole the '48 race from Coke Stevenson. No, Son," Johnny said. He looked straight ahead, squinted and sharpened his focus before continuing, "I'd have to vote for Rockefeller. I'm a good Texas Democrat, like most folks around here, but I've voted Republican in the presidential races ever since the first time I voted against Roosevelt right on up through Goldwater. My only regret is that Eisenhower had to retire after two terms."

"Yeah, I liked Kennedy," Tom said, knowing such blasphemy in front of his father had become safe only since November 22, 1963, "even after Dr. Lee gave that unpaid political announcement of a sermon against him the Sunday before the election, but there's been something about him and L-B-J as Presidents. I never felt *safe* with them in the White House like I did when Ike was. Maybe it's just because I know more about the world. But first there was the Cuban Missile Crisis, and now there's Vietnam."

"Well, maybe Nixon can help you feel safe again," Johnny offered. "I just know we have to get Johnson out of there. If it hadn't been for this war, he would have given everything to the 'niggers' by now."

"How do you feel about The War now, Dad?" Tom asked with requisite care.

"Same way I always did. We've got to take a stand, and stop those Commies somewhere."

"But do you think we can really win it?"

"I know we could if Johnson'd just turn it over to the generals. Quit listening to all the 'weak sisters' up there."

Tom took a breath and said, "Well, Dad, you know, if he doesn't - if it's still going on come the summer of '70 – I'll be there. I guess –"

"No," Johnny retorted reflexively, as if correcting a flawed perception. Then focusing far out in the distant night he added, "Well ... " but his voice trailed off.

After a silence as they drove through the dark end of twilight, Tom noticed a red beacon flash on in the sky before them. He decided to test his father on one of their favorite inside jokes from his childhood, and he asked, "What's that light over there?"

"New tower."

"What's the light for?"

"To identify the tower."

"What's the tower for?"

"To hold up the light."

Tom gave his dad a warm smile, and Johnny returned a wink before adding, "I miss you around here, Son."

Chapter 4

Mid-January

The late morning sun followed Tom as he left East Texas behind on his return to Dallas, WSU and his spring semester. He and his Pontiac Le Mans rolled smoothly along Interstate 20, the scenery made monotonous by winter's scythe. His prevailing emotion during the ride back to WSU was one of relief. During the four-week Christmas holiday-semester break he had been subjected to only two of his mother's all-nighters. One had been the predictable - even traditional - post-Christmas bout with the blues. At half past one of a late December night after several temporary truces when his mother had locked herself in her bathroom to reload, he had given up and had told his father that he was going to his cousin Chet's. It was Johnny's custom on such nights to go to bed during these truces. Being an optimist he hoped that each such moratorium would mark the end of the night's hostilities and that Nancy would come out and go to bed. But having learned from experience, his other reason for getting in bed was to get whatever rest he could against the coming of the next barrage. As Tom meekly told him he was going to Chet's, his father propped himself on one elbow nodding sadly.

Chet Carter was Tom's 33-year-old once-divorced first cousin, the only child of Bowman and Nela. He had been a good friend to Mark, and now, in spite of their age difference, he and Tom had become close. Chet taught History at Stover County Junior College. A lifelong resident, he was viewed by the locals as unconventional, a free spirit. His ready smile, generosity and willingness to help with any worthwhile cause made his independence palatable to the community. He lived across an alley from his parents in a cottage they owned. Other than their close geographic proximity, the Carters' willingness not to interfere in Chet's life was legend in New Fredonia.

Chet had genuine love and sympathy for Nancy Windham, and it rarely took the form of pity. He had known her when she was younger and happier, and he had kept alive the imprint of who she was and how enjoyable she had been to be with in those days of his childhood. Through Tom's late teen years he was often drawn to the peace and good humor of his cousin's cottage. Chet's understanding of Nancy and his love for her helped temper Tom's spells of resentment toward her. Chet was a night person who survived well on five hours rest. Tom had arrived at his house a number of times after midnight and had never found him asleep. His rollout couch, though lumpy and uncomfortable, was always available to Tom. His arrival at a quarter of two that early morning had been no different. Chet asked for no explanation or details and offered only bed coverings, milk and Oreos. Tom stayed over and returned home the next morning to a shaky peace.

Then a couple of nights before Tom's return to school and perhaps, he feared, in anticipation of it, Nancy spent an evening drinking heavily. Tom had been in Springfield with Meredith all afternoon and had brought her back to New Fredonia in the evening for a come-and-go open house given by Glenda Bell's parents honoring the college students of New Fredonia before they returned to school for the spring semester. Tom and Meredith had left the party around nine to return to his house. As they had on several occasions, they occupied the dark, spacious living room on the other end of the house from the Boys Room, where his parents were watching television. But soon after they started listening to music and necking, Tom picked up the familiar sounds of his mother's anger - though muffled by the distance and the music. He went cold from habit and from fear of embarrassment in front of Meredith when he realized that it was "one of those nights". After twenty minutes of uninspired, distracted kissing, he excused himself on the pretense of going to the bathroom. He found her in his bedroom drunk, and Johnny was past trying to control her. After running through his standard litany of reasoning with her, pleading for her at least to be quiet until he and Meredith left, and finally threatening his disaffection from her, he determined the situation to be hopeless. He returned to the living room, told Meredith he was feeling ill, and hustled her out of the house. As he drove her in near silence to Springfield, she gave no indication of having heard anything. Tom was grateful – either for her not having heard or for her pretense.

Returning the twenty miles north from Springfield in the clear, chilled January night, the purr of the heater and the soft green dash lights seemed to insulate Tom both from the cold outside and from the dread of what awaited him at home. Since receiving his license at fifteen and getting a used Ford Falcon a short time later, cars had provided Tom with two basic necessities - escape and sanctuary. By himself or with friends or girlfriends he had covered every street and alley in New Fredonia and most of the roads in Stover County. When things got rough at home and he was not directly involved, he was gone. He credited Chet, the Falcon, and later the Le Mans with keeping him sane until he could make his break to WSU. So as he approached the southern outskirts of town, he determined to make one more loop of the Dairy Queen before deciding whether to go home or to go to Chet's. Finally, he drove slowly past his darkened house. He ventured in and went straight to bed though not to sleep. That night his prayer that all would remain quiet was answered.

But now as he approached Dallas and caught sight of its skyline, his thoughts went once more to Clair. At the Bell's party Jennie Corrigan, a friend of Tom's, and Clair's closest friend, had cornered him away from Meredith and had urged him to call Clair. She quickly made the point that Clair still wanted to be his friend. Meredith had joined them before they could talk further. So the day before he left, he had called Clair's house. Her grandmother had answered, but he did not identify himself and he did not think she had recognized him. It had been so long. Tom was almost relieved. It was as if he had fulfilled the minimum requirements of an obligation to his heart. But there was a nagging sadness - again, an opportunity lost. As he thought of Clair while drifting along a monotonous stretch of Interstate 20, his reverie revisited their last time together almost three years prior.

He remembered each detail of their having shared a picnic on her grandmother's patchwork quilt by the pond at the back of Gramma's farm and in the shadow of Scatter Mountain. He thought of how idyllically it had begun as they had eaten well and then had lain on the quilt kissing softly, of their laughing in each other's arms as they thrust their hands skyward in the Sign of the Wild Goose Moon, and of their capturing fireflies in a mason jar and reveling in the magic of their release. But his memories proceeded to how bitterly the evening had ended when he demanded much more than soft kisses and to the verbal assault with which he punished her for her reluctant refusal.

As the Dallas skyline came into view, Tom closed his latest review of this chapter in his life. He continued to carry the regret of his behavior as well as, if nothing else, at least the obligation of an apology if the opportunity ever came.

* * *

Tom opened the door of Room 332 McCartney Hall. His new roommate stood in the middle of the long, narrow room between the two beds that nestled against either wall. A bit taller and slimmer than Tom, his clothes - from the unbuttoned ecru button-down collar that sprouted from the loose-fitting chocolate brown wool sweater to the tan corduroy slacks - looked comfortably rumpled. His thick dark hair was wiry and unruly. As their eyes met he ducked his head slightly and gave Tom a smile that was shy bordering on surreptitious. Tom immediately liked the glint in the dark brown eyes that complemented his smile. He instantly presumed that this was the face and carriage of a fellow traveler whose prescription for dealing with the world, its conventions and its inconsistencies, was, like his own, a generous dollop of irreverence seasoned with whimsy.

Tom approached him and extended his right hand. "Tom Windham. Ah'm a Suthun Bayuptis fum Eas' Ticksis," he announced.

"Brandeis Wasserman," his roommate replied. "I'm a Suthun Jyeww from Wayus Tennesay." As they laughed and shook hands, their eyes locked for a second – Brandeis squinting slightly as in earnest assessment - and Tom felt it was going to work.

"Brandeis Wasserman?" Tom queried. "With a handle like that I'm surprised when you registered they didn't just place you out straight through law school, size you for a judge's robe, and ask you what court you wanted. You have a nickname? Brandy, or anything? Or do you go by Brandeis?"

"Brandy?" Brandeis replied, as if taking offense. "No, I go by Brandeis. I know the whole five syllables is a mouthful, but one of my overriding goals is to live a life free of cutesy-ness. I think that necessarily excludes nicknames. So tell me, what happened to *your* roommate?"

"Sure thing, *Woz*," Tom replied with a wink. "Grades got him. He'd apparently just squeaked by as a freshman. Then he had some sick time last semester. Lost the thread. Had to drop out. It got to be a real bad deal. He was so down the last month or so. Just kind of gave up. What about yours?"

"Oh, the usual," Brandeis began matter-of-factly. "He was an undercover CIA operative having what was thought to be a homosexual relationship with the Russian language prof whom he had been led to believe was KGB but was really undercover FBI, and it all blew up when they were trying to consummate their relationship at the top of the first incline on the roller coaster during the State Fair and the Russian prof-KGB-FBI man discovered my roomie was a girl. So he-she had to move to a women's dorm. You know the rules: no girls in the men's dorms."

"Really?" Tom queried in mock earnestness.

"Well, no," Brandeis replied. "Really, he knocked up his girlfriend, and they got married over Christmas."

"So, you got everything over here or can I help you move," Tom asked.

"Just a few boxes to go, if you don't mind."

"Anything in your car we need to get?"

"I don't have a car," Brandeis stated.

"Really?" Tom asked, with too much surprise.

"Well, I have one, but it's old and was in pretty bad shape after driving back to Memphis before Christmas. Oh yeah, let's get my plyboard over there, too. You know, Culver was built at the same time as McCartney. Looks like they used the same cookie cutter for the rooms." Looking up at the tops of the closets, which flanked the door and were essentially wooden cubes built into the front corners of the room, Brandeis said, "It spans the opening over the door from closet to closet. It'll give us a lot more storage space. Good for luggage, life-size blow-up dolls, that kind of stuff. What do you think?"

'Ingenious', Tom thought, glancing at the expanse of the door opening. "Sounds great."

Traversing the Men's Quad's web of sidewalks horseshoed by the three men's dorms, the boys discussed their classes. Tom learned that Brandeis was indeed pre-law by way of political science, and he reveled that he was tentatively general business with history and/or law school seen as options. Brandeis did not talk in terms of options. The inevitability of his path seemed set by the fact that his grandfather, his father, and his uncle were partners in a Memphis law practice. As the boys talked, Tom began to notice a hint of effeminacy in Brandeis' speech not dissimilar from that of two friends he had grown up with in New Fredonia. Like them, it was short of sissiness, but still discomforting.

Their discussions returned to course work and to the game of "Who Do We Both Know?" as they left Brandeis' boxes in their room and went to Tom's car to unload it. Exiting the back door of the dorm toward the parking lot, Tom heard a familiar greeting.

"Hey, Tom-cat, how's it hangin'?"

Turning to the burly figure approaching, Tom replied, "Limply, Joe Joe. Quite limply."

As he drew near Joe Joe shifted his cigarette from his right hand to his left and covered a deep, gravelly cough with a fist. Extending a meaty right hand to Tom, Joe Joe's scruffy few days' growth of beard, puffy face with baggy eyes, and short, curly dark blonde hair plastered forward onto his forehead gave him the appearance of having been up for days. The lifeless collar of his white oxford cloth button-down peeking out of his navy parka and his creaseless faded jeans completed the picture.

"Did you git any for Christmas?" Joe Joe asked in greeting Tom.

"Just mistletoe, no stockings," was the best Tom could come up with. Then turning to Brandeis, Tom made introductions. "Joe Joe Bartlow. Brandeis Wasserman. He's my new roomie. Joe Joe's just down the hall from us, and he lives on a ranch on the Canadian River north of Amarillo."

"Out where a man's a man," Joe Joe boasted.

"And the sheep know it?" Brandeis chimed in.

Breaking into a grin and a nod, Joe Joe queried as they shook hands,

"Brandeis, did you say?" But before Joe Joe could get any mileage from the name, the three boys standing in the parking lot jumped from the path of a white Corvette as it slid slightly while making a sharp, fast turn just in front of them. All three watched longingly as the sports car made another quick turn and disappeared from sight.

With its husky exhaust note still reverberating through the parking lot, Tom said, "God, I love that new 'Vette. What a brutal-lookin' 'muthah'."

"Yeah," Joe Joe added, "that T-top is so tough." Then after a moment, "Do you know who that was? Justine Lecataret. She got it at Thanksgiving. One of the first 68's off the line. Yeah, I saw her in it during finals over on The Drag at an intersection. I was walking across and looked in this car. All I could see was this cockpit full o' tit. Boy, I'd like to offload a few thousand of my favorite wigglies into that Kappa Kappa Kapussy."

"Stay pithy, Joe Joe," Tom said.

Taking their leave of Joe Joe, Tom and Brandeis began unloading Tom's car. In the three trips required to empty the Le Mans, Tom filled Brandeis in on some of their third floor/south hall neighbors. He pointed out the room of Topper Burke and Clayton Terwilliger, the Australian swimmers upon whose door was still taped a hand-scrawled "Bah Humbug - Christmas Finals" sign. The Aussies, who kept mostly to themselves, were noteworthy principally for being the only jocks on third floor. As they passed the room next to their own, Tom gave Brandeis the rundown on Jack Putnam and Harvey Groesbeck.

Jack, whom Tom called Blackjack, was a product of military schools, and he wore grey slacks, light blue shirt, navy tie and navy jacket to class every day. His was often the only made-up bed on the third floor on a given day, and it was the only one in the Men's Quad on which one could bounce a quarter.

Tom smiled broadly as he described the wired enthusiasm of Harvey Groesbeck. The plump, jovial sophomore from Waco had Tom's vote for "most likely to become a TV news anchor". His consuming interest in current events was matched only by his commitment to disseminate the information he gathered to his friends, classmates, and anyone else within earshot.

Tom chose to temporarily forego Brandeis' introduction to another side of Harvey - his highly successful entrepreneurial venture. For aside from the gang shower in the communal bathroom, there was a single large private shower behind a translucent door. A vestige of a time when it was reserved for use by the floor director, Shower Number Nine was now open to use by anyone on the floor. But it was Harvey Groesbeck who had capitalized on Number Nine's privacy by attaching to one wall a laminated copy of the legendary Sophia Loren-*Boy on a Dolphin* poster. Suspended from the towel rack, Harvey had hung a plastic cup. On the masking tape label that he had applied was printed "25 cents - Honor System". The clink of quarters in the cup could be heard throughout the night and early morning in the bathroom, but the residents of the floor were never so blatant or indecorous as to form a line at the shower door. It was the general consensus along the hall that a girl could be impregnated by merely sitting on Number Nine's floor.

Next door to Tom and Brandeis on the west side were Bob Tolbert and Pete Wheeler, "townies" from East Dallas and Oak Cliff. Pete was pre-med and spoke science fluently and almost exclusively. Bob was noteworthy for his Peter Lorre-eyes and receding hairline. The latter had given him early notoriety for his ability to buy liquor without an ID since age fifteen. During his first semester Tom had gravitated more to Harvey and Blackjack's room and to Joe Joe's, which was on the other side of Bob and Pete's. Joe Joe's roommate had also moved out of McCartney between semesters and into his fraternity house. For the time being Joe Joe had his room to himself as did Rodg Messing, the floor director, who lived at the end of the hall nearest the elevator.

A senior from Iowa, Rodg was like no one Tom had ever met. Articulate, idealistic, willing to push aside the veil and share real feelings, yet with a quick sense of humor and a sufficient leavening of pragmatism, Rodg was to Tom what Mark could have been if Mark's best qualities had been nurtured and his most destructive squelched. Rodg's avowed intent to join the Peace Corps upon graduation was the perfect finishing touch to Tom's image of him. Through the autumn, though, Tom had been unable - even reluctant - to draw as close to Rodg as he sometimes wanted. His fear was that he did not meet Rodg's standards - that he would fall short as a friend by being inadequate in one or more of the qualities that he attributed to Rodg - and that Rodg's rejection of him for his inadequacies would give Tom conclusive evidence that he was not a worthwhile person. Through nineteen years of life Tom had been able to avoid any one-person jury as capable as Rodg, who combined a detached objectivity with such a set of impeccable moral and ethical credentials. Though Rodg had never hinted at any inclination to render such a judgment, Tom feared closeness to him against the day - however unlikely - when, with a certainty and a finality not unlike a brand on a calf's flank, Rodg might choose to do so.

Having unpacked, Tom shrugged and stated, "Time to face the music."

"What?"

"Dinner," he stated profoundly. "McCartney Mess Hall. It won't be pretty. It may not even be edible."

As they left their room, Brandeis said, "Whoa. Let me make a pit stop."

"Sure," Tom said, smiling. "I need to, too." Entering, Tom motioned Brandeis toward Shower Number Nine. "For future reference you might want to go in and take a look."

Brandeis popped open the door. A second later his laughter reverberated off the mint green tile walls. "Is this for real?"

"Was up all last semester," Tom replied. "It not only covers all of Groesbeck's expenses; I think he even sends money home."

Still laughing, Brandeis emerged and closed the door. "So," he asked, "how often do *you* avail yourself of Number Nine's ... what? Pleasures, convenience, attraction?"

"Pretty rarely, in fact. No, you see I subscribe to the Finite Number of Shots Theory, and I don't want to waste my lifetime limit on my hand."

A sly grin traced across his lips as Brandeis asked, "Have you gotten to waste any on anything else?"

Surprised first that they had already gotten to *that* question, and second that he had left himself so wide open for it, Tom shrugged, "What the hell. No. But when my time comes, I'll have a full clip."

"All-right," Brandeis replied with a laugh.

"What about you?" Tom asked.

"Nope, I've remained true to my hand."

Chapter 5

The next day Tom, Brandeis and Joe Joe walked briskly through the morning chill across campus to Zimmerman Coliseum, a giant red brick block of a building. "The Zim" and the acres of close-cropped grassy plain beside it called the ZPL (Zimmerman Parking Lot) flanked WSU on the west. As they entered The Zim, Tom relished the excitement he again felt about the registration process just as he had five months earlier. To his further joy he found himself absent the fear and apprehension he had carried into registration the prior autumn. He liked the size and scope of the event: the endless rows of tables covering the basketball court, the departmental signs hoisted on poles marking the various academic fiefdoms, the frequent shouts of joy - principally from gaggles of Greek co-eds - as they scored scheduling coups, and the haggard expressions of the faculty members dealing with the tidal wave of self-absorbed, unyielding students driven to a frenzy by their desire for the perfect day/time/prof/subject combinations. Billed as the Third Annual Final Non-Automated Registration, the process employed the antiquated ritual of flustered faculty members leafing through reams of class schedules and entering students' names on a first come-first serve basis until a class roll hit capacity. WSU's continuing software problems with its computerized enrollment and registration system had over the past two years become a worn-out joke, a dog too old to kick.

On the way from their dorm the three boys had discussed their registration goals. Brandeis planned to sign up for Labor Law, Business

Law, and a political science course along with some remaining core requirements. Tom, as he straddled the fence between Business and History, knew he needed the second half of "Principles of Accounting" and of "Man and His World". He hoped he could get into Dr. Briggs' "European History 1815 to the Present", but he knew that it would be much sought after. Joe Joe's plan for registration was to find four courses after ten in the morning and before two in the afternoon, preferably M-W-F only.

"That was hell," Brandeis judged as the three rendezvoused after registration in front of The Zim. Joe Joe had been waiting for them awhile.

"Did you get all the law courses you wanted?" Tom asked.

"Yeah. How about you? Did you get Briggs?"

"Yes, God help me, I did. Joe Joe?"

"Here, read my new door sign," Bartlow said, brandishing a piece of cardboard.

If today starts with a T
Leave Me Be!

*   *   *

That evening, with the beginning of classes a day away, the 332 McCartney crew decided to treat themselves to a dinner out. At Brandeis' suggestion they went to Jamie's on Lemmon Avenue for "fancy" quarter-pound hamburgers, curleque fries and hot red beans with chips.

"You want to go see a movie after?" Brandeis asked over their burgers.

"Sure. What's on?"

"There's something new that's supposed to be good at NorthPark. Can't think of the name of it," Brandeis said.

"Who's in it?"

"Nobody I know, really ... except Anne Bancroft."

"From *The Miracle Worker*?" Tom asked.

"Yeah."

"What's it about?"

"No idea," Brandeis replied, "but the ad in the paper looked weird in a good way. And my brother had mentioned it to me."

"Yeah, I'm game. So, is your brother older or younger?"

"Younger by two years. His name's Ted —"

"Ted?" Tom asked, feigning wonderment. "How did he avoid being named Learned or Oliver Wendell or something catchy like that?"

"Just lucky, I guess," Brandeis replied, and then more seriously, "I guess the level of expectations were less, or at least different. Do you have any brothers or sisters?"

Tom blinked and caught his breath. "No," he replied with precision, relieved - however temporarily - at the convenient tense Brandeis had offered him.

* * *

The opening scene without credits was of the passenger compartment of a commercial jet. The pilot's voiceover announced the plane's "descent into Los Angeles". The next scene, which kicked off the credits to the familiar strains of Simon and Garfunkel's "Sound of Silence", was of a young man who had been showcased in the previous scene. It became apparent that he was being transported along an airport terminal's moving sidewalk.

Tom did not recognize the actor, but he immediately identified with him. Innocence, vulnerability, curiosity, affability, insecurity - all these from this smallish, sad-eyed young man with a large nose and well-squared sideburns.

Late in the credits, as they watched Dustin Hoffman give passersby curious, almost pained, glances, Brandeis asked, "Is he homosexual?" Tom replied with a negative shake of his head and a hummed 'I don't know'. Tom intuitively liked this character on the screen, and he was irritated by Brandeis' suggestion. Through the first half of the film, they laughed along with the crowd frequently and grunted in understanding and identification with certain situations, but they did not speak to each other. On that rainy day, though, when Elaine's face blurred with tears, when Mrs. Robinson, suddenly a shriveled old woman in black, withdrew to the stark white corner of the upstairs landing, and when Benjamin Braddock's world imploded, Brandeis went silent. Without ever looking at him Tom noted uncomfortably that Brandeis was no longer laughing or even sighing appreciation along with him and the rest of the audience. Subconsciously, Tom identified the mood swing as one of which his mother would be capable, but as he had learned to numb himself against her behavior and to go on with his life, so he ignored Brandeis' silence and remained deeply and optimistically involved in the movie.

At the film's climax Tom experienced a thrilling surge of elation - even victory. Then he looked at Brandeis and saw that he was crying. He was being quiet about it, and he was holding his hands over his eyes, but there was no doubt that he was crying. The house lights came on, and the crowd - mostly sporting sweet, warm smiles of appreciation, and like Tom, of vicarious triumph - began slowly to file out. Tom stayed in his seat next to his roommate, but he began to feel embarrassed by and more uncomfortable with Brandeis' behavior. 'If I had wanted crying', he thought, 'I could have stayed in Noofer.' He knew that he would be back to see *The Graduate*. Like his other few favorite movies he knew it would become a dearly loved, rarely seen friend that he would, by chance, bump into over the years at revival houses and eventually on television – however edited. But Brandeis' reaction disturbed and perplexed him. Trying to put the best face on the situation, Tom finally made a comment about the effect of "witnessing pure art", which he immediately recognized as both inadequate and overblown. After a minute in their seats Brandeis composed himself, and they left the empty auditorium.

Boarding the Le Mans, Tom asked, "You want to go riding around some?"

"Yeah," Brandeis replied quietly.

After stopping at a Dairy Queen, Tom drove north on Preston Road through Renner and Frisco, turning back at Hebron. As they discussed the movie, Tom was comforted to learn that Brandeis had enjoyed it - possibly even as much as himself. Brandeis' comments evidenced a recall of dialogue and situations that surprised Tom. Though he never named the source of his tears and, in fact, made no mention of his behavior at the end of the movie, Tom noticed that he kept returning to the shallowness and hypocrisy of the adults in the movie - to the superficiality and materialism of their lifestyles.

They returned to campus and as Tom was pulling into a parking space near McCartney, Brandeis said, "A psychiatrist I know told me once that it just didn't matter a hell of a lot what you had - what you owned - or how you used it. What mattered was what you felt, that you expressed what you felt, and that you expressed it honestly."

"A psychiatrist?" Tom asked. "How do you know *him*?"

Brandeis hesitated before answering, "The hard way."

Following a leaden silence, Tom asked, "Did he help you?"

"Yeah ... he does."

Chapter 6

Late January

Standing at the urinal contemplating his penis, Tom suddenly launched a withering fire at the cigarette butt below him. He mused at the coincidence that he and Mark had stumbled on many years before. Since his father frequently used the toilet in the Boys Bathroom as an ashtray and given Tom's penchant - instilled in him by his imaginative older brother - toward the devising and playing of war games, in his boyhood Tom had created such a game involving his urine stream and the cigarette butts that he often found floating in the toilet. By the time he devised the game Johnny had switched from unfiltered Lucky Strikes to filtered Winstons. The filter and the higher quality of the paper had increased the level of difficulty. When, after his first year of college, Mark was able to smoke openly at home, Tom found more opportunities to play the game and to hone his skill. Given the field of combat, the unnamed activity was a naval war game.

Tom's version required that he direct as strong a urine stream as he could strain his bladder to deliver and for as prolonged a period as his bladder accumulation allowed toward a point on the saturated butt's white paper just behind the burned, blackened tip. Obeying a self-imposed soldier's code of honor, though, he never drank liquids strictly for the purpose of stockpiling ammunition, and he rarely put off urination just to increase his firepower.

The cigarette butt represented an enemy battleship, and victory at sea entailed the breaking off of the burned tip from the body of the butt, which signified the sinking of the ship. Doing so also sent the individual flecks of tobacco spilling into the sea of the bowl. Each of these tobacco grains represented an enemy sailor killed in the attack. Thus if Tom's bladder pressure were down or if his ammo dump were low, he could still inflict light to heavy damage by loosening the blackened tip sufficiently to send some number of the ship's complement to their deaths and the battleship limping back to port - although the sunk, the damaged, the unscathed, and the nicotine sailors living and dead, all quickly faced the common destiny of spiraling down into Davey Jones's Locker.

Tom and Mark discovered during their last summer together that Mark played a variation on the same game. Like Tom's version the butt was a battleship and each grain of tobacco loosed from it represented a sailor killed. But for Mark the ship was sunk by separating the filter from the white wrapper, and the major twist in his game was that the separation of the blackened tip meant that the ship's captain had been killed. Tom remembered thinking then that Mark took a more personal view of combat.

Like the prior semester the first two days of class after registration had consisted of ten- to fifteen-minute introductions of professor to students and of handing out first assignments. Noteworthy during these two virgin days was a statement that Tom made in "Man and His World" that he regretted as soon as the words left his lips. Dr. Longoria, his discussion leader for the class, had asked each student to answer roll with his views on Evolution. Normally a first year course, but one for which Tom had taken no equivalent at Stover County J.C., he listened in lonely dismay as freshman after freshman parroted what Tom perceived to be a brash, arrogant, and altogether overly enthusiastic acceptance of Darwin's theory. As his turn approached, a Southern Baptist fervor took hold of him. In this classroom where God had suddenly become the underdog, Tom felt compelled to make a stand.

"My religious beliefs do not allow me to accept the Theory of Evolution." The words were out before he could draw them back. No stir, as he had quickly feared, occurred among his classmates, but the cold chill of unwelcome recognition - of a current error banked for future punishment - came over him as he made eye contact with the plump, plain, severe Dr. Longoria. Tom saw her mentally record him as a narrow-minded, backwoods religious fanatic as surely as if he had jumped atop her desk and demonstrated his snake-handling skills while speaking in tongues.

Now as Tom completed his toilet game (enemy battleship damaged but still seaworthy), he shifted mental gears to mull over the discomforting approach of his last first class - the biweekly lab of his biology course. "Requirement" correctly defined any science course in which he would be enrolled.

He made his way up campus across the Common, the large treeless expanse of manicured lawn interrupted only by an azure-tiled fountain and pool and a complex grid of sidewalks, which was the center and focal point of the original campus. It was surrounded by WSU's oldest classroom buildings - including Old Wesley where he had "Man and His World" and sociology, and Peller Science Building, which was his current destination - plus the library, the auditorium, and the Student Union Building (The SUB). As he walked, he noted in appreciation and in spite of the landscaping's wintry pallor, the solid grandeur and strength of the homogeneous Georgian architecture employed in these buildings. The rich, dark red brick and the thick bone-colored columns, familiar to Tom since his earliest childhood visits to Dallas, made WSU look, in his view, like a college campus should look.

Noticing a familiar face, Tom yelled across the Common, "Hey, Freddie!" The target of his address was walking away from him amid the mass of students that had just escaped their last afternoon classes in Old Wesley, and his target cringed his head down and continued to walk while glancing from side to side.

Tom waved and smiled as he approached. But as the figure - now ten yards away and walking against the flow of students that Tom was being swept along by - waved and with a smile of recognition yelled back, "Tom Roy!" Tom cringed his head down and continued to walk while glancing from side to side. Reaching to shake hands, the baby-faced, long-haired young man instructed, "That's 'Fred', just 'Fred'."

His given name a conflation of the first names of his father's and of his mother's favorite movie cowboys – Tom Mix and Roy Rogers, respectively – Tom had used the separation provided by his WSU sojourn to jettison his middle name based on his evolving notion that such appendages branded their users as unsophisticated. Consequently, smiling broadly and nodding in perfect understanding, Tom instructed, "That's 'Tom', just 'Tom'."

Tom had known the former Freddie Slater since both were in the fourth grade, a week in the summer after which they had shared at the Baptist encampment on Lake LaSalle, south of Springfield. Bethany Baptist Church was a denominational sister to First Baptist New Fredonia, and the boys thereafter ran into each other often at church camps and activities.

After Freddie was the first in his high school class to get a new car - a midnight blue Mustang and among the first in the county - Tom saw more of him because Freddie's hometown, the much smaller Bethany fifteen miles to the west of New Fredonia, had drawn a void in Dairy Queens. Tom remembered Freddie's father Alf as being stern but caring, and Johnny had informed Tom that he was a wealthy lumberman and landowner in Stover County. It was not until high school that the fruits of that wealth had become evident to Tom when Freddie had landed the Mustang seemingly seconds after receiving his license. But with that information Tom had come to like Freddie all the more because, with or without the money and with or without the car, Tom had always gotten the same Freddie - now Fred.

"Yeah, I heard over Christmas you were transferring here. How're you liking it so far?"

"I think I'm going to really like it. U-T was fun, but it was sooo big."

"Were you in a fraternity down there?"

"Yeah, I'm a Mu Nu," he frowned, "but I don't know how active I'm going to get in the chapter here. Down there it helped a lot to be in one just to meet people, because you never had more than one class with anyone or even with anyone in your dorm. But the fraternities are just so out of touch, so mired in the fifties - the eighteen-fifties, that is."

"Where are you living?"

"Postlethwaite."

"Are you headed for the SUB now?" Tom asked.

"Yeah."

"Well, I'd buy you a D-P, but I'm headed up to Peller for Bio lab."

"That's okay. I'm on my way to a meeting there anyway, and it starts in about ten minutes."

"So you've already gotten involved in something here, huh?" Tom asked with a bit of wonder and a touch of envy.

"Yeah. SCAR, Student Coalition Against Racism."

Tom jerked his furrowed brow back in surprise. "Hmmm. So ... who's coalescing?"

"Whites, blacks, any other colors that want to," Fred answered with a hint of defensiveness.

"So did you get both of the 'nigras' on campus to join? And the three Koreans, too?" Tom asked with a laugh.

"Tom, there are sixty-three blacks on campus," Fred replied, just short of sharply.

Realizing Fred's sensitivity on the subject, Tom continued more carefully. "What does the group do?"

"Well, we just organized. Right now, it's more of an ad hoc organization to deal with a 'whites only' washateria south of campus on the Drag."

"You mean Rutledge's?" To Fred's nod, Tom said, "Why, that's a 'Wazoo' institution. It's always been there, and I guess it's always been 'whites only'."

"Yep, and it's time for it to change. Now."

"Don't you think he has the right to refuse service to anyone he wants to?" As the words borrowed from the popular store sign spilled from his mouth, Tom's mind flashed to the ultimate fight scene in *Giant* - to Sarge standing over the blood- and salad dressing-stained Bick Benedict and dropping the framed sign on his chest as the final soaring strains of "Yellow Rose of Texas" peeled forth from the Wurlitzer.

"Not if the only reason is the color of their skin. No-siree, I don't," Fred shot back.

Tom's eyes opened wider. 'What happened to *him* in Austin?' he wondered. Tom was surprised to hear what he considered a Yankee Liberal point of view issuing forth from this fellow East Texan - and Southern Baptist, to boot. 'I hope he hasn't said any of this stuff in front of his father,' he thought, remembering Alf Slater as a man, like his father, most unlikely to be supportive of any such radical notions. To them there were two kinds of black people - the vast majority who were simply "nigras", and those who performed useful services for them and who 'stayed in their place' while doing so, thus earning them the honorary title of "good nigras". Since everything except a few water fountains and restrooms in New Fredonia were essentially no less segregated in 1968 than they had been in 1954, and since he had heard no complaints about it either from Vashti, the Windhams' maid, or from Felton, the shoeshine boy at Dorsey's Barber Shop, Tom assumed integration to be a false issue and one that agitated only white liberals and a handful of troublemaking blacks while bothering the general black population not at all. But hearing the confrontational edge in Fred's voice and seeing the idealistic fervor in his eyes, Tom became aware that there might be another side to the issue. It was not, however, anything he was interested in debating - either for two minutes between classes here on the Common with an old friend who had turned left or, for that matter, with anyone under any circumstances. Therefore, understanding it to be an issue upon which one man of goodwill and one man who avoided confrontation at all cost could differ, Tom chose to change the subject. "Mmm. I see your point. Say, are you dating anyone steady now?"

"Yeah," Fred answered tentatively, still in his combatively idealistic mode, but trying quickly to jerk himself back toward small talk. "Well, no. I thought she was going to come up here this semester. She's from around here. But after I'd made my plans, she chickened out and stayed at U-T. Decided she didn't want to be this close to home. So we kind of broke it off over Christmas. We're free to date other people." After a moment's reflection, Fred asked, "What about you? You dating anyone?"

"Yeah, Meredith Blaine from Springfield. She's a freshman at the college there. Do you know her?"

Shaking his head and drifting again, Fred asked, "What about Clair Kennerly?"

"What do you mean?" Tom replied.

"I just remember y'all used to be pretty hot 'n' heavy after each other. Didn't know if you might have come back around."

Tom bit his lip and began to shake his head slowly. "Nope."

After an awkward silence Fred gave Tom a pat on the shoulder and said, "Catch you later. Gotta go change the world."

* * *

In the basement of Peller the nauseating scent of formaldehyde greeted him as he walked down the long row of two abreast black-topped, chrome-fixtured lab tables. Tom noticed index cards with two names on them taped in the center of the tables. On the second row from the back he found "McKenna-Windham".

Looking up from the sign at his partner, Tom's mouth dropped open slightly before peeling into a grin. Her fixed, oblivious gaze at an object on the table in front of her awarded him the momentary luxury of staring McKenna up and down. He was drawn first to her deep-tanned face. It was of a bronze he had seen previously only on magazines and on billboards, and, even then, only in the summer. Her skin tone contrasted dramatically with her thick platinum hair cut in bangs and turned under at the neck. Venturing down, her loose-fitting "Tri-K" sweatshirt strongly suggested a figure the delectability of which from the waist up would match that clearly defined as a certainty from the waist down by her skin-tight Levis - into which he wondered how she had ever gotten.

As she turned to face him and a split second later flashed a canned Panhellenic smile, though, Tom's mouth closed into the pursed grin of the Independent in the wrong place at the wrong time. He thought he detected disappointment behind her sparkling blue eyes.

To make matters worse, he noted her full name - Siobhan McKenna - on her notebook and greeted her uncertainly, "Si-o-bun?"

With a giggle doubtless giggled countless times, she corrected him, "That's Sh-Von. Kind of like 'Chevrolet'. It's Irish. Very Irish."

"Fine, Sh-Von," he cracked, "but I'm from East Texas, and it's pronounced 'Shivalay' there."

Her open laugh in response encouraged Tom that she was thinking he might work after all. "And you're - ?" she asked.

"Bawnd. James Bawnd." But as she glanced down at their index card, he corrected with a raised index finger, "Make that ... Windham. Tawm Windham."

"Where in East Texas are you from, Tawm?"

"Liiittle bitty town. Probably never heard of it. New Fredonia. North of Springfield." Her vacant expression and slight shake of the hair replied that she had heard of neither. "What about you?"

"Chicago," she replied, going hard and nasal on the "cag".

"D'home o' d'Hawk?"

"Blow yo' pad down, Jim ... er ... Tawm."

As they laughed at their Lou Rawls homage, their smiles were matched and easier. After a moment Siobhan directed her focus and Tom's back to the object at which she had been staring when he arrived. "Jeremiah," she stated in introduction. "Meet Tawm."

Tom nodded courteously at the lifeless, shiny green frog - its stiffened legs splayed grotesquely. "Pleased t'meetcha, podnah," Tom began, offering a hand to shake.

Further pleasantries were interrupted, though, by Dr. Hickman's call to order. More at home in the lab than in the lecture hall Tom noted, the professor quickly reeled off instructions for the dissection of the frogs. The McKenna-Windham team approached the removal of Jeremiah's epidermis with equal gingerness - their four pinky fingers splayed as preciously as Jeremiah's legs were grotesquely. They took turns snipping away skin in small patches trying to avoid holding and tugging on the leathery cover with their fingers. Unfortunately, Hickman started to give time deadlines for the completion of skin removal after which he pledged to begin innards identification - ready or not. Tom's and Siobhan's willingness to pull and yank at the frog's skin increased in inverse proportion to the dwindling of the allotted time. Finally, as Tom held and Siobhan ferociously ripped the last shred of skin from the cold, lifeless amphibian, she breathed a triumphant sigh and exchanged a full-bodied shrug of accomplishment with Tom. Thus 'blooded' together, they survived the remainder of the lab uneventfully.

At the end of class as they began to swap favorite moments of their trip through a frog, Siobhan was whisked away by two breathless Tri-K sisters, who barely acknowledged his existence. As Tom shelved the remains of Jeremiah, he considered his good fortune at being partnered with Siobhan. She was remarkably beautiful, and that would give him a fair amount of conversational mileage on third floor McCartney. She had turned out to be very friendly, easy to talk to and to laugh with. But not even going so far as to bring his allegiance to Meredith into play, he perceived that the Greek-GDI barrier was ruling in their relationship; therefore, its limit was, by definition, good in-class friends – nothing more.

* * *

*'I wish ... I wish, I wish in vain
That we could sit simply in that room again.
Ten thousand dollars at the drop of a hat -
I'd give it all gladly,
If our lives could be like that.'*

The haunting lyrics of "Bob Dylan's Dream" greeted Tom as he entered his darkened room to find Brandeis napping. Tom was uncomfortably damp and chilled from his walk down campus from biology lab in a drizzle. He agreed as he glanced out the window at the grey, gauzy sky that the afternoon was meant for sleeping. He undressed and wrapped himself in his terrycloth robe. Lying back with his hands under his head, he let the folk-rock mix of Peter, Paul and Mary's *Album 1700* drift over him. When first Brandeis had played it for him, Tom had recognized only "I Dig Rock'n'Roll Music" and "Leaving on a Jet Plane". With frequent replays since, though, they had fallen in rank among his favorites as the melodies, the harmonizing, the moods, the humor, and the messages of the less commercial cuts became familiar to him. The mournful and finally majestic "The Great Mandella" spoke to him, but though he wondered what or who a Mandella was, he dared not ask. And he loved the kazooed racial satire of "Big Blue Frog" as well as the "Scotch and Soda"-smooth "Whatsername".

His thoughts drifted away from the music as he contemplated the somnolent figure across the room from him. Since that first strange day when he had met Brandeis Wasserman, his roommate had seemed to settle down. He was a much more disciplined student than Tom, yet his wry and frequently sarcastic humor remained unabated. Their conversations since that first day had avoided depth, though Tom perceived a mutual understanding that the capability for and openness to serious interchange was there. Brandeis seemed to wear comfortably a sensitivity and honesty about his emotions that would have fit tightly and pinched on an adolescent in New Fredonia - as it had on Mark. On the one hand Tom's background and his experience with his brother made him uncomfortable, as if Brandeis' sensitivity was somehow threatening - its portent dangerous. On the other, though, Tom saw an opportunity in him for the kind of intimate, guards-down discussion of real human feelings for which Tom occasionally betrayed a hunger in spite of the risks.

He awoke in the early evening to the renewed peppering of rain against the window. Arising and moving toward the bathroom, he felt the dull non-sensation of oversleeping - as if his mind were walking a step behind his body. He tried to shrug off the feeling as he forced himself to make pick-ups at the cleaners in preparation for his return the following day to New Fredonia for his first weekend home since the semester had begun. He capped the evening with his second solo reprise of *The Graduate* at NorthPark. It kept getting better.

Chapter 7

"Oh, yeah," Meredith said, "I loved your letter. About registration and everything. That was so sweet of you to write."

The afternoon and evening had been frenetic for Tom. Following the two-hour drive home, he had rushed through a shower and welcome home chat with his parents before driving to Springfield to pick up Meredith and get them to the Beaux Arts in time for the start of *Camelot*.

They had scarcely had time to talk, but now as they headed away from the theatre toward Paco's for Mexican food, Tom said, "Well, you know from last semester not to count on me to keep it up, but I'll try."

"That's something about your roommate - what's his name? Brandeis? Being Jewish and all? I thought they were supposed to try to room you with someone you'd have more in common with."

"Oh, I think they only do that your first semester. After that, you're fair game. Anyway, I'm enjoying Brandeis. He's a neat guy. Real funny."

"I'd just think the two of you would be so different you wouldn't have much to talk about."

Hesitating a furtive moment, Tom replied, "Oh, we do."

"So, how are your classes going?"

"Briggs is great," Tom answered.

"Briggs?"

"European History - 1815 forward. He really brings it alive. It's so interesting; I've already read way ahead in the text. Of course, it's kind of strange taking the second half first and then not getting the first semester of it till next fall. But it'll work because - "

With a frown Meredith asked, "What about your business courses?"

"Well, that's just accounting. That's the only business course I'm taking this semester. And it's just more of the same. Practice sets. Bleahh."

"But when do you get to take more - to really start into your major?"

"If ...I stay with business, I'll get into them next fall. Probably three courses."

"*If?* What do you mean? I thought you were set on getting a business degree."

"I'm just not sure about Business. I enjoy History so much. And the accounting - well, let's just say, it doesn't quite seize my imagination."

"So what are you saying? You're giving up on Business before you even get into it?"

Pulling into Paco's parking lot and bringing the car to a halt, Tom winced at the disapproval in her voice. "Meredith, I'm not sure. I may stay with it. Of course, if I did go History, I could still go Law." Though Tom knew he was making this last offer mainly to de-fang Meredith's disapproval, and in spite of the predictable brightening of her countenance that it had produced, he added, "But I do love History. And I think I would really enjoy going all the way with it. Masters. P-h-D. The whole nine yards."

"Oh, you don't mean that."

Tom stared at her and sighed a long sigh. "I'd hardly have said it if I didn't."

Leaving the car they did not speak on the way into the restaurant. Meredith turned the dinner conversation toward goings-on at Springfield and among her friends. Tom was subdued through dinner and begged off going to her house to watch television pleading weariness from the day's pace and the obligation to visit with his parents. He returned to Springfield the following night for a dance on campus, and Meredith again kept the evening light.

Throughout the weekend Tom enjoyed the peace that Nancy was granting the household. As she had been several times the prior semester, Nancy was so genuinely happy to have her son home that she was able to control both her dark side and the thirst that nurtured it. And Johnny did what he did best - laid low. At the office. At the farm. In front of the television. Sunday morning at breakfast the three agreed to meet at the cafeteria after church for lunch. The aura of togetherness among his family was a needed counterpoint to the dull, distant discomfort that Tom felt about his relationship with Meredith after Friday night's conversation.

* * *

Tom had been raised Southern Baptist, so he worried about God. He took comfort in the Baptist doctrine of "Once saved, always saved", or, as some phrased it, "You can't lose your salvation". Having been baptized in typical small town Southern Baptist fashion - after accepting Jesus as his personal Lord and Saviour at age nine during a revival - Tom frequently wondered, through the remainder of his childhood and teen years, if that baptism "took". He wondered if it was the real thing - whether he had been truly washed in the Blood of the Lamb or if he had simply been dunked in a strange, elevated room filled with tap water by an ordinary man in robe, shirt, tie, and waders. He fiercely hoped that it did "take", wishing almost for some physical sign like the sore that had told him that his smallpox vaccination had.

He had never gone to the trouble of marching down the aisle again to fulfill the Baptist ritual of "rededication". In a small church such as his wherein the congregation was relatively static in size and composition, and all but the small number of children in the church were already baptized, the occasional rededication by mostly the same pool of devout members was understood to be a reward to the preacher for an especially stirring sermon. Or, if there had been a long dry spell of new members or baptismal candidates walking the aisle, it gave the preacher relief from the embarrassment of standing lonely sentinel down front through Sunday upon Sunday of invitational hymns. Privately, though, this spiritual "booster shot" seemed redundant to Tom - like being "born again" again.

Another facet of Baptist doctrine that worried him was the double bind of "Grace" and "Works". Every good Baptist knew he was saved by the Grace of God and not of Works (lest any man should boast). Tom took this as meaning that he was saved because of what he believed about

God and Jesus and not because of what he had done to advance Their Kingdom on earth. Given these two options, Tom often breathed a sigh of relief that he was born Baptist because - on the face of it - all he had to do was believe, which he did easily and readily. He gladly left it to the Church of Christ, the Mormons, and whatever other denominations required it of their members to keep earning their place in Heaven.

Unfortunately, the double bind was applied by Tom's preacher, his Sunday School and Training Union teachers, and any other saints of the church who had his ear. It said that *though* he was saved by Grace and not of Works, *if* he truly believed, *then* he would joyfully, selflessly, automatically want to be out in the World witnessing for God and advancing His Kingdom on earth by winning souls to Him. The obvious fact that Tom was not out there doing those Works brought him back to the fundamental question of whether that confession and baptism experience ten years earlier really "took".

As a visiting college student in his home church on a weekend outside the normal holiday and vacation periods, Tom could have felt uncomfortably "in between" the adults and small children that he joined on the main floor of the sanctuary and the teens and pre-teens who ruled the balcony. But Tom took the high road and with feigned maturity and a certain arrogance, he sat with his parents. He glanced upon entry and occasionally during the worship service at the high school and junior high kids who had rotated up to the balcony seats after him and who would eventually rotate out as he had, only to be replaced in future years by the grade school children and below who now slept soundly in their parents' laps on the main floor with him.

As Tom had done in his recent past, he knew that he was being eyed with envy by the teenagers as ready to make the break from New Fredonia as he had been. He was also pleased by the unstated understanding - even tradition - that visiting college students were exempt - with honors - from Sunday School attendance. The accepted view was that for college students to deign even to show up at church was above and beyond what could reasonably be expected of them. For their four-year hitch in *academe* they were allowed a suspension of the rules that applied to all ages on either side of eighteen to twenty-two. They could use the time as a breather, as many did; as a time to let their beliefs lapse, as others did;

or as a time to evaluate and bring into focus their relationship with God moreso than their relationship with the Church, as Tom was doing.

The church service plodded faithfully through the Order of Worship past announcements, songs, welcome of visitors, reading of scriptures, and more songs, to the offertory prayer. He listened with a furtive grin below his reverently closed eyes for The Phrase. It seemed like months since he had heard it, though he suspected it had been spoken countless times in his absence. And this morning he was not disappointed:

"... and bless the missionaries on home and foreign fields," prayed the deacon delivering the offertory prayer.

Just as Tom had thought to himself every time - which numbered in the dozens - that he had heard that traditional prayer cliché, he countered in his mind with: 'and pity the poor heathens in the Black Forest.' He had shared the counter-thought with Mark when he came up with it around age eight, and Mark had howled in laughter. The hackneyed prayer phrase had not troubled Tom so much as it had presented to him a vivid picture of missionaries being exclusionary - tending their flocks in verdant green meadows - not bothering with the unsaved who might be the least bit of trouble to get to. The fact that the originality and absurdist humor of the counter-thought coming from an eight-year-old had so impressed his teenage brother assured that the prayer phrase when heard by Tom would forever trigger in him the small joy followed by the small melancholy of that most inside of jokes shared only by two and then treasured only by the survivor.

Then, as surely as after the day, night cometh, Tom awaited with unquestioned certainty the choir's special music following the offering. The choir was small and mostly old, but it had within it a sprinkling of the seeds of regeneration that in microcosm demonstrated the remarkable staying power of such small-town East Texas congregations - a daughter singing with a mother here, a son-in-law with a father-in-law there. With a gusto surprising for their number and with thundering organ and piano support, this Southern Baptist choir launched into "A Mighty Fortress Is Our God", generously - yea, magnanimously - recognizing its differences with Martin Luther as being those of degree rather than kind.

Chapter 8

Following lunch with his parents, Tom swung through Springfield to bid farewell to Meredith before returning to Dallas. He enjoyed a sunny drive back and was not surprised upon return to find Brandeis reading - lights out, feet on his desk, chair propped back against the wall - by that same crisp sunlight streaming in the window of 332 McCartney.

"Hey, Roomie," Brandeis said with a looping wave of his arm.

"So, Rabbi Vasserman, just how vas your Sabbath and my Sabbath for you?"

"Werry pisful oont quviet, my son. My translation of ze *Talmud* eento Peeg Latin ees nearink complition. Voud you care to join me at ze ZUB for to celebrate?"

"Zounds goot."

The roommates left McCartney and headed for the SUB. As they stepped off the curb at the intersection of Knight Boulevard, the tree-lined parkway that bisected the campus, and a narrow side street, they were unaware of the cyclist bearing down on them. Their intrusion into the street had ruined her line through the turn, so as she yelled "Hey!" loudly and quickly to freeze them no farther out in the street than they were, she modified her balance on the bike by swinging her left leg open toward them - her knee almost brushing Brandeis as he stopped at her command.

Noting the swinging gate motion of her thigh, Brandeis yelled after her, "Hey, don't do that unless you really mean it!"

Tom, who had been looking the other way down the boulevard, glanced up in time to see a mop of bleached blonde hair atop a royal blue sweatshirt riding away from him. Brandeis' challenge, however, brought the cyclist to a screeching halt as she clamped hard on the ten-speed's handbrakes. As she engaged the kickstand without looking at the frozen pedestrians, Tom recognized her. It was Siobhan. Anticipating an uncomfortable and embarrassing confrontation for his roommate, he of the Big Mouth, and himself, he walked a few feet away from Brandeis and looked the other way and skyward. For his part Brandeis' mouth fell open slightly as he stared in awe when Siobhan finally turned his way. The stunningly beautiful, unsmiling face wore the best tan he had ever seen in any January. As she walked toward him, he tilted his head allowing a smile, as if welcoming the approaching face-off whatever it entailed.

Siobhan stopped two feet from him, locking her legs at attention and resting her knuckles on her hips. "I really meant it, asshole," she declared brusquely and straight-faced. "What are you going to do about it?"

Without hesitating he reached into his breast pocket and pulled out a crumpled laundry ticket. "I've got a coupon for two hours on the vibrating bed at the Whip Inn on Greenville," he responded matter-of-factly.

"You're on. Want me to pump you over there on my bike?"

He slung his head toward the parking lot saying, "My car'll be quicker. You can pump me when we get there."

"You got rubbers?"

Brandeis stuffed the laundry ticket back in his shirt and reached into his jeans pocket. "Which'll it be?" he asked. "Ribbed or ticklers?"

They finally stood silently for a moment staring at each other as pursed, close-mouthed smiles began to wrinkle their lips. "Gone about as far as we can go with this?" she asked.

"That's all my best stuff for years to come," he allowed, now smiling openly. As they laughed, she leaned her hand against his shoulder.

Tom had maintained his distance during their conversation, but had turned and watched the exchange. As he walked up, interrupting their laughter, she put an embarrassed hand to her mouth and said, "Oh ... Tawm! Are *you* with *him*?"

"Frankly," Tom replied, "I have never seen this man before in my life."

She turned back toward Brandeis, who was staring at her intensely. She dropped her hands to her side and said simply, "I'm Siobhan."

Brandeis thumbed through his thoughts and finally replied, "I'm ... Brandeis."

Tom approached them as they stared at each other, and he picked up their hands closest to him. He joined them and rested his right hand atop theirs while lifting his left hand heavenward. Closing his eyes, he prayed, "Siobhan McKenna ... meet Brandeis Wasserman. What God hath joined together, let not Man mispronounce." As Tom moved away continuing toward the SUB, he saw that they had gone dumb and were once more lost in eye contact. "Hey," Tom laughed, "do you two want to be alone or something?" Simultaneously they turned their heads and rolled their eyes toward him. "Oh," he said, and he waited quietly.

Brandeis looked back at Siobhan and said, "We were on our way to the SUB. Would you like to come?" Tom knew Brandeis' normal voice, and he had heard him talk on the phone to his mother and to his brother, but he had never heard him speak in this tone before. There was a sincerity, a tenderness to it.

"Yeah," she answered softly, also in a tone she had not employed in the biology lab. "Brandeis?" she asked. "Is that what you said your name was?"

"Yeah."

"Nice."

As they began to walk slowly away toward the SUB, Tom looked around, and said, "Say, are we going to contribute your bike to the Wazoo theft ring, or do you want to do something with it?"

Awakening from his daze, Brandeis offered to get it, and he walked the bicycle and Siobhan to the SUB behind Tom's lead.

While Tom waited at the snack bar counter for drinks and fries, Brandeis and Siobhan searched the crowded SUB-Rosa Cafe for a vacant booth. Finally eyeing a foursome rising from their seats, they quickly claimed it. Upon arriving, though, both hesitated and passed knowing grins. Brandeis was glad to see Siobhan too was puzzling over whether to sit beside each other or across the booth from the other - and each knew that was what the other was debating: the cutaneous possibility against the visual certainty. Finally, after nervous smiles and giggles, Brandeis offered Siobhan the view. He was encouraged by a barely perceptible disappointment in her expression as she accepted it. Settling into their seats their eyes locked again. As Brandeis opened his mouth to speak, she began to focus on his face - lips, hair, skin, eyes, lips.

"So ... where're you from?" he asked gently.

"Chicago. Well, really a suburb on the lake north of town named Lake Forest."

"How long have you been at Wazoo?"

"This is my third year. I'm a junior."

This information set off alarm bells for Brandeis - the fear being that his underclassman status would be an impenetrable barrier between them. Based on this information, he chose not to volunteer his class level. Tom joined them at the table bearing a tray of three large orders of French fries, a Dr. Pepper for himself, and Cokes for the non-Texans.

Changing the subject away from class status, Brandeis offered, "There are a bunch of you Windy City-zians down here, aren't there?"

"Yeah," Tom said, "do you know Horace Michaels - or, Horse, as we get to call him?"

"Sure," Siobhan replied. "He went to Saint Mike's, my brothers' school."

"He's a floor below us in McCartney," Tom said.

"Yeah," Siobhan added, "Nice guy. He was a year behind me."

With a dawning smile Tom exclaimed, "Oh, you're a junior!" Before Brandeis' knee could strike him, Tom turned to him and exclaimed, "Wow! A junior Wazoo co-ed deigning to be seen in the SUB with a couple of sophomore weenies like us." Brandeis' eyes, followed by his head, rolled northward in disgust at Tom's open-faced naiveté, as if he were the unwilling half of a social murder-suicide.

Crunching on a fry with half of it hanging from her mouth and noting with a malicious smile Brandeis' reaction, Siobhan replied, "Sophomorics, huh?"

Seeking to rescue the situation by moving on, Brandeis asked, "So, which high school did you attend?"

"Our Redeemer. It was the sister school to St. Michael's. Our Redeemer Wildcats - "

"Our Redeemer *Wildcats?*" Tom repeated.

"Yeah."

"So you've always been a Wildcat, huh?"

"From grade one through Wazoo. Forever a Wildcat," she purred. "Anyway, we were the Wildcats, and the boys were Mike's Marauders."

"Were you a Marauder cheerleader?" Tom asked.

"Of course," she responded, with a flip of her hair. "I'm sure it didn't hurt any that I had had two brothers go through Saint Mike's before me. I guess you could say I was a 'legacy'."

"Any younger brothers or sisters following in your footsteps?" Brandeis asked.

"Nope. After she had me, Meg decided to hang up the ovaries."

With Tom agog, Brandeis held an imaginary microphone to his mouth and said, "Thank you, Miss McKenna, for that discreet and subtle response, but please don't think you have to censor your descriptive flair just for our virgin ears."

"Sorry," she giggled. "It just came out."

"So you went to Catholic schools all the way through?" Tom asked.

"All Catholic - all the way."

"Nuns in habits?" Tom queried.

"Yep," Siobhan replied, warming to his unabashed provinciality. "Some of the nuns were sweet and crazy, and a few of them were mean and crazy, but they were all crazy. They were good teachers, though."

"Taught by nuns," Tom marveled.

"Yeah, and they were so out of touch with reality. Outside of the curriculum, their major purpose in life was to warn us of the danger of that other wholly evil species out there in the world: Boys. According to them, every male child born into this world had within him the potential of being the Antichrist. And the things they warned us about were so hysterical. Like white tablecloths."

"What?" Tom asked.

"Never let a boy take you on a date to a restaurant with white tablecloths," she answered, "because the white tablecloth will remind him of white sheets and make him want to take you to bed!"

"Yeah, I can certainly say for myself," Brandeis offered, "I never would think of that without a really obvious hint. But the tablecloth would definitely do it."

"And, let's see. Oh yeah, of course. Black patent shoes. Never ... ever ... wear black patent shoes on a date, because a boy standing directly in front of you could look down at your shiny black patent shoes ... and look straight up your dress off the reflection!"

"Wow! I never thought of that," Tom noted.

"Tawm!" Siobhan scolded.

"Those remind me of my mom's old wives' tales and superstitions," Tom offered. "You know, like Calvin Coolidge's son dying from a blister on his heel after playing tennis. Whenever she saw a blister on me, she'd get hysterical about my not popping it. She lived in mortal fear of me dying from a popped blister!"

"Mother used to tell me the same story," Brandeis interjected, "but she had it all twisted around. The way it came out with her, I couldn't take tennis lessons!"

"And then there was poor ol' Zachary Taylor," Tom said with a laugh. "He supposedly died of eating too much strawberries and cream on a hot day - "

"Or was it cherries?" Brandeis asked.

"So you heard that one, too?"

"Oh, yeah. Between him and Coolidge, I finally decided it would be more expedient to promise never to run for President - just to avoid a premature sports- or dessert-related death."

"What about fish and milk?" Tom asked.

"What about 'em?" Brandeis asked.

"Eating fish and drinking milk at the same meal. It'll kill you!" Tom exclaimed. "Didn't your mothers ever warn you of that one?"

"No."

"Surprised you two survived childhood. Sure. No salmon croquettes. No fried fish. Nothing. No fish with milk at the same meal or instant death. For anyone. Not just Presidents and their immediate families.

"I loved milk, and I loved salmon croquettes. But I lived in fear that I might negligently have chocolate pie for dessert after salmon croquettes, and I just *have* to drink milk with chocolate pie. And Bam! Grim reaper time. Those fish meals were scary. Of course, we didn't have fish that often, and," glancing at Siobhan, "never on Friday."

"What?" Siobhan asked with a disbelieving laugh.

"Hey, I told you I was from East Texas, and a Baptist to boot. Growing up in 'Noofer' – that's 'localese' for New Fredonia - any good Southern Baptist would rather die than eat fish on Friday. It would suggest an acquiescence to the dark evil of the global Catholic conspiracy."

But Siobhan laughed and said, "Good idea. *We* definitely have a cellar full of weapons. But how did you know Noofer was our next target?"

"Easy. We tortured the Catholic in town until he spilled the beans. Actually, he was a priest, drunk on leftover Communion wine. Okay," Tom said, "last one. My parents made sure that I lived in mortal fear throughout my childhood that my dog was going to bite someone and break the skin, and it was going to have to be checked for rabies. Because, I don't know what the threat was in Illinois or in Tennessee, but in Texas if there was the slightest hint that a dog *might* have rabies, they would - and this is the expression we were always told - 'cut its head off and send it to Austin'. I grew up with this image of the bus station in Austin being the central processing center for hacked-off dog heads - arriving daily in big hat boxes from all over the state. And I wasn't sure whether rabies was detected by lab analysis of its brain or by the scientific reading of the expression on its face! Really strange."

"Ever have that happen to one of yours?" Siobhan asked.

"No way. And they could've bitten my arm off, and I wouldn't have turned them in."

After a laugh, a momentary silence fell on the trio. Still holding the conversational podium, Tom shifted gears and queried, "Pardon the cliché, but I've got to ask, where'd you get that tan?"

"London," she replied smartly. "Well, Acapulco actually, but we did go to London over semester break, too."

"Really?" Tom continued, wide-eyed. "I love England."

"Oh … when were you there last?" she asked.

"I've never been there. I just love England, and things English. Where all did you go? In England?"

Before she could answer, Brandeis broke in, "Oh, and no, I've never been there either, but my brother's ex-girlfriend's cousin once read a travel book about England and Scotland … oh, and Wales, too."

Realizing that she might be coming off haughty and experiencing a rare sense of concern about her own haughtiness, Siobhan responded to Tom with unadorned information. "We went to London and stayed four days there just before Christmas - shopping, seeing shows, sightseeing.

Then our dri-. Then we drove up to Oxford and Stratford-upon-Avon. We had Christmas at the Lygon Arms in Broadway. It was just beautiful. It's a gorgeous country, even in the dead of winter. Of course, Paddy - that's Daddy - was cursing the 'Bloody English' the whole time. And Meg - that's Mom - is just as Irish as he is, but she likes to go to England anyway because she understands what a knockdown great-looking country it is - and historic, too - not like anything we have over here. So after Christmas we ferried over to Dublin and toured all of Daddy's old haunts – especially the Guinness brewery. Then we kind of crisscrossed over to Shannon and flew back from there. We'd done it two summers before, but it was more fun this time because they let me go to a lot of the pubs with them, and that's where the wonderful characters are - the real spirit of the place."

"But what were you saying about Acapulco?" Brandeis asked. "You went there, too?"

"Yeah," she replied, her eyes sparkling as her memory crossed the border. "Oh, it was great. We stayed at Las Brisas. And I'm never staying anywhere else. Have either of you ... ever been to Mexico?" she asked carefully.

Before Tom could answer, Brandeis offered with feigned eagerness, "No, but my grandparents went there back in the fifties and brought me back a really neat carved baseball bat."

"Really?" Tom asked absent pretense.

"Yeah," Brandeis answered, and then laughing at himself, went on, "yeah, as a matter of fact, I loved that bat. It *was* real neat." Then offering Tom his moment, he said, "You went there last fall, didn't you, Tom?"

"Uh-huh," he answered, "but only to Mexico City."

"Yeah, but you went by yourself, didn't you?" Brandeis continued.

"Really?" Siobhan asked.

"I went to see the Grand Prix there in October," Tom reported. "But what about England? What was your favorite place there?"

"Oh, Tom, that's hard to say," she began, grinning deliciously. "But let's see. I loved the Cotswolds. Pretty little honey-colored stone houses in quaint villages with names like Chipping Campden, and Bourton-on-the-Water ... and Stow-on-Wold. And Stratford was wonderful. We saw *The Taming of the Shrew* at the Royal Shakespeare Theatre there. And from a deck off the theatre through a grey fog hanging over the Avon, I saw the silhouette of Holy Trinity Church where Shakespeare's buried. It was this eerie, magical moment."

Brandeis noted Siobhan's momentary embarrassment at having made a more serious, more self-revelatory observation than she had intended as Tom embellished her description, saying, "Yeah, I've seen a picture of that view of the steeple. Down the river from a raised position - between trees on either bank. The picture I saw was on one of those rare sunny days. I'll bet it was something to see through a fog." After a moment's silence, Tom asked, "But what did you think about London?"

"Ooo, London is fabulous. All the history there, and now all the great clubs, too. But those people have so much love and respect and pride in that old city. You hear it from all the cabbies and the tour guides. Even the store clerks. And it's the most ... civilized city I've ever seen. All class. Like Dr. Johnson said, 'If you're tired of London, you're tired of life'."

Just then a tall long-faced co-ed with waist-length black hair wearing a "Harvard - WSU of the East" sweatshirt approached the table. "Chevy," she said in a deep gravelly voice. "The meeting starts in five minutes."

"Oh, Thia," Siobhan said, "this is Brandeis, and this is Tom. Tom's my bio lab partner."

After swapping "hi's", Thia asked, "You coming?"

Siobhan looked into Brandeis' eyes and smiled. "No, I'll make the next one."

Unperturbed, Thia replied, "Okay. See you later." And to Tom and Brandeis, "Nice to meet you guys."

Once she was out of earshot, Brandeis asked, "Chevy?"

"Yeah, a lot of people call me that."

"Well, you don't mind if I keep calling you 'Shivalay', do you?" Tom asked.

As Tom and Siobhan laughed, Brandeis said, "Did I miss something?"

"Hey, Wasserman, Chevy and I go way back. Why, just the other evening, we skinned a frog together in a most intimate setting. Just her, me, Jeremiah, who used to be a bullfrog, about thirty of our closest friends, and fifteen other pickled frogs."

Regaining the floor, Brandeis asked, "What meeting?"

"Oh," she replied, "a ... political meeting."

"Are you for Clean Gene?" Brandeis asked.

Looking at her in anticipation of a response, Brandeis observed a change in her expression - in the glint in her eyes. She dipped her head slightly, and her eyes opened wider as if her mask of playful sarcasm fell away before him, and an honest, defenseless Siobhan was revealed - exposed. "No. I want Bobby to run," she stated with a mix of familiarity and reverence. "He can bring us together. He's the only one who can. Not just end the war, but really bring us together."

Picking up on her newfound sincerity, Brandeis observed, "He sounds pretty important to you."

"He is." After another awkward moment, she smiled and said, "Gee, guys, sorry to bring things down like that. Hey, he probably won't even run. He says he won't run against Johnson, but there are groups of us all over the country who are trying to get him to."

"Are your parents Kennedy people?" Brandeis asked.

"Dyed-in-the-Donegal-wool Democrats. And, yeah, they worshipped J-F-K. The way we see it, the torch was passed to Bobby."

Tom looked perplexed and asked, "I'm glad you're here and everything, Siobhan, but ... it just seems strange. You being such a Kennedy fan - and coming to college in Dallas. How'd you pick Wazoo?"

Nodding as if to validate his question, she replied, "Daddy's in the construction business, and I came with him several times over the years when he's had projects down here. I love the town, and during those trips I'd been out here to Wazoo to visit friends from Chicago who came here." Then after a pause, "I don't blame Dallas for the assassination - but by the same token, I don't spend a lot of time driving past the School Book Depository or the Triple Underpass, either."

"So, what's your major?" Brandeis asked.

"A double in Business and music."

"Music?" Tom asked.

"I play the piano."

"Are you good?" Tom asked, before he could stop himself.

"I'm a lot better than good," she replied.

"Yeah, Trevor Bob Taylor from Noofer is at U.T. - "

"Trevor Bob?" Siobhan interrupted. "Is that really his name?"

"Sure. His mom's English; his dad's New Fredonian," Tom explained offhandedly. "They met in a London bomb shelter during W-W-Two. Brought her home. They had a kid; went halvsies on the name. Anyway,

Trevor Bob is at U-T in music and math. His mother was a concert pianist, and she trained him. Of course, Trevor Bob was just your typical, every-class-has-one genius. He knew his multiplication table through twelve when he walked in the door in first grade. Of course, all the rest of us only knew our sevens."

"Your whats?" Siobhan asked.

"Chevy," he began impatiently, "every boy growing up in Texas learned how to multiply by seven before they learned how to add or subtract. Seven points for a touchdown and extra point. That was before the two-point conversion, of course, and in high school you hardly ever saw a field goal or a safety. So we just learned from age four or five - 7, 14, 21, 28, 35, and so on up to about 77. You hardly ever saw more than eleven T-D's in a high school game."

"Fascinating information, Tawm," Siobhan mused. Then as it had throughout their conversation, her gaze gravitated back to Brandeis' dark, penetrating eyes. "So what about you, Mr. Wasserman? You've been milking me for all this information. What's your story?"

In the best Charles Boyer he could muster, he replied, "I shall remain a man of mystery, for I may yet change my major to 'Life of Crime'. No questions, no pictures, please."

"He's from Memphis," Tom began to tick off matter-of-factly, "he's pre-law; he loves movies; he can lift ten times his weight; his only weakness is Kryptonite." Then looking at Brandeis, he asked breezily, "Leave anything out?"

"Just the Olympic medal and the Peace Prize."

"Sorry. Hey, y'all want to go see a movie?" Tom asked.

"I love 'y'all'," Siobhan stated.

"We love you, too," Tom answered.

Waving him away, Siobhan went on, "No, I mean, I love to hear you Southern boys say 'y'all'. It's so endearing. I really miss it when I go back to 'you guys' country. But, yeah, a movie sounds great. What?"

"Got any ideas?" Tom asked Brandeis.

"Yeah, have you seen *Wait Until Dark*?"

"No."

"No."

"Heard anything about it?" he asked.

"Only that it's supposed to be pee-in-your-pants scary," Siobhan answered.

Glancing at his watch, Brandeis said, "Let's hit it."

As they rose from the table, Tom said earnestly, "There's just one thing I've got to say, Siobhan."

"What's that, Tawm?"

"The fact that you are a Liberal Democrat Irish Catholic ... makes you the most exotic woman I have ever met in my life."

*　　　*　　　*

They settled into their seats in the darkened theatre with Tom and Brandeis on either side of Siobhan. As the movie began to play itself out, they exchanged whispered observations about the against-type casting of Alan Arkin and Richard Crenna in these roles as villains and about the delicate vulnerability of Audrey Hepburn - made the more delicate, the more vulnerable by her character's blindness. As The Scene approached, the threesome was caught unaware. Brandeis had been out to buy popcorn for Siobhan, and she was munching on it vigorously. Tom had bought a Dr. Pepper. They were experiencing obvious relief that the Arkin character seemed to have been put away. Then like the most primitive animal in the jungle, he leapt out of the dark, and all three realized the worst fears of their most horrible childhood nightmares.

Siobhan let her popcorn box tumble where it may as she grabbed with both arms for Brandeis' neck. Tom emptied his drink in the floor and on his jeans as he reached for the armrests. Brandeis simultaneously shrunk into his seat and lifted his knees into a tuck, so that Siobhan's grab for his neck resulted in her burying his head in her bosom and holding onto his wiry mop of hair. Their three screams were but a small part of the cacophonous shriek that filled the auditorium. Tom intently watched the struggle that ensued to its conclusion. When he finally looked around at Siobhan and Brandeis, he saw them still clutched together, and Brandeis was applying a comforting pat on the back. When he whispered to them, "It's okay; it's over," he won no response. His ensuing, "Hey, guys, it's alright," brought a slight separation, but they spent the remainder of the movie joined at the armrest. Her joyous expression was warm and reflective; Brandeis' was that of The Chosen, home from Babylon. Glancing across Siobhan at Brandeis a couple of times during the film's denouement, Tom registered hope for his roommate - and not a little envy.

They left the theatre speaking animatedly about the movie and especially about The Scene. As they approached the car, Siobhan and Brandeis glanced at each other and at the two-door bucket-seated Le Mans. When he opened the door for her, Siobhan snipped the Gordian Knot by suggesting, "Why don't I sit up here with … 'y'all'?" Brandeis nodded gleefully as Tom rolled his eyes skyward.

Returning toward campus from downtown, Tom said, "Hey, let me take y'all down a really fun stretch of road." He drove up into Highland Park, Dallas' exclusive interurb, to the intersection of Fitzhugh and St. John. Heading north on St. John, he worked his way up and down through the gears along the twisting tree-canopied street. His passengers watched him revel in the sharp turns, switchbacks, and changing radius bends offered by the route.

"Tawm, we're going to have to get you a Saint Christopher's for this little jalopy. Might should even drop it by the Vatican for a kiss," Siobhan allowed.

"Yeah, I've been offering him my Star of David necklace to hang from his mirror," Brandeis offered. "I have it on good authority that Golda Meir carried it around in her purse all one afternoon while she was grocery-shopping in Milwaukee."

"Star of David?" Siobhan queried.

"Yeah," Brandeis replied with a smile.

Lifting herself barely from his lap, she blurted out, "You're a Jew?"

"*Bona fide*' Son of Abraham," Brandeis declared.

Sitting back down in his lap, Siobhan began to laugh - and then to laugh uncontrollably, holding her face in her hands and rocking her head toward the windshield.

"Don't worry," Brandeis jested, "I've been polled."

"No, no," she continued to laugh, "it's just so funny - what Paddy and Meg would think. And Father Martin - and -"

Joining her in laughter, Brandeis allowed, "Yeah, it would kind of set Avrum and Shirley on their ears, too. Not to mention Rabbi Blitstein."

"You," Tom began with feigned disgust, "You… non-Protestant heathens."

Upon their return to campus Siobhan realized she had left her bicycle chained to the rack in front of the SUB. Tom dropped Brandeis off with her to walk Siobhan and her Peugeot home to Blake Hall. After putting the bike away, Brandeis walked to the dorm's front steps with her. There she turned to him and with a mischievous grin, said, "I have a request."

"I'll see what I can do".

Is it alright if I call you Bran?"

"Sure."

"Good," she began and then dipping her head while looking up at him, added, "because there may be times I'll need to say your name fast, and I may be ... out of breath."

*   *   *

Tom and Brandeis lifted their trays from the cafeteria line and strode out into the expanse of McCartney Mess Hall. Seeing Joe Joe at an otherwise unoccupied table, they joined him as he was sugaring his Frosted Flakes. The threesome gobbled down their breakfast with a minimum of *non sequitur*-strewn conversation until Joe Joe excused himself to return to bed, it being Tuesday. Shortly the 332 two were joined by Rodg Messing and by Clark Ferring, Rodg's counterpart on second floor. The young men ate industriously, continuing their inconsequential small talk.

When Brandeis glanced up and waved at someone passing their table, though, Tom was surprised to note as he was waving back that it was a tall, lean black student. "You know him?" Tom asked with curiosity.

"Yeah," Brandeis replied casually. "That's Danzell Johnson. He was in Culver with me last year. Neat guy."

"Huh," Tom sighed, with sufficient disapproval to irritate his roommate.

Deciding to explore Tom's boundaries in this area, Brandeis went on, "Yeah, he's a dancer. I know his girlfriend, too. Emily Watson. Last year she and I were in that "Man and His World" experimental theatre workshop that they didn't bring back this year." To Tom's blank nod, Brandeis declared, "Emily is one beautiful girl."

"Is she black?" Tom blurted out, catching the attention of Rodg and Clark.

"Yeah," Brandeis huffed. "She's black. She's from around here but lives on -"

"Well, so which is she?" Tom asked. "Black ... or beautiful? I mean, is she a nigger or is she a knockout?" Tom asked, laughing at his alliterative turn of phrase. "It's one of those 'either-or' things." Brandeis replied with stunned silence.

Hearing Tom's last remark, Rodg turned and stared coldly at him. Picking up on the cessation of conversation at the other end of the table and sensing the glare, Tom turned and stared back into Rodg's injured frown - his eyes squinting behind his small round wire-rims and his lips pursed as if holding back comment.

"What?" Tom asked, opening his hands, in reply to Rodg's look.

Rodg continued to stare for a long moment, but he did not answer Tom. Finally, he turned to Brandeis and asked, "Did you go hear Phil French last night?"

"No," Brandeis replied, thrilled not to be on the receiving end of the floor director's unspoken wrath.

"Did you?" he turned and asked Clark Ferring.

"No. What did he have to say?"

"You know, he's head of SCAR, Student Coalition Against Racism, and they've decided to picket Rutledge's Washateria, the one with the 'Whites Only' sign up." Tom could feel his ears reddening as his face became flush, but he remained silent. Looking back at Brandeis, Rodg continued, "They're looking for volunteers. You might want to call Phil."

"What's the administration said about their doing that?" Clark asked. "I mean, they *are* an authorized student organization, aren't they?"

"Yeah," Rodg replied. "From what he said, though, I don't think he ran it by them."

"Gutsy move," Clark stated.

"Yeah," Brandeis agreed.

As the three discussed the validity of SCAR's planned boycott and picket line, Tom dealt with the dagger Rodg had plunged into his intellect - with the brand he had applied. There had been few moments in Tom's life when he had been so acutely forced to re-evaluate such a basic and previously unchallenged attitude as his regarding race. He had inherited his father's view, which was that common to the coffee break crowd at the Swan Cafe in New Fredonia and, he had assumed, to that of much of white America. His attitudes had been intellectually challenged on occasion through the Kennedy and Johnson years of the early Sixties, though his view still held that most of the Freedom Marches, sit-ins, and demonstrations were staged by white liberals and Northern blacks - the notorious "outside agitators". But the flames and gunfire of Watts and the other urban battlegrounds of the summers of the mid-Sixties generated a fear in him that confirmed the correctness of his earlier segregationist instincts. His direct connection of racial activism with the threat of physical violence and property destruction had, until now, given him the comfort necessary to support the validity of his old views. But after his conversation with Freddie Slater, he who was born of the same cauldron; after his observation of the "normalcy" of the few black classmates he had had the prior semester; and now, receiving the unspoken condemnation of Rodg Messing, this young man whom Tom saw as having a clear-eyed, unbiased handle on absolute right and wrong in a modern world, Tom knew it was past time for self-examination and course correction. He knew the old habits of thought - those born of inherited signals and reinforced by simple and handy reactions to fear - could no longer be complacently condoned in his attitudes toward an entire race of people with whom he lived.

Looking back at Tom, Rodg said, "Well, to quote Phil - and he gave a damn good speech - 'sometimes you just have to give the finger to the world ... and go ahead and do what's right'."

Tom buckled his lip and nodded.

"And Tom," he added, raising his index finger to support his imperative, "don't use that word again."

Chapter 9

Early February

"You better ask Tolbert," Joe Joe advised from the neighboring stall. "I've already struck out with most of the liquor stores in Dallas County. All the clerks know me. Some of them just laugh when they see me come in. I been through so many fake ID's, sometimes I forget my own name. Anyway, you ought to go to Tolbert. Everyone does. But listen," he offered in a furtive tone - lowering his head as if trying to whisper through the opening under the metal stall wall, "if you guys just want a girl to spill the cream with, why don't you let me line you up with this 'Metscan' girl who cleans the rooms at the Whip Inn - Lana Estacado. She's drained my case a couple of times like I ain't never had it done before."

Holding his head and shaking off an incredulous laugh, Brandeis replied, "Thanks for the offer, Joe Joe, but I guess we'll just stick with the booze."

Taking Joe Joe's advice, Brandeis visited Bob Tolbert. Finding him casually throwing off a hand of solitaire while Pete Wheeler studied at his desk, Brandeis said, "Hey, Bob, I hear you're the man to talk to about the purchase of libations."

"Don't know about that, but I'd be glad to buy you some beer. You want a six-pack?"

"Well, I've got one little problem. No wheels."

"No problem," Tolbert replied. "I'm pickin' up a couple cases for a frat buddy on Two. I can get you what you need, too. What'll it be?"

Peach brandy," Brandeis replied through an embarrassed grin.

"What? You got a cough?" Bob asked with a derisive leer.

"Hey, it's Windham's birthday. He can't see his girlfriend because it's the middle of the week. Won't even go out because he's got a major history exam. And that's the only thing he says he'll drink."

"You got it. What do you want? A pint?"

"Smallest size they've got".

"Probably a pint. Maybe a half-pint. I'll see if they have a teaspoon dispenser."

*   *   *

Brandeis opened the door of 332 to find Tom pouring over his history text while munching a gooey chocolate chip cookie from the batch his mother had sent. Glancing up at Brandeis, Tom allowed with disgust, "This test is gonna be a 'muthah'."

Brandeis returned a sly grin as he slowly lifted the bottle from its brown paper bag.

"Whatcha got there, Woz-man?"

"Oh, I just didn't think we should let the occasion of bidding adieu to your teenage-hood go by without a mild celebration. Or a wild one if it turns out to be."

"Peach brandy!" Tom noted with a laugh. "You sure you're not trying to get me drunk? You probably got a carload of big-tittied Tri-K nymphos downstairs just ready to have their way with me after you get my defenses down with hard liquor."

"No, I was much more egalitarian about it. We have the Homecoming Queen and her entire court. Each sorority on campus is represented."

"I must not disappoint," Tom allowed, reaching high on his shelf for his bottle of British Sterling. Sucking in his stomach and pulling out his jeans, he splashed several drops into his underwear.

Brandeis approached him and handed him the bottle. "Just thought you might want to celebrate. And since you don't have anywhere to go, and nothing to do but study, I figured you couldn't get in any trouble staying home and knocking back a bottle."

"Where's yours?" Tom asked.

"Hey, I'm the one who's going to drive you back to your bed."

"Well, just don't try to have your way with me before the queen and her court get their chance."

Brandeis grinned uncomfortably for a second before he laughed. Tom broke the seal on the bottle, unscrewed the cap, and took a whiff of the contents. "I guess I like it because it reminds me so much of that sweeter-than-sweet cough syrup Mom used to get me if I played my cards right," he said, and he started to take sips.

After a half hour of off-and-on discussion of school goings-on Brandeis asked, "You talked to Meredith yet tonight?"

"No, she's got a sorority thing. She said she may call later."

"She sounds like a neat girl. I'm really looking forward to meeting her. When's she going to be up?"

"Oh, she and her parents'll probably find some occasion to come to Dallas during the semester. They come over here shopping a lot."

"Must really feel good to have someone special like that."

Tom could feel his limbs and his tongue loosening. He propped his feet on the bed, laid his forearms on his knees, and rested his head and shoulders against the wall. "I don't know. Meredith and I don't seem to have that spark. We get along okay. She's pretty. Fun sometimes. But we both seem to be holding something out. We'll never admit it. But both of us always seem to know it. That's why we don't talk a whole lot about the future. I talk about what I want. She talks about what she wants - and she talks about what she wants for me to want. But neither of us talks about us."

"Are you going to recognize that spark when you feel it?"

His inhibitions floating away, Tom replied, "Yeah."

"Well, if you haven't felt it yet with Meredith, are you going to grow into it?"

"No, probably not. I know what it feels like. I'll recognize it if - I'll recognize it when I feel it again."

"Again?"

"Have you ever felt it?" Tom asked.

"No," Brandeis said. "I've never felt that special about a girl."

"Well, have you ever felt that special about a guy?" Tom laughed.

"No," Brandeis replied quickly and seriously.

"Just kidding," Tom allowed. Brandeis face remained solemn for a moment as Tom watched him. "Hey, I was just kidding."

Brandeis looked away from Tom and out the window into the wintry chill of the Men's Quad. "I had something real strange happen to me over Christmas. A friend of mine from high school was in town over the holidays - home from Vanderbilt. And he called me to go see a show. We went out, got some pizza, went to the show. And it was still early, so we got a six-pack - he has a good fake I-D - and went back to his house to watch some T-V."

Tom anticipated what was coming, and he dreaded it. He tried consciously to sober himself up - focusing his eyes on Brandeis and trying to focus his mind - so that he could handle what he feared his roommate would say. His face was tingling, and his nose and lips were numb from the peach brandy he had been drinking too rapidly for his normally alcohol-free system. Reflexively, he wrapped his arms around his knees and closed himself up like a turtle with only his head exposed.

"We watched a movie together," Brandeis continued. "We were sitting on a couch in his den, and we both had our feet propped up on the coffee table in front of us. We'd both had a couple of beers, and I was feeling sleepy." Tom's face registered an anticipatory wince, which Brandeis noticed. He continued, knowing that Tom was already ahead of him. "At one point I dozed for a minute, and when I came to ..." Brandeis said, taking a breath. "And when I came to, he had his hand on my thigh. He was looking at me square in the eyes with this pitiful smile on his face ... that seemed to be asking if it was alright."

Tom shrugged, shook his head, and emitted a disgusted sigh. Finally he asked, "What did you do?"

"Tom ... for a second there, I didn't do anything. It really didn't feel bad, but I knew it was wrong. We'd been close friends in high school. I really liked the guy. I really *like* the guy now."

"Oh, damn," Tom moaned.

"But I moved away from him - let his hand fall on the couch. We stared at each other for a long time without saying anything. And then he started into this discourse, backtracking, real defensive, about how he really liked girls, but how he'd always had this special feeling for me. The guy was really mixed up. I knew he'd never had any girlfriends in high school, but then I guess he knew I'd never dated that much either. He told me he'd been dating at Vandy. He didn't say anything else about him and me. But, Tom…I did not protest too much. It scared the crap out of me. I still don't know how I felt about it - how I feel about it."

Are you going to see him again?" Tom asked. "Do you want to?"

Brandeis hesitated. "No, no, I really don't think I want to."

Don't *think* you do?"

"No, I don't want to."

"I just can't identify with that at all," Tom declared. "It grosses me out. You hear jokes about that stuff a lot, but ... I never thought ... well, I've never had an experience with it, and I don't ever plan to."

"Well, I didn't plan to either," Brandeis said, "but I do like the guy. He's a friend of mine. I care about him."

"Friendship's one thing, but that's something else all together."

"Yeah, yeah, I know. It's just that - "

"It's just that nothing," Tom interrupted. "That's really sick."

"Tom, I don't think it's sick to want to be loved."

"Well, that's what girls are for," Tom shot back. They fell silent for a moment, each avoiding the other's gaze. Then Tom asked quietly, "Have you told anybody else about this?"

"Only my brother," Brandeis answered. "It was real good to have him to talk to about it. His reaction at first was a lot like yours, but he's a pretty sensitive guy. He loves me. We've shared a lot. I guess it's rough for you not having anyone like that."

Tom rose from his bed and looked out the window into the darkness. His defenses down, Tom voiced his thought, "I did ... but I don't anymore."

Brandeis looked at Tom curiously. "Who?"

A hot tightness seized Tom's throat as he turned to face Brandeis. He answered deliberately, "Mark. My brother."

Brandeis was silent for a moment trying to grasp this gap in information that had existed for almost a month. He tried to dial back to any mention Tom had made of having a brother. He could not remember an instance when he had, and he thought that sometime in the past Tom had given him the impression that he was an only child. "You never told me you had a brother," Brandeis finally said.

"He was six years older than me ... and he died ... when I was fourteen."

"I'm really sorry, Tom. But I don't remember your ever saying anything about him."

"No, I haven't, but I think about him a lot."

"I'm sure you do. I can't imagine what that would be like. I love Teddie. He's a part of me."

"Yeah, so is Mark."

"How did he ..." Brandeis began. "How did he die? An accident?"

After a long hesitation, Tom answered, "No." Then focusing beyond the wall behind Brandeis, he added, "On purpose."

"You mean ..." Brandeis began to ask and then paused. "He ..."

"Yeah," Tom answered coldly. "I mean he took a twelve-gauge shotgun ... put the barrel to his heart ... leaned over it ... and pulled the trigger." Tom's voice was icy, disembodied, like nothing Brandeis had ever heard come from his lips. "... Left himself to be found in a pool of blood by his parents at the lakehouse. With a note beside him," Tom continued, now with an edge of bitterness, "that really gave a lot of comfort to those of us he left behind." Brandeis was silent - in shock, but Tom answered his unasked question. "It said, 'This is a suicide note. No one is responsible for this but me.'"

"Your parents *showed* it to you?"

"No, I found it."

"My God, Tom," Brandeis began, shaking his bowed head. "My God, I'm so sorry." Then after a long pause, "So how old was he?"

"Twenty. I'm about to catch up with him."

"What? Oh - "

"Yeah, April 20, 1968. I'll be as old as he was when he died."

"So what does that mean?" Brandeis asked carefully.

"Oh, I'll probably just note the day. Take a look at where I am, and what I've become. I can hardly compare where he was with where I will be. He was a lot smarter than me, but I guess I'm obviously ... more stable. And, no, you needn't worry," he added with a grin but with a theatrical profundity, "I'm not ready for that ... Final Disappointment."

Brandeis countered with a smile and said, "That's good to hear, but I hope you don't mind if I call my 'shrink' anyway and ask him what it means when people start quoting Peggy Lee lyrics."

They shared a small laugh. Breathing easier, Tom offered, "Hey, let's call it quits on the 'True Confessions' portion of this evening's program." With both of them emotionally exhausted and Tom still woozy from the liquor, an unspoken moratorium on dialogue set in, and the roommates flopped back on their beds for some easy conversation backed up by *Album 1700*.

Chapter 10

With the mental adrenalin available to students in their subjects of choice, Tom kept the previous night and its emotional and traditional hangovers at bay until the completion of his history test. Then zombie-like, he plodded through the remainder of his classes aided most by the consumption of huge portions of wheat bread and dinner rolls chased with a pint of milk at lunch. By mid-afternoon he headed home toward McCartney. In spite of the previous night's benign conclusion, his mind fought a reluctant skirmish between his out-of-synch body's urge to plummet into bed and a nagging anxiety about being with Brandeis again. By the time he opened the door of 332 his mood had not improved.

"She said 'Yes'!" Brandeis declared, elation dawning, as he put down the receiver. "Siobhan McKenna said 'Yes'! I've got a date with her!"

"Yes?!" Tom exclaimed, suddenly returning the sunbeam smile of his friend as he grabbed his arms and shook him. His anxiety evaporated instantly.

"Yes! Yes! Yes!"

"My Lord, Wasserman, do you realize what you've done? What this means? You've not only dated up a whole class, you got a date with a Tri-K." Thrusting an imaginary broadsword skyward, Tom continued, "You've crossed the Aegean! My God, I can't believe you had the guts to ask her."

"Hey, your guys win a six-day war - kick some ass in the Sinai. It gives you all kinds of confidence," Brandeis crowed. "But I've got one problem."

"What's that?"

"No wheels."

"You mean you want me to chauffeur?"

"No, I've given it some thought, and since I'm wheel-less, I guess I can take her over to the Wildcat for pizza, and then we can walk down to Schneider Plaza and see whatever's on at the Vista."

"No way, Woz-man. She'd be laughed off sorority row," Tom scolded. "Okay, here's the deal. I'll break my blood oath to Dad ... and loan you my car."

Brandeis' eyes brightened, but his manners intervened as he replied, "Oh, no, you don't have to - "

"Oh, yes," Tom offered, "if you're going to go, you might as well go in style; so, for this one special night in your life, the 'Luh Mahnz'. I mean, what were you planning on doing - *walking* her over to the ZPL after the movie?"

"Oh, I think the ZPL would be a little ambitious for the first date."

"Son, what were *you* looking at when she was giving you those looks she was giving you at the SUB the other day?" Tom asked.

"Hey, I'm going to take it real easy with her. I don't want to blow it. But, really, thanks for the car. This is great. Now I can take her down into town. At the Casita Linda they're having a revival of *Casablanca*," he said pensively, his image of the date starting to form in his mind.

During the ensuing two days before The Date, Brandeis was amazed and appalled as Tom took on all the most frightening characteristics of a Prom Mom getting him ready for "The Most Important Night of His Life". Sending his shirts to the cleaners, demanding that he buy a new sweater, having his pants pressed, Tom even glanced up once as if to suggest that he might get his hair cut. To this, Brandeis clipped off "No" before the suggestion left Tom's lips. Finally, he got the message that Brandeis was losing patience when he asked, "You're not planning on coming along in the car and taking pictures when I pick her up, are you?"

And then Date Night came, and, true to form, as Brandeis was trying to escape 332, his roommate was still picking lint off his new sweater.

But as he walked away down the hall, Tom stood in the doorway and said, "You look great. Go get her."

Turning to Tom in his starched light blue oxford cloth shirt under a burgundy lambswool V-neck sweater above perfectly creased tan corduroy slacks and Weejuns polished at Tom's request by Blackjack, Brandeis replied, "Of course you think I look great. I look just like you."

*   *   *

Brandeis arrived at Blake Hall at prime date pick-up hour. After leaving his name at the desk and requesting that Siobhan be rung, Brandeis joined the club of expectant males in Blake's delivery room. His fellow members donned in the gamut from dress suits to jeans, he felt oddly out of place in this gathering that he had visited so rarely during his three semesters at WSU.

Co-eds came and couples went, and finally Siobhan, who chose to make her entrance down the old lobby's ornately-banistered winding staircase, began her descent. A bedazzled Brandeis watched her in. With a white rabbit jacket draped over her arm she wore a forest green scoop-necked, long-sleeved wool knit minidress. Having seen her only the one time in her sweatsuit and never before dressed out in full date regalia, Brandeis unabashedly and uncontrollably stared her figure up and down. Her breasts spilled bounteously and tan from the top of the dress, which then tapered dramatically to her narrow waist before filling out roundly at the hips to the flare of the skirt. Her tanned, athletic legs finished the picture. Finally, Brandeis looked back at her face and offered her the smile of a child whom Santa had blessed and in excess. Her face, framed by her bobbed and banged bleached blonde hair, was incandescent - dominated by her sparkling blue eyes. Her lips were full and succulent and were adorned with the palest of pink lipsticks.

"You look nice," she offered sweetly.

"You are ... beautiful," he proclaimed with near-reverence. Trying to snap back to the event at hand, he awkwardly murmured, "Are you ... ready to go?"

"Sure," she replied eagerly.

Following an exchange of nods between Siobhan and the desk clerk, he gently took her arm and led her to Tom's car. After ceremoniously opening her door and depositing her inside, he took the driver's seat. But looking around at her, he again lost concentration noting her flagrant beauty in the soft glow from the dash.

"So, where'd you like to eat?" he finally asked. "What do you like around here?"

"Well," she replied, with much more experience at how this was supposed to work, "did you have anything in mind?"

"All I had in mind was Wildcat Pizza, and Tom informed me that that was totally unacceptable. And ... having seen your outfit, I think he was probably right."

"The Wildcat sounds great!" she announced with genuine excitement. "I love their pizza."

"Me, too! The Wildcat it is."

As Brandeis drove across campus, he experienced feelings of a confusion that were to be an unwelcome third party intermittently throughout the evening. He was enjoying being with Siobhan as much as he had the previous Sunday at the SUB and at the movie - and more. But he also felt the pressure to be "cool", to be entertaining and funny, to be whatever it took to impress her to the point that she would be interested in dating him again - and again. His fear was that she had been attracted to him Sunday by something he said or did or by an aura that he created then that he might be unable to replicate and sustain. He had trouble allowing himself to accept the comfort offered him by her obvious enjoyment of his company.

Conversation was difficult over the din of the Wildcat crowd and the jukebox in the background, but while they awaited their large "Kitchen Sink" plus anchovies, they rehashed *Wait Until Dark* and were reminded of their body lock in response to The Scene. Siobhan, who had been sitting a quarter of the round table away from Brandeis, scooted her chair toward his. Following suit, he was rewarded with occasional shoulder and knee brushes, which were exceeded in enjoyment only by the continuing magic of looking into her eyes. Through the lengthy wait for their pizza they swapped information about Chicago and Memphis, their neighborhoods, and favorite features of their respective hometowns. Siobhan proudly crowed about the pan pizza at Gino's East. She also described the ominous beauty of a fog bank rolling in off Lake Michigan. Searching for examples of Memphis' uniqueness, Brandeis ticked off

Beale Street, Elvis's home at Graceland, and the ducks at the Peabody Hotel. Siobhan listened with rapt attention to Brandeis' description of the ducks' daily regimen of taking the elevator to the lobby fountain each morning at eleven and returning ceremoniously to their penthouse digs each afternoon at five.

"They sound so cute," she squeaked.

"Yeah," he added, "you ought to see them. They waddle and quack down this red carpet from the elevator to the fountain with this old fellow urging them along."

"I'd love to see them," Siobhan said into his eyes.

"I'd love to show you," he responded.

"568," announced the pick-up counter.

In the presence of this dream date and in his continuing quest for coolness, Brandeis put his pizza-eating know-how aside and bit down on his first bite without blowing on it. He was unable to muffle his pained exhalation and his rapid grab for and guzzling of Coke. Siobhan vicariously winced in pain and then shared a knowing grin with him while she blew vigorously at the tip of her first wedge. After his drink Brandeis assessed with his tongue the damage to the roof of his mouth. He found the familiar residual shards of scorched skin dangling there for him to play with over the weekend.

The positive result of his mis-bite, though, was Brandeis' discovery that he could behave in an un-cool manner in front of Siobhan without fear of ridicule or disaffection. It was finally becoming clear to Brandeis that she *liked* him.

They left the Casita Linda arm-in-arm, humming "As Time Goes By".

"I loved that movie," she announced with a full-bodied exhalation. "It was so beautiful. And *she* was so beautiful."

"And those looks they gave each other at the airport," he added. "Wow!"

"Oh, and they were so in love in Paris. I felt so sorry for him in the rain at the train station."

"Yeah, and at the end, I didn't know how it was going to come out, but I thought there was going to be some way they'd all get away together." After walking silently for a moment, Brandeis stated solemnly, "I think it was the most aesthetically pleasing film I've ever seen."

"The most 'what'?" she asked.

"Aesthetically pleasing," he replied, his pretense threatened.

Where'd you get that?"

Leading her in laughter, he admitted, "I read a lot of movie reviews. Ahem, excuse me - film reviews."

"Aesthetically pleasing, huh?" she mused, and, without warning or plan, gave him a hug at the waist.

Just as naturally he reached around her and pulled her to him. Her softness, her warmth, and her compliance overwhelmed him. Unsuccessful in his attempt to quell or even to control the delirious joy that was gripping him, he smiled down at Siobhan and said, "God, this feels good."

"Yeah," she replied softly through an easy but sincere smile, "it does."

They arrived at the Le Mans' passenger door, and she stood by him while he unlocked the car. He turned and was facing her. They both wanted him to kiss her, but he did not. He opened the door for her and glanced at his watch. Ten o'clock. Too early, he thought. Ensconcing himself in the driver's seat, he asked, "What do you want to do?"

"I'm open."

"Hmm," he stalled, flipping through the limited entertainment reference guide in his mind. "Oh, yeah," he finally offered, as if having divined the correct answer on an oral quiz, "how about 'Quarter of Three'?"

On a rundown section of The Drag south of campus, Quarter of Three was an anachronism clinging tenuously to the fifties - a jazz club/coffeehouse. Almost swamped by the British Invasion, it held on principally because of an intense interest at WSU in jazz, which, in turn, was stoked by the school's nationally renowned jazz band program.

"Sure," she replied tentatively, for she knew, as she assumed Brandeis also did, that Quarter of Three's crowd was split between Greeks and "Artsies" - both groups in which Siobhan knew she fit most comfortably but in which she feared Brandeis might feel out of place.

Although he had never been inside the club, Brandeis had passed it a number of times. He recognized its flat black plaster exterior and rickety awning over the entrance. Entering, the couple was greeted by the hostess, a frail young woman with a blanched complexion in '50's Beat attire. As she escorted them across the room, he threw over his shoulder, "Walk this way", and swung his hips twice. She followed his orders but with an exaggeration that her hips and her dress easily allowed her. Watching her, he lost concentration momentarily. The table he walked into barely shook and no drinks spilled. The spirited fellow-Wazoozers seated there laughed and gave him a gentle shove back on track.

The interior walls carried out the flat black motif with professionally scribbled graffiti etched on them in white. A smoky haze hung in the stale, poorly ventilated air of the club. On the way to the table, Brandeis had noticed Siobhan waving at two rowdy tables eliciting "Hey, Chevy's" from each of them. He had looked but had recognized no one. He felt himself being watched and being evaluated as he passed. The hostess led them to a tiny, round wall-side table away from the stage. Scrawled diagonally down the wall above them was:

'I saw God, and She was Black'

"I love that one," Siobhan said. As she glanced toward the stage, she squealed in glee and pointing vigorously, said, "Hey, look, it's Hawk and Coy."

"Who?"

"Hawk Antoine and Coy Delacourte," she replied. "They're Sigma Sigs from N'Awlins," she drawled. Hawk was at a trap set while Coy nursed a sax. On break, they had watched her cross the room. When they saw that she had seen them, Coy nodded her way and Hawk fired off a rimshot. Brandeis experienced the momentary fear of having sleepwalked naked into a stranger's garden party. He worried that he would either lose her attention to the groups of her friends present, or worse, that she might feel obligated to stay with him while wishing she were with them. But his fears proved unfounded, as, after her initial recognition of her compatriots, she turned her undivided attention to him.

The long-nosed hostess returned to take their orders. With a "what-else-would-we-order-here" tone, he glanced at Siobhan and coolly queried, "Espresso?"

"Of course."

Indicating with his forefinger and thumb, he stated, "*Dos espressos.*"

After a half hour of amateurishly eclectic jazz, two more espressos, and fitful conversation running the gamut from fluffy to snide, Brandeis' discomfort from the absence of ventilation was confirmed by Siobhan's protest, "I'll never get all this smoke out of my hair."

"Are you about ready to leave," he asked. She nodded and they made for the exit.

Returning to campus at half past eleven, Siobhan fell silent in anticipation of Brandeis' next move. As he drove through WSU, he took the street bordering the ZPL on the east. Glancing out into the acres of the vast parking lot adjoining The Zim, both saw the array of haphazardly parked vehicles strewn across the grass - all with their lights off, even the two cars making their way out of the lot and the one entering. Siobhan and Brandeis wondered with less and more degrees of anxiety, respectively, whether he would lead them into the campus ritual of parking at the ZPL; for the ZPL was the unofficially authorized make-out zone for WSU students. By an unwritten understanding rooted in tradition - on the order of the English Common Law - between Wazoo students, administration, and security, it was off limits to campus police, and they patrolled only the perimeter. While some students without dates used the ZPL for weekend beer parties, most could be found in backseats under blankets fogging their windows.

With a coward's sigh Brandeis turned right toward the dorms, and Siobhan withheld comment. Arriving back at Blake Hall, she took Brandeis' hand as they ascended the steps and said, "Come inside for a minute."

Passing through the phalanx of fellow early returnees receiving and administering goodnight kisses on the semi-circular columned porch, she led him through the lobby to the parlor of Blake and to a seat beside her on the piano bench. She began to play "As Time Goes By" - first simply, then with rhapsodic frills. He gently placed his arm around her waist as she played, closing his eyes periodically to fully absorb the feel, the sound, even the fragrance of the moment, against the distant, plaguing fear that this might be all - the fear that tomorrow she might awaken and regain her senses and laugh him off as a weekend's aberration. Just in case, he wanted all of his senses filled with the memory.

But at the completion of the piece she smiled warmly at him, and his apprehensions fell away. "When did you learn to play that?" he asked. "I thought you had never heard it before."

"Just now. I'm sure I've heard it ... but I had never played it before."

"But you mean, you've never seen that music before?" he asked in amazement.

"No, I heard it tonight ... and I wanted to play it for you," she said. With a smile, she added, "I told you. I'm good."

Their eyes locked and their smiles eased away. Bereft of further small talk and lacking either the courage or the confidence to initiate large talk, Brandeis said, "I guess I'll go."

Siobhan nodded and whispered, "Okay."

She walked out with him, taking his hand at the door. On the steps he turned to her and asked, "Can I see you tomorrow?"

Too quickly, she answered, "Yes." They laughed, and she corrected herself by repeating more quietly and in a measured tone, "Yes," before adding with a coy smile, "How early?"

"How about breakfast?" he answered hopefully.

"Like I said, how early?"

"Eight?"

"I'll be ready."

She walked down the steps with him toward his car and out of the glare of the porch light. Finally he turned to her, and as she leaned into him, he enveloped her in his arms. He felt the full warmth and softness of her body. He moved in to kiss her with his lips slightly apart. When their faces met, though, he found his lips awkwardly alone and engaged only by her probing tongue and her open mouth. To her surprise he pulled away, smiling, and said, "Hey, I didn't know we were going straight to France." The laugh that followed was followed as quickly by silence – and then by The Kiss.

Chapter 11

Mid-February

Tom opened the door of 332 to the familiar sight of Brandeis hunched over his desk, the only light in the room his table lamp.

"Whatcha up to?" Tom asked.

"Writing Mother."

"Filling her in on Chevy?" Tom teased.

Smirking off his roommate's non-response, Tom dumped his load of textbooks and multicolored spiral notebooks on his bed. Sifting through them, he picked out his survey on Europe since 1848. Flipping on his light he eased back against the wall on his bed and located the Franco-Prussian War of 1871. But before he could get deeply into the reading, Harvey Groesbeck entered and left the door open behind him. The open door suggested to Tom that Harvey's visit would entail only a news brief and not an in-depth investigatory report. Harvey's look of sincere concern, though, also told Tom the news he was there to disseminate was serious - hard news - not the *Guinness Book of World Records*-type human interest stories that Harvey enjoyed so much to tell and Tom enjoyed so much to hear. No two-hundred-pound pumpkin cultivated on the ancient site of a Franciscan monastery's latrine this.

"What's new at the news?" Tom asked, referring to Harvey's prized position as reporter for *Cat Tracks*, the campus gazette.

Before he began his reply, though, Harvey saw Jack Putnam look in the door. He motioned to his roommate saying, "You'll want in on this." With a solemn profundity patterned after Chet Huntley delivering news of the death of a head of state, Harvey began, "The wire service reports that've been trickling in on these battles in 'Nam the last two weeks have been real scary. They really caught us with our pants down. Almost took Saigon. All of a sudden, there and in provincial capitals and towns all over the country, the Cong just came out of the woodwork and hit everywhere. Westmoreland had been telling us we had them under control and were winning the war. And, like magic, suddenly they're everywhere - anywhere they want to be. I was thinking this thing might be over before I got out, but it looks more and more like I may get to report on it." The latter statement he began with an unmasked enthusiasm that trailed off into a masked enthusiasm amid mild embarrassment.

"I think you can count on that," Tom opined. Brandeis kept his head down continuing to scribble his letter.

"You know, they were real sneaky about it. They started during the Tet holiday, when there's usually a truce." As Joe Joe passed the open door, Harvey offered, "The press has dubbed it the 'Tet Offensive'."

Joe Joe stopped suddenly in the hall, stepped inside the door wearing that rarest of his expressions - righteous indignation - and exclaimed, "Tit?! Offensive?! Why that's a contradiction in terms!"

As Harvey protested, "No, no, I said –", Joe Joe expounded.

"Tit's the most wonderful thing God ever placed on a woman's body or in a man's mouth. I can honestly say," and he assumed an oratorical pose, "I never ate a tit I didn't like."

"No, I said 'Tet'," Harvey explained with amused exasperation. "Tet. It's the name of the Vietnamese New Year."

"Oh, well, yes, of course," Joe Joe winked, as he dropped onto Brandeis' bed.

"Well, we can all laugh," Harvey continued, "but it won't be so funny for you when you're slogging around in a rice paddy. The war's worse than ever, and L-B-J just keeps dumping more of our guys into it, to where it looks like it'll finally get around to us."

"Yeah," Tom said, "I remember, growing up, playing war, playing with toy soldiers, fighting the Krauts, the Japs, the North Koreans. We re-fought the Civil War, the American Revolution. War games were just such a natural part of that time ... but none of us ever died from it – never imagined we'd have another war."

Brandeis turned toward the room and said, "Listen, it's a crazy war, and it doesn't have anything to do with America." Tom and Jack grimaced their displeasure with Brandeis' comments. "Well, it doesn't," he contended. "What are we doing taking sides in a civil war - an internal struggle - ten thousand miles away? All the people and the weapons and the money we've thrown at it are just totally out of proportion with what's going on over there - with what our interests are."

"Well, I think our interests," Tom rejoindered, "are to stop Communism there, and keep it from taking over anymore of Asia and moving out to Japan and Australia and - "

"Come on, don't 'domino' me, Windham," Brandeis interrupted. "I think we can stop them somewhere short of Disneyland. Probably even Waikiki."

"I just know it's the place to be right now if you're a journalist," Harvey observed. "So in two years if it's still going on, I'll be there."

"Hey, in two years if it's still going on," Brandeis added, "we'll all be there. Or in Canada."

Previously silent but absorbing the information and attitudes expressed, Jack finally joined the discussion, stating, "Well, when I *can* get over there, I sure will."

Scanning the campus view out the window, Tom said, "I love America. From sea to shining sea. And I would fight for her in a minute, if she were in danger. But Woz, I guess I understand what you're saying. This isn't like World War Two where the Japs attacked us from one side and all of Western Civilization was threatened on the other."

"So you think we should be able to pick our wars, huh?" Jack retorted. "Would you have fought in Korea?"

"Yeah," Tom answered defensively.

"What about World War One? What about the Spanish-American War? American soil never trod by enemy boots. Would you have signed up for those?" Jack asked.

"Yeah, I would have."

"But Jack," Brandeis asked, "how would you have felt if the British or the French had sent huge armies over here to decide the Civil War?"

Before Jack could reply, Tom stated, "Listen, if called upon to go,

I'll go. But honestly, when it just comes down to me - just me, without regard to world politics - just Tom Windham, well ... I guess I'm just plain scared. And I guess my first fear is simply that I wouldn't come back. I love this life and this world, and I'm selfish enough that, of course, I don't want it all to end. But my other fear would be that twelve months over there - three-hundred-and-sixty-five days - would drive me crazy. Because I just can't imagine there'd be a single, solitary, safe moment that whole year when I wouldn't feel threatened with death. Just like those battles you were talking about, Harvey. The enemy's everywhere, and you can't tell friend from foe. Everyone's in green and so's the jungle. And I hate to think what that would do to me. I hate to think what it would do to my mind. That's what really scares me. I might could get a desk job somewhere or - God knows what - something off the front line, but ... from the moment I touched down in that transport plane to the moment a year later when I escaped - got back to The World - I'd be afraid I was going to die. Every moment. I can't imagine living like that, and I hate to think what it'd do to me."

"I just know it's our generation's war," Harvey stated, "and it's probably the only one that I'll get to cover."

"I hope to God it is," Brandeis said.

"And I'm just afraid it's slipping away - or at least the best part of it. We've never been in a war for more than four years. That's about where this one is."

"Right," Brandeis said, "but we've never been in a war like this one."

"Yeah, but look, it's sixty-eight," Tom reasoned. "It's an election year. Don't you think Johnson'll end it sometime before November?"

"I think Johnson's in too deep to end it," Brandeis responded. "I don't think he can get us out."

"No," Harvey agreed, "and especially not after this. This Tet thing."

"It's swallowed him up," Brandeis stated. "And if Kennedy doesn't come out, I guess Eugene's our man."

"You really think someone could beat Johnson?" Tom asked.

"I think Johnson's beating himself," Brandeis answered. "The deeper he gets into it, the more he loses his vision of how to get out."

"I can't believe you would want us to lose this war," Jack huffed.

"It's not our war to win or lose," Brandeis shot back. "And it's that attitude - that almighty American ego - that got us into this and that's killing kids our age ... right now. And the only difference between us and them is that their daddies couldn't afford to put them in college."

"So you'd just have us walk away," Jack observed with disdain.

The three noncombatants looked at Brandeis as he returned Jack's stare. He replied evenly, "Yes."

Jack threw up his hands and, exhaling a dismissive sigh, walked out of the room. Regretting the exposure of these raw nerves among friends, Tom offered, "You know, I do think sometimes about the unfairness of us being here, just being able to sit in an air-conditioned dorm and talk about it - and them being there, living it every day. Some of them eighteen year-old kids who didn't even have the right to vote for or against the old men who sent them there."

"It's really a paradox," Harvey observed, "that they're old enough to die there, but they weren't old enough to vote for or against us going there."

"If you're old enough to be drafted to fight for your country, you ought to be old enough to vote, too," Tom stated, parroting the popular cliché.

"Yeah, and if you're old enough to go to war for your country, it ought to be legal for you to buy a beer or two the night before you ship out," Brandeis offered.

"Damn right," Joe Joe said, indignantly. "And if you're old enough to vote, it ought to be legal for you to buy yourself a few beers."

Tom and Harvey smiled blankly at each other as Brandeis tossed his smile out the window. Then glancing at his watch, Brandeis exclaimed, "Holy - !" and looking around at his friends said, "Gotta go, guys. I'm running late." Quickly pulling his business law text and a notebook from his shelf while slipping into his Weejuns, he darted from the room.

"So where's he off to in such a damn big hurry?" Joe Joe asked.

In a sing-song falsetto Tom answered, "Studies with Chevy."

"Is he still seeing her?" Joe Joe asked over Harvey's query, "Who?"

"Siobhan McKenna," Tom answered in Harvey's direction, followed by, "Yes," to Joe Joe.

"A lot?" Joe Joe asked.

"Oohh, only about every night and every day. They study together; they eat together; they sit googoo-eyed in the library staring at each other all tangled up together. It's disgusting. I'm so happy for him, I could kill him."

"When did all this start?" Harvey asked.

"Two or three weeks ago."

With a devilish grin Joe Joe lowered his head and queried, "He gittin' any?"

Before offering his unsubstantiated opinion to the negative, Tom caught himself and answered, "Joe Joe, you'll have to ask *him* that. I'll just say that ... I haven't personally seen him getting any, but I've sure seen her all over him every time I've seen them together."

"Wow!" Harvey exclaimed. "Siobhan McKenna?!"

"Siobhan McKenna," Tom and Joe Joe repeated in unison.

"She's a knockout," Harvey declared.

"Yeah," Joe Joe observed with a frown, "but I hear she's a real pushy broad. You know, the kind of girl who'd get in your car on the first date and change all the settings on your radio buttons."

"Listen, she could reset my buttons anytime she wanted to," Harvey marveled.

Chapter 12

Early March

The curious figure sat crouched on the back steps of Pitts Hall facing the parking lot that separated it from the back of McCartney. As Tom pulled out of the lot in time to beat Dallas's Friday rush hour traffic on his way home for the weekend, the short, round figure - clad in a black wool cap, sunglasses, a heavy black wool pea jacket, and jeans - crossed stealthily to the rear entrance of McCartney. Scaling the backstairs and pulling down the cap as two hall residents passed, the figure bustled quickly down the third floor's south hallway and tapped lightly on the door of 332.

Brandeis, wearing only his Levis, opened the door. Before she took off the sunglasses, he had already recognized Siobhan. His open grin was quickly overcast by his sudden cognizance of where she was. He cast neck-whipping glances up and down the empty hall while grasping the shoulder of her coat and pulling her into the room. Closing and locking the door, he turned to find her doffing her cap with her thick, blonde bush of hair falling down around her face. He started to speak, but she covered his mouth with her hand. Stepping away from him, she unbuttoned and opened her coat. The pillow, which had been her only undergarment, fell silently to the floor, followed by the jacket. The sight before Brandeis was virgin to him in spite of two weeks of near-nightly sessions in her 4-4-2 convertible in the ZPL. Though Siobhan had happily and encouragingly let his lips and his hands run free, she had until now been patient with his restraint.

Brandeis stood for a moment in the most envied of quandaries. He wanted to reach out and bring her to him, but he was so in awe of the view that he hesitated to give it up. Realizing his sweet confusion, she smiled and came back to him. They stood for a long time in the middle of the room clad only in their jeans locked in a soft, wet kiss. Finally, Siobhan whispered, "Bran, it's time. It's our time."

*   *   *

Two buzzards picked at an object in the road as Tom crested a hill east of Grand Saline and swept down toward them in the Le Mans. First, one bounded off the asphalt in a slow motion takeoff; then the other picked up its afternoon snack and began its ascent. The dead snake dangling from its beak swung lazily below the bird's malevolent expanse as it flopped above the road. Finally proving too heavy to take aloft, though, the buzzard dropped the lifeless serpent in the high grass of the parkway.

Tom's co-pilot was more than the normal queasiness and unease that he felt approaching a weekend in New Fredonia, because in addition to the unpredictability of his mother's state of mind, Tom felt ambivalent about his relationship with Meredith. Their recent phone conversations had been uninspired, obligatory, and sprinkled with awkward dead spots wherein neither seemed interested in sharing intimacies or even in communicating information. And they had not shared a genuine, honest laugh in some time. Tom did not roll over the details of this discomfort in his mind, but rather, his silent passenger was a dull, unspecified foreboding.

To provide himself a change of pace, Tom had taken Highway 80 to East Texas instead of his usual route down I-20. Through Terrell and the smaller towns of Wills Point, Edgewood, Grand Saline, and Mineola, Tom was reminded of the many trips to Dallas through his childhood that had followed this route from New Fredonia west before the interstate opened. The memory of those years was of a happy young family of four - before the wheels came off. Before his brother had come of age and had entered frequent and destructive combat with his mother. Before a pall of unhappiness had sinisterly drifted over his mother leaving her subject to the fits of depression that had stolen the caring, loving heart of the family even before Mark's death finally killed it forever. Occasionally, he could dial back to a time of family happiness - a time of comfort and security within the unit of the four of them. He could pick out some birthdays, some Thanksgivings and Christmases, some special family moments, and a few family trips - when he did not remember the insecurity, the discomfort. But those were isolated moments, often gifts of a selective and optimistic memory and insufficient to offset the overriding emotion of dread - dread of the next confrontation, dread of the next outburst.

Tom stopped in Mineola for gas, a restroom break, and a Dr. Pepper. Upon returning to his car, though, the attendant brought to his attention excessive and uneven tire wear on his right front tire. He also remarked that the tires all around were showing their age. Never the mechanic, Tom chastised himself little for the uneven wear, though he did remember that he had been driving for some time under a requirement for an inordinate amount of steering wheel pull to the left.

Upon arrival at home, he greeted his father with, "Hi, Dad. Time for new tires on the old Luh Mahnz."

His father looked back at him blankly for a moment, and Tom repeated his automotive maintenance requirements. With a sigh of resignation, he said, "Okay, but it's not cheap keeping you in that school, you know."

Taken momentarily aback by his father's mention of finances, Tom replied, "Fine, Dad, I'll just drive them till they wear down all the way and then start patching them."

"I'm sorry, Tom," his father replied through a pained expression. "I'll give you a check and you can go over to Springfield tomorrow and get some new ones. Do you know what kind you need?"

"Sure," Tom replied, searching his mind and remembering that it was marked somewhere on the tires.

Just then his mother entered fresh from her Friday afternoon comb-out at Roxie's. Arriving at WSU the prior fall, Tom had looked in vain for the row upon row of beauty shops he had assumed would be required to service the manes of the school's three thousand-plus co-eds, for based on the example of his mother and her friends, outpatient hair care was a two- to three-visit per week multi-hour social requirement. Not an option, a requirement. Meredith, who admitted sometimes rolling hers on empty frozen orange juice cans and sleeping on them, maintained that she visited beauty salons rarely and only for cuts and trims. Tom assumed her to be a tonsorial aberration.

"Do you like it?" she beamed, framing it in her open hands but not touching it, as if a magnetic field protected it.

"I love it," he replied, as he hugged her and administered a peck on the cheek. Tom was happy to see her genuine smile, and he was encouraged by the positive attention she had given to her appearance. He also noted the freshly painted-on dark brown eyebrows applied at Roxie's. They again replaced those that his mother had plucked to a then-fashionable pencil-thin width in her teen years never to have them fully regenerate. He had not yet had to use the information, but he had banked it against the day he might need to defend himself to her on charges of giving oneself over to faddishness or outrageous fleeting fashion.

After briefly catching them up on his course work, he rushed through a shower, tapped his father for date money, and headed out the door. From the front porch his mother called after him, as she had done innumerable times before, "Have a good time, Tom, but be careful. Just be a good boy, and people will like you."

Returning to his room to gather his dirty laundry, she noted with curiosity that his previously blank small green chalkboard on the wall next to his closet had written on it the cryptic inscription: "042068".

* * *

Tom pulled up in front of the two-story Williamsburg-style home of the Blaines in the new heavily wooded Blystone subdivision of north Springfield adjacent to the Pine Hills Country Club - the "right" club, where the town's old money gathered and played. The rich dark red Chicago brick exterior along with its massive size and cost befitted Springfield's most successful ophthalmologist and one of its most prominent attorneys. The political viewpoint of the doctor, which he freely and frequently expressed, was to the right of George Wallace whom he reluctantly supported for president, but whom he criticized for having compromised his "bar the door" segregationist principles. Mrs. Blaine had a quick and aggressive courtroom lawyer's mind and tongue. Less conservative and leaning toward apolitical, slower of wit and committed to conflict avoidance, Tom was intimidated by Meredith's parents and generally fumbled inarticulately through those times that he was required to wait downstairs for Meredith with either of them for any length of time. He had become most grateful to Harvey Groesbeck for the current events data that Harvey imparted to him, which he in turn regurgitated through a reactionary filter to Dr. Blaine when pressed.

This evening Meredith was mercifully punctual. Her promptness, though, seemed less an enthusiasm to be with him than an interest in arriving on time at Hubbard Auditorium on the campus of Springfield College for her part in "Freshman Follies", a series of skits put on by the school's fraternities, sororities, and service clubs. She was excited about her role in the chorus of Gamma Alpha Mu's sketch. After dropping Meredith off early at the stage entrance, Tom found a seat down front among the performers' friends and families who had arrived early - but comfortably away from the Blaines whom he had spotted upon entry. Watching the performance among strangers, Tom observed energetically corny skits ridiculing hippies, communes, and alternative lifestyles; parodying the movies *Bonnie and Clyde* and *The Graduate*; and a bad Beatles imitation. He mused at how out of touch the Greek organizations were - both here and at WSU - with what he considered to be the day-to-day lives, concerns, and conflicts of the average students on both campuses.

He remembered when during the prior semester Jack Putnam, whose language was generally exemplary and pristine, had had to explain to Tom the "GDI" label that had been playfully ascribed to him by a fraternity friend. Laughing it off and not daring to reveal his ignorance to the friend, Tom had hauled his quandary back to the dorm and had asked Blackjack to fill in the blanks. With a pained reluctance, Jack threw off, "God Damn Independent". Tom had been momentarily stung by this revelation, but he had since come to understand that, first, it placed him firmly in the majority of Wazoo students, and, second, at this point in American college life it was viewed by many of those so labeled in a positive light. For whether they had sought Greek citizenship and been denied it or had either purposely or by inaction avoided it - the latter being Tom's course - the fact of Independence suggested a turning away from the traditional, the anachronistic, the old ways of earlier generations. Tom had not done so against the certainty that he would have had to explain it to his parents, but several of his friends had proudly placed "Gamma Delta Ioda" decals on their cars. Even still, sitting there alone - among, but not of, that shallowly jubilant and congenitally like-minded crowd, Tom could not deny a grudging envy of the bright patina of camaraderie around him - even if pretentious, eggshell-thin, store-bought.

At the show's conclusion Tom met Meredith at the stage door entrance. Intermixed with her post-performance bouncy energy and adrenalin was what Tom considered an unsavory leavening of finger-pointing and name-calling directed at members of rival clubs whose sketches she held in lower regard than her own. Her cuteness in other ways had generally been a sufficient offset - for Tom's purposes - to this unfortunate aspect of her personality. But this night he found himself making the choice to take more prominent exception to her pettiness. And he wondered why.

As they ordered dinner at Paco's and gobbled down hot sauce and *tostados* in anticipation of it, Meredith continued to enlighten Tom as to the weeks of preparation she and her sorority sisters had put into their sketch. Though the bent of her narrative had become more positive, Tom's nagging annoyance with her persisted. Then as the waitress arrived with their entrees, Tom glanced through the plastic-vine-laced latticework between their table and the restaurant lobby.

Clair had not seen him, and, ignoring Meredith, he watched her enter. The sight of her was exhilarating to him, but the subsequent image that entered his view brought him crashing back down. For it was Gene Ray Driggers who put his hand to Clair's back as they followed the hostess to their table. Tom had been a freshman when Driggers was a senior at New Fredonia High, and he remembered him as a mean-spirited thug whose mere presence in the hall carried with it an ominous threat. While slickly handsome with his dark pompadour, Gene Ray had been linked during high school to several of the more attractive, less popular girls from out on the county - but none like Clair, or at least Clair as he remembered her. As they moved to a table behind him, Tom found himself revolted and upset.

The remainder of the meal was an awkward experience for Tom. He wondered whether Clair had seen him and was now watching him. On the chance that she was, he found himself continuing to be distant from Meredith, and he instinctively controlled any physical displays of enthusiasm or of interest in her. His attitude toward Meredith before Clair's entrance made this withholding on his part the more natural.

At the completion of their meal as they rose from the table and Meredith moved toward the exit in front of Tom, he could no longer restrain himself. Risking the fate of Lot's wife, which he remembered Gene Ray's glare as being capable of inflicting, Tom turned to look at Clair. She was staring at him with the same strength and sincerity that he had seen in her eyes at Fat City on New Year's. Buckling his lip into a pained smile, he nodded at her and only after that did he note that Gene Ray was also looking at him. But Gene Ray's gaze was a blank look of wonder suggesting that he remembered Tom's face but neither who he was nor where he had known him. To Tom, Clair's beauty remained natural, unadorned, and somehow tied to the way he knew she had felt about him. As he knew he must, he turned away from her, but he carried with him the visual and emotional imprint of the large soulful eyes, the small sensual mouth, framed closely by the ripples of rich golden brown hair.

Meredith invited him back to her house to watch the late movie, and he unenthusiastically agreed. By the time they arrived, her parents had removed themselves upstairs, leaving the comfortable, expansive, glass-walled den to Meredith and Tom.

Returning to the den with Dr. Peppers while Tom checked the newspaper's television listings, she said, "I mentioned to Mother your idea of going to Law School, and, of course, she was very excited. But she said either Business or Pre-Law would still be the way to go undergraduate. She said that going the Liberal Arts route would just be a waste of time."

He glared at her for a long moment before unleashing his reply. With a mix of indignation and defensiveness laced liberally with sarcasm, he said, "Thank you so very much for that information. Did you and your mother also decide where I should attend Law School?"

Standing above him holding their drinks, she, too, took the defensive. "Well, Tom, I was only trying to help. I just didn't want you to waste the next two years taking *History*, when you could be taking courses that would really be helpful for you in the future."

"History may be my future," he shot back, and then smiled into himself, glancing around to see if Casey Stengel were hiding behind his brain.

"What would you do with History? Teach?" she asked scornfully.

"I might. I love history, and it's one of the few things I've ever studied that I've had any real interest in - that I enjoyed just for the sake of it, and not for if it could ever earn me a living."

"So what are you going to do to ever earn a living?" Meredith asked.

"Hey, cut me some slack. I'm a twenty-year-old sophomore. I'll get it figured out in the next couple of years. But if nothing else comes to me, I can always pick up the title business from my dad."

Sensing the latter to be an avenue not to pursue, Meredith returned to her original thesis, "Well, are you really thinking about Law School or Business?"

Letting Law School lie, he answered, "I'm just not sure I'm cut out for business."

"I don't see how you can say that. You've made all A's and B's in Economics and Accounting."

"Those were all basics. Principles courses."

"I know what has you down on Business," Meredith declared.

"What's that?"

"It was that Business Statistics course last semester. The one you took the first part of, and then you didn't take the second."

Surprised by her dead-on insight, Tom felt uncomfortably revealed. His experience in Business Statistics had been the root of his disaffection with the Business School and with the pursuit of the business degree that had been his original goal. "B-Stat" had been an unwelcome revelation for Tom, because it seemed to have defined an intellectual limit or capacity that heretofore he had never had to face - except in the sciences, which he had always known not to be his realm. But B-Stat, and what he considered an insufficient aptitude on his part to grasp the guts of it, was the first intellectual wall he had ever hit separating him from a life goal. Through high school and in discussions with his parents and friends, his intention, if not his passion, was to obtain a business degree and then to offer himself up to the financial world in return for riches untold. But barring that path lay Business Statistics, a subject with which he experienced difficulty from the start. His inability to get under its skin and to grasp the meaning behind the formulae frightened him. His solution for his short-term first semester goal, which was to pull down a "B" in the course, was to memorize and to learn by rote sufficient data to test out at 80 or above. He had been able to do that, but the effect of the experience on his confidence, first, that he could obtain a business degree while maintaining a high GPA, and, secondly, that he could become a "successful businessman", was primal. The concept of "enjoying" a career in business was peripheral to him. The requirement that he be "successful" at it was fundamental. The thought process that led him away from business because of his experience in B-Stat was one that he had never consciously laid out before himself, though it appeared to be one that Meredith's mother had laid out before her. At any rate, late in the prior semester, a switchman deep in Tom Windham's psyche had re-routed him onto a new track and had mentioned to his life in passing that perhaps he should make a career of something he enjoyed - just for itself, just for the experience, and not for the lifestyle that it could buy him. This had been a concept anathema to the Protestant Work Ethic that the town of New Fredonia, New Fredonia High, and the First Baptist Church of New Fredonia - though not his parents - had sought through a boyhood to ingrain in him.

His reply of silence to her bull's eye observation squelched her conviction and gave her to understand that she had cut far too close to the bone. Performing a stammering backpedal, she commenced to bring the dialogue back to a comfortably trivial level. With an assist from the automatic override from Tom's highly developed conflict avoidance system, she was successful.

After two hours of watching a movie on television and engaging in spotty, perfunctory necking, Tom rose to leave. Meredith walked him to the door where she yielded up a somnolently passionate goodnight kiss. As he started to walk toward his car without suggesting plans for the following day, Meredith, whose dating code included the strict requirement that he - not she - should put forward such plans, could offer only an anticipatory but firm, "Tom."

Looking back over his shoulder and knowing that he owed her either an elaborate explanation or an acceptable excuse, he said, "I think Mom wants to do something with me tomorrow afternoon. I'll give you a call."

His choice not to make plans for Saturday night told her in volumes that they were in trouble, but her pride won out over her concern. She only huffed, "Okay," as she slammed the door.

Of the many things that their relationship had going for it, two that stood out were Tom's natural inertia and the sight of Clair Kennerly with Gene Ray Driggers. For Tom dreaded change, and the thought of initiating it without a very attractive alternative - at least in mind, even if not in place - made it the more unlikely.

He arrived home with nothing resolved - all in flux. But the house was dark and quiet, and that was its own victory.

Chapter 13

"Ooooh, Bran," Siobhan cooed as they lay in a naked tangle on Brandeis' bed. With the dim pre-dawn light of Saturday morning peeking timidly in the window of 332, the lovers kissed lazily - still drugged from their latest round of love-making. Suddenly shivering from their cooling perspiration and from the wintry radiation through the uncovered window, though, she reached down the bed and pulled the sheet and his heavy green Army blanket over them and tightly around their necks. Her fists holding the blanket snugly between their chests, they rested silently for a minute before Siobhan pulled away slightly and with a wicked grin and a whisper, adjudged, "That was soooo gooood."

"First hard in the mornin' - hardest hard all day," Brandeis explained with feigned nonchalance.

"What!?" she laughed in a suppressed squeal.

"It's a phenomenon Joe Joe apprised me of. Never had had occasion to ... put it to the test before."

"Well, you can tell him you proved his thesis - in spades. You just can't tell him when, where, or with whom. But goodness, the things you boys talk about," she scolded. "Sounds like the things we girls talk about."

As she adjusted the sheets, an updraft brought a grimace to his face. "What's that smell?" he asked.

"Us," she replied with a broad grin.

Squinching his lips, he bobbed his head and stated, "Smells pretty good." After another moment of kisses and body rubs, he stared at the ceiling and asked, "What were you thinking about while we were making love?"

As he looked back down at her, she dipped her head and replied, "I wasn't thinking. I was making love."

Absorbing her reply with a smile and a nod of understanding, he asked, "Well, how was I?"

"Like I said, good. Daaamn good."

"Sorry about making that mess the first time - and the second time," he allowed.

"Hey, when it's good, it's going to be messy," she whispered while gnawing on his ear. After holding each other silently and still for a long moment, Siobhan admitted, "I've *got* to go pee." Untangling herself from him, she began to don her costume for another clandestine trip down the hall. They shared hungry, loving glances as he sprawled naked in bed watching her dress. But when she laid back on Tom's bed and started pulling her jeans up, she asked, "Don't have any pliers, do you?"

"Pliers?" he wondered.

As she tugged at her jeans, she asked with a laugh, "How do you think we get these things zipped?"

"You're kidding?" he giggled as he took pleasure in observing her wiggle into the flesh-hugging Levis.

"Uhn-uhn," she replied. "Sometimes, to get the right leverage, I even have to get Thia to do it."

"Please, I'm already turned on enough," he said through a muted laugh.

"Got it," she said as she sprang from the bed and swung a tightly-bound hip in his face.

As soon as she returned, he slipped on his Levis and followed suit. Coming back to the door of 332, he scanned the vacant hall jubilant both that she had had the courage or the madness or both to come and that they had had the good luck to pull it off. Opening the door and closing and locking it quickly behind him, he was stunned to turn and see Siobhan's naked silhouette framed in the horizontal stripes of muted light as she stood at the window and looked out through the Venetian blinds. She did not look at him as he dropped his jeans, crossed the room to her, and gently wrapped his arms around her waist and her breasts.

Sucking in a passionate sigh, closing her eyes, and dropping her head back onto his shoulder as he pressed against hers, she whispered, "Oh, Bran, I love you so much."

"And I love you. My God, I had no idea. This is the best. The best."

*   *   *

"Mom, want to go see a movie with me this afternoon?"

The question caught his mother off guard as she served Tom his breakfast. She cocked her head with a broad smile and began to nod. She considered several questions - all to the point of 'Why me? Why now?' - but assuming an explanation might follow, she merely said, "Sure, I'd love to."

Also assuming the questions that were running through her mind, Tom explained carefully, "There's a movie I'd like you to see: *The Graduate*."

"Who's in it?"

"Anne Bancroft's the only one I think you would know. She was the teacher in *The Miracle Worker*."

His mother nodded vaguely, "So, how do I rate? Why aren't you taking Meredith?"

"Meredith's already seen it, and I'd just like for you to. It's ... I've seen it several times, and it's about the ... best movie I've ever seen. And I can't tell you exactly why I feel that way about it. Anyway, I'd like for you to see it, because I think you'll like it, and I'd like to know what you think about it. Is it a date?"

Again choosing not to probe, she answered, "We're on."

After breakfast Tom drove to his father's office off the town square. The square was already crowded with farmers and families from out on the county in town for a Saturday of shopping, banking, haircuts and hairdos, and a Saturday matinee at the movie house. After collecting his signed blank check for the tire store, Tom left for Springfield. He noted en route that the front-end wobble had become quite pronounced.

Arriving at Grubbs Tire Company on the north side of Springfield's downtown, Tom turned himself over to Jerry Grubbs, the store manager. Grubbs laid out the options to Tom of the three Goodyear tire models available, and he gave Tom the pros and cons of each. Trying to avoid making obvious his inexperience in such matters, Tom selected the medium-priced, middle-of-the-road option, repeating the points that the store manager had made concerning it.

Tom whiled away much of his two-hour wait for the tire job at the nearby Austin Street Newsstand - scanning racing magazines. After the newsstand he made a pass at The Record Shop and flipped aimlessly through albums. Remembering from his recent past having stopped there specifically to ogle one album cover in particular, he was disappointed at the absence from the shelf of the outrageously erotic *Whipped Cream* by Herb Alpert. It had been the openly acknowledged stuff of wet dreams among high school boys of the mid-'60's, incidentally giving many an introduction to jazz trumpet.

Leaving there with no records, he ambled back to Grubbs' shortly after eleven. The new tires were husky and aggressively attractive to Tom with their pinstripe whitewalls. He filled in the check for the invoice amount and gave it to Jerry Grubbs who disappeared into his office with it. A minute later Grubbs reappeared devoid of the congeniality with which he had treated Tom earlier in the morning. Gruffly he declared, "I called the bank, and this check's bad. There's insufficient funds in the account to cover it."

Tom was stunned. He fumbled through a confused apology before asking, "May I use your phone?"

"I think you'd better," Grubbs replied.

Experiencing a type of embarrassment previously unknown to him, Tom slipped past Grubbs into the office. As he dialed the number of his father's office, an anger rushed through him. It was a novel anger - righteous and parental - to which he felt clearly and unequivocally entitled as a result of the unfair injury this humiliation had heaped upon him. When his father answered, Tom stated with punishing indignation, "Dad, you gave me a hot check to pay for the tires. It bounced. They won't take it."

"Son - "

"They called the bank," Tom interrupted, "and the bank said it was a bad check."

"I'm sorry. I don't understand," his father stated. "They must have talked to the wrong person at the bank."

Having quickly and cleanly emptied his vitriol regarding the matter and sensing that to heap more punishment on the direct hit he had already scored would be overkill, Tom backed off to seek a solution. For the fact that he needed to leave there on a new set of tires was not lost on him. "So what do you want me to do?" Tom asked with a strong residue of belligerence.

"Let me call the bank. I'll call you right back."

Tom returned to Jerry Grubbs' desk and apprised him of the situation. "That's fine," Grubbs stated, "but you're not leaving here with those tires until somebody puts the cash in my hand," and he plunged his forefinger into his open palm.

After an eternity of two minutes, the phone rang and he handed it to Tom. Still shaken, his father said, "I gave you a check from the wrong account. Come on back up here, and I'll give you another check."

"Dad, I don't think he'll take another check," Tom said. "He wants cash."

At that his father was quiet for a moment before stating with an unguarded desperation, "Well, come back up here. I'll get the cash, and you can take it back to him."

"Dad," Tom said slowly, "I don't think he'll let me leave without the cash. The new tires are already on the car."

"Oh, Son. Let me speak to Mr. Grubbs."

Grubbs had been watching and listening to Tom's end of the exchange, and as Tom handed him the receiver, saying, "Here, my dad wants to talk to you," he gave Tom a pained smile. Tom felt relief flow over him as he watched the return of the kindly tire store manager to whom he had brought his car so long ago that morning.

He hung up the receiver, turned to Tom and said, "Son, go on back up to New Fredonia. Your dad's gonna give you the cash and you can bring it back down to me."

Tom returned smoothly and quickly north on the newly aligned front-end and the fresh Goodyear shoes. He smarted all the way home from the humiliation he had suffered, continuing to roll it over in his mind lest he lose the pain of injury and, with it, the upper hand he had seized over his father. His analysis went no farther into the subversive joys of victimhood. He did not consider what he would do with the upper hand nor its meaning or value, and certainly not its impact on his father. But for a boy at the brink of his twenties, to be so purely right on a point and for his father to be so perfectly wrong was so rare a circumstance that he was wont to give it up. All of that changed when he arrived at his father's office and saw him. At that moment he knew that the humiliation of this father before his son was incomparably more hurtful than the humiliation that he had experienced before a stranger. Tom instantly jettisoned the script he had planned en route from Springfield, and he gave his father the floor.

Handing Tom an envelope, he said, "Here, take this to Mr. Grubbs. This is the cash. This'll take care of everything."

Looking at him, Tom only knew that he did not want his father to hurt anymore, and he said, "It's okay, Dad. It really is." This won a weak smile from his father. Then Tom had a thought. "Dad, I need to use the phone."

"Mom, I'm up at the office - "

"Oh, Hon, your back from Springfield."

"Yep," he said, "and I'm ready to go back again. Ready for our date?"

"I didn't know we were going so early. Well, yes, I will ... ah, I am."

"Good. I thought we might go over there and have a late lunch and then see the movie."

"Okay. Just come on home and pick me up. I'll throw something on."

His father had heard the conversation, and as Tom left his office, he looked at him with pain and apprehension, and began, "Son - "

Sensing his father's plea, Tom offered, "Dad, don't worry. I won't say anything to her about it." His father nodded his thanks, but Tom understood his own rationale to be purely selfish, given the combustibility of the information were his mother to learn of it.

Son and mother shared an enjoyable ride to Springfield filled with light conversation. He remembered to reduce his speed for her sake, and, for her part, only once did she white-knuckle the armrest and dashboard while stomping an imaginary brake on her side of the floorboard. He provided her with an update of goings-on at WSU and of his relationship with Meredith - both heavily filtered.

After lunch Tom casually mentioned to his mother that he needed to stop by the tire store to pick up his receipt for the tires, which would constitute their guarantee. He entered and apologetically passed the envelope of cash to Jerry Grubbs, who was relieved to see him return and who said, "Don't worry about it, son. It could happen to anyone. And don't be too hard on your dad." Tom nodded and escaped.

As they entered and sat in the darkened auditorium, Tom said, "Mom, just watch it and see what it says to you." As it unfolded, she laughed less than the other members of the sparsely populated matinee crowd. Tom was much too keenly attuned to his mother's reactions and non-reactions to enjoy this, his seventh viewing of the film. And as Benjamin Braddock escorted Mrs. Robinson home from his homecoming party early in the movie and she poured him a drink in her jungle-encased den, Tom thought forward to the approaching scene when Mrs. Robinson would entice him upstairs. It suddenly became obvious to Tom that he could not sit next to his mother and watch as the ten-foot tall close-ups of Anne Bancroft's forbidden anatomy flashed quickly on the screen. He excused himself for a Dr. Pepper and popcorn, and he offered to bring Nancy refreshments. He returned to his seat at the end of Ben's "sow some wild oats" interview with Mr. Robinson.

Tom was able to keep his seat through the first seduction scene at the Taft Hotel and through the Simon-and-Garfunkel-backed montage of their summer affair. He remained by his occasionally smiling mother until Benjamin's date with Elaine. But as the dark-shaded Benjamin dragged the virginal Elaine into the seedy, smoky strip joint, Tom again faced the certainty that he could not sit beside his mother and watch the enormously endowed and uniquely skilled stripper twirl her tassels above the head of the tearful Elaine. He excused himself to the restroom and returned as Benjamin said to Elaine regarding his affair, "It's just something that happened."

He felt no further requirement to leave, and he was able to lose himself in the vicarious ups and downs and ups of the Berkeley scenes, the hunt for Elaine and the race to Santa Barbara, and the final showdown in the church foyer. As they walked from the theatre, Tom stated that it was unlike any other movie he had ever seen. His mother, who seemed serious and preoccupied, replied, "No, it wasn't like any movie I've ever seen either."

Noting the negative tone of her reply, Tom chose not to discuss the movie further with her unless she brought it up. To his surprise and concern his mother did not start a conversation almost all the way home, and she replied to his queries or observations with brief answers devoid of elaboration. Finally, a few miles from home she turned to look at him, and he momentarily glanced off the road at her. Then with a perceptible discomfort, she said, "Tom, I know that we've never talked about ... intimacy between men and women, and I don't think you have with your daddy either, have you?" Tom shook his head. "Son, if you do want to talk about ... any of that, I will ... or your daddy will."

Tom smiled while looking straight ahead and said, "Don't worry, Mom, I think I've learned about everything I'm supposed to know."

"I'm afraid to ask where you learned it," she said.

"The usual place," Tom replied with a smirk. "On the street."

They both laughed, though hers was a nervous laugh. They drove on a way in silence, until she asked, "Tom, what's that you have written on your chalkboard? What's that number?"

Tom was silent for a moment as he mulled over what to tell her. He also wondered why he had projected that small piece of melodrama onto the Boys Room wall. Had he thought, he would have known she would have asked him about it. Had he wanted her to, he wondered. He finally chose the straightforward approach. "It's a date. Four twenty sixty-eight. April twentieth, nineteen sixty-eight. It's the day I'll be Mark's age when he died."

She pursed her lips and pondered her response. "What about that date? What does it mean?"

"Nothing really, Mom," he answered, feeling regret for having troubled her. "I'll just be where Mark was in age when he died, and it may be a good day to look at myself and see where I am. It's nothing to worry about, Mom. Honest."

Upon arriving home late in the afternoon Tom responded to an uneasy feeling that to go the entire day without contacting Meredith in any way would brand his attitude toward their relationship with a more negative mark than he was prepared to do. Consequently, he called her house and was surprised to find that she was out. Her younger brother answered and said only that Meredith had gone somewhere with her mother, and she would be in late. Tom's emotional response was a mix of relief and discomfort. He had not wanted to be with her this evening, but he feared that her perception of his message that he did not had been too accurately received and too overtly acted upon. A slow smile and a shake of the head accompanied his realization that he had apparently wanted her to mope about at home thinking of him.

It still seemed strange to him, though, to go a Saturday night at home without a date. He called his cousin Chet to check his schedule. He said that although he had a date later, he wanted Tom to come by and visit before he left.

His mother had been quiet and uneasy since their return from the movie, and his father had not come in from his regular Saturday afternoon of farm work. Not interested in having dinner with them, Tom went through the Dairy Queen's drive-in window for a double cheeseburger, tater tots, and a vanilla shake and spread them on Chet's breakfast table. His cousin nursed a Pabst Blue Ribbon.

After greetings, Chet asked, "What's been going on with you, anyway? Why don't you have a date tonight?"

Tom looked out the screen door into a hazy sun setting through the trees of Chet's backyard. It bathed him and the cozy kitchen in a creamy golden light. "I don't know. I just didn't feel good about having a date tonight."

"Have you and Meredith broken up?"

"No," he answered, holding onto the word too long and leaving it hanging in the air.

"Are you thinking about breaking up?"

"I don't know."

"What's going on between you two, if you don't mind me asking?"

"Very little," Tom replied, "and I don't mind you asking."

"Well, let's go at it from another angle. What's going on with you?"

"I'm really not sure what's going on, and I'm really not sure where I'm going or - or where I'll end up," Tom stated.

Chet smiled warmly and said, "Tom, you're twenty. And you're *going* to be twenty-one, and you're *going* to W-S-U, and you're *going* to be a junior next year, and you're *going* to have plenty of time between now and then and the year after that to figure out where you're going. But you know what? You may not figure it out in four years stacked up one on top of another. And it may come to you in a blinding flash next week or it may slowly reveal itself to you over the next five or ten years. But let me clue you in on one thing. You don't go and go and go and stop. You keep going."

Tom furrowed his brow. "What do you mean?"

"Well, I guess I mean, without getting too philosophical - and warn me if I do - that life is what we do every day, and it's not what we 'end up' doing. We all know what our final destination is - what we're going to 'end up' doing. And believe me, Cousin, that won't be the fun part."

"What I'm talking about is: my major, my girlfriend, what kind of work I'm going to do, even where I'm going to *live*."

"I understand, Tom. All that stuff is perplexing. I really didn't mean to get too abstract. I guess all I'd ask is: what do you like? I know you've taken some Business, and you told me you were taking some History. Without betraying my natural prejudice," Chet asked, "how do you like the History?"

"You know I have the same natural prejudice for it, but can you earn a living at it? I think I heard a girl saying last night that she didn't think I could, and she didn't plan to be the one earning the living."

"Well, I'm teaching it right now, and I do seem to be getting by. But that sure takes me to '*deja vu*-land'. I heard that same complaint more than once from my ex-, as in 'former', wife. But *I'm* not worried about getting rich. And, Tom, if you *are* worried about getting rich, you might should stay in Business. And you *might* get rich, and you might not. And you *might* be happy as a businessman, and you might not. But given that matrix, I don't think you'll get rich unless you're happy at it. I may be wrong, and I'm sure there are some exceptions, but, rich or not, I'd just hate for you to live your life doing something that didn't make you happy - that you didn't enjoy. I think you'd eventually see it as a trap, and you'd resent it deeply - along with anyone you might blame, including yourself, for getting you into it."

Tom nodded and asked, "So you're happy teaching History at Stover J-C?"

Chet hesitated before answering, "Yes, I am happy teaching History at Stover J-C, but I'm not going to do it here for the rest of my life. In fact - " and he hesitated again.

"What's up?" Tom asked.

"Well, did you know I was going to Colorado next weekend?"

"No."

"I'm going to Boulder to the University of Colorado for an interview."

Tom's mouth dropped open into a wide grin and a "Wow!" before an elementally selfish concern betrayed itself on his face. Without thinking, Tom blurted out, "You mean you'd move?"

Chet bit his lip and, nodding, exhaled, "Yeah. Hey, I don't know if it'll work out. I don't know if I'll get on there. But we've talked on the phone, and I've sent a resume and letters and some things I've published, and I know a fellow from college who's in the History Department there. Next summer I'll finish my doctorate. You could come up there and visit me and go skiing. Come up in the summer, too." Tom's half-smile in reply pained Chet, knowing the escape valve he provided his young cousin.

Chet patted him on the back and left his hand on his shoulder. "I'd miss you, Tom. But you have to understand, nothing's happening for me around here. I need for my personal life to move forward, and my professional life, too. I want to go somewhere where my work will be appreciated. Somewhere I can do some writing. And, frankly, somewhere that's exciting. A lot of young people."

"Yeah, I hear Colorado's got that," Tom allowed. "Do Aunt Nela and Uncle Bowman know?"

"Yes, I've talked with them about it. Told them it was a possibility. And, you know them. They're on my side, and they're excited for me."

"Boy, they'll miss you, too."

"Well, it's far from finalized. We've got to see if we like each other. Nothing's signed on the line. But I'm pretty confident that it'll work out."

"When would you go?"

"Next fall - or the end of the summer."

Tom breathed a sigh of relief, realizing he would not be leaving as soon as he had feared. "I thought you had been dating someone - someone who might be important to you."

"Oh, I've been dating one or two women that your Aunt Nela wishes were important to me. Anyway, we'll see how the Colorado thing works out. Tell me, though. Aunt Nancy tells me you really like your new roommate. What's he like?"

Tom's face brightened as he described Brandeis to him - his sense of humor, his background, and his appearance.

"Sounds like an interesting guy, and a lot of fun. Does he date anyone?"

Tom's eyes rolled as he informed Chet, "Does he ever! Only about the toughest-looking girl at Wazoo."

"Really?" Chet asked with puzzlement, "Because who you described didn't sound like B-M-O-C material. Not quite the Campus Casanova."

Tom threw up his hands, "I guess it was 'just one of those things'. But however it happened, let me assure you, they're ate up with each other."

"Do you know her?"

"Yeah, she's my biology lab partner."

"Well, what's *she* like?"

"She's a lot of fun, too. And she's blonde, and big-busted, and beautiful ... and big-busted."

"I'm getting the picture. But Tom, I've got to impart to you one of the saddest but truest facts that Man has to face in this life." Patting his shoulder, Chet asked, "Are you ready?"

"Yes, my wise and experienced cousin. Please, impart."

"Tom, here it is. Big tits ... sag." Tom dropped his face into his hands and heaved a sorrowful sigh. "I know, my boy, I know. It's hard to have to hear that. Chin up, Tom."

"I ... I just don't know if I can go on ... knowing that," Tom moaned.

"Well, I just wanted to make sure you heard it from a friend."

"Thanks, Chet, thanks." After a laugh, Tom went on, "I don't know, though. Siobhan's may defy the Law of Gravity. I've seen her bra-less in a wool sweater. And going back to my in-depth training in geometry, I think I'm ready to postulate the Siobhan McKenna Theorem: that an imaginary line extending out directly from and at the same angle as her nipples would run parallel to the Earth's surface - pre-Columbian - to Infinity."

"Siobhan McKenna?" Chet asked.

"Yeah, great handle, huh? As she says, very Irish."

"She sounds more like she'd be a freckle-faced redhead."

"Hey, who knows what her true hair color is," Tom mused, "but no, no freckles. Peaches and cream with a tan."

"Hang around this guy, Tom. It sounds like you could be very happy with the ones he throws back. Hell, so could I." Glancing at his watch, Chet frowned, "Sorry, buddy, but I've got to get out of here. Got to run over toward Bethany and pick up my date, and then we're off to Springfield."

"Who are you going out with?"

"Janelle Waverly," Chet replied. "She used to be Janelle Sorrells. She's divorced. Do you remember her?"

"Sorrells? Is she one of Dory's older sisters?"

Chet nodded and said quietly, "Yeah, she is. I guess you do know her. Mark dated Dory, didn't he?"

Tom smiled, "Oh, yeah. He sure did." Glancing reflectively out the back door, he went on, "Dory Sorrells Day."

"What?" Chet asked.

Tom shook his head as if to clear it. "Oh ... I was just remembering. July twelfth, Dory Sorrells Day."

"Her birthday?"

"No," Tom answered. "I asked Mark that, too. No, he said it was just a day they celebrated together. Took me years to figure out why."

Chet draped an arm over Tom's shoulder and squeezed him as he nodded, "Glad he had that to celebrate."

"Yeah, me too."

"But they didn't date for more than one year, did they?" Chet asked with puzzlement. "How did they celebrate it more than once?"

"I don't know if they got together or if he just sent flowers or a note or called or what. But I remember even his last summer him telling me that he had been in touch with her."

"Yeah, I should have remembered that about him. All his old girlfriends still loved him. I don't think it was ever their idea to break up." Chet looked down and fell silent.

*   *   *

Tom circled the Dairy Queen once, and he was not surprised by the absence of familiar faces. Like the balcony of First Baptist, it, too, had been turned over to succeeding high school classes. After that he decided to drive The Course.

Devised by Tom and Jonathan Meador while cruising Stover County's backroads, The Course was a 27-mile road racing track they had laid out from New Fredonia on the east side of Stover County toward Bethany in the west, then south and southeast toward Springfield, and back across the county and home. Because of the original layouts of many of the old county roads along property lines - with a leavening of county politics involved - some excellent sweeping bends, tight banked turns, and changing radius curves had been incorporated into these narrow two-lane pikes tying the towns and the farming communities of the rural county together. The fastest section of The Course was the two-mile straightaway going down a hill, across Holly Creek bottom, and up a lower hill on the other side. To Tom it was the Mulsanne Straight - The Course's equivalent of the four-mile-long high-speed section of the Le Mans circuit. Although Mulsanne was longer and flat, the straight across the marshy bottom did parody Mulsanne in that just across the Holly Creek bridge there was a subtle bend - the "kink in the straight" - which, as at Le Mans, was to be taken flat out with just the most delicate tweak of the steering wheel.

While out on the county's deserted roads he considered his options for the remainder of the evening, and he realized how long it had been since he had watched Saturday night network television, or, for that matter, any night network television. He had seen some Christmas specials during the holidays and a number of football games, but he mused that Wazoo had drastically cut back his opportunities to waste his life in front of a TV. With no television in his room and only an aging boxy black-and-white in McCartney's lobby, he remembered that the only program he had watched at WSU the prior semester was the late August final episode of "The Fugitive". That had been different. It had been a generational duty to usher Dr. Richard Kimball home.

Arriving home after his drive Tom rolled into the driveway and parked behind his mother's Buick. As he closed the car door, he heard the familiar shriek - muted by the walls of the house, but unmistakable and chilling.

Chapter 14

Tom's heart raced, a tightness gripped his throat and chest, and a shudder ran through his body leaving chill bumps. He considered his options as he closed the car door. Chet was gone; Meredith was gone. Johnny's pick-up in the garage told him that his father was inside taking the brunt of the assault. Noting it not to be late in the evening, he birthed a hope that his return might quiet her as it had on other occasions when she had not yet gone so far over the edge that she could not pull herself back and control herself in Tom's presence and for his benefit.

Entering the house with the hope that he could spare Johnny further abuse and against the fear that it was already too late, he opened the front door and quickly shut it loudly. And as quickly and as loudly, he followed with, "Mom, Dad, I'm home."

His parents were in their bedroom, he could tell, as he heard her in a low, controlled voice. He walked past their door and back to his room. Leaving the door open, he turned on the television, also loudly. Momentarily, his father joined him. He was wearing a fresh scratch, which, to his Sunday School class the following morning, would be a farming or gardening accident. As was in his powers, his father tempered to a casual frown the grimace to which he was entitled.

"I'm surprised to see you home on a Saturday night, Son. Is anything wrong?" he asked with sincere concern.

Passing on the irony of his father's question, Tom answered directly,

"No, Dad, I just didn't have a date tonight. I thought Mom would have told you." Tom looked back at the screen.

"You and Meredith having a spat?"

Tom's stomach and his emotions were churning. He was less practiced than his father at carrying on casual conversation under the conditions extant. He further felt that he had at least temporarily and possibly for the evening - if they were both very lucky - brought to an end for Johnny another night of his mother's nightmarish behavior. Nor was he anymore concerned about the embarrassment at the tire store. He and his father were again allies in a larger, more violent battle zone. He simply did not want to talk about anything that might entail or even bode conflict. So he lied. "No, Meredith had somewhere to go with her mother tonight."

"Oh. What are you watching?"

"Nothing. I just turned it on to *Mannix*. Is there anything you want to watch?"

"No, this is fine. But just a minute. Let me go get something. I'll be right back."

His father left the room, and Tom cast an ear down the hall. He heard him close the master bedroom door behind him. Through the door came the familiar spine-chilling tones of his mother's seething whisper. The individual words were unintelligible, but the inflection and the rhythm of the delivery betrayed the anger and hatred she was communicating to this man she had loved, had married, had born two children to, and had buried one with. Tom wondered again how and why his father lived with it. Then the door opened and closed again. Silence followed and minutes later his father joined Tom in the easy chair beside him at the foot of his bed.

Tom glanced at the tall glass his father was working with a long teaspoon. He realized that his father had mixed his special cornbread and buttermilk concoction and was churning it into a pasty pulp which history had shown he did intend to consume. Noting his son's observation and aware of his prejudice against buttermilk, Tom and his father shared their inside joke with Johnny's smile and Tom's, "Yuck."

But their amusement was short-lived as they heard the master bedroom door open. Both waited, and Nancy did not join them. Both listened, and she did not go to her bathroom. Both then assumed that she had ventured to the guest bedroom at the other end of the house where Tom knew, having found empty liquor bottles and beer cans in the cabinets and drawers of the guest bath, that she went to drink.

At ten o'clock Johnny excused himself pleading weariness from an afternoon of farming. Tom understood that Johnny's plan was to get to bed and get to sleep before Nancy came back, in hopes that his somnolence would remove him from the target zone upon her return.

Uneasy and not sleepy, Tom stayed up to watch the news. But during sports at the end of the newscast, he heard the master bedroom door open, and it was followed immediately by the startlingly high-pitched screech, which from experience told him she had sunken deep into a drunken stupor. With a disembodied and perversely sing-song cadence, Tom heard his mother scream, "So Johnny's gone to sleep! So Johnny's gone to sleep! Poor tired Johnny!" Next he heard her slam the bedroom door with a ferocity that reverberated through the Boys Room.

Frozen in his chair, Tom's worst fears were realized as seconds later she appeared in his doorway. Wild-eyed and tousle-haired, her puffy face was contorted into a maniacal grin. "Y'all are just alike!" she screamed. "Are *you* going to sleep, too?! Y'all are just alike!"

Too paralyzed with fear to do otherwise, Tom responded as he always did to her opening barrage - meekly, apologetically, and with great care. "No, I'm not asleep," he said, wide-eyed, pushing himself back into his chair.

"Of course, you're not!" she screamed. "You're going out to look for whores, aren't you? Just like him!"

"No, I'm not –"

"You're just like him!" she continued to yell. "Just like him!"

Tom did not respond, knowing better than to agree, and knowing that he did not disagree. His mother started to cry loudly, and amid her sobbing she asked, "How could you take me to see that movie? How could you? That woman was just like her. That awful old tramp was just like her! Just like your daddy's whore!"

Tom closed his eyes, sighed, and said, "I'm sorry, Mom. I'm sorry. I'm so sorry."

"How could you do it? How could you?" she moaned loudly. "Didn't you see she was just like her? That dirty old whore! She was just like her! Just like his whore!" Tom replied with silence. "Oh, I know you'll stand up for him," she cried. "You're just like him. You're both against me. You want to get rid of me. Then you could have your whores together!"

"Mom, please don't say that, please. Mom, you're wiped out. Please, why don't you try to go to bed?"

She screamed again and louder, "That's all y'all want! Y'all just want me to shut up! To go to bed!"

"Mom, this just doesn't do any good. It doesn't help anyone."

"I love both of you," she screamed, "and you want whores! That woman was so horrible! So ... dirty! How could you take me to see that?"

"I'm so sorry, Mom. I didn't have any idea you'd take it like this. Please go to bed," Tom pleaded.

She walked close to him and drew back her open palm. Tom sat frozen in the chair and offered no defense. She had made the same threatening motion to him before and had never followed through. He had grown to hope that she would, assuming her guilt over finally doing it to be at least sufficient to bring one night's battle to an end. But again she gritted her teeth and snarled fiercely close to his face, but she did not strike him.

As Tom sat immobilized, she dropped her face into her hands and sobbed. She turned, opened his door onto the patio and went outside, slamming the door behind her. He turned his eyes back toward the television screen, but no words, no pictures registered in his mind. The horrible dread of the rest of the night was ruling.

After ten minutes, though, Tom began to fear for his mother's safety. He had not heard her return to the house. It was cold and he knew she was wearing only a nightgown. He also thought of the swimming pool - in the dark, in her emotional state. Finally, leaving behind the momentary comfort and quiet of his room, he walked out into the dark in search of her.

It was an overcast, moonless night, but from the lights of the street across the vacant lot that bordered theirs in back, he saw her sprawled and sobbing on the diving board. Her being outside created another problem for Tom - that of discovery by the neighbors and the resultant additional heaping on of embarrassment and humiliation that her screaming and ranting at this hour could bring. He hoped that she was not so far gone that the strictures of appearances before the community would still mean something to her.

As he approached her, he discovered that she *was* too far gone. She looked up at him and yelled, "So you finally came out to look for me!" He reflexively shushed her. "Oh, God!" she wailed. "Yes, I must be quiet!"

Tom noted at the corner of his vision a light coming on in the kitchen window of the Allens' house adjacent to the lot behind theirs. Intent on quieting her, Tom changed his tack. "Mom, I love you," he began gently. She moaned and started to cry again. "I love you," he repeated as he approached her and placed his hand on her shoulder. "And if you love me, you'll stop doing this and come inside with me now, please."

"I do love you, Tom, but I can't help it."

"Yes, you can, Mom. You've got to."

"I can't, Tom. I can't!" she cried, and she started to sob again loudly.

Again Tom's reflexes betrayed him. "Sshhh," he urged.

To this she whipped her head up, her hair flying back wildly and snarled, "You don't care about me! All you want is quiet - just like him! You don't care if I'm happy or sad ... or living or dead ... just as long as I'm quiet!"

"Don't say that, Mom. I do love you. I do want you to be happy. I want you and Dad to be happy." A desperate thought shot through his mind as he searched for some new approach - something that would get through to her and end this emotional carnage. Sitting beside her on the diving board, he held out one hand palm up, and said, "Mom, what we've all got right here, right now - what you've got, what Dad's got, what I've got, is one pile of shit." She jerked her head back and frowned at him but did not speak. He went on, "There's nothing we can do about that. We've been working on this pile of shit for a long time, and it stinks and it's horrible, but it's ours. Now we can push it aside ... or put it away ... or throw it away," he said, motioning with his arm as if throwing it in the water. "Or we can keep going on like this and make another pile of shit of the rest of our lives," and he held both hands palms up as if each were filled. "I say let's go from here. Let's don't make anymore. Let's stop doing this -"

Finally interrupting him, she once more gritted her teeth and yelled, "I can't believe you'd talk to me like that! I can't believe you're using those words! I thought you were a good boy. You *are* like him. You're just like him! I wanted you to be a good boy." She began to sob and moan again, throwing her face down on the diving board.

Tom stood up quickly and backed away from her. "I've got to leave," he said. "I've got to get away from here."

She looked up at him and pleaded, "No, don't leave me! Don't leave! Please!"

"I've got to, Mom. I'm getting out of here. I can't take this anymore."

"No, no, don't leave. I'll stop. I'll stop."

He turned and walked quickly into the house leaving her screaming for him to stay. He slipped into his Weejuns, donned his Wazoo parka, and hurriedly looked in on his father. His face turned to the wall, Johnny appeared to be asleep. Tom heard the back door into his room open, and he walked quickly out the front to his car - his heart and stomach churning with fear and upset. He started the engine and began to roll down the driveway as he saw her run out the front door toward him. She was beside his car before he could clear the drive. Fearing what she might do to herself, he stopped. She stood beside his door as he rolled down the window.

"Mom, I've got to go. I can't stay here."

The voice he heard in reply was one transformed. It was gentle, loving, and pleading. "Please stay, Son. I love you. Please don't go. I'll never do that again. You're right. I'll change. Please stay. I love you so. Please don't go."

"Mom, I have got to go. I can't stand this. I've got to go. I love you, too."

"Tom, where are you going?"

"I'll go to Chet's," he lied.

"Will you come back tomorrow?"

"I don't know."

"Son, please don't go. I'm so sorry. Please forgive me. I love you." All the while that she spoke, she wiped the moisture from her face and brushed her hair back with her fingers trying pitifully to make herself presentable, or, at the least, less threatening. "Will you come back?" she asked.

"Mom, of course I'll come back. But not tomorrow. I'm just going on back to school."

"Tom, I'm so sorry. I love you so much."

"I know you do. I know. And I love you. And I love Dad. But I hate this part of our lives more than anything."

"I know. I know, Son. I'm so sorry. I won't let it happen again. I promise, if you'll just come back."

"Mom, I'll come back. I'll come back."

"Tom, please hug me and tell me you don't hate me."

He got out of the car, hugged her and said, "I love you, Mom. I could never hate you. I just hate *this*. I hate this when it happens, but I love you."

"I know, Son. I'm so sorry. I'll change. I won't let it happen anymore."

Tom nodded. "I've got to go now, Mom. I'll be back. Don't worry. And I'll be careful."

He gave her a kiss on the cheek, and she hugged him tightly. Holding him close, she asked, "What does that date in your room mean to you?"

Pulling away, he answered, "I told you."

"Yes," she replied, "but what happens on that date? What are you going to do?" she asked, holding on precariously to her composure.

"Nothing, Mom, nothing. I'll probably just take a look at myself. It's just a day to stop and look. I'm sorry I wrote that there."

She was silent for a moment before saying, "Son, please don't kill what's left of me."

"Oh, Mom," he said, shaking his head, and he hugged her again. As he let her go, she pulled away and, almost politely, put her hands at her sides.

As he backed out of the driveway, beneath the puffy eyes, the frazzled hair, the swollen face, was the sweet warm smile of the mother he could not help but love.

*   *   *

Tom drove by Chet's, but he was still out. At half past eleven he set out for Dallas. As he cleared New Fredonia and headed for the interstate, it occurred to him that he had left his luggage at home and, more importantly, his clean clothes - or at least the pile of dirty clothes he had brought home with him the prior day. He did not, however, consider going back for them. He counted himself fortunate for not having any homework to do over the weekend; therefore, he had taken no books with him. He was sorry to have left his father to whatever fate the rest of the night might hold for him, but he enjoyed an undesignated hope, if not optimism, that the shock of his departure would quiet his mother. He hoped it would give her something to think about instead of something to scream about. He was surprised - but proud of himself - for having taken the authority to remove himself from the field of combat. What he did not review was any connection between the movie, the chalkboard entry, and the night's events. He knew there was culpability there for the taking, but he graded her actions or reactions to be totally out of proportion to his.

It was just past two o'clock when he arrived at McCartney. By then he had pushed back the specific details of the conflict he had left behind and the disaster of a weekend that he had experienced, and all that was on his mind was crawling into his safe, quiet bed in 332. Unlocking and opening the door with the hall light backlighting him, Tom was greeted with a strange sight. Covering the floor were three family-size Wildcat Pizza boxes, dried cheese and tomato sauce entrails a greasy testament to their long since devoured contents. Joining them on the floor were a half-dozen empty, syrup-stained Coca-Cola cups, two pair of jeans, and a pillow. Investigating upward Tom beheld the familiar army-green wool blanket atop Brandeis' bed, but the figure beneath it was outsized - twice the size of his roommate. As he reached back and flipped on the overhead light, he noted the figure's two-toned, two-textured hair. The light brought Siobhan and Brandeis to, and after a moment's slow-motion movement the two faces, frozen in shock, whipped toward Tom.

When he closed the door and looked back at them, Siobhan gave him a wickedly joyous smile. Even with her face, lips, and eyes totally devoid of make-up, it having been kissed, licked, and sweated off through thirty hours of lovemaking, she was still beautiful - more radiant from the sheer, obvious happiness in her face. The former virgin beside her was another story. As he stared back in stunned silence at his roommate, for the first time Brandeis' eyes appeared larger than Siobhan's.

"What time is it?" Brandeis whispered desperately. Before Tom could answer, he added, "What are you doing here?"

Glancing at his watch, Tom whispered, "It's about two in the morning. And I live here." Then choking back a laugh, "What's *she* doing here?"

Propping herself on one elbow, the army blanket draped over her shoulder and hanging precariously across her chest, Siobhan replied in a Mae West voice, "So what does it look like I'm doing here, Big Boy?" Tom did not answer, lost for an instant of reflection on his happiness for his roommate - and in hopes that the blanket might move. Switching back to her normal full-bodied tone, Siobhan declared enthusiastically, "Hey, the nuns always told us to nail a Christ-killer whenever we got the chance." Nodding toward Brandeis, still frozen against the wall behind her, she added, "This one even gave me the stake."

Chapter 15

"Who was that funny-lookin' little fat boy I saw in the latrine yesterday?" Joe Joe asked, his elbow propping him up in the doorway of 332.

Brandeis replied with a stunned stone face. Tom's mind raced before he looked back at Brandeis and asked, "Wasn't he a high school buddy of yours?"

"Yeah," Brandeis quickly agreed.

"Well, he was a weird-looking little muthah," Joe Joe observed. "Wore his cap into the head. Never said a word. Always looked down."

"I ... I guess he felt sort of out of place here," Brandeis offered.

"So that's why you had to bunk in with me?" Joe Joe asked, turning to Tom. To Tom's nod, he continued to query, "But what were you doing coming in in the middle of the night?"

Now it was Tom's turn to reply with a blank face. Drawing a void in excuses, he replied, "I just felt like coming back. Can't get enough of this place. What about you?" he asked Joe Joe. "Did you have a big date last night?"

"Aw, it wasn't that big. I had another date with Dixie Merrill."

"Hey," Tom said. "Something getting serious there?"

"Hell, I'm not, but she sure seems to be."

"What do you mean?" Brandeis asked.

"She's been puttin' out like crazy. That's what I mean."

Seized by a raw curiosity, Tom asked, "Well, how far've you gotten with her?"

"All the way."

Tom asked with unabashed amazement and unguarded envy, "Last night?!"

"Sure," Joe Joe bragged. "Last night. Last weekend. The weekend before that. Hell, she folded on the first date."

As Brandeis' wince toward his desk blossomed into a smile, Tom glanced at him and whispered, "Did everybody here get some last night but me?" Then looking back at Joe Joe, he asked, "Where do y'all do it?"

"Back seat of the Bonneville in the Z-P-L. Where else? Couple of times I did take her to the Whip Inn. Yeah, she's been collectin' my runoff for several weeks on a pretty regular basis ... but I don't know. Maybe I'm gettin' tired of her ... or gettin' tired of the routine ... or something. But it seems like I've had better nights in bed with my hand."

"And more," Brandeis offered dryly, before Tom added, "Many more."

"I'll tell y'all my problem," Joe Joe whispered seriously, "as long as we can keep it between the three of us. I don't have *any* trouble gettin' it up with Dixie or with settin' my tadpoles free ... the first time. But after that ... the next time, seems like it takes me forever before I can loose the juice ... if I can at all. I'm worried I'm losin' interest in the whole proposition."

"You got any ideas for him, Woz?"

"Haven't run into that problem lately," Brandeis replied.

Tom shook his head and smiled in wonderment at his sated roommate. "No advise from me," he offered. "I can't quite get past my envy of having the problem in the first place."

Shaking his head as he turned to leave, Joe Joe offered, "Aww, don't worry, Tom-cat. Just keep your chin up. Some girl'll come along and sit on it."

* * *

Tom had waited in Joe Joe's room until he received Brandeis' midmorning call that the coast was clear. Joe Joe had followed Tom to his room, though, and it was only now as the cowboy closed the door that the roommates could speak freely about the weekend.

"Gyyaahh!" Tom exclaimed skyward, shaking his head. "Well?" he asked.

"Well, what?" Brandeis responded behind a self-satisfied grin.

"Well, a million things. Geez, where to start," Tom wondered. "How'd you talk her into doing it? And how'd you do it? And how'd she get in? And how'd she get out?" After a hesitation, "And what was it *like*? Had y'all planned this before I left and you hadn't said anything to me about it?"

Brandeis bit his lip pensively and then responded, "No, it wasn't anything that we had planned. And, like Joe Joe said, she just looked like a little fat boy who was visiting someone in the dorm. And, we just didn't go out any."

"That was obvious," Tom observed.

"Hey, I got it all cleaned up," Brandeis laughed.

"Well, how'd she get out of her dorm overnight?"

Meekly offering a peace sign, Brandeis whispered, "Two nights."

"*Two* nights!?" Tom shouted. As Brandeis nodded, Tom shook his head in disbelief. "Two nights."

"Yeah, it worked great. She just checked out to spend the weekend with Thia. Her mother lives here, and from what Siobhan says, she's a real free spirit. Very open-minded. She let's Thia pretty much come and go, and she doesn't nag too much about what she or her friends choose to do."

"So when did she get here?"

"Right after you left Friday afternoon."

Still shaking his head in amazement, Tom said, "You lucky dog. You worthless, undeserving, flea-bitten lucky dog."

Yeah," Brandeis answered slowly, nodding.

Changing his tone, Tom observed, "You're different, you know."

"Really?"

"Yeah, mainly you just really look happier."

"I really am," Brandeis replied evenly.

"Then I guess it's everything it's cracked up to be?"

"Tom, it's that and a hell of a lot more. It just *feels* so damn good. The best feeling I've had in a long ti- The best feeling I've ever had."

"So it appears you've been yanked back, kicking and screaming, from the yawning jaws of gaiety."

Brandeis' expression changed to a more pensive pose than Tom had expected before he replied, "Well, I've learned a lot about love this weekend – and sex," he added with a grin. "But I guess what I've learned helps me understand love better. And whether it's between a boy and a girl, or a boy and a boy, or a girl and a girl, it's something we should all look for – and hopefully find – and hopefully keep. I never had thought about it like this before, but right now, it feels like love is what we're here for. It sounds crazy, but now I can understand my Memphis buddy better. Now I know what he was looking for." Suddenly embarrassed at the depth and the bent of his statements, Brandeis laughed lightly and added, "Got more than you bargained for, huh?"

Tom had followed the tone of Brandeis' monologue to a more serious place within himself as well. Nodding in understanding, he said, "Yeah, I think that kind of feeling in me has been – oh, I guess, blunted – over the last couple of years. I hope I get back to it. Nice to be reminded how good it feels." Then joining his roommate in a momentary embarrassment, he fell silent in search of a conversational course change. Finally, looking around the room, Tom asked, "Well, did she just now leave?"

"No, we got up early, and she went out before me. And then I followed her a little while later. We went over to Kip's and had breakfast. Speaking of which - it's lunchtime. Are you ready to go eat?"

Tom glanced at his watch. "It's only eleven o'clock."

"I don't care," Brandeis replied. "I'm starved!"

Hypnotically staring at his steaming cup of coffee as he slowly and methodically stirred a half teaspoon of sugar into it, Brandeis finally asked after minutes of silence while they had rapidly consumed their blandly seasoned plates of mess hall chicken and dressing, "What about *your* mystery woman, the love of your early youth?"

Surprised by the question, Tom considered his reply through an overlong silence. "I guess when you're so head-over-heels in love, you wonder why everyone else isn't – or if they are but don't know it."

"It's okay. You don't have to go into it."

"I know, I know. It just caught me off guard. No, there's no great mystery. Her name is Clair Kennerly. She lives in Promise, down the road from Noofer - between there and Bethany. I've known her all my life. She grew up in Noofer. We went to grade school together. She had a real tough early life. Her father ran off when she was a baby, and her mother died when she was eleven or twelve. Twelve, I guess. And that was when she had to leave Noofer. She moved to Promise - just eight miles down the road - but she had to transfer to Bethany schools, which is another four or five miles on down. So we pretty much lost touch through junior high. You know the problem."

"Sure," Brandeis nodded. "No wheels."

"Right. But we'd see each other every once in awhile in Noofer or Bethany at a football game or at *Harvest* or something like that. And always - every time - I guess from the time she was nine or ten on, she always looked at me and talked to me like no one else did. It was real strange between a boy and a girl at that age - or, rather, between a girl and a boy, because I really didn't notice anything different about how I felt ... except maybe how easy it was to talk to her. But she always really made me feel - made me know - that I was special. Special to her - and just special for being me. And then, long about the time I turned fifteen, and I got - "

"Wheels?"

"Wheels. I noticed that all of a sudden she was this beautiful sophomore just down the road at Promise. And I could just tool on down there, pick her up for a date, take her places, be with her, and have all that specialness that she gave me all to myself - whenever I wanted to."

"So you started dating?"

"Yeah, off and on at first - not a whole lot. We'd see each other a lot, but not like formal dates. I went out to her farm pretty often. She lived with her grandmother, her mother's mother, who she called Gramma - and who I got to call Gramma. A really sweet old lady. Gee, I guess she's deep into her seventies now. I've never been very close to either of my grandmothers. Neither one of them was really your basic 'over the river and through the trees' type. Dad's mother was real frail all the time I was growing up, and she died three years ago. And, of course, Mom's mother is this crazy old lady who runs a truck stop, and doesn't have the time or the inclination to be a grandmother.

"But Gramma really cared about me, and cared so much about Clair. She hovered and she coddled and she nursed. She did everything she could to make up for the love that Clair was missing by not having parents, I guess. Yet, she did anything but spoil her. Clair was really her partner in that farm. I've never known any kid who had her head on as straight as she did - about everything in the world - except maybe about how she felt about me. I guess I was her weakness. And sometimes we'd talk about that - about how special I was to her - and how special she was to me. And we'd wonder where it came from. But she was the one who really thought about it more than I did. By that time, the main thing I was interested in was getting her in the backseat.

"We dated for a couple of years - through our sophomore and junior years. And neither of us dated anyone else during that time. But it was funny. We had known each other for so long and been friends before we started dating for so long. It was like we never had to or never did stop and say, 'We're going together,' or stop and say, 'we're going steady.' We just ... dated. And, pretty soon after we started dating, we started going parking. And that was a real revelation to me: how good that felt. Just like you were saying this morning. Except all I'm talking about is just some necking, where everybody kept their clothes on." Under his breath he added, "Damn it. And she really liked it, too. But then, she liked everything about being with me. And I loved being with her. But, *that* became the priority. That became what I was always angling toward. And, of course," he noted with a weary exasperation, "it's hard for you to just get to one level and stop. Or, at least, it was hard for me. I got frustrated and wanted more. She knew it. I hardly tried to keep it from her.

"And by the end of our junior year, I started trying to spring the 'if-then' trap on her. You know, 'if you love me, then you'll do so-and-so'. And then we were both frustrated. She was just so damned mature. I wanted to go all the way. I wanted to real bad. But she knew she wasn't ready to, and she *really* knew I wasn't. And yet, every time we went parking, or got together - and we had some wonderful picnics." Tom smiled and looked away in reverie. "We'd go up on Scatter Mountain above her farm or to the pond behind it." Then looking back dejectedly at his roommate, he went on. "Anyway, we'd go farther and farther - faster - and then stop. We did that for months. And, I guess - yeah, there's no guessing about it. One time, what I said was, in effect, an ultimatum. And I lost. She said 'no', and I blew up and said a lot of stupid, horrible things. God, she cried. And I took her home, and she was still crying when we got there. I drove away, and I never called. We didn't see each other our senior year. She stayed out of Noofer, stayed at home and went to school - didn't go to games. And I stayed out of Bethany and never drove past the Promise turnoff at less than seventy." Spent, Tom propped his elbows on the table and his chin on his interlaced knuckles.

"What's she like, Tom?" Brandeis asked. "I mean - smart, dumb, funny, sad, loud, quiet?"

"She's really a neat girl. She's got a good, quick sense of humor, but she's pretty quiet. Loves to read - and read and read. If she wasn't with me or doing homework or working chores with Gramma, she was reading. We used to go on picnics, and she'd take a book - with the understanding that I could rub around on her and kiss on her while she was reading. She really liked that," Tom added wistfully. "And, yeah, she's real smart - and pretty. Dark blond hair. Big blue eyes. Works outside with Gramma a lot and has these beautiful pink cheeks. Didn't wear a lot of make-up. Didn't need to. She made me feel so special, and I really ... blew it. I really did. I know it."

"Well, Tom, why didn't you ever call her to say you were sorry?"

"Aw, Woz, because I really felt like I had said too much and hurt her too much. Really ended things. And I later heard she was dating somebody else, and I started dating Meredith."

"And does Meredith give you what Clair used to? Or have you been holding out on me, and she's been giving you what Clair wouldn't?"

"Quite obviously," Tom replied, "no and no."

"Well," Brandeis nodded, "from everything you'd said, I'd guessed she wasn't."

"No, and I never have really pressed her about it either."

"So why was it so important to you then, and it seems less so now?"

"Well, Woz," Tom answered expansively, "have I ever told you about my golf game?"

"Noooo."

"I love golf," Tom began. "Love to play it. Love that *rare* sound of the solid crack of a ball coming off my driver heading long and straight down a fairway. I've been playing it - or playing at it - since I was about twelve, but I've never been that good at it. I just never had a summer that I could play it day after day to really see if I could be good at it. But I love to play the game, even though I'm very inconsistent - very up-and-down - have good days, bad days - good holes, bad holes. When I do it well, it feels great. When I do it lousy, though, I'm certain that I'm being punished by God - for some character flaw - or for just general character deficiency."

"So," Brandeis reasoned, "why don't you just act nice before you play golf? Be a Good Samaritan. Help little old ladies across the street - whether they want to go or not."

"Oh, no, my Hebrew friend," Tom declared. "What you are talking about is Good Works. It is by Grace that par is saved, not of Works, lest any man should bogey. No, God could see through it if I just consciously performed some acts of goodness. It would not reveal the truth of what was in my heart. Golf is the 'character check'. It's what's inside me that counts. And my golf game goes up or down right alongside the struggle within me between good and evil."

Shaking his head clear and with a smile, Brandeis said, "Okay, so let's bring this back around to sex."

"Sure," Tom replied. "Same principle. Well, if not the same principle, at least the same involvement level from God. Direct. Daily. I've dated several girls besides Clair in high school and after, and before Meredith and I started going together. And I've gotten pretty far with a few, and nowhere at all with a lot more. And I guess I've always felt like God had his hand in it - figuratively, of course. Anyway, after Clair, and then after a few other girls that nothing happened with, I guess I finally came to feel like God must be saving me for something - or someone. So with Meredith, when it didn't happen right off, and when she never even had that same feeling or intensity about me that Clair had from the start, I suppose I felt like God was still saying, 'Nope, not yet. I'll let you know when.' So I don't worry about it that much anymore. But I do wish he'd give me credit for good behavior - and improve my golf game."

"My God, Windham, you are so weird. But one more question. Where's Clair now?"

Glancing at his watch, Tom replied with melancholy, "Probably standing beside Gramma at the Promise Open Door Baptist Church singing 'Just As I Am', the invitation hymn. But Friday night, she was at Paco's with Gene Ray Driggers."

"Who's that?"

"Local thug *par excellence* a couple of years ahead of us in high school."

"Are they going together?"

"I don't know," Tom replied, shaking his head in disgust. "Maybe I'm just meant for a monastic life. Ascetic. Celibate."

"Lighten up, buddy," Brandeis said. "Anyway, wouldn't you be hard pressed to find a Southern Baptist monastery. I don't even think there's one in Nashville."

After a moment of introspection, Tom's expression cleared and he asked, "What's your mother like?"

Brandeis responded with a quizzical look before replying, "Well, let's see what my shrink and I have come up with. Domineering, smothering, single-minded, oppressive. Perfectionist, disciplinarian - but loving - and deeply involved with her children and their well-being. She loves me. Just ask her. Why? What's going on?"

"Mine's as crazy as a loon. And she's trying to drive me just as crazy. I'm sick of it, and I dread the next time I have to go back there. I suppose that's going to be Spring Break, and it ain't gonna be fun." Brandeis began to speak and then hesitated. "What is it?" Tom asked. "Hey, it's open season. Take your best shot."

"I guess I'm just surprised ... that she wouldn't be ... very careful with you ... after what happened with Mark."

With a bitter scowl Tom looked down and away and said, "Sometimes I think she was just warming up on him."

Chapter 16

Mid-March

"So the interview went well and you loved Boulder, huh?" Tom asked as he and Brandeis shared a large "Kitchen Sink" with Chet at the Wildcat.

"You mean 'interviews'. Seems like I talked to everyone in the department and half the administration. But I think they liked me, and I liked them."

"So you're going?" Tom asked seriously. Chet bit his lip and nodded, a modicum of pain showing on the face he gave Tom. But with an uncharacteristic and fleeting flash of maturity, Tom read his favorite cousin's expression and said, "I think that's really great. It'll be a good experience for you, and now I know what I'm doing on Spring Break next year."

Chet smiled with relief. "Yeah, you'll love snow skiing. I can't believe I waited till I was thirty-three to try it," Chet allowed.

Leaving the Wildcat after lunch, Brandeis noticed Chet stop on the sidewalk. Assuming that he wanted to speak to Tom privately, he offered his hand with a, "Nice to meet you, Chet." Then pointing at Tom, he added, "Check you later, Roomie."

"There he goes," Tom yelled after him, "the man who put the Woz back in Wazoo."

Just before jaywalking across the Drag, Brandeis twirled toward Chet and asked, "Say, Chet, did you say you were thirty-three?"

"Yeah."

"Just a piece of advice. You'll want to steer clear of Jerusalem in April." And spinning, he plunged into the traffic on the Drag - zigzagging through it and emerging unscathed on the campus side.

Chet had been through Dallas the week before on his way to Boulder, but Tom had been in class. He had left Tom's clothes and luggage with Rodg Messing. Tom's mother had included a letter containing the familiar apologies and promises of forbearance from future such scenes. They were unusual to Tom only in that they were in print. But in spite of their having been committed to paper, he discounted their contractual viability and discarded the letter.

"Where do you go when you want to go for a ride around here?" Chet asked. "I'd just like to talk with you for awhile. And catch up. Okay?"

With the knowledge that they had caught up only two weekends prior, Tom warily replied, "Let's just head north on Preston."

Quickly finding themselves rolling past the fields of maize and alfalfa that apprehensively awaited the northward march of Dallas development, they exchanged for several minutes scholastic pleasantries and unpleasantries about Chet's teaching experience and Tom's learning experience. Finally, though, Chet went to the crux.

"Aunt Nancy asked me to talk to you."

"Surprise, surprise."

"Tom, she loves you very much ... and she's very, very troubled."

"I know both of those things," Tom said. "But right now, the 'troubled' part is winning out over the 'love' part. It's way out in front. I just don't want to be around that. I'm not going to be."

"Tom, I just wish you had known her -" Chet began, but Tom cut him off.

"You've said that to me before. It makes me real envious that you and Mark got the good part, because, frankly, I don't remember much of it. I mean, I can remember way back when she was only 'nervous'. Back then the Vitamin B shots seemed to help at least for a few days at a time. Or maybe they just helped because she thought they did. But it is just not in my consciousness when she was a 'happy person'."

"Well, she once was," Chet said quietly.

"So what happened?"

"Come on, Tom. You lose your child, especially someone like Mark, and that's it. You're devastated for the rest of your life."

"No, that's too easy, Chet. I remember her before ... Mark ... did what he did. They went at it with each other day after day after day, and night after night. I remember all the crying, all the yelling and screaming at each other. Dad having to come down on Mom's side, as if she was someone Mark had to respect - just because she was his mother. Something must have knocked her out of kilter way earlier on."

Chet stared ahead up the straight, rolling band of asphalt. "I'm sorry, Tom. I was never sure how much of that you got, and how much they were able to keep from you. That must have been hell."

"It still is."

Nodding, Chet continued, "I've thought about Aunt Nancy a lot. It's so hard to see how a kid like my dad could come out so happy, so untroubled, and the other child - from the same family - be so insecure and so at odds with life. I think you can lay a lot of it on her mother. From what I've seen and from what Dad's told me, Granny gave her a real hard time growing up. Jerked her love back and forth. And probably, frankly, made it obvious that my dad was her favorite. I'm no psychiatrist, but it seems like Aunt Nancy was always trying to win her love, and her father's, and just never realized that they were incapable of giving her what she wanted. And it wasn't any reflection on her or the kind of person she was, but I'm afraid that was the mistake she made. She thought she was the problem. And she always seemed to think that if she just did enough or did the right thing, she'd get more love from them. She was so wrong. I don't think they have it in them. And my dad just didn't need it like your mother does. And he got more than she did anyway.

"And then she was gifted with this creative, imaginative, brilliant son, and all she could think of doing was trying to get him to fit in the mold. I sometimes wonder if she ever really thought about what she was doing, the way she was treating him. I think way down inside, in a place she never could see or figure out herself, she thought she was doing the right thing for Mark - by trying to make him conform so he would get the love from people that she always missed. She never understood him and, in her defense, was probably just incapable of understanding him. She tried to apply the same rules to him she thought worked for her. And they never did - for either of them. And it just drove him farther away."

"So have we found the culprit?" Tom asked caustically. "It was Granny ... who killed Mark?"

Chet shuddered. "Oh, Tom, I almost wish it could be that simple. I know you'd like to have an answer to that question even more than I would - as much as your mother would. It's just not that simple, and it never will be. And I hope some time in your life you'll be able to do something I've never been able to do and that I'm still working on. And that is to accept that I'll never know ... and to go on anyway."

"Sometimes I'll think I have, Chet. I'll go for days without thinking about him. But too many things happen that remind me how much I miss him - how sorry I am I don't have him."

"Hey," Chet said, "there's a lot of him in both of us. Sometimes I'll be in class. One of my students will ask me something about the Civil War, and this incredibly detailed narrative on some obscure but infinitely interesting point about that war will usher forth, come from within me. And with my students sitting there agog, I realize it was one of Mark's anecdotes - one that he threw out along with a thousand others. And this one stuck, and so many of the others did, too. They're just ... there ... and they're our gift from him – to enjoy and even to pass on. History, sports, movies, music, all that stuff he loved and shared with us."

The cousins drove on in silence for several minutes. Finally Chet noted a city limits sign, and said, "Gunter? We better turn around and head back before we cross the Red." After U-turning short of the sleepy little town's center and beginning to drive south, Chet asked, "Will you come home this weekend?"

"No."

"Will you come home next weekend?"

"No. I'll be back for Spring Break."

"This really hurts Aunt Nancy. I wish you'd call her or write her or something."

"Chet, weekend before last really hurt me. I've got plenty to do over here. I like being here. No one yells at me - without cause. I'm not going to put myself through that again. And if it happens at Spring Break, I'll leave again. I don't know where I'll go, but I swear I'll leave."

"Is that supposed to be a message for me to give her?"

"No," Tom answered, "that's just what I've decided for myself. I can't believe the two of them can stand for their lives to be like that."

Chet pondered a response for a moment and then shaking his head, agreed, "I don't understand it either. But Tom, I love you, and you know whenever things get rough for you at home, you've always got a place to come."

'Until the first of August I do,' Tom thought.

After stopping at the Dairy Queen in Van Alstyne for Dr. Peppers, Tom and Chet spent the rest of their visit lamenting the sad state of University of Texas football and its three-year wandering through the wilderness of mediocrity. Stopping behind McCartney, the cousins bade farewell. But as Tom approached the back entrance, he heard Chet hail him once more. Tom spun toward him and was surprised by what he saw. Chet thrust his arm out the car's side window and pointed a familiar hand sign at Tom. 'Wild Goose Moon', Tom noted. Having neither given it nor received it in a long time, he nonetheless reflexively responded with the same sign toward his cousin. As Chet drew in his arm and motored away, Tom followed him, his arm outstretched, with the sign.

A flood of memories gushed over him - of Mark, who had originated it, and of Clair, the other member of the surviving trio who knew of it. The wind blew chill across campus and Tom shivered momentarily at the back door of McCartney as he called up the memory of Clair standing on Gramma's front porch laughing giddily at the end of a date and returning the same farewell that Chet had just given him - the Sign of the Wild Goose Moon. And he thought of her by the pond. Clair.

*   *   *

On the first flight of stairs on the way up to 332, Tom remembered that he needed to buy a book for required "Man And His World" reading. Backtracking down to the first floor and heading through the lobby, Tom noticed Joe Joe descending the main stairway toward the door.

"Hey, Tom-cat," Joe Joe called out. "How's it hangin'?"

"By a thread, Bartlow. How 'bout you?"

"Where you headed, boy?"

"Over to the bookstore," Tom answered as he flung open the double doors. They walked out together into the darkening, chilled evening. Violets and musty reds and oranges silhouetted the campus's aging live oaks and outlined its buildings. Walking quickly but hunkered against the cold, the boys made their way across campus.

"What do you have to get at the bookstore?" Joe Joe asked with the feigned concern of the requirement-only reader.

"*Candide*. Did y'all have to read that last year in "Man And His World"?"

Joe Joe searched the sky for an answer. Suddenly the light dawned, and with a mischievous grin he replied, "Oh, yeah, isn't that the one where the pirates check the pussies?"

"What?!"

"Oh, hell!" Joe Joe said. "There I go giving away the best part."

"So what do you need at the bookstore?" Tom asked.

"Huh?" Joe Joe replied, taking his turn at incredulity. "Naw, I'm not going to the bookstore. I'm heading over to the Drag. Going over to the Drop Zone to hear Pi Makers."

Waving Joe Joe off at the steps of the SUB, Tom entered the sprawling student center building. Homing in on the 'Literature' sign in the bookstore, Tom walked quickly through a hallway intersection and was forced to spin dexterously out of the way of the similarly oblivious girlfriend of his roommate. Laughing at their near miss, they stopped to talk. Glancing down, though, he noticed her right foot wrapped in a bandage with white antiseptic gauze protruding from it.

"What happened to your foot?"

"Oh," she began, betraying embarrassment, "nothing really. I just ... cut it on some glass ... at the ZPL."

"Yeah," Tom observed, as if he knew, "you've got to be careful of those broken bottles out there."

"Right. So. What are you up to, Tawm?"

"Looking for *Candide*. Do you know where it would be?"

"Ahh," she noted. "Cultivate your own garden."

"Funny," Tom observed. "That's not the line Joe Joe quoted."

"Say, have you and Bran worked everything out about this weekend?" To the vacancy in his squinting eyes, she backtracked. "Oops, hasn't said anything to you, has he?"

"Y'all know I'm going to be here this weekend, don't you? I mean, I could bunk with Joe Joe, but I'm going to need the room during the day," he said with a tentative smile.

"Oh, sure. That wasn't what I meant. That's not what we -. I blew it. Forget it. Let Bran tell you."

"Okay."

Embarrassed, she waved and said, "Gotta run. See you."

Leaving the bookstore, a wave of melancholy swept over Tom. It was with a guilty ambivalence that he realized his sadness was that he had lost his new best friend to happiness. He knew that Brandeis' priorities for his waking hours had become, first, to spend time with Siobhan; a distant second, to maintain good grades; and much farther behind in third, to comply with the minimum requirements - that minimum still being highly stringent - of his parents. Tom was sad that his relationship with Brandeis was now somewhere behind those three. He did not resent Siobhan because he knew how happy she made his roommate. He also understood his drive to excel in his studies. In that realm he had always envied Brandeis' energy, determination, and self-discipline; although, each of those had been pushed aside to varying degrees to accommodate the wide swath that Siobhan had cleared in his attention. And his mother simply *demanded* her role in his life.

But, as he had compartmentalized and assigned to steerage Chet's request for understanding of his mother, so he pushed back his sadness at the passing of his moment of primacy in Brandeis' life.

Walking down the sidewalk away from the bookstore and toward the Drop Zone, he glanced up and saw Siobhan's 4-4-2 in a parking space. As he passed it, he did a double-take and bent over in laughter at the sight of the cardboard taped over the kicked-out rear passenger-side window.

Chapter 17

"Give it to me," Siobhan urged hungrily in his ear between kisses.

Siobhan lay naked and golden outstretched before the fire crackling in the outsized, aging, soot-stained rock fireplace. Brandeis lay on his side flush against her, an elbow and hand propping his head as he caressed her body. Working his lips down from hers to her neck and to her breasts, she stretched her arms out on the floor above her head and arched her back. Brandeis rolled onto her. She caught her breath when he suddenly pushed her thighs apart with his. Finally, wrapping his arms beneath her and pressing her breasts into him, he complied with her command.

The glow of the flames danced erratically off the glistening bodies of the young lovers and off the heavily varnished knotty pine walls and rough-hewn rafters of the cozy bedroom suite they occupied. As her breathing became more urgent, Brandeis pushed off the floor with his hands and propped his upper body above her. Gazing down at her dreamily, he saw her hair soaked and askew from his perspiration more so than her own; her face, her body auric in the glow of the fire. Finally, she reached up and pulled him close to her. Momentarily tightening her body and then totally releasing it, she cried out and then followed with a rhythmic moan before ending in a soft, loving whimper. His release quickly followed hers as they heaved for breath against each other.

After a minute's stillness, they rolled on their sides and kissed each other gently and contentedly. But she soon pulled away and gave him a curious grin. "Bran," she said, her tone a mixture of fear and discovery, "Bran, I'm in love with you."

As he retracted his head also, he smiled and observed, "That doesn't seem to make you too happy to say that. What's wrong?"

"No - no, baby," she said. "I *am* happy. I am *very* happy." Looking at him and shaking her head as if in disbelief, she went on, "It's just that this has never happened to me before, and I always thought when it did, it would be with somebody ... big and blond and tan. Maybe even with a brogue. And for damn sure with a crucifix."

At this they laughed, and Brandeis kissed her quickly. "Well, babe, sorry. You got yourself a skinny, bone-white, wire-haired Son of Abraham."

"You look *damn* good to me," she said, glancing his hard, glistening body up and down as she smiled, grabbed his hair in back, and brought his lips to hers.

Both suddenly started, though, as the tiny cuckoo clock on the wall announced eleven o'clock. "Oh, time for the movie," Siobhan said with enthusiasm. Then looking at her spent lover, she asked, "Do you feel like watching it or do you want to just go on to sleep?"

He nodded, "Sure, just let me get a Coke. That'll bring me to."

"Okay, I'm going to the ladies' room for a minute. Get me one, too." Rising to their knees, each scanned the other's shining body again and neither could deny the other one more embrace. Still kneeling, Siobhan reached for the silk panties that she had already had on and off three times this Friday evening. Before putting them on again, though, she passed them by her face and took a whiff. With a grimace, a wave, and a "whhooo", she announced, "Ain't enough Tide in Texas", and tossed them in the fire.

In a chat earlier in the week following Business Law class with Jeb Garrett, a neighbor of Brandeis at Culver the prior year, Jeb had mentioned his bachelor older brother's cottage near White Rock Lake in East Dallas and its availability for the weekend. Brandeis had quickly leapt at the opportunity. The wicked flicker in Siobhan's eyes when he had coyly presented the prospect to her gave him to know all he needed about his wisdom in accepting Jeb's offer.

And now as the dying light of the fire competed with the blue glow from the portable television atop the dresser, a small pool of Siobhan's tears welled on Brandeis' chest as she laid her head on him while he stroked her hair. With John Wayne blinking against the rain that soaked through his shirt, an apprehensive, young Maureen O'Hara clung to him while they waited out the storm in the ancient grey cemetery.

"I've never seen the Duke look so ... vulnerable," Brandeis marveled. "So human."

Siobhan did not move, but, sniffing back tears, responded, "Up in Lake Forest right now, Paddy and Meg are probably doing the same thing we're doing. You can always find *The Quiet Man* on a late movie on some channel around Saint Patrick's Day up there. The difference is, Paddy's already been into the Dewar's and he's singing along with all the songs. His voice gets so sweet and high, nostalgic and melancholy, when he starts singing those Irish pub songs."

"Do you really think they're doing what *we're* doing?" Brandeis asked.

Siobhan remained still but Brandeis felt her smile as she replied, "Hey, his didn't fall off when he turned forty, and hers didn't close up."

"What a thought. I just can't quite imagine Avie and Shirley still ... doing it. I'd really like to meet your parents. You think they'd buy it if you introduced me as Brandon O'Wasserman?"

At the film's conclusion they watched the romantic couple posing happily in a pastoral scene. Then the vivacious Irish lass turned and, smiling naughtily, whispered in John Wayne's ear. His reaction was one of genuine surprise and mischievous delight as he turned and chased her across a shallow, rocky brook.

"What did she say to him?" Brandeis asked. Siobhan shook her head as she rubbed his stomach but did not respond. "No, really, what did she say to him? It must have been great."

"Who knows?" she replied.

"Did you see his reaction? It was so unexpected."

"I love that movie," Siobhan observed. She kissed her way up his chest to his neck and to his lips. Observing his sleepy visage, she suggested, "You want to call it a night?"

"Yeah," he answered. "I'd call it an unbelievable night. An incredible night." After he turned off the television, they dozed off in each other's arms.

* * *

It was nine o'clock Friday night when Tom received the first call from Shirley Wasserman. Tom had let Brandeis' telephone ring a number of times before he picked up to take a message for him.

"Oh. Hello, Mrs. Wasserman," Tom stammered. "I'm Tom, Woz-uhh, Brandeis's roommate."

"Oh, how do you do, Tom," she said matter-of-factly. "I need to speak to Brandeis."

"He's not here, ma'am."

"Where is he?"

"Out ... with some friends," he responded. 'Why didn't I say 'on a date'?' he asked himself with exasperation.

"Oh?" she replied with a cold curiosity. But choosing to pursue no further information, she said only, "Please have him call me upon his return."

"It could be late," Tom ventured.

"Why? Where is he?" she asked sharply.

"Oh," Tom recoiled. "I don't know. But it's a weekend, so he could be out late."

"Well, have him call me," she directed.

"Yes, ma'am. I will."

With the click of receivers Tom exhaled a breath of relief. He instantly established the fiction in his mind that Brandeis was going to be out past the time that he was going to bed - which was technically true - and that he had, therefore, been unable to give him the message from his mother. She did not call again Friday night, and Tom went to bed early without thinking again of her call.

Returning from his Saturday morning shower, Tom was greeted by the ringing of his roommate's telephone.

"Hello, this is Tom."

"This is Brandeis' mother."

"Oh, Mrs. Wasserman. I'm sorry. I didn't give Brandeis your message last night. I had already gone to sleep when he got in, and I forgot to this morning."

"Is he there now?" she asked coldly.

"No, ma'am. I'm sorry. He took Siobhan to breakfast this morning, and then I think they - "

"Who?" she asked.

"Siobhan."

"Siobhan? Who is *that*?"

Tom's mind raced, though not quickly enough. After an overlong pause he replied, "Uhhhh, that's ... someone he has a class with, and they're ... working on a project together."

"What class?"

"B-Law," he shot back, knowing that he was digging the hole deeper with his every word.

"What?"

"Business Law. Let me have him give you a call ... as soon as he gets back."

"Yes, you do that. When will he be back?"

"I ... don't know," Tom answered, obviously rattled.

Suddenly understanding that Tom was shaken, it was as if Shirley Wasserman had instantly played back her words and their tone and had realized that she had exposed her fangs. She converted to a gracious nonchalance. "Well, Tom. That's alright. Not to worry. Just ask him to give me a ring when he returns, please. I'm sorry," she laughed. "There was just something I needed to talk to him about. It'll wait."

"I'll have him call you, ma'am," Tom replied, still anxious to get off the line.

"That will be fine," she said pleasantly.

Hanging up the receiver, Tom stared out the window and shook his head in disbelief - at the performance he had just heard, at the performance he had just given, and at his roommate for not having told his mother about Siobhan. The vision of Brandeis on a psychiatrist's couch flashed across his mind's eye. He then leafed quickly through his campus directory for Jeb Garrett's number. There was no answer; nor was there ten minutes later, nor when Tom returned from breakfast.

After an afternoon of studying and research at the library and shopping on The Drag, Tom returned to 332 to prepare to go out with Fred and Harvey. He could hear the phone ringing as he approached the room. He determined not to answer it, but after more than twenty rings he realized that she was going to stay on the line until someone responded. Picking it up, he was greeted with a breathless, "Brandeis!"

"No," he answered. "It's Tom."

"*Where is he?*"

"I don't know," he replied calmly, expecting her at any moment to revert to the pleasant Mrs. Jekyll as she had during their last conversation. "I've been missing him all day, and it looks like from the clothes on his bed that he's gone out again."

"With that *girl?*"

"I don't know. Probably not."

"Well, leave a note for him to call me," she directed.

"Yes, ma'am, I will."

Tom again rang for Jeb Garrett. After five rings Tom was ready to give up when Jeb answered. Tom sucked in a breath ready to speak and then fell silent.

"Hello," Jeb repeated. "Who is this?" Then after a short pause, he exclaimed, "Adios, Homo!" and slammed down the receiver.

'Let them have their weekend,' Tom thought. 'He can't catch any more hell for one more night than he will anyway. Mothers,' he concluded with disgust. 'It's us against them.'

Tom went out with his friends and returned after eleven. Brandeis' phone was ringing, so he went to the lobby and watched television until midnight. Coming up the stairs he met Rodg Messing.

"Do you know where Brandeis is?" Rodg asked.

Having already prepared his story for Mrs. Wasserman, Tom said, "I think he's spending the night with a buddy of his."

"Who? Where?"

"I don't know. I think a friend of his from Culver last year. And I don't know if he's in another dorm or if he has an apartment. Why?"

Rodg half-smiled and asked, "You mean *you* haven't heard from her?"

"Oh, Woz's mother? Yeah, she's called. I told her I didn't know where he was."

"Yeah, well, she was pretty upset." Cocking his head and staring into Tom's eyes, he asked, "Are you giving me the straight stuff?"

"Yeah," Tom replied uncomfortably.

"What if I called to check on where Chevy is right now?"

"I don't know."

"Okay, but tell him to call his mother as soon as you hear from him."

"Okay."

Tom was not sufficiently out of earshot of Rodg when he blew out an enormous sigh of relief. Rodg smiled and shook his head.

Soon after his return to 332 Tom answered Brandeis' phone on the second ring. To Mrs. Wasserman's frantic query, he replied innocently, "Oh, did he not get you? Well, I left a note, and he wrote on it that he was spending the night with a buddy of his."

"Do you expect me to believe that?" she asked menacingly.

"Well, yes. That's what the note says. I'm sure he tried to call you."

"I've been here all evening," she stated coldly.

"Oh, well, don't worry. I'll tell him to call you in the morning."

"Yes. You do that," she commanded before hanging up loudly.

Tom rose early Sunday and determined it to be a good day to attend non-denominational services at Proctor Chapel. He dressed hurriedly and exited his room early. Changing clothes quickly after church, he managed to avoid more than a minute at a time in 332 for the rest of the day, and he only left the telephone ringing twice.

*   *   *

The pre-dawn chill of Sunday morning in the poorly heated bungalow found Brandeis and Siobhan entwined under two blankets, a bedspread and a frayed, aging quilt - where they had also spent most of Saturday. Brandeis untangled himself from the warmth and softness of Siobhan in her naked slumber. Leaving his underwear beneath the sheets, he slipped on his heavy wool socks, his rumpled corduroy slacks, his plaid flannel shirt, and his worn wool crewneck sweater. He turned on the side of the bed and smiled at the shock of blonde hair that was all of Siobhan that showed from beneath the covers. Leaning down on the pillow beside her, he reached under the layers of covering. Finding the sensitive spot at her waist and the small of her back, he watched as she sighed and arched her back. With her eyes still closed she brought a smile from beneath the blankets as he leaned over, pressing his mouth against her ear.

"Let's see if we can get lucky this morning," he whispered.

With a dreamy confusion she purred, "Again? Sounds good."

Brandeis smiled and replied, "No, there's somewhere I want take you. I want to show you something. I think it'll be worth it."

"What could be better than this?" she asked softly. Then squinting her eyes open, she groaned, "Bran, why do you have all those clothes on? Why don't you just get back in here with me?" Lifting the covers to reveal the substance of her offer, Brandeis' glance caught her ample breasts, her narrowed waist, and the rise of her hips.

He softly rumbled with regret as he looked away and said, "Trust me. I'll get on top of that just as soon as we get back."

"Well, do I have to get dressed?" she moaned.

Without replying he grabbed the softer of the two blankets - a Tartan plaid lambswool - pushing the other covers aside. He wrapped the blanket snugly around her and lifted her out of bed. Enjoying the spontaneity of his actions and the anticipation of whatever experience this was that was so important to him as to wrest him from her bed, Siobhan kissed him on the cheek and, smiling contentedly, buried her head in his shoulder. He carried her to the 4-4-2 parked in the dark, earthen-floored one-car garage and carefully placed her in the front seat. Easing into the driver's seat, he found her holding the blanket around her and leaning against the opposite door.

As he backed out of the driveway, she snuggled her bare feet under his leg and wiggled her toes. He took a deep breath and glanced at her. Now fully awake, she wore an eager smile that flashed from her blue eyes and brought out her dimples.

Frere` Jacques Cafe on Garland Road gave off a friendly, yellow glow against the pre-dawn darkness as Brandeis pulled up. He returned to the car with strong, steaming chicory coffee and a grease-stained sack of beignets laden with powdered sugar. First circling south of the lake through a somnolent East Dallas neighborhood, he finally turned and drove north along the western lakeshore, periodically looking east at the violet sky of the approaching dawn, until he reached a vacant parking area with a clear view of the eastern shore of the lake. He parked the car on the grass close to the line of low reeds that separated land and water. Tiny mudhen silhouettes bobbed in the waves offshore.

Brandeis eyed Siobhan noting on the blanket a liberal sprinkling of powdered sugar. He smiled at the white dot of sugar on her nose and traces at the corners of her mouth. "Wait there," he whispered. He got out and went around the car to her side. They nuzzled as he kissed the sugar from her nose. Then he lifted the bundle of blanket and beauty out of the car and sat her down on the hood. After tucking the blanket under her feet, he climbed on the hood behind her. As the cool breeze drifted off the lake into their faces, she leaned back into him resting her head on his shoulder as he nuzzled her ear and neck.

The sky had lightened from violet to pink and a half-dozen thin, striated clouds to the north gave off a coral glow. Above the pink sky was a corona of aqua before it merged with the receding shades of dark blue. "Look", Brandeis said, as the yellow of the approaching sun began to filter into the pink. Siobhan raised her head from his shoulder and Brandeis pressed his face into her thatch of hair as the golden glow of the sun's dawning reflected off the lake and into her face. Intermittent gusts of wind blowing across the water brushed her hair back, and it caressed his cheeks. Squinting into the oncoming brightness, she scanned the horizon noting the symmetry of the picture before her - the thin clouds to the north above the darkened trees and lake, the approaching orange ball of the sun, and the spire of a church - reminiscent to her of that of Holy Trinity's at Stratford - rising above the trees to the south.

As the wind died down, the white clouds of their breaths mingled while they silently watched the sun rise quickly to its blinding fullness. Brandeis finally said, "Let's go."

"Okay", Siobhan whispered, and he helped her off the hood. She leaned against the front fender and slowly shook her head. Then opening the blanket to him, she said earnestly, "Oh, Bran, I do love you." As he came to her, wrapping his arms around her under the blanket, she enfolded him, whispering, "Yeah, it was worth it."

Chapter 18

Early April

"And the dawn comes up like thunder out of Garland 'cross the way," Brandeis announced as he propped himself against the side of the built-in chest of drawers that doubled as his headboard. The brilliant red-orange sunrise through a retreating morning haze shown through the open window of 332 and gave Brandeis's naked upper body and face a pinkish tint that caused Tom to double-take when he glanced around from his desk. Breaking from the study of European history, Tom gazed out the window and nodded.

"So, what are you going to do on Spring Break? Start studying for Finals?" Brandeis asked with a laugh.

"Right," Tom scoffed. "No, I really haven't thought about it much. I'll probably just lay low. Rest up. Go see some movies. Catch up with some friends. And, of course, the regular stuff: break up with Meredith; fend off my mother's attacks."

"I feel for you, buddy. Hey, if things get too close, hook 'em up and head on up to 'd'city det gave birf to d'Blues'."

"Yeah, keep a light on. That jackass tapping on your window one of these spring nights may be me. Oh," Tom said, changing suddenly to an excited tone, "one thing I'm going to try to line up out of Dad is a trip to Indy for the Five-Hundred at the end of May. I read in the paper that Jimmy Clark was testing there last week and is going to be driving one of Andy Granatelli's turbine cars in the race. I'd give anything to see that. What about you? Are you and Chevy going to get together anytime during the Break?"

"I wish," Brandeis moaned. "No, I fear Shirl's going to keep me pretty close to home after weekend before last."

"I'm sorry I couldn't have handled that any better for you," Tom said.

"No, no. It sure wasn't your fault. I know you did everything you could to cover for me. It was just dumb of me to think she wouldn't check on me and then do everything short of flying down here to track me down."

"Yeah, I was glad I talked her out of *that*."

"If I'm lucky," Brandeis stated, "I'll get to go up to Union City to my grandmother's farm."

"What about Chevy? London, Acapulco, the Big Apple, Monte Carlo? Which will it be?"

"Hey, that girl's fallen for another man. Didn't you know? R-F-K. That's all I hear. Ever since McCarthy cleaned LBJ's clock in New Hampshire and Bobby decided to come out and sweep up the pieces, that girl has been floating around on Cloud Nine –"

"Whoa," Tom interjected, "mixed metaphor overload."

"Sorry. Anyway, you should've seen her the night her father called her and told her Kennedy had decided to run. You remember the look on the Mother Superior's face in *Sound of Music* when she was singing "Climb Every Mountain"?"

"Oh, yeah," Tom nodded. "You mean," and he began to sing in a squeaky falsetto, "*Climb every mountain, chevrolet every stream*."

"Yeah, that's the one. I mean, it was this worshipful, beatific ... countenance. Yeah," he nodded, "it wasn't just an expression. It was a countenance. And she's just kind of drifted around campus like a novitiate in the Order of Saint Bobby ever since."

"I've seen the look," Tom assured him. "At revivals. Don't worry. They get over it."

"Good."

"You're not telling me our boy's been going without, are you?" Tom taunted.

"Well, she hasn't gone *that* far."

"You two amaze me," Tom said. "I hope you're using some kind of protection. I mean as often as ... "

"Just livin' on luck - and an occasional rubber - when she thinks it might be time. It's kind of a Catholic thing," he said with a laugh. "Personally, I subscribe to the view that doing it with a rubber on is like washing your feet with your socks on, but - "

Checking his envy, Tom shook his head and said, "Back to Kennedy. I just don't get it. I don't see what she thinks he can do."

"Oh, just end The War and bring our country back together. That's all, I think." Tom did not reply, and an awkward silence followed. Finally, Brandeis went on, "Anyway, she's off to work on his campaign in Indiana next week. Her dad lined it up for her. He's apparently one of your typical fat cat contributors."

Looking pensively out the window, Tom said, "What's amazing to me is that LBJ just hung it up like he did. Good-bye, White House. Good-bye, Air Force One. Good-bye, Power. Good-bye, Glory. Hello, Johnson City. Hello, White-faced Herefords."

Brandeis suddenly snapped his fingers and said, "Oh, I was supposed to ask you. Do you want to go to Coy and Hawk's party with us tonight? Billed as *The* Pre-Spring Break Blowout to see and be seen at."

"Well, I wasn't invited," Tom replied. "I wouldn't want to crash - "

"No," Brandeis explained. "I'm sorry. Siobhan told me to tell you you were, and I forgot. And she wanted you to go with us."

"Where will it be?" Tom asked warily.

"At their apartment, just off campus, behind The Drag. There'll be a crazy group of people there - not just Greeks."

"I don't know," Tom said.

"Aw, come on. After this test of yours, and before we've got to face what we've got to face next week, we deserve a party. Come on, it'll be a kick. Justine Lecataret'll probably be there. She may take one look at you, throw you in her 'Vette, and make you her personal sex slave as you spend Spring Break cruising Route 66 from one dingy motel to the next."

"Eat your heart out, Marty Milner. I'm there."

Siobhan was waiting on the steps of Blake Hall when Brandeis and Tom arrived on foot. Sedately attired in a navy miniskirt and a white knit top, she ran to Brandeis and draped herself around him for a long kiss before pulling away and asking, "See anything unusual?" Posing quickly with her arms akimbo and then spinning, she gave her perplexed boyfriend a clue by looking down at her feet and spreading her legs slightly.

"Oh, you've got new shoes on," he guessed.

"These things are old as the hills," she said. "But come closer. What kind are they?"

"They're black patents," Brandeis answered as he drew nearer. With a suddenly devilish glint he stopped directly in front of her and looked straight down. Smiling broadly, he whispered to her out of earshot of Tom, "And the fact that you don't have any panties on could definitely get me encouraged." Grabbing her around the waist he lifted her off the ground with a kiss.

"Oh, no, sisters, sisters!" she cried. "You were right. He *did* get the wrong idea. Get me to a nunnery - fast!"

*　　　*　　　*

They opened the apartment door to a din of laughter and loud conversation in competition with the jazz combo - Hawk on drums and Coy on sax - set up in the living area and jamming around the fringe of "Take Five". Brandeis faded behind Siobhan as she entered to a chorus of "Hey, Chevy's" from the assembled, and Tom sneaked in behind them. The assembled comprised an eclectic mix of Greeks, Jocks, musicians, and GDI's - some invited, some invited by invitees, and a smattering of benign crashers who simply assumed that they had been out when their invitations had come. The large apartment was shared by the hosts and John Wiviott, a Sigma Sig to whom Siobhan introduced Brandeis and Tom.

"You two ought to hit it off great," Siobhan offered. Tom and John gave her matching quizzical looks, and she went on. "You're both car racing nuts!" Their expressions continued in unison with mild embarrassment unfolding into curiosity.

"What kind of racing do you like?" John asked.

"Formula One, endurance sports car," Tom replied.

"Le Mans, Sebring?" John asked.

As Tom nodded, Siobhan blurted out, "Le Mans? Hell, he's been there."

"Really?!"

"Yeah," Tom replied. "In '65."

John thought for a moment and then offered, "Let's see ... Rindt and Gregory in a Ferrari?"

"You got it," Tom said.

"God help us," Brandeis stated. "Windham has found a kindred spirit. These two could bring this party to a halt. They could make this crowd plead for The Quiet Game."

John went on, "What was it like? Was it incredible?"

"Labor and birth aside, it was the most incredible twenty-four hours of my life."

"That was the year of the 427 GT-40's, wasn't it?"

"Finned 427 GT-40's," Tom corrected, "that flew for a few hours and then broke. And that raunchy Cobra Coupe. God, that muthah would take the uphill bend past the pit straight before the Dunlop Bridge like it was on rails - with those big, fat nine-inch tires. And there was no body lean - just pure, unquestioned adhesion."

"Yeah, that was the one when the lead Ferrari broke late, wasn't it?" John asked.

Tom thought for only a second as his focus extended through the den's glass doors past the smoking grill on the patio to the park-like common area beyond. "There was a moment on Sunday afternoon near the end of the race when I had returned to the main grandstand at the start-finish line across from the pits. There was a yellow Ferrari in the lead. Yeah, yellow," he said incredulously, noting John's appropriate surprise that it was not red. "I think it was a private entry," he went on, eliciting a nod of understanding from his host. "Anyway, the grandstands were packed, and we were all straining to see the lead car make the turn at Maison Blanc and barrel past us. We'd been giving it a cheer every time by. It took about four minutes to complete a lap. So as four minutes since its last pass came up, there was great anticipation in the crowd. The temperature there in northern France had made two forty-degree swings. It was eighty at the start at four o'clock Saturday afternoon, and it had gotten down to forty in the middle of the night when I had just kind of keeled over against a wall and stole an hour or so of sleep. And now it was back up into the eighties, which made the track temperature probably somewhere over a hundred.

"I remember straining for a view down toward Maison Blanc. And then this perceptible moan rippled through the crowd, starting down at the end of the grandstand closest to the corner. I looked and saw the yellow Ferrari, and the heat waves coming up off the track made it look like jiggly lemon jell-o with racing numerals. Because of the heat and the distance I couldn't tell if or how fast it was moving. But then some other cars started coming up behind it and passed, and I could tell it was rolling slowly - trying to limp into the pits. It had blown a tire, and once it crawled in, it took them several laps to repair it. I was across the track from the pits, and as the Rindt-Gregory Ferrari stormed by to take the lead, I saw one of the yellow Ferrari's mechanics throw down his tools in disgust. It was quite a moment, and that was how they ended – one-two."

At the end of his monologue Tom's head drooped slightly as if vicariously expressing the disappointment of the losing car. His audience of three joined him. Looking up at him and then around at Brandeis, though, Siobhan said while grabbing Tom's arm, "Sorry, Bran, and give my regards to R-F-K. I want this man. He has known Life - at its fullest."

Playfully punching Tom's shoulder, Brandeis said in his David Niven accent, "Good show, old sport. I must say, I perfectly understand. Shall we have cocktails?"

"How about Bud or Coke?" John offered with a laugh. "They're in the kitchen."

"Let's leave these car nuts to themselves," Siobhan suggested, and wrapping her arm around Brandeis, they made their way through the crowd in the den to the kitchen. Clad as simply as she was, Siobhan still left in her wake a sea of college boys' longing looks. One was from Joe Joe, who had brought Dixie Merrill and who waved with a hoisted Budweiser from near the patio doors. After grabbing their beers from the overburdened ice chest, they went out on the patio where they found Thia helping two Mu Nu's. They were grilling shish-kabobs, and Brandeis and Siobhan helped themselves to the latest batch.

Hawkins Antoine, taking a break from the combo, joined them. "Sounded good on the drums in there," Brandeis allowed as they shook hands.

"Thanks. So where're you off to tomorrow?" Hawkins asked.

"Just home to Memphis. Say," Brandeis whispered, "is Justine Lecateret here?"

"Yeah," Siobhan added. "We kind of promised a friend we brought with us a 'viewing opportunity'."

"Just missed her," Hawk sighed. "She left with the wrestling team not five minutes ago."

"Hey, Chevy," Thia asked, "can you go in the kitchen and cut us some more meat cubes. And pick up another bag of the pepper and onion slices in the 'fridge, too?"

Making her way back across the room, she was happy to see Tom and John still lost in car talk - oblivious to the progressively boisterous mood of the increasingly inebriated crowd. Before going to the kitchen she detoured down the hall to use the bathroom. Taped to the first closed door she encountered was a Polaroid snapshot of an erect penis. She backed away from the door and laughed aloud through a covered mouth. The drunken couple propped against the wall joined her in laughter as she gasped, "You mean it's the -"

"Right," the co-ed slurred. "The 'ladies' is one more down and on the left."

As she approached the door, she saw another snapshot taped to it. This time she was not surprised but was shocked that a fellow female of the species would be involved in such a graphic exercise in bathroom identification. Leaving the bathroom moments later and laughing her way toward the kitchen, she saw a Polaroid camera on a lamp table. Shaking her head at the accompanying realization, she reflexively scanned the room for likely models.

Meanwhile, John had reluctantly excused himself from Tom to resume his informal chores as host - a task, which at this point principally involved attempts to dissuade the celebrants from destroying the leased furnishings and the premises themselves. Tom found Brandeis on the patio working up a sweat over the open flame. Upon seeing him, Brandeis asked, "Would you feel ditched if Siobhan and I snuck out a little later? We could come back by and pick you up if -"

Tom considered for only a second. "Don't even think of coming back by. Hey, this is your last night together for ... almost a fortnight. I understand and -"

"Almost a fortnight? Wow, how British of you."

"Yeah, John and I were talkin' British racing trash - you know: Clark, Hill, Moss, Pete Hawthorn, Duncan Hamilton. It'll do it to you. Anyway, y'all go ahead. Hey, you know I hate beer. I'm already the most sober guy here, and my lead is only going to lengthen. I may end up taking *all* these people home. I'll have my choice of rides."

A prominent member of the majority to which Tom alluded, Joe Joe, bleary-eyed and shiny-faced, was in the kitchen alone when Siobhan entered. She acknowledged him with a nod and began to cube the sirloin with a butcher knife.

Running his eyes up and down her rear view, he made his way past her in the narrow galley kitchen intentionally brushing the front of his jeans full against the back of her skirt. Without turning she leaned closer to the counter and said, "Watch it, Joe Joe."

After reaching deeply into the watery ice and slinging the chilly excess off the can and his hand, he eased behind her and leaned into her again, saying, "Hey, Chevy, let's us get out of here."

"What?!" she exclaimed, pushing him away with a backward shove of her shoulders.

"What I'm saying is, I feel the urge to purge a surge."

Attempting to remain detached, she said offhandedly, "Why don't you just ante up a quarter and go take a shower with Sophia?"

"Won't work this time," he explained. "I need a warm, wet target."

Finally spinning to confront him with the bloody blade's point inches from his rodeo belt buckle, she watched as he backed hard and swiftly into the opposite counter. Twirling the knife adroitly, she offered him the handle and said, "Here, go heat up a watermelon." Then glancing quickly below his belt and back up at his face, she added, "Or maybe in your case, a grape*fruit*."

His legs winced together, Joe Joe scooted crab-like down the counter and out of the kitchen as Brandeis entered. "What was that about?" he asked, having quickly observed Joe Joe's pained expression as he left.

"Why? What did he say?" she laughed.

"Oh, just a passing reference to the sanctity of excrement. What happened?"

"Nothing. I just had to squash a roach. Here, make yourself useful. Grab this tray of vegetables. I'll get the sirloin cubes."

Siobhan and Brandeis made their way through the crowd as the combo played an extended jazz version of the Wildcat Fight Song in an effort to perk up the sagging crowd. Delivering their provisions, Siobhan feigned haughtiness, "Cynthia, my dear, I present you with ... the raw meat."

"Thank you ever so much, my beloved Miss -"

She stopped in mid-sentence when she heard the combo's drummer hit a rapid, out-of-rhythm drum roll and then slam the sticks against the snare's frame as he stopped playing. The silence of the drums was followed quickly by that of the sax and then by the clarinet and bass. Brandeis, Siobhan, and Thia swung their heads to look into the living room. The crowd that less than a half-hour earlier had filled the apartment shoulder-to-shoulder had either left, sat down on the available furniture, or collapsed on the floor; therefore, the three had a clear view across the living area to the apartment's front door. At the door was Fred Slater accompanied by Danzell Johnson. Siobhan smiled when she saw Danzell - before placing his appearance in the context of the occasion and the locale. She looked around at the combo. Coy wore an arrogant sneer and was holding his saxophone down from his lips as if the interruption of his playing was only temporary. But looking at Hawk, his face of anger framed by the Confederate Stars and Bars over the fireplace, she saw the active hatred that she had witnessed on rare occasions growing up in Chicago and even fewer times on this collegiate island of WSU. She watched as Hawk left his drumsticks on a snare and started to rise from his stool.

Without taking her leave from Brandeis and Thia - indeed, without even giving them a look - she walked quickly into the room. Intentionally brushing by Hawk, she made her way past several burned-out celebrants toward the new arrivals, yelling out on the way with forced gaiety, "Danzell! I'm so glad you could come!"

Sensing trouble, Fred had already moved a step ahead of Danzell. For his part the handsome, lanky young man was scanning the eyes of the crowd into which he had ventured. "Chevy", he replied, pointing at her as she approached him.

Without hesitation she gave him a quick, friendly hug, and, looking at Fred for the first time, asked Danzell, "Who's your friend?"

Smiling broadly at her reverse pivot on the situation, Danzell answered, "Chevy, meet Fred Slater. Better known as, 'the guy who got me into this'. Fred, this ol' dog is Chevy McKenna, a fair hand with eighty-eight."

"Hi," Fred replied meekly.

"Good line, Fred. You're gonna bowl her over," Danzell laughed. Pointing a thumb at Fred and addressing Siobhan, he said, "He's a lot better at initiating racial confrontations than he is at meeting beautiful ladies."

"Let's go get you guys something to drink and some food." Turning to the crowd and noting from the corner of her eye that Hawk had not moved, Siobhan announced loudly, "Everybody! This is Danzell Johnson, best dancer at Wazoo, and Fred Slater, ladykiller!"

'Freddie, you idiot,' Tom thought as he stood beside John Wiviott, with whom he had resumed conversation.

"He wasn't invited," John said coldly.

'Nor were half the people here,' Tom thought. Then smiling into himself, he mused, 'Gee, maybe he meant Freddie.'

'I guess she's for real,' Brandeis thought, his feelings a mix of discomfort with the situation and pride in Siobhan, as she cleared a path toward him for her escortees.

Leaning uneasily against the patio rail having left Dixie asleep in the hallway, Joe Joe stared lasciviously at Thia's tall, lean frame and thought, 'I'll bet she could plant her feet flat on my shoulder blades with her tongue in my mouth.'

Coy turned to Hawk and said, "Let's just play the music. There's nothing to do about this. Come on. It's Spring Break." Hawk's expression remained menacing, but he slowly settled onto his stool and picked up his drumsticks.

Passing out of the kitchen, beers in hand, Fred saw Tom and gave him the oversmile of recognition of he who knows few in a crowd and is overly heartened to find an unexpected acquaintance present.

"Hi, Fred-, Fred. Ready to head for Bethany?" Tom asked.

"Hi, Tom-, Tom," and they shared a laugh. "Yeah, see you on the interstate. Danzell, you know Tom Windham, don't you?"

"Sure, we've taken our chances with McCartney's dining hall food together before, haven't we? Hi, Tom," he smiled as he reached out his hand. With the eyes of Fred, John, Siobhan, and, from a distance,

Brandeis focused on Danzell's extended hand and then leaping to Tom's face, none noticed the millisecond of hesitation before he extended his hand to shake. Smiles of relief graced three of the observers' faces.

"Yeah," Tom exhaled. "You're going to love that shish-kabob out there."

Siobhan made introductions on the patio and helped Fred and Danzell serve their plates. But five minutes into the ensuing political discussion the propensity toward which President Johnson's surprise announcement of Sunday prior had sparked on campus, Siobhan caught Brandeis' focus and gave him a wink and a nod toward the door. He excused himself to the restroom, and Siobhan followed suit. Rendezvousing in the kitchen, they kissed passionately.

"Let's go somewhere and make love," she whispered.

"Done," he replied.

Pulling away slightly with concern, though, she asked, "But what about Tom? He came - "

"I talked to him. He's going to get a ride or walk. No problem."

"Good boy," she purred. "You get a special treat," and they locked lips again.

Joe Joe eased to Thia's side at the grill, and she regarded him warily. "Need any help?" he asked.

"You bet. You want to turn all these for me?"

"Your wish is my command, Madame."

"You're Joe Joe Bartlow, aren't you?"

"Guilty. But don't believe everything you've heard," he replied pithily.

"Don't worry. If I did, I'd be wearing a garlic wreath, a crucifix *and* a chastity belt."

They bantered harmlessly as he turned the shish-kabobs and removed those that were done. "Want to put some more on?" he asked.

"Sure," she replied. "Hand me that bowl of beef cubes over there."

Dipping his head with a sly cut of his eyes, he grasped the bowl and, holding it away from her, said, "I'll give you the meat, baby, but you gonna have to work for the gravy."

Kissing again hungrily at the apartment door, Siobhan and Brandeis pulled slightly apart at the distant but distinctive crack of open palm against cheek. "Let's get out of here," he said.

Ten minutes after their departure and as other partygoers began to crawl off home, Harvey Groesbeck came in against the tide. He inquired of a departing Chi Lambda after Brandeis, but received a vacant stare. Entering, he scanned the living room until he spied Tom near the patio door conversing with Fred and Danzell. "Tom," he called out, relieved to have found him.

The ashen, grimacing face that Tom saw approaching him gave him a start. Unguardedly, he answered, "Harvey, what's wrong?"

Harvey hesitated before replying, noting with concealed surprise Danzell's presence at a party hosted by a group of Sigma Sig brothers. But he finally spoke, "Martin Luther King's been shot."

"Is he - ?" Tom began.

"He's dead. Shot in the neck by a sniper at a motel in Memphis."

"Oh, my God, no," Fred said, his eyes bulging before he glanced up at Danzell.

The young black man stared through the messenger - his mouth barely open, his eyes glazed and unfocused, his brow furrowed - as if a last, best hope had vanished. Tom reached for Danzell's muscular arm and patted him with a cupped hand. "I'm ... sorry. I'm really sorry."

Controlled rage bleeding through, Danzell did not look at Tom but raised his focus to the Confederate flag behind the band and said with difficulty, "You should be sorry for all of us. It's going to get bad. It's going to get real bad."

"It already is," Harvey said "I was looking for Wasserman. Are he and Chevy still here?"

"Why?" Tom asked. "Is Memphis burning?"

Nodding his head, Harvey sighed and replied, "And Chicago, too. Of course, they already had the National Guard out in Memphis because of the garbage men's strike, but that's nothing compared to this. It could turn into Watts all over again. And all over the country. Are they here?" he asked again.

Shaking his head, Tom answered, "I don't think so. I -"

"I saw them leave," Fred said.

"They're probably at the ZPL," Tom allowed without a smile.

"Yaaahh-hooo!" yelled Hawk Antoine, straddling his stool with a drumstick raised triumphantly in each hand. "Someone *wasted* Doctor Martin Luther King, *Junior*!" The news had reached the party from a phone call and had been filtering through the crowd while Harvey was informing Tom, Fred and Danzell. Hawk's cheer was joined by only a few of his friends. The crowd's reaction was more one of disbelief and uncertainty. But as he continued to celebrate the news, he intentionally glanced toward Danzell, and their eyes met. Hawk gave him a sneering grin, and Danzell tightened in anger. He started toward him with Fred, Tom, and Harvey in tow. As he approached Hawk, who was showing a brave front while checking the exits, two burly Sigma Sigs joined the combo who stood as a shield in front of the drummer.

Fred grabbed Danzell's arm short of the Sigma Sig perimeter, and he spun with rage in his eyes to face Fred. "Stop! He's not worth it!" Fred yelled.

"Come on, dancer," Antoine mawked, once Danzell had stopped.

"What did King stand for?" Fred pleaded.

"And what did he *get*?!" Danzell replied.

"This is *my* apartment," Hawk declared. "Y'all just git outta here, y'hear! Git out!"

Coy left the battle line and walked into No Man's Land. Approaching Harvey, whom he knew through *Cat Tracks*, he said, "We don't want any trouble. I'm just going to declare this party over and get everybody out of here. How about if you and your friends ... just ... go on?"

"Good idea," Harvey replied, as Tom and Fred nodded.

Turning to Danzell, Coy cleared his throat and said, "It was a bad thing what happened."

"Come on," Fred said to Danzell, giving him a nudge toward the door.

Danzell took one step, and then in a lunge that caught both sides and the observers off guard, he mounted the raised brick hearth, ripped down the Stars and Bars, and threw it in the soot-filled fireplace. He then walked slowly and unmolested, along with his escort, from the apartment.

* * *

With the Beach Boys' "Wouldn't It Be Nice" soaring in the

background, Siobhan rested her feet on the smooth cheeks of Brandeis' butt. Whispering soft words of love into her ear as he mouthed it, Brandeis' hands ran free across her body as if trying to memorize it against the coming of the next day's separation.

The sound of the door being unlocked and opened below them caused them to freeze their motion. It was the last labored breaths they took after Tom entered the room, along with the stacks of luggage dumped unceremoniously on the two beds topped by Brandeis' clothes and the "little fat boy's" costume, that instantly gave Tom the picture. "It's just me," he whispered as they bounced nervously nonetheless from his thump on the bottom of the plywood shelf covering the entry to 332. He smiled noting it to be slightly bowed under their weight, and said, "I'll go on down to Joe Joe's."

"Thanks," Brandeis answered, having regained his composure. "You can come back after midnight."

"Oh, yeah," Tom replied, remembering the girls' weeknight curfew. "Well, good night," he whispered, with Benjamin Braddock-like goofiness. Closing the door and losing his smile, he stood still for a moment with his hand on the knob. Finally, he released it and walked down the hall. He had decided that the young lovers could go the night without knowing that their hometowns were afire and that their world had changed once more.

Chapter 19

Spring Break

"Passover in Noofer," Brandeis observed, as he and his girlfriend saw Tom off from the parking lot behind McCartney. "What a trip. Oh, yeah, Windham. We called ahead. You ought to start seeing the palm leaves laid on the road for you, oh, about five, six miles out of town."

"Thanks, guys. Of course, I expected nothing less." Looking back around into Siobhan's eyes, he asked, "So what are you going to do now?"

"I talked to Daddy, and Kennedy is going to suspend his campaign for the time being. I'm sure he'll go to the funeral. And if he starts it back up next week, I guess I'll go to Indiana."

"So you're going back to Chicago right now?"

"Yeah, looks like it," Siobhan replied.

"Can't you just fly somewhere else and meet your parents? New York or Acapulco or somewhere?"

Siobhan laughed him off. "I'm not a jetsetter."

Glancing her quickly up and down, Tom remarked, "Well, you're a damn good facsimile thereof." Then holding her shoulders and looking her squarely in the eyes, he said, "If you're going back to Chicago, you be careful."

"Yes sir," she said with a salute. When Tom did not laugh, she added, "Don't worry. I will."

Turning to his roommate, Tom observed, "And off you go into a war zone, too."

"Hey," Brandeis mugged, "don't you know the problems of three little people don't amount to a hill o' beans in this crazy world?"

"We're not at the airport, are we?" Tom asked.

"No," Siobhan laughed, "but I'd better get his sweet buns out there, or we're both going to miss our flights." Then losing concentration as she looked at Brandeis hungrily, she added, "And they *are sweet*."

Tom opened his arms to his friends, and they joined him in a triple hug. "Y'all be careful. I love you."

"We love you, too," Siobhan said.

"Chin up," Brandeis said. "We're all only going to be gone for - what? Less than a fortnight? Listen, why don't you just have a great time in Noofer. Cause a disturbance at a theatre. Stay out all night. Get laid. Or get laid all night in a disturbing theatre."

With one more hug from Siobhan and a wave from Brandeis, Tom started to enter the Le Mans. He stopped, though, and turned with the Sign of the Wild Goose Moon extended toward them.

"What the hell is that?" Brandeis asked.

"I've decided to admit y'all to the Wild Goose Moon Club," Tom replied.

"What are you doing with your hand?" Siobhan asked.

"That's the Sign of the Wild Goose Moon. It's an Indian term for the April Moon. I guess that was the month the geese flew back north after the winter. Least that's what Mark thought. He told me about it, and he came up with the hand sign."

"How do you do that?" Siobhan asked, extending her arm out toward him.

"Touch your little finger to your thumb, then your ring finger to your forefinger, and your middle finger'll just stick out straight. And, no, it's not a perverted way of giving someone The Finger."

As Siobhan and Brandeis practiced, she asked, "Did the Indians come up with the hand sign?"

"No, Mark did. He heard the expression once - I guess, while he was in Boy Scouts - and he liked it. He told me he came up with it once while he was 'just twiddlin' his fingers'. See, the extended middle finger is the long neck and the head of a goose. The next fingers touching are the wings - you know, the way they look kind of swept forward when they're landing. And that little space made by the crook of your pinky touching your thumb - see, look at it from the side - that's the moon."

"Yeah, I see it," Siobhan said through a smile of discovery.

"The Sign of the Wild Goose Moon," Tom repeated. "Well, so much for today's lesson in Indian lore."

"So what does this make us, blood siblings?" Brandeis asked.

"That's exactly what it makes us," Siobhan stated as she hugged each of them.

"Don't guess I can put off leaving any longer," Tom said as he boarded the Le Mans. Peeling out of the parking lot, he pointed the Sign of the Wild Goose Moon at them out the window, and they responded in kind.

* * *

Tom was greeted at the interstate's entrance by a cool, cleansing spring shower. Its dark, low-hanging clouds brought up headlights among the heavy Friday afternoon traffic exiting Dallas. Tom enjoyed driving in the rain - the feeling of encapsulation in his cockpit. Alone in his car this afternoon in the rain, though, with his destination New Fredonia, there was no longer any undesignated, indefinite time that he would have to deal with what he would find there. The time was two hours. Since he had less control over it and because he had a plan for dealing with it if it should come, he was less concerned with the problem of his mother's imbalance.

No, his problem was Meredith. They had talked on the phone once each week since last he had been home, but their conversations had entailed nothing of greater depth than their recounting of current events at WSU and at Springfield College. Substance had been avoided, and Tom had sidestepped a confrontation over his having stayed away for four weeks by a very simple tactic. He had lied. He had told Meredith that he was having problems with his grades and that he had a series of time-consuming projects and research papers to complete and tests to study for. She had been a willing accomplice to this fiction. Her reaction to his absence had been passive, and his flimsy explanations had been accepted without question and with a hint of relief. What had been noteworthy to Tom had been the absence of the words, 'I miss you', from their telephone dialogues. Consequently, approaching home, Tom was at a loss as to what steps he should take when he found himself within twenty miles of her. They had set no specific time for a date but had spoken only generally of seeing each other over Spring Break. The awkwardness was mitigated by the fact that she had already had her break two weeks prior and was now off only for Good Friday, which was near the end of Tom's holiday.

Pulling into his driveway, Tom glanced at the trinity of lanky pine trees that hovered over the corner of the front yard. His grandmother Windham had planted them the day Mark was born. The two trees in front framed the taller, setback center tree in a pattern of arboreal Gothic. Tom had occasionally wondered how his deeply religious but personally distant grandmother had known the center tree would grow taller. Given their genesis, Tom hardly minded having to rake their needles every summer.

His mother had been waiting at the window, and as Tom pulled to a stop he saw her pause at the front door to announce his arrival to his father. She walked quickly with a warm smile across the driveway to him, and Tom's spirits were greatly lifted by her appearance. She had cut her hair short and rinsed out the grey resulting in an appearance reminiscent to Tom of her ten years earlier. But for her eyes, she looked like the mother of his early youth, the way he remembered her - the way he wanted her to be. Her smile, even in her eyes, was unconditional. He saw joy without hesitation and without apprehension. His father trailing soon behind her bounced clear-faced and youthfully toward him. Tom hugged his mother as he and his father swapped affectionate pats on the back.

"Oh, Son," she said, "I'm *so* happy you're home."

"Servants!" his father yelled toward the house with a clap. "Bring forth my best robe! Place my finest ring on his finger! Kill the fatted calf! The Prodigal Son returneth!"

"Servants!" his mother yelled after him. "Spare the fatted calf! We're going to Paco's!" Under an uncertain twilight sky fleeing toward night the Windham family laughed together, and Tom – again - dared to hope.

After unloading his trunk and backseat full of dirty clothes, Tom took a quick shower and changed clothes before the drive to Springfield.

They returned home to the apple pie that Vashti had left for him. He had earlier apprised Meredith of his plan to dine with his parents Friday night, thereby putting off for at least one more night any resolution or non-resolution of their situation. Stuffed, happy, and relieved, Tom went to bed and slept the sleep of the Prodigal Son come home.

*   *   *

Late Saturday morning Tom gathered his nerve and made the call.
"Meredith?"
"Oh. Hi, Tom. How are you?"
"Fine. I'm home."
"Good."
"I wanted to see if you'd like to get together and do something tonight."
After the briefest hesitation she answered, "Well, I can't tonight. I have something to do at school."
"Then could I come see you this afternoon?" he asked.
"Sure," she replied. "That would be fine."
Having effectively put off for a month any detailed consideration and resolution in his own mind of where he would like for their relationship to go, Tom gave himself the twenty-minute drive to Springfield to clarify those matters. Assuming her feelings to be static - inert - and accepting of whatever he would want to do, he considered various scenarios - from an angry, hostile breakup with all bridges and much of the surrounding landscape put to the torch; to a cool, antiseptic Noel Coward-style breakup wherein both parties continued to call the other "dahling"; to an open-ended, all-bridges-left-standing moratorium until either or both exhibited an unbearable case of the "hots" for the other; or, finally, to maintenance of the status quo. The latter he divided into subsets wherein he either explained his distance over the last month or things simply proceeded as if nothing had happened. On the outskirts of Springfield he totally lost his nerve and opted for the latter and the sub-latter.
Stepping out of his car in front of Meredith's house, he was greeted by a perfect seventy-two-degree East Texas spring day. It was the first time since his return that he had noticed the absence of the constant drone of Dallas and the presence of the clean, cool, spring-scented air of Home. The sun, high and heading west in combination with a light

breeze, softly kissed him as he rounded his car to find Meredith waiting for him on her front steps. Clad in khaki shorts and a polo shirt, her face was turned sunward and her eyes were closed but not squinting as she soaked up this beautiful day. Hearing him, she rose with a smile and gave him a hug but not a kiss.

Pulling away but holding her arms, he said, "I missed you."

"Did you?" she asked, before adding, "I missed you, too."

"You want to go for a ride? Get something to drink?" he asked.

"No, it's such a pretty day. Let's just sit here on the steps."

"Okay."

"So you got your big history test behind you?" she asked.

"Yeah," he shuddered. "It was a bear."

"And your research paper?"

"Yeah. How've things been going for you?"

"Oh, it's been hard being back in school after the break."

"Yeah, I'm sorry ours weren't together," Tom said.

"So what're you going to do this week?" she asked.

"Probably just catch up with some friends; plus, Dad has come up with some *work* for me, of all things. He wants me to paint the barn's tin roof out at the farm."

"That should even out your tan," she said with a laugh.

"You mean my *burn*," he replied. "And then I was hoping we could get together some. Go out on nights when you don't have to study." She did not reply, and he asked, "What do you have going tonight? On Saturday night? A sorority thing?"

"Tom, we need to talk." Stunned and speechless with the full knowledge of exactly what such a lead-in meant, Tom did not reply. "This past month," she began uneasily, "and the way we left it the last time you were here, I really haven't been sure what you wanted for us - what you wanted from me."

"I know. I should have talked to you more about it."

"Yes, you really should have."

"Well, I'm sorry. I'll try to do better. So ... what are you doing tonight? At school?"

Gathering herself, she replied, "I'm going to the one-act play competition ... with an A-K who asked me out."

"Oh," Tom said, recoiling with surprise. "Who?"

"You don't know him. He's from Mississippi."

"Have you ... been dating him?"

"No. He's asked me out before ... and some other boys have, too. But I didn't feel right about dating anyone without telling you. So I'm telling you."

"So do you not want to date *me* anymore?" Tom asked.

"I don't want to date you exclusively anymore."

"Exclusively?" Tom repeated. "Sounds like someone's parents talking."

"No, it's me talking. I'm going to date other people."

"So, should I not ask you out?"

"Maybe not for awhile, Tom. You hurt me by pulling away from me like that. I didn't know what it meant. I didn't know what I had done wrong, if I had. Or if you had found someone at W-S-U that you wanted to date. I thought that might have been what you were doing the last few weeks."

"No, it wasn't," he declared quickly.

"Oh," she responded.

"Well, I'm sorry we didn't talk more this month. I guess it's just kind of the way I am."

"Yeah, I guess it is, Tom, but it makes you real hard to keep up with - hard to get close to."

Uninterested in further ex-girlfriend analysis of his shortcomings and upset at the prospect, Tom rose from the steps and looked down at Meredith, who returned his gaze. "I think I'm going to go on. I feel ... bad about this."

"I'm sorry if I upset you," Meredith said. "I guess it had to come out sometime."

"Yeah, it did," Tom said, trying to hide his agitation. "I understand. I just - I just need to go on."

"Okay, Tom. I don't know what to say next either. There are a lot of great things about you," she said, blinking back tears, "but I couldn't tell which of them were for me. I just never knew how you felt."

"I know," he said quietly, hanging his head. "That's a problem I have. Well, I'm going to go on. I'll ... I'll - uhh, if you feel any different, give me a call ... or I'll give you a call in a few weeks."

"Okay," she nodded. Rising, she said, "Here, give me a hug." After an awkward hug she kissed him softly on the cheek and walked inside.

Driving home from Springfield, Tom battled his upset and unease. His initial feelings were related more to the rejection than to the loss. But what came later that triggered the unease was the realization that he was now back in the dating marketplace, a situation that he recalled without fondness. But only moments north of Springfield the name that he had closed off in a dark corner of his mind since last he had seen her with Gene Ray Driggers came to the fore, and he began the slow process of introspection and accumulation of courage that might lead him to call Clair.

After church the following day Tom spent the afternoon catching up with Chet, who had confirmed his Boulder position and was unenthusiastically completing his lame duck semester at the junior college. The unencumbered cousins went to Springfield in the evening and split a Pizza Classic "All-The-Way" and a viewing of *The Lion in Winter*. On the way home Tom rehashed his break-up with Meredith, though without mentioning Clair. Unsurprised by the news, Chet mentioned a conversation he had had with Bethany banker George Collum at a recent *Harvest* committee meeting regarding the banker's daughter Elizabeth, a high school senior – the bottom line being her mooning over and her father celebrating the end of a relationship with a boy from out on the county whom he detested. Chet further related that Mark had dated her older sister Karen, and he remembered losing her as one of Mark's regrets. Noting Tom's non-plussed reaction to his information, Chet eschewed his *yenta* role and, as Tom dropped him off at his house, merely referenced the number of fish in the sea.

Arriving home just before eleven, Tom impulsively called Memphis information and obtained the number of Avrum Wasserman. Brandeis picked up on the second ring.

"Hello," he whispered.

"Hey, Woz, it's your ol' roomie!" Tom said as he looked at his watch. "Gee, I didn't realize it was this late. Sorry. Were you asleep?"

"No, no, that's okay. What's going on?"

"Well, just wanted to let you know that I had hung it up with Meredith. Broke the poor kid's heart."

"Really?"

"No," Tom laughed. "She quit me before I could quit her. Remember? Kind of like in second grade. Yeah, she had a date lined up for tonight before I was even cold in the grave."

"Are you kidding?" Brandeis asked, though his tone gave away his lack of appreciation both of the humor and of the irony of the situation.

"No, she hung me out to dry," Tom said. Then tuning in to Brandeis' lack of enthusiasm, he asked with concern, "How are things going there?"

"Oh, curfew, federal troops, the usual."

"No. I mean how are things going for you - there?" Tom asked, the auditory memory of Brandeis' mother fresh on his mind.

After a pause Brandeis answered in a whisper, "I'll tell you about it when we get back." Then in a normal voice, he asked, "So what are you going to do this week - now?"

"Chet and I just went to see *Lion in Winter*. Highly recommended. Never knew that Dick, the Lionhearted, was a homo, though. Kind of brings into question what Robin Hood and his Merry Men were so merry about, doesn't it? But O'Toole and Hepburn were great. You and Teddie ought to go see it."

"Maybe we will. So tell me," Brandeis asked, "have you called Clair yet?"

It was Tom's turn to hesitate before replying, "I'm not sure what her status is. She's probably dating Driggers ... or someone."

"Well, are you going to find out?"

"Yeah ... yeah, I probably will."

"Your parents like her, don't they?" Brandeis asked more quietly.

"Well, yeah, I guess they do. They don't dislike her. Is that what's going on up there? Are you getting the third degree?"

"Yeah," Brandeis answered. "Listen, I'm probably going to head back early. So I'll be there when you get in. And they're talking about getting me a car to bring back."

"Wheels?! What kind?"

"I don't know," he replied unenthusiastically. "I think my mother's looking for a one-seater. Anyway, I'll probably head back next Sunday."

"Easter?" Tom asked incredulously.

"Don't you remember? There is no Easter."

"Oh, yeah," Tom laughed. "It's just the kickoff day for Post-Passover Depression for y'all, right?"

"You got it."

"Have you talked to Chevy?"

"Yeah."

After waiting a moment and receiving no elaboration, Tom asked, "Not in a position to discuss it, huh?"

"Nope."

"Okay. Well, is she okay?"

"Yes." With Brandeis' hand over the phone, Tom heard him say a muffled 'Yes, ma'am. I will. Goodnight'. Tom, I can just talk for a second. Call Clair. Don't miss the chance."

"Okay," Tom answered, surprised by the urgency in his friend's voice. "I will."

Chapter 20

"Let me see the sports, Dad," Tom requested. It being other than football season, his father passed the cleanly creased, unopened sports section of the *Dallas Morning News* across the breakfast table.

"Aawww, nooo!" Tom stated with shock and anguish.

"What is it, Son? What's wrong?"

The words came slowly and with injury. "Jimmy Clark ... is dead."

"The racing driver?" Johnny asked.

"Yeah," Tom responded numbly.

"What happened?"

"He crashed at ... " and then Tom paused to read down into the article. "At Hockenheim."

"Where's that?" Johnny asked.

"It's in Germany. Just a minute. Let me read it," he exhaled despondently.

"I'm so sorry, Son. I know how much that upsets you."

"My Lord," Tom said with exasperation. "He died in a Formula Two race."

"What's Formula Two?"

"It's a big notch down from Formula One." Shaking his head, he declared, "What a waste. What a horrible waste."

"Well, what was he doing driving in it?"

Johnny's question did not register with Tom as he continued to read the article. Recognizing his upset and his disorientation, Johnny fell silent.

"It just says here, he lost control and hit some trees. Broke his neck. I've heard about Hockenheim before. It's very fast with a lot of trees. I can't believe this. I ... just can't believe it." Tom explained, "You know, he's the one who won the race I went to in Mexico."

"I remember you telling me about him. He's the great one, isn't he? How many wins did he have?"

"Twenty-five. One more than Fangio." Tom continued to stare blankly into the newsprint, as if in hopes of finding some clue as to why a personality of such note - a man of such moment - would die while practicing his trade at a minor event. It was as if the builder of the Empire State Building had died by falling off a ladder while repairing his roof.

Staring at the picture of the mangled car in the woods, Tom stated quietly, "Thank goodness he didn't burn. Thank goodness he didn't go like ... Bandini." With that statement made, Tom could not escape the horrible picture emblazoned in his mind of the lifeless figure of Lorenzo Bandini clad in his Nomex suit lying by the foam-covered wreck of his Ferrari at the sight of his crash at the Chicane in the prior year's Grand Prix of Monaco. He remembered clearly, as he had watched *Wide World of Sports'* coverage of the race, the re-igniting of the flame by the French television crew's helicopter wash - how the small blue plume of fire danced on Bandini's chest until again put out by the firemen, and how it left his helmet, his goggles, his face, and his body covered with the extinguishers' white powder, like Death's Dew.

After Johnny had to excuse himself to go to work, Tom returned to the Boys Room. He reached high on a shelf of his closet and pulled down his 1967 Formula One World Driving Championship chart. He retraced Clark's final full season, noting again with anguish - and now with final anguish - the run that Clark and the new Lotus 49 had made at the title and how they had fallen short. Tom knew and understood that it was a blood sport, and he had seen Bandini and other of the lesser stars of the Grand Prix circus die in crashes, but until that day he had thought that the best could and would make it through. Fangio had survived. Stirling Moss had been retired by his accident at Goodwood. The great Nuvolari - to quote Ken Purdy's Moss biography - 'had died in bed, hating it'.

Having been made aware of Tom's upset, his mother was sympathetic and more attentive than usual to his needs during the day. And when his Aunt Nela arrived for her daily visit, his mother invited him to join them and offered him a piece of the lattice-crusted cherry pie that Vashti had baked for him. Tom took a large piece of the pie and a glass of milk to his room, begging off on joining them.

Consuming his pie and milk in solitude, he continued to pore over his racing magazines and to mentally revisit the prior day's tragedy. The general sensation was that an aspect of his life - unique in its significance - had changed for the bad, and it would not be back as he had liked it before. That evening as he watched television, he smiled at some things. And the next day he laughed at others. The day after that, laughter came more easily. But he knew there would never be another Jimmy Clark, and he knew that his absence - underscored by the memory of the way he had passed - would forever lessen his enjoyment of racing. He felt great grief at the loss of this person he had never met, but whom he would never forget and whose loss he knew would remain a small sadness he would carry with him always.

As the week drifted by, Tom fell into a pattern of painting the barn for two or three hours in the cool of the morning and a like time toward twilight. In between he enjoyed Vashti's wonderful noon meals. After lunch he generally circled the Dairy Queen and washed down his meal with a Dr. Pepper while looking for friends.

He found that he took any opportunity to be out of the house. In spite of the harmony - often genuine in appearance - that his parents were displaying, he still viewed the Boys Room as the night watchman's cottage next to the ammo dump. He did not want to be there when the spark - and it could be anything, as he well knew - set off the explosion that he could not keep himself from thinking was out there - at the end of the next conversation, around the next conflict, just over the next rise of voices. He found himself watching his mother's eyes for signs of her mood, for assurances of her sobriety. He could not fully enjoy the peace in his house for fear of its cessation.

He was able to discuss some of these feelings with Chet, but Tom's discomfort ran deeper. Having been content to spend a month away from Meredith when he felt that he could be with her on his terms when he so desired, her choice to remove herself from his life left him disoriented, especially in the evenings when he at least would have had her companionship - however out-of-kilter their personalities had proved to be.

And then there was Clair. After his Sunday night talk with Brandeis, he had confirmed to call her. The news of Jimmy Clark's death the following morning, though, had left him upset all day, and it blunted his interest through to mid-week. Finally, he called her Wednesday night. The busy signal was almost a relief to him. The busy signal five minutes later and five minutes after that, though, became a spur. When finally on his fifth try the line was free, it surprised him and he was momentarily flustered.

"Hello," a male voice answered.

Dropping his telephone etiquette, Tom blurted out, "Who is this?"

"This is Gene Ray Driggers," the answer came back coarsely. "Who the hell is this?"

After a hesitation, Tom stammered, "Uhh, wrong number," and hung up. He did not call again.

*   *   *

Before heading for the farm late Thursday afternoon, Tom stopped at the Dairy Queen and took his most recent *Road & Track* in with him. At the counter he was surprised to find Troy Hewitt. Two years Tom's junior, Troy was the brother of Bruce Hewitt, with whom Tom had graduated. The Hewitts were a farming family in Piney, and Bruce had gone through twelve grades of New Fredonia schools with Tom. Contrasted to his older brother's lanky, dark-featured good looks, Troy's face was scarred by acne, and his long brown hair was slicked back and greasy.

"Hi, Troy, I didn't know you worked here."

"Oh, Tom. Yeah, after school and on weekends."

"Think you can mix me up a vanilla shake?"

"Sure. Large or small?"

"Big as you got." As Troy started to work on the shake, Tom asked, "You about ready to graduate?"

"Yeah, I think they're gonna let me out."

"So what're you planning on doing when you get out?"

"Probably go down to Houston and join the fire department. Eddy's down there now."

Tom remembered Eddy, Bruce's older brother by barely a year, as being similar in looks to Bruce but with half the personality and intelligence. Tom was not surprised that he had dropped out of college, remembering that he had gone to Stover County J.C. out of high school. "Are you in the fire department here?" Tom asked.

Troy sloughed off a laugh. "Naw, don't need to be yet, but joining the H-F-D'll sure beat stomping around in the rice paddies. That's where Bruce is, you know."

Tom lifted his hands from the counter and retreated a step in surprise. He had neither seen nor heard from Bruce Hewitt nor heard anything about him since the night they had graduated high school. "No, I didn't know that."

"Yeah, he's at Cam Rahn Bay." Crossing his fingers, Troy added, "Five months to go."

"Did he marry Lorena?" Tom asked, remembering Bruce's high school girlfriend.

"Yeah, they've been married more'n a year. Have a new little baby Bruce ain't even seen yet."

"A baby?!" Tom marveled. "Well, what'd they have - a boy or a girl?"

"Had a little boy. Looks just like his Daddy - all legs and dick."

After a guffaw, Tom asked, "So where're Lorena and the baby living?"

""With her parents – well, actually in a trailer house out behind her parents - till Bruce gits back."

"So what have y'all heard from him lately?"

"Aw, he ain't one to write much, but he says they take a lot of 'incoming'. Says those Gooks are just like a pesky grassfire on a windy day. Think you got 'em stamped out one place; they'll spring up somewhere else. Go over there and they'll come back up the place you just left."

"What does he do? He's not in the infantry, is he?"

"Naw, he unloads cargo planes at the airfield there."

Taking a seat in a booth by the window, Tom stared blankly at his magazine. His blues about having a date that night with neither Clair nor Meredith seemed trivial in comparison to the hand Bruce Hewitt was playing. Tom could not help but question the equity of his sitting there in the air-conditioned comfort of the Dairy Queen with the spring sun filtering in through the tinted glass - drawing on a vanilla shake, reading the "Miscellaneous Ramblings" section of *Road & Track*, and off on holiday from his ivory tower in Dallas - while ten thousand miles and one college deferment away a former classmate and new father sweltered on the tarmac at Cam Rahn Bay with a nervous eye cast over his shoulder as he emptied ammunition and supplies from the guts of giant C130's and refilled them with body bags.

Chapter 21

Easter

"Low in the grave He lay - Jesus my Savior."

The choir began slowly and dramatically in the solemn, restrained tones laced with anticipation so familiar to Tom from many Easters past in First Church New Fredonia's hushed, overcrowded sanctuary. The mood of the first verse before the chorus was somber, pessimistic, and defeated, and the overstuffed choir with its excess spilling out of the choir loft into folding chairs trailing down toward the pulpit captured that mood.

"Waiting the coming day - Jesus my Lord."

Their lugubrious delivery brought Tom and all of the other regulars in the congregation, who knew what was coming next, to the edge of their seats. As they approached the chorus, the expectation, which seemed tangible, airborne, caused the assembled to catch its collective breath. And then it came:

"Up from the grave He arose (He arose),
With a mighty triumph o'er His foes (He arose);
He arose a Victor from the dark domain,

*And He lives forever with His saints to reign.
He arose! (He arose!) He arose! (He arose!)
Hallelujah! Christ arose!"*

Victory! Triumph! Glory! It was all there in the melodic combination of choir, organ, and piano that was as upbeat, as affirming, and as joyous, as its lead-in had been doleful. And amid it all Tom listened, and was not disappointed, to hear the deep, booming voices of the ageless Carl Laurence and his equally senior law partner, James Alton Pell, reverberate through the auditorium on each of the bass echoes in friendly competition with the organ's longest bourdon pipes.

Tom eased back into his seat to receive the rich sensory thrill of the choir's rendition of "Christ Arose". His smile of appreciation of this fleeting, but profound once-a-year sensation was akin to that he experienced each October with his first bite of a Fletcher's Corn Dog at the State Fair of Texas. As he did with the initial taste of the golden brown, fresh-out-of-the-deep-fryer, piping hot, batter-encased wiener on a stick, Tom closed his eyes to help empty his psyche of distractions while he absorbed through every pore the three verses and each thunderous chorus of "Christ Arose".

After this breath-taking special music, moved for Easter Sunday to the start of the worship service from its usual spot between the offering and the sermon, Tom glanced around and noted his parents seated in folding chairs in the aisle toward the back of the auditorium. In keeping with another Easter tradition at FBC-New Fredonia, because his parents had attended Sunday School - as most of the regular members of the church had - they were displaced from their customary pews by the Christmas-and-Easter-only "worshippers" (rabble) who passed up Sunday School in favor of snatching up the choicest seats in the sanctuary for the worship service. As he had taken a seat among strangers, having also foregone Sunday School - as was his right as a collegian - Tom had smiled and thought of the lunch topic to come.

For as was an additional Easter ritual, Tom knew that these holiday intruders - these fair-weather Christians - would be skewered by his mother over the chicken-and-dressing at Hallie's Cafe after church. His favorite among her annual declamation of their sins was his mother's indignation at their practice of "saving places" for their still-later-arriving co-conspirators (their families). Though most did this gingerly by spacing themselves generously over a pew and extending their hands out on either side or by placing Bibles or articles of clothing in the reserved seats, his mother had reported instances - to Tom and his dad's muffled amusement - of the children of these fifty-Sunday-a-year infidels actually *lying* across a pew and insolently warding off "the good people of the church".

Beyond the special music and this observation, though, the remainder of the service went downhill from Tom's perspective. While disappointed, but not surprised, that Dr. Lee made no mention of the Palm Sunday loss of Jimmy Clark in his sermon, at its conclusion Tom shook his head in disbelief and exasperation that for the second Sunday running the pastor had been able to avoid mention of the death of Dr. Martin Luther King, Jr. With the nation simultaneously afire and in mourning on the Sunday prior, Dr. Lee had deviated from his prepared text only to call for respect for the nation's laws and respect for property without mention of the spark that had ignited the firestorm. By this the following Sunday, with the fires out and Doctor King six feet under, Browning Lee was comfortable to deliver a business-as-usual, no-nonsense, three-days-out-and-back Easter sermon.

The revelation of that church service, though, did not hit Tom during the pastor's prayer after the sermon, nor even during the invitation (rededications - 2; new members - 0). It was not until the benediction that Tom realized that the only element of the service that was different was one member of the congregation: Tom Windham. Browning Lee had only spoken what he believed, and the preacher had had no reason in the last week or the last two weeks or the last year or the last twenty years to be rocked from his beliefs. Movements had come and movements had gone and so had their leaders, but he was unchanged. And he spoke to a like-minded congregation. True, he had given them what they wanted to hear, but he had not done so fraudulently or hypocritically. For it was he and a long navy-suited, silver-maned, white-carnationed line of predecessors in the pulpit of the First Baptist Church of New Fredonia who - based on their shared fundamental Baptist theology - had shaped the religious beliefs, many of the attitudes, and even some of the practices of the congregation that he looked out on that Easter morn. Tom realized that it was he who had changed; that had Martin

Luther King been assassinated the Thursday before Palm Sunday 1967, he would have been agreeing with his father and nodding with the congregation at the appropriateness of Browning Lee's omission of the name of Doctor King or any reference to his movement from both his Palm Sunday and his Easter Sunday messages. Tom was surprised at himself. Had Ol' Wazoo and its unlikely agents, Fred Slater, Rodg Messing, Danzell Johnson, and even his roommate, insidiously pricked awake a social conscience, he wondered? Given his racist upbringing, he was stunned that a fundamental change in mindset may have occurred in him without his being aware either of its genesis or of its progress.

*   *   *

Upon return home from the predictable Easter Sunday lunch and spurred by his brief "conversation" with Gene Ray Driggers, Tom decided to make a call.

"Elizabeth, this is Tom Windham ... in New Fredonia." And with an awkward laugh into the telephone, he said, "Do you even know me?"

With a laugh of her own, she replied, "Sure, Tom. Navy sixty-six Le Mans?"

"That's me." After a nervous momentary pause, he said, "Listen, Elizabeth, I know this is *real* short notice for tonight, but this is my last night in town before I go back to W-S-U, and I was wondering ... would you like to go out and do something?"

"Ha!" she exclaimed. "Pops told me you might call, and I told him he was full of it! Geez. No, I wish I could, but we're doing our Easter contata tonight at church and the mother and the father would simultaneously have cats if I didn't show."

"Oh, okay," Tom said. "Sure, I used to do those at First Baptist on Easter night. Is it a 'Petersen'?"

"Sure. Didn't he do them all?"

"Yeah," he laughed. "Well, I know how long you've been working on it—"

Cutting in, she said more seriously, "But I'm glad you called and asked." And after only a second's hesitation, she added, "So ... give me a call the next time you're in town ... sailor."

"Okay, Elizabeth. I will."

"But, Tom, when you call me, call me Lizza."

"Okay, Lizza. I'll be back in two or three weeks, and I'll give you a call before then."

"That's a deal, Tom. Sorry about tonight."

"Hey, I understand. Well, rock out."

Tom spent his last night at home watching television alone in his room.

*   *   *

He awoke early but slowly Monday morning with the eager anticipation of returning to WSU prodding him toward consciousness. Before he opened his eyes and became fully alert to the day, though, negative feelings began intruding upon his mind. Finally he focused his hearing without opening his eyes, and he realized that the source of his discomfort was the familiar angry hiss of his mother's voice two walls away. The recognition brought his eyes open, but froze his body in place. The sound continued, but it was different because there was no variation in modulation - no hysterical highs, no foreboding silences. In hopes that he was misinterpreting a conversation between his parents, he rose from his bed and crept out of his room and down the hall.

Their bedroom door was barely cracked open. Tom peeked in and saw his father's back as he stood before their dresser mirror tying his tie. A few feet behind him at the foot of their twin beds stood his mother with her neck craned forward toward him. In profile he saw her eyes squinting and her mouth grimacing viciously. In the few seconds that he dared to watch and listen he heard his mother say - with passion but not rage, with spite but not madness - in a clear undistorted voice, "I hate you."

As chilling as his mother's words was his father's non-verbal response as he lifted his right hand from tying his tie and without looking at her, casually waved her off. Tom did not know what had gone before, and he did not wait to see what would follow. He returned to his room in a daze, and he quickly showered, shaved, and dressed. While packing his bags, he heard his father leave for work. As he finished packing, his mother knocked lightly on his door, and he froze with apprehension. But when she entered without his answering, he saw that she had applied her smile.

"Tom," she said, "already packed?"

He looked at her closely. Her eyes were clear and no more puffy than usual. "Yes," he said carefully. "I've decided to go back a little early." He walked across the room and gave her a hug. Sniffing silently, he noted no aroma of liquor. Pulling away, he looked at her closely and confirmed that she was as sober as he.

"Why?" she asked. "Why are you leaving early? What's wrong?"

Thinking quickly, he replied, "I talked to Brandeis. He's coming back early. He's got a new car, and he wants to show it to me."

"Oh, well, let me go make you some breakfast. Did you tell your father?"

He winced inwardly at her casual mention of him - this man she hated. "No, but I'll stop by the office and say goodbye to him."

When she left the room to make his breakfast, he stood numbly for a second and then felt a chill run through his body. He collapsed into one of the easy chairs at the foot of his bed. Folding his arms at his stomach, he doubled up - his face almost to his knees.

'My mother hates my father,' he thought. 'Stone cold sober, my mother hates my father. And he doesn't care. I love him, and I love her, but there's no 'them' to love anymore. So I guess there's no 'us' anymore, either. After I'm gone - after I'm out of this house - there won't be anything to keep them together. They'll get a divorce. Mom'll go crazy. And Dad'll go bad. God, help me. God, help them. And, God, help me please.'

After feeding him breakfast and voicing her farewell cliché in the driveway ("Just be a good boy, and people will like you"), his mother returned to the Boys Room to pull the sheets off his bed. Walking into his room, she glanced at the wall beside his door and froze. There written on the green chalkboard that she had wiped clean a month earlier was: 042068.

Chapter 22

Struggling into 332 with his luggage, Tom found his roommate sitting expressionless on his bed, his thatch of brunette ringlets, uncut since January, pressed against the corkboard wall above it. It was not as happy a friend that he returned to as the one he had left - less than a fortnight ago. Realizing that - for himself - he had left troubled and troubled he had returned, he felt it incumbent upon him to comfort this friend who had obviously brought new problems with him from home.

Tom asked sympathetically, "What's up?"

Searching the ceiling for the answer, Brandeis finally replied, "We got trouble – up there in River City."

"Your mother?"

"No one but."

"Siobhan?"

"Not just Siobhan. The entire worldwide Catholic conspiracy."

"What did she say?" Tom queried.

"Oh, first she hit me with the 'Four-Six' combination." To Tom's look of confusion, Brandeis replied with four fingers raised, "You know, four-thousand years of Hebrew history." Then adding a thumb and another forefinger, he went on, "Six million Jews exterminated in the Holocaust. She really went tribal on me."

"So what does that have to do with Catholics? And how'd she find out Siobhan was one?"

"Siobhan called once while I was out. Shirley got her *full* name out of her."

"Oh."

"No, you can't quite pass that one off as Buddhist. Of course, I pointed out to Mother that, hey, at least she wasn't Moslem. She was unimpressed."

"Well, clue me in. What's so horrible about Catholics? I mean, I know what the Baptists think. But what problem do the Jews have with them?"

"To hear Shirley tell it, Pius the Dozenth did everything but turn on the gas at Auschwitz."

"Now, correct me if I'm wrong, but I got the impression from you that after you and Teddie *bar mitzvah*'d, your family didn't darken the synagogue door that often."

"Well, that was then," Brandeis answered. "After Siobhan's call she decided we all needed to dust off our beanies."

"She wasn't mean to Siobhan, was she? I mean, she didn't say anything nasty to her, did she?"

"No, of course not. She was courteous, civil, and, no doubt, pleasant. And when she got off the phone and I came home, she merely pointed out to me that I'd never be able to replace my genocided European brothers and sisters, the responsibility for which lay directly in *my* pants, with half-breed Papists from a Catholic harlot."

Tom was saddened by the hopelessness he saw in his friend's eyes. "What's this summer going to be like?"

"Ohh," Brandeis sighed. "Yeah, this summer. I was supposed to clerk for Father and spend some time on my grandmother's farm. Now she's talking about sending me to - get this, Israel."

"Israel?!" Tom exclaimed. "Lord, she might as well send you to 'Nam. I mean, a war zone's a war zone! What does she want you to do in Israel? Be a border guard on the Golan Heights?"

"I don't know. Return to the Bosom of Abraham. Get in touch with my Hebrew roots. Stay away from agents of the Vatican - especially beautiful blonde ones. She's really gone crazy over this."

"So I guess you didn't get to go to, where's the farm, Union City?"

"No, she had me under her thumb all week."

Tom chose to raise a question in an area that he had hitherto voluntarily treated as taboo, though Brandeis had made rare references to it over the semester. "What about your psychiatrist? Did you or your mother talk to him about any of this?"

"No, not yet," Brandeis answered quietly. "I've switched to someone down here, you know, and I haven't gotten to see him since all of this came up." After an awkward silence, he asked, "Oh, did you have a date with Clair?" Tom shook his head. "Did you call her?"

"Yeah, I called her. She was ... otherwise engaged."

"Oh. I'm sorry." Patting a six-pack of Coca-Colas beside him, he said, "Hey, I've got an order in with Tolbert for some rum. Siobhan's not coming in till tomorrow night or Wednesday. I've just damn well decided to drown my troubles, and you're welcome to join in."

Tom walked past Brandeis as if he had not heard his offer. Propping his hands on the frame above the window, he looked east toward Promise. They did not speak for a minute until finally Tom tripped over a pleasant thought. "Hey, did you get 'wheels'?"

Laughing, Brandeis replied, "Yeah, almost forgot to tell you. *You're going to love it.*"

"What is it?" Tom asked excitedly.

"Given my mother's senses of humor and of propriety, it's the perfect car. The smallest two-seater she could find."

"What kind is it?"

"Come on down. Let me show it to you."

Walking through the parking lot, Tom exhibited a great deal more excitement as observer than did Brandeis as exhibitor. Tom spotted it before his roommate had the chance to point it out. "It's a *Sprite*! You got a 'Bug-eyed' Sprite!"

"Pardon me," Brandeis corrected. "My sports-car-buff younger brother tells me the British refer to it as a 'Frog-eyed' Sprite."

"Yeah, that's right. They do. Listen, that's the most fun car I've ever driven in my life. You got to let me drive it."

"I'll let you drive it all you want to."

The tiny car's paint job had oxidized to a flat pale blue. Its weathered tape-patched cloth top appeared to have started its life black and had greyed considerably, though not respectably.

"Let's see," Tom conjectured, "it's got Plexiglas sliding side windows instead of the side curtains. So I guess it's a '61, if those are the originals."

"Yeah, that sounds right," Brandeis agreed, amused by his roommate's overawing interest.

"You say your parents picked this for you?"

"Yeah. I'm not kidding. She wanted the smallest thing she could find. I mean, how much trouble could I get into with a girl ... in this car?"

With a side glance at Brandeis, Tom observed, "Hey, she's never met Siobhan."

As he pulled into the parking lot near them, Brandeis waved down Tolbert and collected his delivery.

"Whoa," Tom protested. "We've got to take this little baby for a drive. You can't go up and get sotted yet." A light dawning, he said, "Wait. I've got to run to my car and get something." He returned donning a tight pair of saddle-hued calfskin driving gloves. "I've been saving these for a car worthy of them," Tom explained.

Installing himself in the driver's seat, Tom looked at the quaint but familiar dash layout and grinned broadly. "Oh, I have missed this car." Dipping his head slightly and clearing his face of expression as if to sharpen his focus, his Driver persona overtook him. Slowly he lifted his hands and placed them just above nine and three o'clock, lacing his gloved fingers into the grooves of the small non-factory wood grain steering wheel. He turned the key and smiled remembering the separate ignition button that he had to depress. Reaching toward the center of the tiny dash, he pushed the button while giving it gas. He closed his eyes and reveled in the rowdy exhaust note. They left campus and at his first opportunity Tom wound the engine out in first, second, and third, shaking his head in enjoyment of the unique feel and sound of the Sprite. Brandeis, who had recently spent ten hours in its cramped, uncomfortable cockpit, watched his friend with amazement. He did not understand Tom's passion for this car, but he understood Passion.

*   *   *

"But when Irish eyes are smiling ..." Brandeis crooned out the open window of 332 to Tom's sober amusement. After taking a sip of Brandeis' first rum-and-coke concoction early in the evening, and then taking another, Tom had realized two things. First, it was too strong and could make him drunk and sick quickly. Second, it did taste dangerously sweet, and he was not interested in finding an alcoholic drink that he liked. He had decided instead to enjoy the evening observing the progressive inebriation of his roommate. The floor was re-populating as its tenants returned from holiday, and 332 enjoyed a number of drop-ins during the evening.

By ten o'clock Brandeis was wild-eyed and far gone, and Tom had put away the rum and gently moved him away from the window. Collapsing on his bed, Brandeis mumbled in a fair Barry Fitzgerald accent, "My love for Siobhan is ... impetuous ... Homeric." Then laughing, he asked, "Have ya' e'er seen *The Quiet Man*, me'boy?"

"Sure," Tom answered. "Beautiful flick. John Wayne before he started playing John Wayne. I really liked it."

"Aye, me'lad, as did I, as did I," Barry nodded soulfully. "And at the end of the picture, were ya' seein' the fair couple sparkin' and courtin' by the brook?"

"Yeah - I mean, aye, I did."

Brandeis' countenance took on a perplexed, quizzical glare as he dropped accent and wondered aloud, "What did she whisper in his ear?"

"What?" Tom asked.

"I've got to find out what the hell Maureen O'Hara whispered in John Wayne's ear - when he was so surprised, and he laughed and chased her across the brook," Brandeis announced with determination.

"How are you going to find that out?"

Tom watched the gears turn - slowly. As they finally meshed, Brandeis' face brightened into a curious grin. "Well, I'll call John Ford. He can tell me. And he's only a director, so he shouldn't be that hard to reach, you think?"

"Probably waiting by the phone," Tom nodded in agreement. "But why not just call Maureen ... or the Big Guy himself?"

"Well, I will if Jack's not home. He let's me call him Jack, you know."

After two unsuccessful but - for Tom - highly entertaining conferences with long distance operators Brandeis was on the verge of trying to reach John Wayne, when they heard a single loud knock on the door followed by a thud against it. Tom went to the door and opened it. Joe Joe collapsed through the doorway and landed hard on the floor. He rolled over and offered the room a foolish grin, which gave Tom to know that he now had a pair of drunks on his hands. Joe Joe rested on the floor trying to orient himself to his new surroundings.

"Who you calling?" Joe Joe asked.

"The Duke," Brandeis replied nonchalantly.

"Is he in town?" Joe Joe asked as evenly and without surprise.

At this Tom took it upon himself to explain to Joe Joe the point of Brandeis' attempts to reach John Ford, Maureen O'Hara, and John Wayne in Beverly Hills. In his advanced state of stupor Brandeis' efforts sounded reasonable to Joe Joe, and he was even drawn into the project.

"What about Ireland?" he suggested vaguely. This won Brandeis' attention, and he focused on Joe Joe as best he could. "Where was that little village in Ireland where the story -" Joe Joe went on before being cut off.

"Inisfree!" Brandeis yelled enthusiastically, rising to his feet too quickly and wobbling. "That's it. I'll call Inisfree!"

"Who are you going to call there?" Tom asked.

Brandeis' face gave off a perplexed frown only for a moment before it cleared and he cheered, "The pub! Yeah, I'll call ..." He hesitated as his off-duty brain cells leapt to attention to do combat with the alcohol. Suddenly his chin dropped into a smile and the light dawned in his eyes. "Pat Cohan's Pub! No ... Pat Cohan's Bar!" he shouted triumphantly.

As Brandeis launched his effort to reach an information operator in Ireland, Tom noticed Joe Joe roll over and prop himself on his elbows. He thrust an inquisitive index finger toward Brandeis. "Woz," he began seriously, "as important as your question about what she whispered in his ear is -" and he paused to gather his thoughts - "I think the much more important question about that movie - and really, about all of Maureen O'Hara's movies - is ... whether or not she has freckles on her titties! I mean, all that red hair - Irish to the core - I want to know -" But leaving his thought hanging, Joe Joe's eyes rolled back, and his extended arm fell limply to the floor - followed by his head.

Brandeis reached down and, grabbing a thatch of his hair, lifted Joe Joe's head from the floor to measure his level of unconsciousness. A dim light flickered momentarily as he belched, "Pilgrim," and it faded to black.

Resuming his conversation, he slurred, "That's Inisfree, operator ... Sure, be glad to ma'am. That's I-n-i-s-f-r-e-e-e-e ..."

*   *   *

RACISM IS A SCAR ON THE SOUL OF AMERICA

The black marker lettering of the placard was running slightly in the afternoon mist as Tom rolled slowly by Rutledge's, having finished his first day back in class. He smiled at the **NO BLEACH, PLEASE** sign that followed in line. Carried by a damp, scruffy contingent of five of the SCAR faithful, Tom silently applauded their endurance and their tenacity. *Cat Tracks* and the Dallas papers had dropped significant coverage of the daily vigil after its initial headlines splash in February; although, the student journal had made occasional references to it, and an infrequent "letter to the editor" had kept the issue breathing on campus. But the picket line had never wavered. When Bo Rutledge opened his door in the morning, they arrived. When he locked up at night, the last rotating team of picketers left.

Tom picked Fred Slater out in the group in front of the store. His sign read, **RUTLEDGE - WASH YOUR DIRTY LAUNDRY**. Dressed in a long, well-worn army green coat and Levis, his wet, tangled hair tripping down over his collar, Tom saw in Fred the proud, haggard face of commitment. He pulled into a parking space past the shop. Almost at Fred's side before he saw him, his Stover County neighbor greeted Tom with a momentary wariness.

"Well, what brings you down to this end of The Drag? Slumming?" Fred asked through bleary eyes.

"Just thought I'd come by and see what kind of fun y'all were having," Tom replied casually, as he got in step with Fred and walked in a slow repeating oval on the sidewalk in front of the door.

Fred laughed, "Just here exercising our shoes, right Emily?"

The black co-ed in front of them whom Tom did not recognize and whose sign pleaded, **LET MY PEOPLE WASH**, turned and replied with a smile, "You got that right. This is my third pair of Keds in two months."

Holding his hands out palms up to catch the drizzle, Tom asked, "So y'all have been doing this all this time come rain or come shine?"

Fred and Emily shared a laugh. "This is nothing," she explained. "You should have been here in February and March!"

"Yeah," Fred broke in. "It was colder than a wi-. Well, you can imagine how cold it was. And then there was the sleet and the rain. Oh, yeah, Tom. Sorry I didn't introduce you. Emily, this is Tom Windham, native of New Fredonia, a mere dozen miles from Bethany, which you will remember to be the capital city of northwest Stover County. Tom is a noted G-D-I and an alleged Southern Baptist."

"Guilty," Tom admitted, raising his hands.

"Oh, no," she laughed. "Not another one of you East Texas fruitcakes! Go ahead. Offer me some watermelon. Offer me some greens."

"And who would I be offering them to?"

"Sorry, Tom, where are my 'mannahs'?" Fred continued. "Tom Windham, this is Emily Watson."

Tom looked closely into the almond eyes and the beaming smile of the co-ed, and he concentrated to bring forward a connection with her name that he related to his roommate. Holding his mouth awkwardly open and snapping his fingers when the link finally fell into place, he blurted out, "You're Danzell Johnson's girlfriend, aren't you?"

Smiling even more broadly, she replied, "Yeah, you know Danzell?"

Shaking his head, Tom said, "Just met him once ... at a party." Still staring and smiling awkwardly at her, he thought of his roommate and added, "You *are* beautiful."

As Fred laughed and turned away, Emily slapped her chest in stunned amusement. "What a line!" Fred interjected. "Get many girls that way?" As Tom joined them in laughter, Fred went on, "You obviously don't remember how *big* Danzell is!"

"Sorry," Tom said, waving his misunderstood comment away. "Let's try this. It's real nice to meet you."

"Well, it's nice to meet you, too, Tom," Emily smiled as she shook the hand he offered.

At the end of an awkward moment when the laughter had died down, Tom said uneasily, "So, either of you need any relief for awhile?"

"What?" Fred asked with unguarded surprise.

"I asked if I could relieve either one of you ... in the line."

"Thanks," Emily answered matter-of-factly. "But my shift's almost over. My replacement'll be here in a minute."

Fred tilted his head in wonder at his friend. "Don't give me the missionary gaze, please," Tom said with a smile.

Shaking his head upright, Fred pulled out of the line and quietly said, "Sorry. But ... why?"

Wiping the drizzle from his face, Tom looked away and then looked back at Fred. "I'm not sure. King. Danzell ... and Emily. Me. What's right. What's wrong. Here, give me the damn sign."

Fred handed him his picket sign and leaned against a utility pole as Tom took his place in the line.

* * *

Siobhan unlocked the door of her room quickly and, leaving her luggage in the hall, went straight to her telephone. With the fifth unanswered ring of Brandeis' phone she slapped the top of her dresser, hearing in her mind the twang of Paul Simon's guitar in a Santa Barbara service station.

"Joe Joe." As she said his name, she remembered the details of their last encounter and smiled.

"Called to make up?"

Ignoring his habit of being himself, she asked, "Do you know where Brandeis is?"

"Naw. I saw those two tadpoles wiggle off a hour or so ago. Don't know where they were going. Probably a movie, knowing them."

"Well, if you see them, please tell Brandeis I'm back."

Hanging up the phone, she was startled as a shadow appeared in the door and said, "Chevy?"

She whipped around and sighed, "Thia -"

"What's your luggage doing piled out in the hall?"

"Sorry. I've been trying to find Bran, and I'd forgotten about it."

"Oh, he called -"

"And?"

"He thought you must be getting in late, so he and Tom went to the swim meet."

Entering the natatorium, the aroma of chlorine and the weight of the humidity reached deep into her lungs. She spotted the tousled curly locks of her boyfriend, and she quickly made her way for him in the stands. Tom saw her approaching, but she shushed him from a distance, and he complied. She circled behind them, but the space beside Brandeis was occupied while that beside Tom was vacant. As she approached down the row beside them, Tom moved to his left and Siobhan stepped in beside Brandeis. Backlighting from an overhead fixture framed Siobhan's hair and face as Brandeis looked up in wonder. Her focus on his face was pure and exclusive as she eased down into the empty seat. He took one quick scan of the crowd to consider their audience and then looked back at her.

"To hell with them," she whispered as she kissed him full on the mouth. Tom propped an elbow on one knee, cupped his chin in his hand, and looked away wistfully. After pulling away from their long kiss, she said, "Hi, Tom," and waved at him with a pianist's ripple of the fingers.

"Welcome back to sanity," Tom allowed.

"Oh, I don't know if Dallas is sane. Maybe just indifferent; or worse still - inert."

"What was it like in Chi-town?"

"We didn't see anything out where I was, but from the plane we saw some of the smoke. We went to Mexico early last week."

"See any jetsetters there?" Tom asked.

"Smart ass."

"Great tan," Tom offered. Then observing first himself in jeans, then Brandeis in scraggly cut-offs, and finally Siobhan in her coordinated white shorts set, blonde hair and bronze skin, he added, "Yep, that's us - Atchison, Topeka ... and St. Tropez."

As she leaned into Brandeis and placed her hand on his bare thigh, she whispered, "Can we get out of here?"

With as much restraint as he could muster, he answered, "I told Clayton and Topper we'd watch them in the relay."

"When's the relay?" she asked, squeezing his thigh.

"Last," Brandeis replied through a cracking voice.

Tom observed the action beside him with amusement. He finally interjected, "Aw, Chevy, you really ought to stay and watch some of this." Pointing to the swimmers preparing to start a freestyle heat, he observed, "You don't want to miss these guys - their bodies shaved smooth -

launching themselves off the starting boxes, plunging into the frothy surf, surging back and forth and up and down the length of the pool."

"Cute, Tom. We'll all look forward to your description of the diving events."

Sweat beaded on Brandeis' brow as he asked Tom, "What's coming up next?"

"Oh, to have a camera for this." After an appropriately timed pause, Tom said casually, "Breaststroke."

"Windham, you bastard," Brandeis said through a thin smile. Siobhan leaned back, throwing her face toward the ceiling with a single laugh.

Rising from the bleachers, Brandeis said, his eyes smiling at Siobhan, "Tom, please make our apologies to the Aussies."

After another long kiss outside the Nat door, Brandeis led Siobhan to his Sprite parked in front. "Cute little car," she observed. Then putting her face in his and draping her hands on his hips, she whispered, "Take me somewhere and make love to me. Now."

Motoring into the ZPL, they found the lot packed. The brief wheelbase of the Sprite gave them the opportunity to feel twice every dip and bump of the well-worn ground, rutted by the spring rains and the back-from-Break traffic. Coming to a halt and killing the percolating motor, Brandeis asked, "Is this okay? I'd take the top down to give us more air, but -"

She leaned across the seat and shut off discussion with her open mouth against his. With his last rational thought he depressed the clutch and jammed the shift lever up into first - allowing maximum clearance in the cozy cockpit of the Sprite. As Siobhan began to pull Brandeis toward her side of the car, his left knee thudded against the steering wheel. Soon he found himself crammed into the passenger seat beneath her.

As they surged against each other while kissing hungrily, articles of clothing began to be unbuckled, unzipped, unsnapped, unlaced, and finally pulled up or down and off. Crouched astride him, Siobhan bent her head low below the convertible top, her blonde hair framing his face. As not only the springs of the little bucket seat, but also the car's shocks, squeaked beneath them, Siobhan began to moan with pleasure. Responding to her quickly, Brandeis made an uncontrollable upward thrust. Siobhan cried out, arched her back, and jerked her head skyward. Fortunately clearing the top's metal supports, her head ripped cleanly through the Sprite's weathered canvas top. Still panting vigorously, she opened her eyes, grinned broadly, and looked up at the blanket of stars overhead as they made room for a brilliant oval moon.

Brandeis looked in disbelief at the headless lover above him. "Maybe we should have gone ahead and taken the top down," he said as he shook his head and smiled.

Ducking her head back into the car, Siobhan's face was aglow. "Oh, Bran," she began in a full-bodied tone. "Oh, that was wonderful. God, how I love you."

"Siobhan McKenna," he said dreamily, "I can't believe you did that, but, oh, how I love you, too."

"Come up here, Bran," She said, as they disentangled. "You've got to see this sky."

Straddling the driveshaft tunnel with a knee in each seat, but still ducking below the remaining canvas, Brandeis shrugged, "What the hell," and ripped the opening wider so they both could stick their heads out of the shredded top. "Yeah," he mugged, "what a sky."

"Oh, you old fuddy-duddy," she laughed. Changing to a purr, she kissed him long and softly. But pushing away slightly, she announced, "Hey! That's the Wild Goose Moon!"

"Yeah," Brandeis acknowledged through a widening smile. Simultaneously, they worked their fingers awkwardly before launching their hands skyward in the Sign.

Aware at last of an outside world, they brought their arms down. To their amusement, but not to their surprise, they scanned the neighboring cars thinking that their passionate antics had gone completely unnoticed. After a few seconds, though, the driver of the car parked facing the Sprite saw the exposed heads. He flashed on his headlights only to be mooned by the unmatched pair of cupric and alabaster buns framed in the Sprite's front windshield. Before Brandeis and Siobhan had time to react to this exposure, the car horns in the immediate area began to honk loudly and repeatedly against the ZPL code violator. For the flashing of headlights was infinitely more taboo ZPL behavior than anything the naked lovers in the topless Sprite had just done. The headlights were quickly extinguished.

Chapter 23

042068

Tom had been raised Southern Baptist; so he had a biblical familiarity with numeric irony. As certainly then as things happened in threes, sevens, twelves, and forties in The Bible, so, Tom had reasoned, was there importance to the day he had been alive for twenty years, two months, and nine days. When, earlier in the year it had occurred to him that on April twentieth he would reach that age - the same as Mark's when he ended his life – he had no specific idea what he would do to note the date and its passing. But over the following months when occasionally he thought of its approach, he began to conceive of the day as one of reflection and contemplation. He visualized himself in his briefs on his bed for much of the day, perhaps in the lotus position. He started to view '042068' as a day to add up his accomplishments and lay out for himself the current sum worth of his positives. Most of two semesters of accounting, though, had introduced him to the concept of liabilities, and he considered giving some weight to his downside as well. He discarded the latter notion along the way toward the date, however, based on the view that at this stage in his life none of his mistakes had been fatal either for himself or for anyone else and all could be chalked up to experience. To further restrict the exercise he put aside the notion of forecasting or projection. The past and the present were enough to deal with and provided ample material for the one-day Tom Windham Symposium.

The other matter under consideration, though, was Tom in comparison to Mark. This factor had always been present in the setting aside of the day, but beyond that, the mechanics of the comparison were hazy. Tom had ruled out a straight-up competition of specific accomplishments. Yes, Mark had been valedictorian; Tom had finished only seventh in his class. True, first was hard to beat, but, he had granted himself, seventh did have biblical significance. He did not question that Mark had come into the world with vastly more native intelligence than he, and he also knew that his brother had added many more folds of grey during his stay than he had. But Tom also knew that he was not going to die on April twentieth or on the twenty-first, that in spite of the shortfall of his intellect, he would outlast his brother. But was there any meaning in that? Was God rewarding mediocrity with longevity?

For Tom to set aside a day of commemoration, though, involved a healthy portion of redundancy. He had for years spent stolen moments of contemplation going over Mark's life, his accomplishments, and his gifts to Tom. He knew that too many of the memories were drowned out by the volume of the discord of the final few years, but he remembered the positives more. In observing other brother acts, he was often surprised by the lack of communication and the infrequency of cheerleading. The brothers Windham had always talked, and Mark was Tom's biggest booster. He had been on Tom's side with a perfect absence of sarcasm, cynicism, or embarrassment. He remembered his big brother saying more than once, "We're the closest relative each other has, so we need to stick together."

Tom had shared the irony of the date with Brandeis and then had forgotten he had done so. It came as a surprise to him then on that Saturday afternoon to receive a call from Siobhan on his line.

"How's it going, Tom?" she asked carefully.

"It's going fine, Chevy. How's it going with you?"

"Well, okay, I guess."

After a long silence, Tom asked, "Were you looking for Woz?"

"No. He's picking me up a little later. I just wanted to call and check on you. Make sure everything was okay."

Detecting concern, Tom asked, "What's the deal, Chevy?"

After another silence, she said, "Well, you know ... it's April twentieth, and I just wanted to make sure -"

Realizing that his roommate had shared the information with her, Tom interrupted, "Oh yeah, well," and it became his turn to hesitate. His first emotion after mild embarrassment that Brandeis had told her about April twentieth was appreciation of his friend's concern.

Before he could respond further, Siobhan said, "Tom, you'll never hear me admit this again, and I would deny it under torture, but ... I think there's a lot to you." She followed a second later with an embarrassed laugh.

"Thanks, Chevy," he said evenly as he recalled his mental wonderings early in the morning regarding this date on which his chalkboard inscription reached fruition. "Well, I'm not sure what Woz told you, but, suffice it to say, I've decided to live on," he said with a light, uneasy laugh. "Yeah, I laid here this morning and figured out that I'm a worthwhile, original, and interesting person, and a child of God. And I deserve a life - and not one compared to anyone else's. My own."

"Good for you," Siobhan replied, surprised at his openness. "But you didn't ever really think about ... doing otherwise, did you?"

"You mean suicide?" he asked.

"Oh, Tom," she gasped.

"No. Of course not. Not actively anyway. But when you've got it in your past, it's always this dark specter hidden away in the back of your mind."

"I'm sorry. But remember what they warned us about in "Man and His World". Death is an eternity of "Lawrence Welk" re-runs."

Entering 332 after an all-afternoon stint at the library, Brandeis found his roommate staring pensively out the window.

"Where've you and your mind been off to?" Brandeis asked.

With a laugh Tom came back, "Oh, just thinking about your girlfriend. Don't mind, do you?"

"Hey, join the club. I've learned to put up with a lot of that. I only got nervous when Harvey asked me for a full-length picture of her."

"Really?"

"No, but I'm expecting him to any day. Anyway, what were you thinking about her?"

"Oh, I just think she's a really neat girl." After a hesitation, he continued, "She called me this afternoon. You had told her sometime about what today was."

"What is today?"

"It's April twentieth," he answered, narrowing his eyes to judge when or whether Brandeis would remember its significance.

"So? Oh, oh, yeah. This is the day you reach ... Mark's age ... when ..."

"Yeah, when he died."

"Oh, well, was I not supposed to tell her?"

"No, that's alright. She just wanted to make sure I was alright - let me know she was thinking about me. Like I said, it was nice of her. I really hadn't had time to think about it that much myself." Tom looked back out the window and shook his head. "I guess I had had that debate on Evolution in "Man and His World" too much on my mind."

"What?!" Brandeis asked. "You didn't tell me about that. You have a debate to prepare for this close to Finals?!"

"Yup."

"That's crazy. Who assigned that?"

"The lovely and desirable Miss Longoria, my cow of a prof," Tom said. "She said she realized it was late but -"

"On Evolution?!" Brandeis exclaimed. To Tom's nod, Brandeis asked, "You mean there are two sides to that question? I thought that one was pretty well tied down."

"Well, you sinner, there sure is if you happen to be of the 'Suthun Bayuptis p'suasion'."

"Windham, you crazy asshole, you didn't!"

"'Fraid I did. Hell, I had to. They were pickin' on God."

"When?"

"Oh, back at the first of the semester. I'd hoped Longoria had forgotten about it. Unfortunately, she has the memory of that animal she most closely resembles."

"And you're taking the *negative* against Evolution?!" Brandeis finally began to laugh through his frown of disbelief. "When? And do you have a partner or a second or anything?"

"Yeah, she threw one other Christian in the pit with me. It's week after next, so she knows we don't have hardly any time to research. Like a doomed man getting to choose his last meal, I got to choose my partner first. I picked Carla Mazzalevski. She's the sharpest kid in the class, the one who speaks up the most ... and she's got the thickest glasses."

"Good choice. Are you and her getting together this weekend?"

"Tomorrow afternoon. She's over at the Libe right now researching for archaeological and historical evidence. Y'all mind giving us the top shelf tomorrow?" Tom smirked.

"It's all yours." Lost in thought for a moment, Brandeis finally allowed, "Carla sounds good ... but, gee, I just wish you could have gotten Frederic March."

In the evening Tom was preparing to go to a movie with Fred Slater. Knowing that Fred was due momentarily, Tom picked up the phone. Nancy answered on the first ring. "Hello," she said anxiously.

"Mom."

"Oh, Tom," she answered with unguarded relief.

"Mom, everything's okay. I'm sorry if I worried you."

"Oh, I love you, Son."

"I love you and Dad, too."

* * *

As Tom chomped into his Charco's Number Two Double - a double-meat charcoal-broiled hamburger with hickory sauce and chopped onions heaped on a poppy seed bun - Fred sheepishly answered his friend's question, "I think we're ... pretty close to a settlement."

"Rrerree?" Tom responded, his mouth full.

"Yeah," Fred confirmed, looking away uncomfortably.

"So Rutledge is going to integrate the washateria?" Tom asked, swallowing.

"There'll be something in *Cat Tracks* about it in the next few days," Fred stated glumly, glancing sideways at the crowd at the pickup counter.

"We're just glad to get it settled and over with before Finals and the end of the semester."

"So what does the settlement call for?"

"I'm not sure," Fred replied testily. "I'm not in on that. I'm just a foot soldier, a private. And I'll be relieved to get off that picket line. I don't know what the final language will be."

"I guess it feels good to know you can actually change things ... for the better." Looking beyond Fred and with a half-smile, Tom reflected, "Maybe Chevy's right. Maybe our generation can get some things done. Maybe there is hope for this old world."

"So, what do you want to see?" Fred asked.

Remembering a brief conversation at the Dairy Queen over Spring Break with K.C. Smith, the music and education minister at the church, Tom replied, "This may be a little off the wall, but since we've seen about everything that's come out lately, let's try something I've heard about over at Park Forest."

The only cast member that Tom recognized in the credits was Pippa Scott, and not far into *For Pete's Sake*, he was surprised - even considering the source of its recommendation - to realize that he was watching a Christian movie. At first he felt some awkwardness about the subject matter, but the contemporary setting and approach of the movie made him progressively more comfortable. No *Stars in My Crown* this. The protagonist, played by an actor Tom did not recognize, was wonderfully human. The character was capable of weakness, uncertainty, regret, and anger, but he overcame his frailties and life's knocks with a positive faith in God - a faith devoid of self-righteousness. As the film rolled to completion, Tom gave his cynicism a rest and allowed in the feelings and the questions – and the ancient Hope: The Hope that had lead him at age nine down the longest aisle he had ever walked; the Hope he had grappled with through his teen years and against because of his teen years; the Hope he knew it was now popular to snicker at and to hold up to ridicule; the Hope that might just fall on the side of the Angels.

Tom was embarrassed at having taken a college buddy to a Christian movie. His comments on the way back to campus verged on apology, but Fred - with his similarly small-town Baptist upbringing - empathized with his friend and gave him relieving assurances as to his enjoyment of the movie and its story. Begging off on a late pizza, Tom excused himself from Fred in the plaza of the Men's Quad and returned to the darkened 332. After opening the door, he took his hand away from the light switch and walked across the room. Pulling out the chair from his desk, he swung its back close to the windowsill. Raising the sash, he sat down straddling the chair and propped his arms atop its back.

Peering deeply into the night, he looked up into the sky as high as the open window would allow. He beheld a host of stars far enough removed from the competing campus and town lights that their brilliance was not muted by them. Looking into those stars as he had never looked into them before, he tried to peer as deeply into space as he could - attempting to locate the smallest, dimmest speck of light in the canopy of sequined darkness. As he looked, he unleashed his mind to ask the elemental questions that were always there beneath the surface but to which he rarely gave specific voice:

'Are You out there, God? Where are You? I want to understand You. Did You do all this? Thousands and tens of thousands of suns larger and smaller than our own. Millions of planets as insignificant in size as this Earth. And yet we're all we really know about? We're really that special to You? Just this few billion people down here? A planet peopled with Baptists and Catholics, warmongers and Democrats and vegetarians, and a huge underclass - a majority - of poor, uneducated, frightened, hungry souls. Are we really important to You? Did You do all of this? Did You just set it in motion? Were You only a First Cause? Did You just give us the rules to play by and then leave us alone? Or are You here every day? Are You in this room ... right now? Are You watching? Are You keeping score? Is there going to be a Judgment Day? Has Mark already had his? Is he in Heaven? Is he in Hell? Am I going to Heaven ... or am I going to Hell? Do I have any control? Do I have any say? Or is it already decided and I'm just playing out my part? Did You make all this? Someone did. I guess it was You. I guess it had to be one source. I don't think any group could have argued and compromised and come up with this. I think it had to be born of one vision.' A memory of one his father's favorite well-worn quotes came to mind and brought a smile to Tom's lips. 'For God so loved the World that He didn't send a Committee.'

'I want to understand You. I want to understand all of this. But maybe that's it. Maybe that's the key. Maybe You *are* incomprehensible. Anyone who could do all of this would be - for a mere mortal, for an infinitesimally small being like me - by definition, beyond comprehension, beyond my understanding. So is that it? It comes back to faith? It comes back to my accepting? But do I accept it just because it was what was drilled into me all my life in Sunday School and church and Training Union? Do I accept it because it was the faith of my father and my mother? Do they have it? Is it enough that they had it and don't have it now? Surely they don't have it now, or they wouldn't live their lives the way they do. Am I supposed to accept the Bible by faith? Every word of it? Did it all happen? Did Jonah go into the fish and come out in three days? Did You stop the sun in the sky for Joshua? Did You bring down the fabled walls of Jericho?'

Looking down from the sky for the first time, Tom looked at the weathered wooden window casement and focused on an exposed wood grain where the paint had peeled. 'Was that tree Your idea? Did You think up the concept of seeds, so that from one miniscule grain planted haphazardly in the earth or merely dropped or blown to the ground and then watered by the rain and nurtured by the heat energy of the sun that this enormous tree could grow and then be harvested and split up and milled to create this window frame in this building of brick and glass and steel and wood?' Looking even closer - at the strip of paint peeled back from the wood - Tom asked, 'And was it Your idea to let animals and plants die and decay and blend over millions of years into the oil that made this paint and lubricates my engine? Did You know that was going to happen when You did that? Was that the Plan?' Tom smiled again. 'Is this part of a tyrannosaurus rex that You knew from birth that was spread on this windowsill five years ago by a painter who You knew - even at the time the tyrannosaurus was born - would be born forty years ago and that he would grow up to paint this windowsill? And that painter is still out there somewhere now, and do You know what he's going to paint tomorrow? And do You know, even now, the hour of his death? And if You do, do You already know if he's going to go to Heaven or to Hell?'

Then looking back into the stars as deeply as he could look, Tom thought, 'I can't comprehend how You could have made all of that, but if You could - and I know You did - then I know You could leave Jonah in a fish for three days and bring him out alive, and stop the sun in the sky, and flood the Earth with forty days of rain, and bring Your Son born of woman seeded not by man to live on this Earth for thirty-three years and die and live again and join You in Heaven. You could do any of it. You could do all of it. I guess You did do all of it. And I guess what that sky is saying, and what those stars are saying is, 'Don't try to comprehend. Believe. Look what I did.' Okay, I believe. But now, how does it change me? And does belief get me to Heaven, or do I have to go out and share this message to get there? I hope not, because that's the one I have trouble with. And what about the way I lead my life? I tell dirty jokes. I use bad language. I think a lot about getting girls into bed. I've got the wet dreams to prove it. Does any or all of that disqualify me? Is it okay to do that - to talk that way, think that way, and can I still get to Heaven? And, if so, where's the line? When do I go over it? What do I do or think or say, or avoid doing or thinking or saying, to stay in Your good graces? Or does all that even matter? Is it already decided?

'I think I've come back around, haven't I? I'm not going to get all of this figured out tonight, am I? I'm not *ever* going to get it all figured out, am I? But You *are* going to tell me when I die, aren't You? Whichever place I go, I will get the answer, won't I? Or is that part of Hell - not finding out? Does Mark know now? I know he had the same questions for You. Of course, I'm sure he asked them more eloquently, and he probably thought of them when he was eight. But I hope he's there now - still bending Your ear.

'Okay, so here's where we are right now: I don't understand it, but at least I know now that I'm not supposed to. But I believe. And we'll just have to see what I do with it, won't we?'

Chapter 24

Late April

"Hey, Windham," Joe Joe yelled from Shower Number Nine, "how 'bout some fresh-squeezed!" As a handful of drops of an unidentified fluid came over the tile walls of Number Nine, Tom almost slipped on the floor of the gang shower jumping out of its way. Determining those drops that landed on him to be no thicker or creamier than water, Tom grabbed a can of Right Guard and fogged Number Nine.

As the boys toweled off, Joe Joe said, "Well, did you see where ol' Rutledge fought 'em to a draw?"

"What?" Tom asked. "No. Where'd you see that?"

"'*Pussy Prints*', where else? Topper just brought a paper up from breakfast. Lord, those Aussies get up early."

"What did it say?"

"Well, the gist of it was that he'd take the 'whites only' sign down ... but," and he began to laugh, "he said he still wouldn't let the blacks in." Joe Joe saw Tom wince, and he toned down his enthusiasm. He added only, "He's a tough old goat." To Tom's continued silence, Joe Joe finally said, "Tom-cat, do you realize what approaches just over yon horizon?"

"What's that?" Tom asked, still digesting Joe Joe's information and making the connection between it and Fred's vagueness about the settlement.

"We are one measly week away from Dead Week and two away from Finals."

"Don't remind me," Tom said soberly. "That also means I'm just one week away from defending God against Chuck Darwin."

"You got it, son. So that means this is ... Party Week! 'Cause I never can get anybody to party with me those next two weeks."

"Gosh, Joe Joe, you're right."

"Hell, yes, I'm right. So we need to get the crew together and go do something." After a moment's thought his face broke into a grin. "Nopalito's!"

"What?"

"Mexican food. Lana from the Whip Inn told me about it once when she came up for air."

"So have you been there?"

"Yeah, some of my brothers and I went down there last weekend. If you like good Mexican, you'll love this."

"Sounds great. You can bring Dixie if -. Say, are y'all still dating?" Tom asked.

"Aw," he grinned, "only in spurts."

"Well, then bring her or Lana or whoever. I'll tell Brandeis, and we'll try to round up a couple of old dogs for us."

"Well, Lana'll probably be working. Who are you talking about bringing?" Joe Joe asked.

"Thia."

"Thia and Chevy, huh? Thanks for the warning. I'll wear my steel jock strap."

After his last morning class Tom was able to sit down in the McCartney dining hall and ingest along with his lunch the *Cat Tracks* cover story on the end of the Rutledge's Washateria protest. It was essentially as Joe Joe had presented it. The pickets would be removed in return for the removal of the "Whites Only" signs from the window and from the inside wall. Bo Rutledge had made clear, though, his refusal to integrate the washateria and his intent to direct "the coloreds" toward the door. Phil French of the Student Coalition had been interviewed separately and had responded with the usual abstract generalities about the triumph of principle and the steady tide of change sweeping the land.

As Brandeis approached the table, he found Tom biting his lip and shaking his head. "What's the prob', Roomie?"

Offering him the paper and pointing at the story, Tom said, "I think your girlfriend may be right. Might be time for a suspension of 'business as usual' in this land. Maybe R-F-K *can* shake things up. Cause some *real* change. The sad thing is, people like French and Fred think they've done that - think they've actually accomplished something. Or at least they make sounds like they think they have."

"You're not thinking about transferring to Berkeley, are you? I mean, am I hearing this from the same guy who used 'that word' in front of Rodg not that long ago?"

With a deflating laugh and a quick inward glance, Tom answered, "Yep, the Toms, they are a-changin'. Power to the People. Screw the Establishment." And he jabbed the air with a clinched fist.

Shifting gears, Tom said, "Hey, our friend from beyond the Canadian has come up with a good idea."

"All by himself?"

"Yeah, Mexican food at a new place close to downtown. We thought it'd be a good time to get the group together before we head off into the abyss."

"Which abyss?" Brandeis asked dejectedly. "Finals ... or home."

"Right. Make that abysses. Or is it abyssae? Abyssi?"

"Never thought I'd be so depressed about getting out of school," Brandeis groaned. "But anyway, yeah, you've finally brainwashed me into liking Mexican food. It'll need to be tonight, though, because Siobhan's flying up to Indianapolis tomorrow after class to canvas for Kennedy. Anyway, I thought you were making one last run to Noofer this weekend for a date with …the new one …what's her name? …the jail bait."

"Hey, cut me some slack. Just because I don't dig older women like you do. But no, Mom called and said she and Dad were coming through Dallas tonight to catch a morning flight to Houston, and they wanted to get together with me for dinner. So I had to cancel with Lizza. I think she's really going to be cool, though - if we can ever get together. Anyway, they said they were going to eat with their friends, the Brannigans, and they wanted me to join them. I guess I could just get together with them after dinner. I'll take my car. Say, why don't you ask Chevy to see if Thia wants to go with me."

"Speak for yourself, John."

"No, I'm really not talking about a date. Just somebody to go with."

"I'll mention it to Siobhan. Maybe she can present it to Thia with a bit more enthusiasm," Brandeis said with a laugh. "So what are your parents going to Houston for?"

"A funeral," Tom grimaced.

"Whose?"

"My Uncle Josh's. Actually, he's my great-uncle. He was in his eighties - in an old folks' home. I barely remember him."

"Alright, alright. You don't have to go to the funeral. You've distanced yourself enough."

"I've only been to a few. But that was still one too many," Tom stated, staring out the window. Trying to dismiss his sudden funk, as Brandeis had also fallen silent, Tom asked, "So do you and Chevy have anything ... planned ... for the end of school, which, as Joe Joe pointed out to me, is at hand?" To Brandeis' sudden smile, Tom asked, "What?"

"The White Rock house weekend after next."

"Weekend after next?" Tom asked with surprise. "Won't one or both of you be through with finals then?"

"Both."

"So -"

"So Avie and Shirl and Paddy and Meg don't know that."

As they laughed, Tom observed, "Well, at least I won't be around to chat with your mom umpteen times when she starts calling. Whhooo. Gutsy move."

Suddenly serious, Brandeis looked far out the window toward the lake and said, "There's no telling what this summer's going to be like ... for any of us. We need to have this one la- ... this time together."

*   *   *

Past the southern terminus of the tollway where the road turned into a six-lane one-way expanse of Harry Hines Boulevard, the caravan found the tiny dingy-white clapboard former residence with 'Nopalito's' in neon script on a plate glass window. After parking on the street in front, Joe Joe led the contingent toward the old shotgun house, which Thia pointed out as having a charming lean to it. Inside they found the narrow main room to have clean red vinyl booths - filled with a young

Anglo crowd - pushed against the south wall and leaving room only for an aisle between them and the north wall.

The pungent aromas of Tex-Mex cuisine were second nature to Tom from his surrogate rearing at Paco's, but this was different. Tom had the sensation that he could close his eyes, take a few deep inhalations, and leave sated. The group followed their host through the beer-sign-illuminated front room, past two small, occupied side rooms, and into the kitchen. It was a study in smoke and sizzle and the even heavier concentration of aromas that brought eager smiles to the faces of the party. Glancing as they passed through, they noted the many pots and pans beaten to irregular shapes by years of use and filled with rice and beans and sauces as well as the smoldering sheets of rolled cheese- and beef-filled *tortillas* destined to be smothered in *chile con carne* and devoured as *enchiladas*.

Past the slap of the screen door the fivesome arrived at the backyard patio - its red brick pavers greened with algae – and were led to a large rusting, oxidized white wrought-iron table with a glass top. Lighting came from a mix of Japanese lanterns and exposed bulbs strung low in zig-zags from the roof of the house to the trees and to posts along the fence. The matching chairs - the grime of meals past apparent on them even in the low light - made Tom understand why Joe Joe had recommended wearing blue jeans. The mild evening air in the aromatic courtyard was filled with the high-pitched, tinny sounds of mariachi music crackling out of the ancient outdoor speakers suspended from the eaves of the house.

Siobhan had cheated on the dress code by wearing a full, but short denim skirt. Tom seated himself opposite her and, having come separately in his car with Joe Joe in tow, only now was able to leer at her costume. She wore a white peasant blouse with bands of red, blue, and yellow smocking at the bodice, which matched the bric-a-brac at the bottom of the skirt. The blouse's sleeves were pushed well off her shoulders, and its loosely elasticized neck rested atop her breasts. The red rose above her ear matched the bright lipstick with which she had replaced her normal pale pink.

Siobhan could not be still - clapping her hands, popping her gum, floating her head from side to side, and generally giving herself over to the Latin rhythms; high-pitched, tinny Latin rhythms though they were. Given the setting, the blouse, and the way she moved, Tom felt the evening might not pass without Siobhan kicking and clapping out a Flamenco on their tabletop. He wished fervently for castanets - not totally dismissing the possibility that she had a set in her purse.

Thia had joined Brandeis and Siobhan in the 4-4-2 for the ride over, and both girls appeared to have given Joe Joe a bye on his pre-Spring Break behavior. At his suggestion the party ordered an appetizer of which Tom had never heard. The taste combination of jalapeno slices atop white cheese over refried beans smeared liberally on a *tostado* enthralled him. The waiter called them "*nachos*", and Tom knew he would return to Nopalito's if only for plates of these grease-soaked delights. Though his normal order of soft cheese tacos with refried beans and rice was not on the menu, Tom realized, when he bit into the cheese enchiladas that he was savoring seasonings previously foreign to him. All of his past fifteen years of Mexican food-eating experience seemed a sham. He would continue to eat at Paco's - a lot – but now he knew where the real thing was.

The evening was boisterous, but Tom found himself occasionally drifting into a melancholy triggered by the knowledge that it would end. And for him it would end early, since he had committed to meet his parents at the Brannigans. But more than this night, he feared the end of this mix of friends - the dropping out of some, the changing of others. These people, as they were at this moment, were among the best friends he had ever had, and he knew that went both ways. To shake himself out of the funk, he thought to himself, 'Come on, Windham. Don't ruin what's going on - what feels so good - just because you know it will end. Everything ends. Enjoy now, now.'

Meanwhile, the phenomenon of the evening was the warming of Thia to Joe Joe. Even if encouraged by her matching him beer for beer, they appeared to Tom and the Judeo-Papist pair to be moving well beyond a mere truce. For while Siobhan, Brandeis and Tom covered the gamut from the approaching Indiana primary to Tom's debate to the Rutledge's Washateria settlement, the dark, willowy beauty sat enrapt by Joe Joe's description of his summers spent working the rodeos of the Texas and Oklahoma panhandles and of the neighboring corners of New Mexico and Colorado. His earthy anecdotes seemed to melt Thia's cool cynicism as he told tales of dusty, weather-beaten cowboys, of ornery horses and of dangerous, blood-eyed bulls. He spoke of nights out at sawdust-floored honky-tonks followed by sleepovers under or in dung-encrusted horse trailers. She was enthralled by his descriptions of bursting out of a chute on a fast horse chasing a steer, of lunging from his horse to grab the steer by its horns while digging his boots into the dirt, and of twisting its horns, head and neck until he wrestled it to the ground. Their three friends finally ceased their separate conversation to listen. Other than Joe Joe, only Tom had been to a rodeo, and the rest were in awe.

As he finished his tale, Thia touched his hand and with an awkward, lop-sided smile and dilated pupils, said, "I guess I'm sort of sorry about the slap."

"Huh?" Joe Joe asked.

"At Hawk and Coy's party," she said. "When I slapped you."

"Oh," he laughed, putting his hand to his cheek and wincing. "Yeah, good 'right' you got there."

"Well, you had it coming," Siobhan said with a laugh. "Where'd you get that line anyway? It was so gross."

Joe Joe smiled and answered, "Every bad thing I know, I learned in fifth grade. I've just picked up a little here and there since then, but fifth grade - when I got into junior high - that was the year my eyes were opened," he answered proudly. "We were pretty much thrown in with the sixth and seventh and eighth graders, and I was big for my age then and was already good on a horse. So I got to hang around with all those older boys, and they taught me plenty."

"Yeah," Tom nodded. "I guess that was about when I started hearing dirty jokes, too. But I can't remember hardly any of them."

Brandeis chimed in, "I didn't get much of that stuff till I got to high school. Gee, I feel kind of deprived ... of depravity."

Grabbing him by the neck and planting a kiss, Siobhan cooed, "Well, I hope you've enjoyed my accelerated course."

As Brandeis nodded eagerly, Thia asked, "So tell us, Bartlow, what were some of the classics of your youth?"

"Huh?" he asked.

"What were your favorite dirty jokes?" Siobhan explained.

"Why, I'm shocked," Joe Joe protested.

"Come on," Thia begged.

"Ladies, ladies. No, I just couldn't bring myself to use such foul and vulgar language in your presence. Unless you insist."

"We insist!" they yelled in unison.

After fifteen minutes of his leering delivery, Thia shook her head and observed through tears of laughter, "God, those are so stupid ... and corny ... so why am I laughing?"

"You wouldn't have laughed at my prom date," Joe Joe intoned with sincerity. "I called her my 'melancholy baby'."

"Oh, really," Siobhan said, accepting the bait.

"Yeah, she had a body like a melon and a face like a collie!"

Glancing at his watch, Tom said with great reluctance, "Afraid I've taken it to the limit." Then breaking into song, he added, *"I gotta get outta this place."* Brandeis joined him, *"If it's the last thing we evah do. We gotta get outta this place. Girl, there's a bettah life faw me and you."*

"Song!" Siobhan demanded. Thia chimed in, pulling on the back of Joe Joe's chair "Song! Song!"

Brandeis jumped from his chair and grabbed three of the plastic red carnations from the grimy green vase on their table. Placing one each above Tom and Joe Joe's ears *a la* Siobhan, the third he thrust into the top of his emerging Afro. Forming a chorus line, Brandeis whispered to each before they broke into a brutally off-key *a capella*. *"There is a house in New Orleans, they call the Rising Sun ..."* Tom ended the verse with an attempted high-kick off his end of the 'line'. He then gave a brief instruction to his fellow dancers of the classic Kilgore Rangerette routine, and they ended their program - carnations in their teeth - with knee-kick, high-kick, turn, knee-kick, high-kick.

Returning to their chairs, Joe Joe stopped in front of Thia, bowed, took her hand and kissed it lightly, before backing up and belting out, *"Wild Thang!! You make my Thang stang!"*

*   *   *

Tom left the gang at Nopalito's and followed his father's directions to the Brannigans' house, which was on a cul-de-sac off Inwood Road in the heart of affluent North Dallas. Ward Brannigan opened half of the ten-foot-tall double doors and ushered him inside. Ward was balding, with the remainder of his fine, straight black hair combed wet at a diagonal across his head. He had a noticeable paunch but a firm handshake and a warm, welcoming smile for Tom.

"Come on in," he said, patting Tom's shoulder. "Everyone's back in the den."

The richly grained wood paneling of the foyer and hallway was stained a warm golden brown and was interrupted occasionally by lighted abstract oils. It was unlike anything Tom had seen in New Fredonia - even Springfield. Ward led him to the cavernous den across the back of the house, a multi-level room with a pool table on a raised platform at the far end. One wall was pane after pane of floor-to-ceiling plate glass looking out into the darkness of the North Dallas night.

His parents were ensconced on a white leather loveseat, each of them holding a highball. They wore warm smiles as they chatted with Peggy Brannigan on the brown-and-white cowhide couch beside them.

"Look what I found lurking around outside," Ward laughed. "What can we get you, Son? Coke, Dr. Pepper?" Then glancing at Johnny and raising his glass, "Or does he handle the hard stuff?"

Tom looked away from Johnny's frozen smile and answered, "A Dr. Pepper would be great."

Peggy rose from the couch and offered her hand as Ward introduced her. "You men go ahead and sit down. I'll go get the drinks. Besides, Tom, I think these two old 'shorthorns' need help figuring out how Texas is ever going to get back to the Cotton Bowl."

Tom hugged his mother and then his father, and as they took their seats, Johnny offered, "Well, it all goes back to that blamed Arkansas game in '65, when the 'Horns came back from twenty-to-nothing to go ahead 24-20. And then Broyles sent out that one receiver - Bobby Crockett. And that quarterback of theirs … Britenum … just picked us to pieces right down the field. Pass after pass after pass. Beat us 27-24. Broke our backs and our hearts and our program. And we've just never gotten over it."

"Yeah," Ward agreed, "you know, Coach has said that after we won that national championship in '63, he spent way too much time eating rubber chicken on the banquet tour and not nearly enough recruiting. I mean, sure, he got Super Bill out of Palestine but what good's it done him? He may have something up his sleeve now, though."

Johnny looked at his son while pointing at Ward and said, "This guy's close to the program. He's provided summer employment for several of Texas' top players over the years." Looking at Ward, he asked, "So what have you heard from down there?"

"Well, first, let me tell you, Tom. Those kids work for every dime they get." Looking back toward Johnny, he added, "Aw, I just hear that Coach and his staff have their heads together trying to brew up a little more offensive punch."

"What we need," Johnny reminisced, "is another James Saxton, and a Ray Poage. Tommy Ford. Cotten and Collins. Boy, that '61 team was incredible."

"Well, whatever," Ward shrugged. "We'll all still gather at the Cotton Bowl come the second Saturday in October. See what they're made of when they play O-U. You coming, Tom?"

"Sure," he smiled proudly. "I haven't missed one since '53."

Ward thought for a moment and asked in wonder, "When did you start going? How old were you?"

"I guess I was four or five."

"That's right," Nancy concurred. "We started taking you real young. How old were you before you finally saw Texas beat O-U?"

"Well, I saw Texas lose five times before the 15-14 game in '58."

"That was some game," Johnny said with pride.

"Yeah," Tom began, "I remember Bobby Lackey -"

"Aw, yeah," Ward cut in, "reaching up with that long arm and making that interception there at the end. Killed that last gasp drive of theirs."

As Peggy returned with a Dr. Pepper and found all three men gazing with goofy smiles at each other, she asked, "Which O-U game are they talking about?"

"Fifty-eight," Nancy said.

"I could tell. They have 'the look'."

As Tom started sipping his drink, he asked, "So when are y'all taking off tomorrow, Mom?"

Nancy looked at Johnny and offered, "About ... about eight, isn't it? Or seven-thirty?"

"Yeah," Ward agreed. "I'm going to drive y'all out to Love Field. It's a seven-thirty flight. Johnny, I know you've told me, but whose funeral is this?"

"My Uncle Josh's. My mother's oldest brother. Died in an old folks' home down there."

"Did I know him in New Fredonia?" Ward asked.

"No, he moved off before we were even born."

"What did he die of?" Tom asked with child-like interest.

Snorting a half-laugh, Johnny answered, "Of being eighty-nine."

"Did he have family there?" Peggy asked. To the reluctant shake of Johnny's head in reply, she added, "Rough way to go."

"Yeah, if I got to pick my way to pass," Johnny said reflectively, "I'd be very old, at home, in bed, in no pain, with all my family and close friends and the preacher gathered round," he continued solemnly, "with everyone saying nice things about me and comforting me ... and then I'd get well!" he laughed.

Joining the room in laughter and appreciating the bent of his father's humor, Tom added, "Yep, that'd be the way to go." Shifting gears, he asked, "Say, are y'all going to stay over in Houston?"

"Naw, I think we'll just come on back tomorrow afternoon," Johnny answered. "Maybe we can catch you for dinner tomorrow night before we head home."

"I wish you could just come on down there with us, Son," Nancy said. "Really. Why don't you?"

Tom thought for only a second and replied, "Well, a lot of days I could skip class, but this close to the end of the semester we're getting into the heavy stuff. And if I had a pop quiz in anything, I'd hate to zero out." As he spoke, his distaste for funerals shot through his mind and sealed the decision to pass on the down-and-back Houston trip. "No, I'll just see you tomorrow night. When are you due back in?"

"Around four, I think," Johnny answered. "You can check with Global."

"And I've got a great place to take ... for y'all to take me tomorrow night," Tom said. "Nopalito's." Looking at the Brannigans, Tom asked, "Have y'all been there?"

"No, what is it?" Peggy asked.

"World class Mexican food. It's down on Harry Hines at the end of the tollway."

"In Little Mexico?" Ward asked cautiously.

"Yeah, but it's safe," Tom replied.

"Sounds good, Son," Johnny said.

"Yeah, we'll have to try it, too," Peggy joined in excitedly. "We're always looking for the next great Mexican food hole-in-the-wall."

As the group talked through restaurants to movies, Tom began to feel the weight of the day, and Nancy noticed. "You've got to drive back to campus, Son, and you're looking sleepy. You'd better head on."

As they told him good-bye, Johnny gave Tom a playful hug and said, "So long, Son. See you tomorrow." Tom left his father clear-eyed, happy and in his element.

Nancy walked him to the door and stopped there. "Tom," she said seriously, "thank you for calling me the other night."

"Sure, Mom."

As she gave him a farewell hug verging on desperation, Nancy added, "You're everything to us, you know."

Seeing that she was on the verge of tears, he hugged her again and said, "I love you, Mom. See you tomorrow."

She did not disappoint as over his shoulder he heard her once more advise him, "Just be a good boy, and people will like you."

Boarding the Le Mans, he glanced skyward and rendered up a farewell nod to the pencil-thin slit that was all that was left of the Wild Goose Moon.

Driving alone past the ZPL as he approached McCartney, Tom waved to his roommate and his girlfriend parked somewhere out there. Entering 332 he glanced at the "Signs Come Down" headline of *Cat Tracks* and shook his head in disgust. Sitting down at his desk, he took pen in hand and began to write:

> *Dear Editor:*
>
> *The removal of the "Whites Only" sign from the door of Rutledge's Washateria while segregation is still practiced within is symbolic of the racial situation that has prevailed in this country for the past fourteen years - since the Supreme Court desegregation decision of 1954. Throughout the country, signs suggesting racism have been removed from schools, churches, homes, and especially from people's faces; but in their minds, as is the case inside Rutledge's Washateria, segregation remains as potent, as divisive a force as ever.*
>
> *The student protesters feel that "the picketing has accomplished positive ends". This is true, but only in a*

vague and, at best, superficial sense. The compromise reached by the opposing camps mirrors our society's everpresent urge to seek an easy way out of a problem, no matter how distant the relationship between the achieved solution and the real problem. For to say that the cause of integration will be furthered just by the removal of a sign, but with no accompanying change in policy - no change in thinking - shows marked short-sightedness.

True integration can only be accomplished by the removal of the prejudices which have been nurtured in the minds of white America by three centuries of racial bias. This is perhaps the greatest problem that our generation will have to face, and the answer must be uniquely our own, judging from the way that the problem has been handled thus far.

-Tom Windham

Chapter 25

The Next Day

"We have an unconfirmed report that a Global Airlines jet has crashed near Butler Mills. The plane apparently departed from Houston's Hobby Airport on a flight to ... Dallas' Love Field. We have no information ..."

Tom sat motionless in his underwear in his chair next to the breezeless open window. He chewed in slow motion for a few seconds, then swallowed with difficulty as the phone rang.

"... as to the number of passengers or crew aboard. Nor is there any word of survivors. We will be back ..."

On the third ring Tom rose slowly from his chair. His legs were weak, and a hard cold fear was spreading through his chest and into his throat.

"... to you with further information as soon as it is available."

He picked up the receiver. When first he tried to speak, he choked. Coughing and clearing his throat, he said, "Hello."
"Tom?" The voice was familiar and full of concern.
"Yes," he answered numbly.

"This is Ward Brannigan, Tom. Have you been listening to the radio?"

"Yes."

There was a momentary silence. Finally, Ward said, "Tom, maybe you should come out here."

*   *   *

Motoring across North Dallas, Tom's mind was a blur. His two calls to Global's Dallas office had netted only busy signals. He had moved through the routine of dressing, of leaving the dorm, and now of driving as if in slow motion. He expended minimum energy to steer, accelerate and brake because his limbs were limp, enervated. His eyelids sagged and his lower jaw seemed too heavy to keep his mouth closed. His thought pattern was buffeted to the point of overload by unanswerable questions about the departure and arrival times of his parents' flight - based on his hazy memory of the conversation the night before - relative to the time he had heard the radio announcement. The other thoughts that fought losing skirmishes with his confusion, though, threw a probability graph from his old nemesis, B-Stat, onto the Le Mans' windshield. It reminded him that his parents had flown three - maybe four - times in their lives. The odds were so greatly in their favor, Tom tried to reason, against those of the weekly or monthly business traveler - like Ward Brannigan, whose extensive travel schedule Johnny had once proudly related to Tom - that he drew flashes of empty reassurance that perhaps they were not on the plane.

Drifting down Inwood in early rush-hour traffic, Tom became disoriented and missed the turn for the cul-de-sac on which the Brannigans lived. Finally realizing that he had passed it and that he had forgotten the street name, he U-turned and began to look at the street signs in hopes of stirring a memory. 'Creighton,' Tom realized, as he slowed to turn in. Walking weakly toward the door, he heard a strange message come forward in his mind. 'Don't lose control,' the voice said. 'Be careful. Don't lose control.' Too numb to analyze the thought otherwise, he accepted the internal dictum as a warning to himself to avoid uncontrollably lachrymose episodes as he had experienced at fourteen when Mark died. He felt there was really more to the message than the obvious, tangible instruction, but its deeper meaning was beyond his overloaded brain to fathom.

Ward greeted him wide-eyed and ashen-faced, and Tom saw that his father's friend thought his parents dead. "Have you heard ... anything else?" Tom asked.

Ward rubbed his dry, gnarled lips and replied, "It was ... the plane they were scheduled to be on." As Tom leaned toward him from weakness, Ward reached out to catch him and added quickly, "But we don't know that they were on it. Johnny told me this morning that they might stay longer to visit with the family and catch a later flight. They might not have been on that flight," Ward conjectured hopefully.

"Weren't you supposed to pick them up at the airport, though?" Tom asked.

"No," Ward answered. "I was tied up. They were going to catch a cab back over here for their car," he said with desperation.

"Have you talked to the airline?" Tom asked. "I could never get through to them."

"I finally did."

"And?"

"They're going to check the flight's manifest list to see if they boarded it. I told them you were coming here, and they said they'd call back. Come on in. I was lucky to get through the time I did. I'm sure the lines are all tied up now. All we can do is wait."

Tom entered the quiet house, but he soon heard the muffled whimper of Peggy Brannigan. He did not want to see her. He knew that she had given up, too. He was too emotionally exhausted to deal with her upset, and he had yet to accept the need for her comfort. "I ... need to go to the bathroom," Tom said as they approached the expansive den where he heard Peggy crying softly. "Where is one?"

"Why?" Ward asked with unguarded concern. Then catching himself, he rephrased, "Are you going to be sick?"

Confused, Tom frowned and replied, "No. I just need to go in the bathroom for a minute. I need to splash some water on my face."

"Oh," Ward responded warily. "Yeah. Right down here." Ward guided him to a half-bath.

Tom closed the door and gripped the sink for stability. He turned on the water and wet a washcloth, which he rubbed generously over his face and neck. 'This can't be happening. This can't be happening,' he thought as he shook his head and stared at his sunken face in the mirror. He turned away, understanding the Jewish custom of which Brandeis had apprised him of covering the mirrors at the death of a loved one. Opening the door he found Ward leaning stiffly against the opposite wall staring at him.

"What is it?" Tom asked. "Have they called?"

"No," Ward answered vacantly. "I … just wanted to make sure you were okay."

'Don't lose control,' the voice said.

"Tom, I called Bowman."

Tom nodded and asked, "What did you tell him?"

"Just what we had heard on -"

The telephone rang.

They jerked at its first ring, and Tom followed Ward into the den. Tom's first glimpse of Peggy was all he feared it would be. She had risen from the sofa, and she stood over the phone. Her heavily made-up face, which she had planned that morning to put through nothing more serious than shopping at NorthPark, was scarred by grotesquely uneven blotches of mascara, rouge, and foundation. At the sight of Tom she burst into tears as she opened her arms to him. He accepted her embrace as Ward reached for the phone.

"Hello. Yes, this is he. Yes, he is," he said, looking with pain at Tom. After a long moment's silence, Ward's head fell forward into his hand, and he gasped, "Oh, no. Oh, no. Yes, I will." Tom watched in horror as Ward turned to him with loss filling his eyes. He choked as he said, "They … were on … the manifest. They're gone, Tom."

Chapter 26

The sensations were horribly familiar to him. Sitting in the dimly-lit guest bedroom watching for Chet's arrival on the cul-de-sac, Tom replayed and relived many of the "moment after" experiences that had been part of the morbid ritual of death to which he had been privy six years earlier. From the totally unexpected and unimaginable suddenness and the horrifically imaginable violence of their deaths right down to the delivery of untold numbers of pound cakes on platters with names scribbled on masking tape stretched across their bottoms. From the preciously prayerful words of preacher and laity - always including the proscription that "God never gives you more than you can take" - to the roller coaster of emotions that brought Tom to laugh with those approaching him with joy on their faces and to cry with those - even total strangers both to him and to his parents - who approached him wearing the gaunt face of mourning. From the repeating in his mind of his last image of each of his parents the prior night in this same house to such surrealistically practical considerations as funeral logistics.

The most obvious differences with six years earlier, though, were both the public and the fungible nature of their deaths - aboard a federally regulated carrier in common catastrophe with sixty-seven other souls - no survivors. This time the lexicon of tragedy was expanded to include the gruesome yet impersonal language of identification: finger prints, dental records, FBI interview, jewelry, and so on. Each consideration brought to Tom's fertile imagination horrible images that he could not always shake.

But through the afternoon and evening of tears and numbing grief, Tom had stayed true to his self-instruction. He had not lost control. He had given little thought to why he had so instructed himself, though, and by twilight his mind and body were taut and exhausted. Under the Brannigans' watchful eyes he had retreated into this guest room from the 'open house' atmosphere that oddly follows death to the homes of the friends and families of its victims. But now, even alone, except for the frequent visits of his hosts, Tom began to feel claustrophobic and uncomfortable.

As Peggy peeked in the door, Tom turned from the window where he stood watch. "It'll probably be another thirty or forty minutes before Chet gets here. I'm feeling real antsy, Mrs. Brannigan. I think I'm going to go for a ride. Go get something to drink at the Seven-Eleven. I'll be right back. I just need a little air."

"Okay, Tom. Let me get someone to take you. I think Ward should stay here by the phone, and I - "

"No, thank you," Tom interrupted politely. "I'm just going to go by myself. I just need to get out for a while and get some air. I'm feeling -"

"Oh, no, Tom," Peggy responded with concern approaching panic. "Please, let one of us go with you, or wait for Chet. He should be here very soon."

"But I'm just going to go down to - "

"Oh, Tom, please don't," she implored him. "You're in no condition to be - You shouldn't be ... by yourself ... now."

Tom finally understood her fear. In her view he was at risk of taking Mark's shortcut home. It shocked him speechless for a moment, and he then realized that, for all of his conscious efforts to the opposite, he might be denied the control over himself that he was so fiercely guarding, not because of any questionable behavior on his part but because of his family history. 'I guess I can act as 'in control' as I want to, and I still won't be trusted,' he thought. Reading her fear, he conjured up a discomforting image of finally being physically restrained from leaving the house alone, and the obvious implication of his attempt to leave alone would be that he was 'out of control' and might 'try to hurt himself'.

"Okay, I'll just stay here and wait for Chet," he replied evenly.

"No, let one of us take you. I'm sure you would like to get out for a while," she said carefully.

"No, that's alright."

"Well, can I bring you something? There's so much food in here. Cake, pie, anything?"

"Sure. A piece of pound cake would be nice."

Peggy left with his order, and he sank into the easy chair in the corner of the guest room. The overawing anxiety and insecurity that he felt quickly exhausted him, and he closed his eyes - only to be greeted by a piercing pain in his left frontal lobe. Grabbing for his forehead, he reflexively applied extreme fingertip pressure to the source of the pain and simultaneously tightened his neck muscles against the pressure. Finally opening his eyes, his field of vision in the semi-darkness was momentarily filled with tiny darting specks of light like he had never seen. As they quickly disappeared, he gave them no more heed because of his concentration on the pain that had slowly begun to throb above his left eye. Trying to rise from his chair too quickly, the pain increased and he reached again for his head as if to hold it on. 'Migraine?' he wondered, having had only rare headaches in his life, and those having generally been connectible to particular actions or circumstances. But this was different - both in the suddenness of its onset and in the severity and acuteness of the pain. When Peggy returned with cake and milk, he requested aspirin without discussing the headache.

As he ate and drank, taking care to avoid large gulps of the cold milk, he noted ruefully that the pain had at least relieved the anxiety. Barely in his consciousness, he wondered if it was a trade-off to which he might have to become accustomed.

*   *   *

Chet stood in the guest bedroom doorway silhouetted by the hall lights. "Tom?" he asked, probing the darkness of the room. Tom flipped on a lamp and saw the sad, sympathetic half-smile of his favorite cousin. They stood an awkward yard apart for a moment before sharing a bear hug. Both remained dry-eyed, but as Chet held his young cousin, he whispered, "Oh, Tom. We never could've figured this one, could we?" As Tom shook his head, Chet added, "Aunt Nancy's not hurting anymore."

Sniffing back tears, Tom agreed, "No, no, she's not." For the past four hours Tom had longed for someone who knew him as well as Chet did -

someone with whom he could be himself. Finally willing to cede some of the control that he had imposed so vigorously upon himself, Tom looked into his cousin's eyes and asked, "Chet, what do I do now?"

Chet pulled away from him slightly to place his hands firmly on Tom's shoulders. He considered his response before finally answering, "One thing at a time. That's all you can do. That's all you have to do. You've got a house full of people right here who want to help you anyway they can, and you've got a town full of people back home who feel the same way. Especially your Aunt Nela and your Uncle Bowman.

"Why don't you just tell me what you want to do right now. I'll bet we can do it. If you want to go get in my car and head on back to Noofer, we can go right now and you can spend the night with me."

"I wish it was that simple." Tom grimaced before continuing, his voice cracking, "Chet, they haven't -. They haven't found ... Mom and Dad yet." Chet's eyes widened with pain as the horror of this reality became clear. "I've got to talk to the ... F-B-I tomorrow morning," he said, slinging off the words and shaking his head as he spoke them, as if it were incomprehensible that they were any he would ever have occasion to use.

"Oh, Tom," Chet began, but he quickly composed himself and stated evenly, "then we need to stay here tonight, don't we? And we need to run over to the dorm and pack some stuff for you."

His mind clouded by grief, Tom did not comprehend all that Chet had said. Slowly shaking his head from side to side, Tom finally focused on him and said, "I don't even know how to act – with all these people – and with everyone in Noofer. How do I do this, Chet? I mean, I was a boy when I lost Mark. Now, I guess I'm supposed to be a man. I don't know if I am. How do I act? And ... I don't have Mom and Dad here to tell me. "

Chet weighed the substance of his response, and he dug deeply into his experience with grief and mourning – though knowing that comparables were few. Finally, he said, "Tom, when I was fifteen, I lost my best friend, Troy Cage. He had a brain tumor. He went down and came back and then went down – all the way – over a period of months. Till the day Troy died, I thought he was going to recover and be fine - and we were going to play ball again together and life would return to normal. I was in shock and totally unprepared for his death when it came. I had no concept of death or loss or grief. I didn't know how to give or accept comfort.

"The Cages were country people, and the whole process of death and mourning and visitation and funeral was long and drawn out – and very emotional and, to me, very upsetting. I didn't understand their ways, and I didn't even know what my 'ways' were. On top of the loss I felt so keenly, I was very confused and worried about, as you said, how to act. Mom and Dad did their best to help. But it was Cora Chesterton, our preacher's wife, who made that whole problem of grief and behavior so clear and simple to me. Essentially, she just told me to do what comes natural. Everyone has the right to and should handle it differently – and their own way. She told me that the 'right' way to act was what was right for me. I know you've seen an array of behaviors just today – just like you did when we lost Mark. And you'll see different ones back home. But the way you grieve and the way you act during this time is right, if it feels right. By the same token you should understand when you observe some really different behaviors, but there's nothing that says you have to respond in kind. Nor is there anything that prevents you from removing yourself from an uncomfortable situation."

Tom had listened as intently as his emotional exhaustion allowed, and Chet had watched in hopes that something he said was helping. "Does any of that make sense to you?"

Starting to nod slowly, Tom replied, "Yeah. It's really what I needed to hear. Thanks."

"Sure thing, Cuz. You want me to drive you over to the dorm now?"

"I hate to go back there. I don't feel like seeing anybody, and I don't know what to say."

"Of course you don't. Who does? Don't worry. I'll be with you. And anyway, it's Friday night. Don't you imagine the place'll be pretty well cleared out? We'll just slip in and throw your things in a bag and slip out." As Tom nodded his agreement, Chet said, "But Tom, this is what I mean. Right now we're going to go get you some clothes. When you're hungry, we'll get you some food. When you're tired, you can sleep right here. Tomorrow we'll get through the F-B-I stuff together. In the next few days you've got a funeral to get through, and I'll help you get that behind you. We all will. You can stay at my house for as long as you want to or you can stay with your Aunt Nela and your Uncle Bowman - if you want decent meals," he said, finally eliciting smiles from both of them. "You can even switch back and forth across the alley between us if you want to."

Shaking his head, Tom declared, "I can't go back to my house."

"I know that. No one expects you to."

"Yeah. But what am I going to do, Chet? I mean, I might need to get a job, I guess. Or - I don't even know if I can go back to school. I don't really know anything about Dad's title business."

"Tom, you really don't need to worry about that right now. But let me tell you one thing my dad said before I left. He said that Uncle Johnny had a good bit of life insurance. I don't have any idea what your Uncle Bowman's definition of 'a good bit' is," he grinned, "but I imagine your Dad had you taken care of. Because I'm sure he planned enough for you and for Aunt Nancy." Chet fell silent and dropped his face into his hand, finally weeping. "I'm really going to miss that lady. I'm going to miss both of them."

While heartened to hear that his father had provided for him, Tom gave Chet a comforting hug. Shaking himself back to composure, Chet continued, "Anyway, my point is, you don't have to go out that far. One thing at a time. That's all you have to deal with."

From the host of whispers that drifted by Tom through the afternoon and evening at the Brannigans', he had pieced together a scenario whereby his parents had been aboard an aging turboprop that was felled by an extremely violent cell of the spring storm that had spared Dallas early in the afternoon only to wreak havoc across Central Texas. The Global pilot, based on reasons that died with him, had flown into the storm rather than turning back or attempting to fly around it. The plane had apparently broken up in the air thus scattering its human cargo over a wide area of Trinity River Basin farmland. A much weaker sister storm pushed through Dallas as the cousins drove toward WSU. Tom flinched with the horrible images suggested to him by the sky-lighting flashes of lightning and the violent cracks of thunder. But as they approached campus, the rain abated.

They parked behind McCartney, and as Tom stepped from the car, he stood still for a moment and looked around the parking lot and toward the Men's Quad. He observed the normal comings and goings of a Friday night on campus. A couple walked arm in arm, a mix of rock music flowed from the open windows of the three facing dorms, and the occasional familiar shout could be heard.

As he and Chet walked toward the rear entrance of McCartney, his hope that he could get in and out without seeing anyone he knew evaporated. Finding a lucky parking space close to the back door, Bob Tolbert's Malibu pulled in next to them. As it emptied, Tom recognized Coy Delacourt as well. He did not know the backseat passenger, but he assumed him also to be a Sigma Sig. Approaching the door, Tom pasted on a smile assuming he would have to say something to Bob. Tolbert wore the familiar bleary-eyed oversmile that told Tom he had been drinking. Waving at his neighbor, Tolbert yelled out, "Hey, we've been down to Butler Mills, and that place is a 'wreck'!"

"Yeah, Butler Mills -" the backseat occupant began.

"We're going up to Tolbert's room and 'crash'!" Delacourt shouted through their collective laughter.

"Come on over if you want to," Bob said to the speechless pair. In an inebriated gesture of hospitality he hoisted high a paper sack shaking it slightly and causing its glass contents to clink.

Chet had halted in stunned silence at the door, but Tom looked away, opened it and walked in. The icy glare of the stranger with Tom quieted the three drunks. Fearing that Chet would say something, Tom stood in the door and motioned him through with his head. After a moment's consideration Chet understood and put aside his natural urge to drop the five or six words it would have taken to lay waste to them. He followed Tom in and up the stairs.

Entertainment had been a sparse commodity in New Fredonia in the Fifties. After Tom passed the three revelers, he dialed back to those days and to the last time he had persuaded his father - upon hearing the town's fire siren - to call the volunteers' number (which everyone in town knew) for the location of the fire. As they had done a number of times before, the Windhams piled into their Ford station wagon and chased the fire to its source. It was an aging two-story wide-porched white frame farmhouse from the turn of the century, which had been coaxed to the edge of town by New Fredonia's post-war growth. As the fire brigade launched torrential streams of water into the blazing structure in vain, Tom and his family, along with many of the town's regular fire-watchers plus a number of neighbors, leaned against their cars and observed the awesome ferocity of the flames leaping skyward, relishing the caving in of porches and of walls as the once noble house bowed to the fury of the blaze.

Standing between the observers and the firemen, though, was a large family holding onto one another and crying as they, too, helplessly stared into the heart of the destruction. One of the children, whom Tom, at age eight himself, figured to be around five, turned and scanned the crowd. In his memory her gaze swept the townsfolk back and forth in slow motion. She held back her tears for a moment, and then, still rotating her head to take in Tom, his family, and all those around them, she shouted above the din of the flames, "This is our house! Stop looking! This is our house! Why are you looking?!" Then craning her neck forward as her mother reached for her, she screamed, "Go away and stop looking!"

A few in the crowd had laughed her off and stayed. Most, like the Windhams, left silently. Tom did not ask his father to call about a fire again. As Tom and his cousin scaled the stairs, he fully understood the little girl's wail against the pain and the personal violation of morbid curiosity.

Arriving at 332, Tom's mixed feelings about wanting to see Brandeis were solved by his absence. As he mechanically went about gathering basic clothing, he struggled with whether he should leave a note for his roommate. In his confusion he stood frozen before his open closet. Seeking to help him in whatever quandary had hold of him, Chet said only, "Suit." Shaking his mind as clear as the dull pain of the headache would allow, Tom took Chet's signal and grabbed his tan spring suit off the rack. He matched it with a tie and shirt and remembered dress socks and shoes as well. After gathering his toiletries Chet again interrupted Tom's frozen gaze into his mirror. "Got everything? Ready to go?"

Nodding, Tom opened his desk drawer and pulled out a blank bluebook. Creasing it open to the first page, Tom wrote:

Woz,

I'm sorry I missed you. Something has happened, and I need for you to call me. I am staying at Ward Brannigan's house in North Dallas right now. Please call me there or at Bowman Carter's house in Noofer tomorrow.

- Tom

As Tom finished the note and placed it on his roommate's bed, the party in Tolbert's room cranked up. Following Chet out the door, Tom turned and looked back into 332 - not sure when or if he would return to this safe, simple haven that had given him sanctuary for the past eight months. He shook his head and shuddered, knowing that nothing would ever be as safe and as simple again.

*   *   *

It was late that evening when the first dark thought came. It was after Tom and Chet had returned from WSU and after they had dined on the bounty of mourning. It was after the last visitor had left and after Ward had received the call from the FBI agent confirming the following morning's interview. The thought came after Tom had talked once again to his aunt and uncle and after he had spoken with Browning Lee, pastor of First Church New Fredonia. It was with bitterness that he lay in bed rolling over the contents of that last conversation in his mind. Dr. Lee had given him the straight Southern Baptist mourning line. He had said a great deal about God's Will, about Its movement in mysterious ways, about His tender mercies and The Comforter, and, as Tom had heard so frequently both six years prior and this afternoon, he had stated, 'God never gives you more than you can handle.'

Lying in bed, his angry mental response was that He certainly seemed to have given Mark more than he could handle. And of himself, he thought, 'We'll see. Maybe I can handle it. But You've damn sure taken me to the edge again.' After that he tried to clear his mind for sleep. But when Peggy checked on him at midnight, she found him still staring at the ceiling. At her urging Tom took a sleeping pill that her doctor had prescribed for him. As he tried again to drift off, the dark thought came. And it led to another. And to another.

As the pill finally started to take effect, he spoke quietly into the darkness, "God? Are you there? Please answer me. I feel so alone. God?" Soon the combination of the chemical deadening and the mental exhaustion of grief, guilt, uncertainty, and darkness that had begun to plague him won out, and he fell into an unnatural and troubled sleep.

Chapter 27

Early May

"... and they even asked me what kind of cigarettes Mom and Dad smoked," Tom reported, shaking his head in disbelief and calling up a complete set of memories. "Winstons," he whispered. "And they really looked the part. Short hair, white shirts, dark suits. But, they were nice. Real understanding."

Brandeis nodded, allowing his roommate to explain what he wanted to - to leave unsaid what he so chose. He had found Tom sitting in twilight's semi-darkness in 332. Brandeis had offered himself up to Tom as silent company, as herald of campus goings-on since he had been away, as listening post, as driver, or as passenger. Tom had been quiet for several minutes. Then he began recounting his impressions of the week of grief and loss, comfort and ceremony that he had spent in Dallas and in New Fredonia.

"The whole problem of ... identification ... was a nightmare," he said, while pressing his fingertips against his left temple and then against his forehead. "I had to come back to Dallas Monday just for about an hour ... to look at some ... jewelry. It turned out it wasn't theirs."

"The headache still bothering you?"

"It's a whopper."

"You got anything for it?"

"I've just been stuffing down Anacins. Ward Brannigan's setting me up to see a doctor later this week. Hopefully, he'll give me a prescription that'll help get rid of them," he shrugged. "I've had several the last week. Anyway, I was afraid for a while we were only going to be able to have a memorial service or something like that. They identified ... Dad ... after a couple of days, but ..."

As Tom's voice trailed off, Brandeis said, "Yeah, it was good that you set the date out several days like that, so you didn't have to have separate services -"

"No way I could have done that," Tom said, shaking his head. Continuing to do so, he observed, staring out into the approaching darkness, "I had forgotten how barbaric those things are. I hate funerals. There's all that false grief from the professional 'funeral-ateers' - the Hessian mourners - and it's mixed with all that real grief that you don't know how to express that everyone keeps telling you to 'get out', and you don't know how. Thank God, I didn't open the house, though. That was the only thing that saved me from that mob that shows up for that sort of thing. Once I was able to get back to Noofer late the day after, I could get out and drive out in the country or hide at Chet's and avoid the crowd and the tears and the hugs and the crazy talk that death drives people to burden you with. I think they need to reverse the rules so that the most distant relative is forced to listen to the loudest, craziest mourner; next most distant to the next loudest, and so on down to where the closest relative is blessed with perfect silence and is left alone. And it's really amazing how some people, who you may not know at all, think they can say something that will absolutely change your life and take all your grief away. My God, the ego. The madness."

"Yeah, I've never had much death to deal with," Brandeis said carefully. "A grandfather died before I was born. Everyone else is still around. I can't imagine what it would be like."

Glaring out the window, Tom said, "Tell you what. When I die, I don't even want a funeral. Just tell them to strap my pine box to the back of a Ferrari - like they did Von Tripps after his crash at Monza - and haul me to the cemetery. And while they're lowering me into the ground, just have some glass-shattering soprano sing "Amazing Grace" *a capella*. Either that or have it played by a bagpipe corps - or both."

"Come on, Tom," Brandeis countered. "Don't get so morbid. Anyway, a Ferrari? In Noofer?"

"Good point. Anyway, no funeral and no visitors allowed. Oh, but I'm really glad you and Chevy came."

"Well, there wouldn't have been any keeping her away. I got your note when I got back from the Libe, and after you told me ... what had happened, I got hold of her in Terre Haute the next day. She was ready to turn around and fly back Saturday night, but I told her it would be a few days and that you had gone home."

"I appreciated your call that night, too."

"Yeah, well, I got your note, and after we talked and - and then after I came out of shock - I told Tolbert next door. He turned about as white as a sheet. He felt as bad as he should have about what happened."

"Aagghhh," Tom sighed, batting the air toward his neighbor.

"No, he really did. They all did. Anyway, I could only imagine how upset you were about everything, and then with that on top of it."

"Well, I guess it was nice of them to come to the funeral. Though I wasn't particularly thrilled to see them at the time." Tom leaned back against the wall above his bed pressing his head forcefully against it.

"Aspirin not helping?"

"Naa. I think if I could just push my head through this wall, though, I might experience true relief."

"You want to get out of here?" Brandeis asked. "Go get something to eat and see a movie?"

"That sounds great," Tom replied. "But don't you have a date, or need to study for finals or something?"

"Mind if I bring my date along? I think she'd want to see you tonight anyway."

"I'd like to see her, too."

"You pick. What sounds good to eat?"

"Jamie's. And I don't know what's on in town, but let's see something ... light."

"Speaking of 'light', mind if I turn this one on now?"

"No, that's fine," Tom answered, squinting his eyes closed and opening them slowly. As they approached the door, they were greeted with a knock on it. Looking at each other with surprise, Brandeis answered, "Come in."

Joe Joe shuffled slowly through the door, his head slightly bowed. Nodding at Brandeis, he offered his hand to Tom. Shaking it, he shook his head from side to side and said, " Whooo. That's a tough one to take. Sure am sorry, Tom. Never got to meet your folks, but I'm sure they were fine people."

Tom nodded awkwardly, as he had become accustomed to doing the past week. "Thanks."

"Sure. Well, and ... I'm sorry I didn't come to the funeral, but ... I ... aw -"

"Hey, *I* wouldn't have been there if I hadn't had to. Don't worry about it."

Sensing that Tom would prefer a change of topic, Brandeis asked Joe Joe, "Say, haven't you been dating someone new?"

"Can't keep anything quiet around here," Joe Joe complained.

"So who's the mystery lady?" Tom asked.

"Well, it's Thia, but we've only had one date."

"Thia?!" Tom exclaimed. "Yeah, I thought I saw something going on between you two at Nopalito's. So, give us details. What did y'all do? How was she in hand-to-hand in the Z-P-L?"

"Windham, my boy," Joe Joe protested. "Please. I was a perfect gentleman. Well, I was a gentleman, anyway. Took her to the Vista, and we saw *Elvira Madigan*. Real artsy. This soldier and a pretty girl run off together, and she gets hungry and eats grass and pukes it up. And then she goes out in this field and throws a butterfly up in the air and the guy shoots her. Well, Thia thinks he shot her. It didn't show. I still think he was shooting at the butterfly. You know, like clay pigeons." And raising an imaginary rifle, he called, "Pull!"

"And after the movie?" Tom asked.

"No Z-P-L. Took her back to the dorm, kissed her at the door, and shot off across the lawn." Brandeis beat out a rim shot with his pencil on his desk as Joe Joe said, "Well, anyway, good to have you back. Gotta go."

As Joe Joe closed the door behind him, Tom laughed and said, "Good to know some things never change."

Exiting Blake Hall with her arm around her boyfriend, Siobhan waved weakly at Tom. Approaching him, he saw her eyes redden and glaze over with tears. Stopping close to him and releasing herself from Brandeis, she moaned, "Oh, I had told myself I was through crying."

"It's okay, Chevy. It really is," Tom said.

"But I know you're so sick and tired of sad things. I love you, and I really wanted to ... Ohh," she chastised herself.

Opening his arms, Tom said, "Give me a hug."

Shaking her head, she grabbed Tom and hugged him tightly. "I just never thought ... about ... I mean, I guess I just thought ... all of us would go on forever."

Chapter 28

During the lengthy wait before the funeral Chet had called and explained the situation to WSU administration. Tom returned to campus the day after the funeral. Thus it was that when he walked into his "Man and His World" class on Friday, Dr. Longoria treated him with a care and a deference that was unnatural, even eerie. She took him aside and, following a brief but awkward offering of condolences, explained that another student had joined his partner to present the negative in the debate, and Tom was welcome to observe or to contribute if he had prepared anything he wanted to share.

He took his seat and watched as the unskilled pro-Evolution team clumsily emptied their formidable arsenal - like a retarded giant hunting butterflies with a Howitzer - against his "con" squad. In reply Carla Mazzalevski and her partner struggled valiantly but fruitlessly with their paucity of support, adroitly but thinly glazing an occasional patina of reason over the crackpot ramblings of some of their sources. Their biblical references were greeted with catcalls from the same audience who had raised Tom's ire that fateful first day of class, which, but for the natural laws - or whims - of a God Tom had determined one spring night that he comprehended not at all, would have landed him in this very tournament. And now with another eight months of the scathing cynicism of Dr. Longoria and those in the faculty of her ilk under their belts, the mob had grown even meaner. At any moment he expected them to start screaming, "Give us Barabbas!"

It was into that cauldron and with similar motivation that Tom, to the surprise of his professor, took up the gauntlet when she offered him speaking time at the end of the Negative side's conclusion.

He began tentatively, "I'd first like to thank Carla and Bob for presenting such an excellent case for the Negative after I had to ... drop out. There were just a few things that I had thought of that I'd like to add, if I may." With a slight nod and a wrinkling of her mouth approaching a smile from Dr. Longoria, Tom continued, "We've heard what sounded like pretty overwhelming evidence today from the Affirmative side on this issue. I'm certainly not here to dispute all the scientific findings of Charles Darwin and the army of scientists who followed him in support of his work and who have expanded on it so greatly. Most of the biological, geological, archaeological, and just about every other kind of 'ological' study support the evolution of the species. But the name of the course we're sitting in today speaks of one species that has risen above all the rest, and for no apparent physical reason. 'Man' has dominion over all the other species, just as, coincidentally, the Bible said he would. Man is neither as strong as other animals nor as fast as many nor as large or industrious as still others, yet ... here we are on top. We must ask ourselves, 'How did we do it?' How did we gain such absolute and unquestioned ascendancy given our limited physical tools? Sure, we walk upright and we have pretty advanced levels of manual dexterity, but what's the difference? Gorillas can walk upright ... but then, they're part of our evolutionary chain, right? But so can bears. Monkeys have excellent manual dexterity, but again, aren't they in the evolutionary order toward humans? So what about squirrels, though? Seems like I've seen them and any number of other forest animals exhibit some pretty sophisticated manual skills. All a lot of them would need to catch up with us would be a few weeks of intense training at the General Motors Mechanics' School." Tom was heartened by the few grudging laughs he won.

"No, there's obviously some other difference besides the physical. And it separates us from all the other animals. It is our intellect. The working of the human mind. The feelings that we have. My argument against the whole-hog one-hundred-percent acceptance of the Theory of Evolution is based on that difference - on that vast gap, that chasm - in the intellectual and psychological and emotional capacities of Man as opposed to every other species. Nothing I have heard or read this year, nor any of the research that I was able to do on this topic, has explained that 'quantum leap' to me - that 'linking' of this combination of intelligence, reasoning, and emotional capability from any other species to ours. And the differences are so great, so absolute that the burden of proof goes back against the pro-Evolutionists to prove why the break in this link in their theory doesn't shoot their whole argument down.

"We read some case studies by Dobzhansky on 'inherited traits' during the semester. I don't know if he was trying to be sarcastic or what, but in a section where he touched on evolution, he put forward the argument that if a God as all-powerful, all-knowing, and all-wise as many of us give Him credit for being would spend tens of thousands of millennia laying down a logical path of evidence in support of the theory of evolution, then why can't we accept it. It was obviously what He was pointing to, so said Dobzhansky. To that I say, 'Thank you, Doctor D'. Thank you for agreeing that God made all of this. Thank you for your concurring opinion as to His strength, His power, His control. But given that omnipotence, why then didn't God just *say* that was the way it was. He laid out the whole story for us in sixty-six books. Didn't mention Evolution once. My answer to Dobzhansky and to the Affirmative side in this debate would be that a God with this kind of power could lay out any set of crossed or reversed or confusing signals He was of a mind to, and the answer - the real way it happened - could be some other way altogether. May be the Bible's explanation. May be something completely different that He just hasn't taken the time to mention to us yet. Because there are a couple of things at work here that you probably haven't thought of, and you need to keep them in mind. First, we are - that is, us, human beings - are *incredibly* insignificant to Him in the overall scheme of things. And second, God ... is weird." Eliciting nervous laughs from his classmates, Tom went on, "Strange. Twisted sense of humor. No telling what The Guy'll do next."

Waving at a wound-up, pensive Dr. Longoria, who nonetheless waved back with an ironic smile and a shake of her head, Tom said, "Well, thanks. That's it for me," and he took his seat. But rising again before she began to speak, he said with a grin, "Oh yeah, one other thing. For those of you who would like to hear an argument that kind of reconciles Evolution to the Bible's story of creation, find *Inherit The Wind* on the late movie or at a revival house and check out Spencer Tracy's interrogation of Frederic March, or, better yet, go over to the Libe and read Lawrence and Lee's play." Looking around the room at the amazed expressions on his classmates' faces, Tom waved again and said, "Thanks. That's all. Promise," and he sat down.

The vote went overwhelmingly for the Affirmative.

*   *   *

Driving east away from the sun, Tom replayed the feeling of emptiness that had swept over him as he had left "Man and His World" earlier in the day, having received in the hall outside of class the positive recognition of several of his classmates who had apparently been closet Defenders of the Faith themselves. Leaving Old Wesley Hall and walking across the Common, his reflex had been to call his parents to tell them what had happened and to receive their plaudits and approval. The feeling that followed had been like turning quickly and stepping into an elevator shaft. The void that remained where his parents' support and pride in him had been was enormous, and it was supplanted only by pain and loss. He had never realized how much they had to do with how he felt about himself, nor had he understood how many of the things he did, especially in the area of scholastic performance, were geared to garner their approval.

Uncertainty regarding his financial condition also accompanied him home. Ward, Bowman, and Chet had each urged him not to worry about his finances, and Bowman had been heartened when he found two $50,000 and three $10,000 life insurance policies on his father when he, Tom and Ward had gone to Johnny's office the night before the funeral and had searched his unlocked office safe. Ward, however, who said only that he had had talks with his close friend about his financial status, expressed the dual fears that all of the policies might not still be in force and that there could be cash value loans against them that would deplete their face value. He also warned that there were probably bank loans that would need to be paid off from the life insurance proceeds. A check of the New Fredonia banks had found the three car loans only, though, and to Tom's relief after Ward explained its meaning to him, they found them all to be covered by credit life insurance.

At Bowman's suggestion, though, a call was placed to First State

Bank of Bethany. Ward's call was forwarded to George Collum, the bank president, who confirmed that Johnny had commercial loans at his bank. Collum was uncertain of the balance, but he took the opportunity to ask for Tom and to invite him to dinner Friday night. Thus it was that as Tom motored toward New Fredonia, the uncertainty of the outcome of his meeting scheduled for Saturday afternoon with his Uncle Bowman and with Rocky Woodward, his father's life insurance agent, to determine what he had, and with George Collum this evening to determine how much of what he had he would have to pay, weighed heavily upon him.

* * *

Tom rolled the Le Mans across the cattle guard under the "November Ridge Farm" sign and slowly followed the blacktop drive bordered on either side by symmetrically spaced young live oaks to the circular drive in front of the Collums' two-story farmhouse. Tom perceived an easy, comforting warmth about the house that seemed to be extending its own welcome to him. Its fresh coat of white paint - accented by dark green shutters - glistened, reflecting the yellow and peach hues of the early evening sky. Attired in shirt and tie, he tentatively ascended the steps to the expansive pewter-colored wood plank porch. A well-worn wooden swing was suspended from the bend in the porch before it wrapped around and continued down the side of the house.

Anna Collum answered Tom's rap as if she had seen him arrive and was waiting behind the door. The warmth in her dark brown eyes and in her genuine smile seemed familiar to Tom, but he could not place her. With broad shoulders emphasized by her shaft-like erectness and with her salt-and-pepper hair cut handsomely short, Tom was surprised by how attractive an elderly woman in her mid-forties could be. "Oh, Tom," she said, touching his shoulder to steer him into the house. "We're so glad you could come."

"Well, thank you for the invitation," he replied. Stepping into the foyer he glanced right at the antique-laden parlor and then at the dining room to the left furnished in Duncan Fyfe mahogany, a variation on which sat empty at his house.

George Collum descended the stairs in slacks and shirtsleeves. Now seeing the gentle, round visage of his father's friend next to his hostess, Tom remembered clearly the one time he had met George Collum and his wife Anna. They had come to his house to pay their respects the day after Mark died. For Tom, that day and the day of the funeral that followed had been a nightmarish time of a house absent Mark but filled with strangers, of tearfully grief-stricken displays by distant relatives he had not seen before or since, of the shock of smelling salts during the viewing of his brother, of upsetting speculations overheard. But into that cauldron had come a couple who quietly had given his mother, his father and Tom comfort. He remembered not a word that they had spoken to him. He did remember the sincerity of their concern, the warmth of Anna Collum's embrace, and the understanding among the five of them that there really were no words.

Tom shook the memory clear while absorbing the sincerity of their welcome. Extending a meaty hand the friendly banker from Bethany, his hair thinning toward middle age, asked jovially, "Well, Tom, are you here for dinner, or are you here for a loan?" Having caught Tom off guard, he went on quickly to point out, "The tie, the tie. Don't you know you're only supposed to wear one of those when you go to church or when you go to the bank to get a loan?"

"Oh," Tom laughed nervously.

"Don't you want to take that off or loosen it or something to get comfortable?"

"Oh, but he looks so nice in it," Anna said, and the tie stayed. "Dinner's almost ready," she added as Tom breathed in the aromas of fresh vegetables, baked bread and dessert. "Why don't you men go wait in the den and let me bring you something to drink? What would you like? We have lemonade, iced tea or ice water, and let's see, I'm not sure what soft drinks we have."

George called up in a loud voice, "What color sody water we have, darlin'?"

"Dr. Pepper and R-C Cola," came the disembodied response of a girl from above.

"Well, when are you coming down here?"

"Be down in a minute."

"Better hurry," George urged loudly. "We reeled in a live one, and he looks like a keeper. You'll want to bring your net."

"Oh, Daddy," came the exasperated reply, equaled by Anna Collum's shrug, "George."

"I'd love some lemonade," Tom finally answered.

After picking up their sweaty glasses of lemonade in the kitchen, George led Tom to the den, which had been converted from an open porch on the back of the farmhouse. Its expansive paned-glass wall above knotty pine wainscoting looked out on a manicured back yard of dark St. Augustine grass bordered on the back by more white plank fencing with a meadow rolling off behind it. In the background below the dusky sky was a tall stand of hardwood. Like the freshly painted house, its new bright green spring foliage was made luminescent by the sun's last gasp.

"What a view," Tom said.

"Thanks, but you ought to see it in autumn," George stated. "Those big oaks were there when we got here. Shoot, they were probably there when Anna's parents first settled this land, and Anna and I have been slipping in all those maples you see - the real bright ones. That's what we named the place for - November Ridge. Come back out here 'round the end of October, first of November. That ridge'll put on a show for you."

"Did you cut out the pine?" Tom asked, trying to contribute.

"Anna's dad did that - way back."

Tom knew he had to ask George Collum how much his father owed the bank. Building up his courage to enter this latest uncharted realm, Tom could feel his face heating and his throat drying in spite of the lemonade. "I really appreciate your inviting me out here, Mr. Collum," Tom began shakily. "Have you had a chance to -"

"Hey, fellas," came the playful voice of a girl from behind them.

Spinning, Tom was greeted by an insouciant grin and mischievous green eyes. Her thick strawberry blonde hair was cut short. Coupled with her eyes, her freckled cheeks and thin turned-up nose, Tom read Elizabeth Collum instantly as pert, verging on frisky, and he liked what he read.

"A dress!" George proclaimed, grabbing his heart. "The girl wore a dress."

"Why sure I did, Pops. We are entertaining a ... customer, aren't we?"

Shaking his head and covering his eyes, George made waving hand signs to introduce them. "Elizabeth, Tom Windham. Tom, my daughter, Elizabeth Collum. As you can obviously see, she's handling public relations for the bank."

"Lizza," she reminded Tom with a whisper.

Vaguely recognizing her, Tom realized that she had changed markedly since last he had seen her at Harvest two or three years prior. Her minidress suggested a lithe figure, and, as she stepped down into the den to join them, Tom was cheered to note her height in flats being a good three or four inches short of his.

"Remember me?" she asked, holding her hand on a plane several inches below her eyes.

"Remember me?" Tom replied, mimicking her.

"Weren't you the one I saw upchucking when you got off the Hammer at Harvest a couple of years ago?" she asked with a denigrating grin.

"Certainly not," he replied. "It was the Tilt-A-Whirl. I never even made it to the Hammer."

George continued to shake his head, looking skyward as the young pair shared a laugh.

"Are you going to take any summer school at Stover?" Tom asked.

"Nope," she replied with a carefree twirl. "Just going to lay around and let Pearl fatten me up before they pack me off to Missouri."

"We'll see about that, young lady," her father interjected. "I think I've got a teller window with your name on it about three or four hours a day this summer."

"Dinner is served," Anna called from the kitchen.

Over a delicious meal of pot roast, Kentucky Wonder green beans, mashed potatoes, and cornbread, the seriousness and the stiffness of the visitor was obvious to all at the table. George had dealt with young men who had no business knowledge but who tried to act like they did. And Anna understood the unnaturalness and confusion of grief and of loss. But Lizza could only compare Tom to her peers, and she found this persona simply boring.

No references were made to Tom's parents, but George did hold forth on Johnny's title business sufficiently to determine that Tom knew nothing about it either. As a consequence he offered his assistance whether Tom planned to sell it, to lease it, or to attempt letting his father's assistant manager operate it for him. The discussion brought home to Tom how much he now wished he had accepted any one of his father's many offers to teach him the business. As George's discourse dragged on through dessert - a succulent lattice-crusted apple pie, taken with ice cream by Lizza, plain by Tom, and with slices of cheddar cheese melted on top by the host couple - with Tom courteously attentive and Anna dutifully nodding and agreeing, Lizza became restless.

Fidgeting with her silverware, her napkin, her clothing, she began finally to watch Tom as he watched her father. Observing him closely across the table from her, but turned toward her father, she noted the occasional breaks in concentration as his focus would fix in a distant stare somewhere through and beyond George, and as he occasionally pushed his fingers hard against his forehead and closed his eyes. She even tried placing herself in his situation. The maturity of that approach was beyond her capability for more than a few seconds at a time and the depth of her empathy was shallow. Glancing to either end of the table and imagining both of her parents suddenly gone, though, was empathy enough. The exercise, at least, was sufficient to give her the insight that the Tom Windham she had met this night was most likely not the Tom she would meet under almost any other circumstances.

"... so the title 'bidness' around here pretty much rises and falls with the amount of activity in land sales and oil and gas leasing," George explained to a studiedly serious Tom Windham.

Finding a momentary gap in her father's monologue, Lizza broke in and said, "Tom," and cocking her head with an offbeat smile, asked, "would you like to go to Six Flags tomorrow?"

Tom and his adult hosts had been raised Southern Baptist, so they understood the codes of mourning. The rules were strict, and they were expected to be followed by those among family, friends, and acquaintances given the heavy burden of keeping the mourners in line. It was as if there were, delineated somewhere in the Book of Ecclesiastes, lengths of time from date of death to the acceptability of various activities; and the more public fun the activity entailed, the longer the waiting period. And Ecclesiastes had pushed theme parks far down the list.

"Elizabeth," her mother scolded, with a reflexive, but unintended harshness. She went no further, though, thinking it unnecessary to state the obvious.

Tom, who at the moment of her question, while masking his face with interest in George's discourse, was actually wondering how much his father owed First State Bank and when he was going to find out. Caught off guard by Lizza's offer, he replied with a confused frown.

Misreading his guest's expression as being injury at his daughter's insensitivity to his grief, George came down hard and parental. "Elizabeth, I'd appreciate you not interrupting me, and under the circumstances I think that was an inappropriate question. I apologize for my daughter, Tom."

Waving his hands in front of him, Tom ignored all the subtext and answered Lizza directly, "No, I can't, Eliz- Lizza. I've got an appointment in the middle of the afternoon tomorrow at my dad's office that I've got to keep. But thanks."

Still absorbing her father's disapproval, Lizza replied meekly, "Okay. You just looked like you could use some fun. Sorry."

Before Tom could reply further, Anna said, "Elizabeth, why don't you help me pick up the dishes," giving her request the appearance of punishment.

"Sure, Mom," she replied, as Tom lifted his dessert plate and started to scoot his chair back.

"No, no," Anna protested, waving him away with the back of her hand. "You men go on in the den. We'll take care of this." Flashing instantly to Edna Ferber's *Giant*, Tom smiled into himself at the possibility of Lizza barging in to join in on the "man talk" and his having to tell her, in the pompous judge's voice, "not to worry your pretty little head" about it. But additionally, Tom felt a furtive enjoyment of this piece of playing "grown-up" in which he was about to engage. His fear, though, besides the likelihood that this was the time George Collum would inform him of his inherited indebtedness to the bank, was that he might also offer him a cigar.

As George waited for Anna to bring him coffee, after Tom had pleaded fullness, the men made small talk. Once his coffee was in hand, though, and the women were in the kitchen, George gently began, "Well, Tom, I figure we better talk over this debt your dad had at the bank."

"Yes sir."

"We consolidated his loans the last time they were up for renewal, and the total is right at ... thirty thousand dollars. A bit more including interest." George studied Tom's expression for reaction, but his poker face was holding up. "It's secured by the farm and the cattle and the equipment - you know, the tractor and the accessories and whatnot. Like

I said, we consolidated it several months ago ... but right now, it's in a past due status."

The granite cracking, Tom asked, "You mean I have to pay it right now?"

"No, no, Son," George assured him, giving him a pat on the shoulder. "We'll work with you as much as we need to. Have you found out about your dad's life insurance yet?"

"No, nothing for certain, but I'll find out tomorrow. Uncle Bowman and I are meeting with Rocky Woodward."

George nodded, "Well, I don't know what your plans were as far as the farm or the cattle were concerned ..." George droned on about interest rates and repayment options, but they barely registered.

Tom experienced what had become the familiar tight dryness in his throat. The number sounded astronomical. His worst case fear that his father's insurance policies were no longer in effect distracted him from participating with more than nods and shakes of the head and rote replies through the remainder of the evening's conversation even after Lizza and her mother had rejoined them. With anxiety about his finances and with the now-familiar throbbing pain blasting away at his forehead like a jackhammer on the verge of breaking through, Tom excused himself early, leaving Lizza to read his distraction and the brevity of his visit as disinterest.

Chapter 29

After being coddled through breakfast by Aunt Nela, Tom drove to the post office to collect the family's personal mail before meeting with Helen Meisel, his father's office manager. Opening the box door he was surprised at the sizeable stack of mail that had accumulated since he had last checked it on Wednesday. Neiman-Marcus, Tiche-Goettinger, Dreyfuss & Sons, the Coachman's Shoppe, where he had bought many of his college clothes, and Rolf's, where his mother shopped, were all heard from. Also included were statements from their dentist and from a doctor in Springfield. Sifting through them, Tom continued to find more bills before he finally realized that it was just past the first of the month, and, therefore, a normal volume. The thought relieved him slightly - until he started opening them.

At the raised table in the common area of the post office lobby Tom examined the contents. Anxiety coursed through him as he counted up hundreds and then more than a thousand dollars in charges - mostly past due and several containing warnings or threats stamped in red or hand-written on the statements. The same was true of the doctors' bills. Especially upsetting to him was the Coachman's Shoppe statement because he knew it could only be for the sports coat and slacks he had bought there over semester break in January. Staggered and embarrassed lest any of the townspeople who walked past him might discover this awful secret - or, worse still, might already be aware of it, he reinserted each bill and payment envelope and grasped them tightly to him as he left the building.

Walking up the sidewalk toward his car, though, he was confronted by D.R. Affectionately known through Tom's youth by him and his cohorts as "The Village Idiot", D.R. was a slow-minded doer of odd jobs whom the town - by common, unspoken consent - supported with menial labor, hand-me-down clothes and a rotating non-system of free meals. Johnny Windham had been among his principal sponsors, and D.R. knew Tom and always greeted him with respect, Tom thought, beyond his age or station. To this twenty-year-old whom he had always called "Tom", D.R. hailed him this morning as "Mister Tom", and Tom felt again a mantle being passed. Upset though he was by the burden of the envelopes he carried, Tom stopped to greet D.R.

"Oh, Mister Tom," D.R. began, the tears already welling in his eyes. "I loved your daddy and your momma. They were surely the kindest on God's green earth. Loved your folks. Miss 'em for the rest o' my life; every day o' my life." Indignation came into his voice as he stated, "An' I'll never fly in one o' them airplanes. Never," he repeated, extending his arms as if they were wings.

Tom backed away and glanced around in embarrassment at the foot traffic that gave them a wide berth.

"Promise me you'll never fly in one o' them planes, Mister Tom. Promise me."

Escape became Tom's only goal. He began walking again toward his car, but D.R. walked crab-like along the pavement beside him.

"I knew them things wasn't safe. I always knew. I'd o' never flied in one. Wish I'd warned your daddy and your momma not to."

"Thanks, D.R.," Tom said. "I've got to go." He turned and walked directly across the street toward the courthouse, even though it was away from his car.

"Good day, Mister Tom," he heard D.R. yell after him. "Remember what I said! And promise! Promise me!"

Tom bowed his head and walked quickly across the brick street eliciting the blast of a pick-up's horn as he dodged between the heavy traffic of farmers and their families clogging the square on their weekly trip to town. Trotting onto the courthouse grounds, he ran up a slight incline and stood beneath a shade tree. Heaving deep breaths, he gathered himself for over a minute. He did not look back across the street both out of fear of being harangued further by D.R. and of seeing the watchful eyes of New Fredonia viewing him as the town's new curiosity - his actions and reactions to such incidents providing fodder for its gossip mill.

*   *   *

As his trusty Le Mans cut a path through The Esses midway through The Course, Tom found it difficult to shake the anxiety that the morning's revelations and events had dumped atop the burden of debt of which George Collum had apprised him the night before. After escaping D.R. at the post office, Tom had walked shakily to Stover County Title Company on a side street off the square. There he had met with Helen Meisel, his father's office manager and assistant. The nauseatingly sweet fragrance of her heavily perfumed hug was still on his shirt as he sniffed and shuddered while driving. Having been provided the questions to ask her by Ward and Bowman, Tom was disappointed to learn that his father had done the vast majority of the title work that flowed out of the office. Further, Helen had felt neither capable of nor inclined to pick up the slack by herself. In her early sixties and a chain smoker in failing health, she also had revealed her intention to retire within two or three years. And of the options that George Collum had laid out for Tom regarding the future of the business, Helen had stated that Tom would need to hire a new manager with extensive title experience if he did not plan to sell or lease the business. Having said that, though, she had gone on to warn Tom that if he did not sell the business, whoever he hired as a manager or to whomever he leased it might try to steal the business from him. She had explained that the nature of the trade lent itself to that, and he remembered George Collum also making a veiled reference, which he had not understood at the time, that must have pertained to that danger. To cap off her apocalyptic litany, she had added that any of the attorneys in town might choose to go into competition with him if he did not swiftly move to restore the business to an active management.

After referring Tom to Johnny's loan officer at New Fredonia National Bank to add himself to the company's signature card, Helen had left him emphasizing again the importance of replacing his father with a manager capable of handling the workload as soon as possible. Having been warmly received at the bank by Carl Walther, a close friend of his father's whom Tom had known forever as a deacon at First Baptist, the funds which Tom had hoped he would find in the business and personal accounts and with which he had planned to bring his charge accounts current were measurable in hundreds and not thousands. With sensitivity and with respect for Tom's father, Carl had made clear to Tom that Johnny had been no manager of money. Leaving the bank with a red "$30,000" emblazoned across his mind's marquee, with "past due" flashing on and off in neon, with Helen's urgings to make a swift decision about the future course of the business plaguing him, and with D.R.'s lunatic ravings still ringing in his ears, Tom wanted only to escape.

Yet now, even here, alone in his old sanctuary - the cockpit of a coupe moving at speed - there was no getting away from his own mind, from the messages of panic and malaise that gripped him and would not let go. His distracted half-hour tour of The Course gave him no relief. His problems had chased him from the starting line and, nipping at his heels, had slipstreamed him relentlessly all the way around the county and back to the Carters' house where he arrived for lunch before he and his uncle were to meet Rocky Woodward. His last nightmarish daydream before walking in the door was of a giant auction of his house, the cars, the farm, and the cattle to pay his debts, and of being left with his father's business, which he would lose as a result of his inexperience. His aunt and uncle provided the lunchtime conversation and assumed his listlessness to be a bout of grief as he pushed his food around his plate.

*   *   *

"Johnny had double indemnity on the two big policies," the bright-eyed young insurance agent reported with a carefully respectful smile.

For a split second while he was asking "What's that?" and before he saw his uncle join Rocky Woodward in a relieved smile, Tom feared the meaning of "double indemnity" to be another negative - something that had invalidated the policies and made them worthless. Such an eventuality, Tom thought, would be perfectly in keeping with the revelations of the past twenty-four hours.

Patiently Rocky explained, "It means the face value of the policies - what you get for them - doubles in case of accidental death. Each of those fifty-thousand-dollar policies will pay one-hundred-thousand dollars. So, with the other three ten-thousand-dollar policies you'll be getting ... two-hundred-and-thirty-thousand dollars ... less the cash value loans on the policies."

Tom knew that he was supposed to ask the amount of the loans, but he was too speechless from relief to do so. "How much were those?" Bowman asked for him.

Glancing at his notes, Rocky answered, "Well, let's see, they come to about ... seventy-eight-hundred dollars. So you'll have over two-hundred-and-twenty-two-thousand dollars free and clear."

Tom feared that he would appear avaricious if he demonstrated the true extent of the relief that he felt, but the burden, which he had not spoken of with his aunt and uncle, lifted so suddenly that it took great restraint to keep from jumping with joy. "That's good," Tom sighed with governed relief and a facade of mature seriousness.

"Looks like Johnny took real good care of you, Tom," Bowman said.

"That's exactly right, Tom," Rocky added.

"Thanks, Mr. Woodward," Tom said humbly. "Thanks a lot."

"Listen, I've turned the claims in to the company. We ought to have your checks in the next few days. I'll give you a call and drop them by."

"Thanks," Tom nodded, the relief still sinking in as his uncle gave him a bear hug.

After a run through the DQ's drive-in window for celebratory Dr. Peppers, Tom and Bowman returned to the house.

"Lizza?" Tom asked into the receiver. "You want to go to Six Flags tomorrow?"

*   *   *

Their whirlwind trip to Six Flags on the other side of Dallas afforded Tom his most carefree hours of the past nine days. Rushing first to the Fort St. Louis river ride in the French section, which they had discovered on the drive over was a favorite of each of them, they enjoyed the predictably corny French accent of the river pilot/UT-Arlington student as well as the smoking flash of the fort's cannon followed by a cascading water spout within feet of their launch. They rode off their heavy lunch of greasy fried chicken in the Confederate section with an around-the-park train ride in its breezy open cars before jostling themselves unmercifully in the park's rail-guided jalopies. But as the early May afternoon grew sultry, they made their way for the ice tub-chilled watermelons, slices of which they downed ravenously and without benefit or hindrance of dining utensils. From there they made their way quickly to Six Flags' ultimate combination make-out/cool-off spot: The Cave Ride.

There, in the air-conditioned darkness in a bobbing boat that Tom had winked at an attendant to obtain for just the two of them, Lizza, sitting in front of Tom on the boat's single bow-to-stern bench, had leaned back into him and rested her head on his shoulder. Wrapping his arms around her tiny waist, he nuzzled her neck to her obvious pleasure as the miniature fluorescent spelunkers in the black-lighted displays looked on. With their craft nearing the snow scene, they shared a long, wet, watermelon-flavored kiss as the frigid Arctic winds of the ride's last feature blew across them. Tom felt the chillbumps roughen Lizza's arms as he held her. Emerging through the ride's conclusive double swinging doors into the light below dozens of hot, weary patrons awaiting their turn in the cool, Lizza's head rested on Tom's shoulder - her eyes closed and her lips wearing a blissful smile. Without opening her eyes she reached for his cheek and turned his face toward her waiting lips. As they kissed again, the overhanging crowd broke into a mix of laughter and applause. Bowing as they emerged from their boat, Tom shook his head, not in embarrassment, but in wonderment.

Leaving the ride they held hands and spoke less often, but they smiled at each other more. They picked the Runaway Mine Train as their last ride. By the end of it, though, Tom, who had hoped that his headaches had been caused by uncertainty about his finances and would, therefore, abate with the promise of the life insurance proceeds, felt the familiar stab of pain above his left eye. To make possible their trip while saving Tom an extra turnaround to Bethany and back, the Collums had followed them to Dallas and had dined and taken in a movie while Tom and Lizza did Six Flags. By the time they rendezvoused at NorthPark, Tom's headache was approaching full-blown, and he was barely able to disguise it during his brief chat with George and Anna in the theater parking lot.

As the Collums prepared to board for the trip home, Tom took Lizza's hand, squeezed it, and said with a warm smile, "I had a wonderful time. I'll see you in a couple of weeks, okay?"

Responding with a smile of relish, she replied, "You bet you will." Glancing insouciantly at her parents and then back at Tom, she leaned close to him and gave him a quick peck on the cheek. As George looked away and Anna gave them a syrupy smile, Lizza opened the back door and, lightly scraping a fingernail beneath Tom's chin, said, "So long, Sailor."

* * *

Monday morning at school without classes was a strange phenomenon for the 332 pair. Giving in to the need for more ordered study, though, they walked up campus at mid-morning toward their respective review sessions.

Passing the SUB, Tom asked, "Hey, want to check your mail?"

Sucking in his stomach and pulling his jeans out at the belt, Brandeis looked down and replied, "Mine's fine. How's yours?"

"God, Wasserman, you're gross!"

Tom pulled two envelopes from his box. Under his telephone bill was a letter from Clair. He walked to a nearby common area and opened it.

> *Dear Tom,*
>
> *I cannot begin to tell you how sorry I am about the loss of your parents. They were wonderful people, and I know they loved you very much. I have such wonderful memories of them and of the way they treated me. Like all of those whose lives they touched, I will never forget them.*
>
> *Tom, I can only imagine what a hard time this is for you. I am so glad you have the Carters and Chet and all your friends to help you through this. I hope you count me as one of those friends, and I hope you know I would do whatever I could to help you. I would really like to see you, if you would like to. I've missed our talks, and Gramma has missed you, too. She is doing fine, and she often speaks of you.*
>
> *I hope you know you're always in my thoughts and prayers. I'm never far away. I have probably said too much. I really just want you to know how much my heart goes out to you.*
>
> *Clair*

Chapter 30

Mid-May

The warm wind out of the south rustled the Coastal Bermuda grass that the spring's showers and sun had beckoned forth. Rolling through the open gate of his farm in his father's Ranchero, Tom saw the battered, rusting pick-up of Bailey Harper parked next to the corral. Coming to a stop on the road near the shed, Tom returned his wave as Bailey dismounted his Ford truck.

"Howdy, Tom Roy," the weathered cowboy said through a tobacco-stained smile. Under the beat-up straw hat to which the season had recently signaled his changing was the familiar tan, leathered face of Stover County's resident professional cattleman. Bailey offered a rope-and-reins-toughened hand to which Tom replied with his while holding his ground against the overpowering aroma of freshly spat tobacco juice.

Bailey Harper knew cattle. It was a fact of life, as it had been for more than twenty years, that if anyone in the county needed to buy, sell or trade cattle, move cattle, appraise them, or even feed them while the owner was out of town, the man to know and the man "to be in good with" was Bailey Harper. Now in his late forties he was indispensable to the corps of serious weekend farmers, like Johnny Windham had been, as well as to the growing trickle of retirees who had started buying up Stover County farms and pastureland in hopes of living out their dreams as Texas cattlemen while enjoying their retirement in the quiet, verdant beauty of East Texas.

At Johnny's death it had not even been necessary to place a call to Bailey Harper, Bowman had told Tom. Bailey had immediately started checking the cattle daily, and, though the available grazing provided for most of their needs, he had perfect familiarity with Johnny's supplemental feeding as well.

"Good afternoon, Mr. Harper. I really apprec- "

"Aw, Tom Roy," he said, with a hint of injury, "That's 'Bailey'. It'll always and only be 'Bailey' to you."

"Thanks, Bailey," Tom said with a smile. Tom reacted differently with each of these moments of transition as he grappled with the manhood he had been left to assume three weeks prior. This one he enjoyed.

So, what can I do for you, Son?"

"Well, first I want to tell you how much I appreciate your taking care of the cattle these last few weeks. It's been real comforting knowing they were in good hands. And, of course, just let me know how much your feed costs were or let me have your feed bill or whatever, and I'll write you a check for that - today - or as soon as you can give me an amount."

Looking down and shaking his head while the point of his boot blasted apart a petrified cow chip glazed to the sandstone lane where they stood, Bailey answered, "Aw, you don't owe me anything for that. Wasn't nothin' Johnny wouldn't have done for me."

"No, Mr. Har- No, Bailey, really, I insist. I'll pay you whatever it's cost you."

He stared back at Tom with the hint of a smile playing on his lips. His liquid blue eyes were deep-set under heavy, greying eyebrows. His eyelids folded down at the corners and led to fans of creases up his temples and down his cheeks from a lifetime filled with days of sun and nights of laughter. "What can I do for you this evening?" he asked.

Tom finally mirrored his easy smile and said, "Well, I need for you to sell the cattle."

His hands stuffed in the back pockets of his faded jeans, Bailey nodded as he took another poke of his boot at the remainder of the dried manure. "Be glad to do it," he said, and followed with a spit. "I'll take 'em over to the auction next week."

"How many head do we have?" Tom asked. "Seems like at Easter Dad said it was about fifteen or so."

Bailey continued nodding and, squinting his eyes in calculation, said, "Yeah, you got the ol' bully boy and then eight momma cows and their calves. How's ever'thing else going for you. I mean, I'll take care of this. You know that."

"I know, and I'm grateful. This helps a lot. Everything else'll work out."

"Well," Bailey said, "I can sure handle the rest for you. 'Bout the only other thing I can offer you is, whenever things get too tight for you, why don't you just come on over to the house some morning about seven and 'go around' with me one day."

Tom knew from descriptions passed down from his father that to "go around" with Bailey Harper was to spend the day driving from farm to farm and pasture to pasture that he owned, leased or serviced for an owner. It entailed feeding cattle, checking on sick ones, making minor repairs, and generally "just piddlin'", while stopping frequently for coffee breaks at the Swan and at a sprinkling of the small cafes and general stores around the county.

As an added enticement, Bailey laughed and said, "I can always use me a good gate-opener."

"I'll probably take you up on that," Tom allowed.

"Well, I mean it. It's a firm offer, and don't forget it. It'll sure take your mind off things. Johnny went around with me once or twice, and we had ourselves a time." Walking away and refitting his hat, Bailey rewarded Tom with the rare view of his sweaty greying hair and his bald spot in back, pale white from its rare views of the sun. Waving as he began to mount his truck, Bailey stopped, turned and said, "Tom Roy."

"Yes," Tom replied with a quizzical tilt of his head at Bailey's serious tone and look.

Returning toward him, Bailey shook his head and said, "Anybody in the county'll tell you, 'Bailey Harper's not one to mettle in another man's bidness'." Winning Tom's nodding assent, he went on, "But I have to ask you. Are you planning on selling ... The Land?" As he asked, Bailey spread his hands out palms up and looked slowly from side to side at the farm.

Noting the worshipful tone in which he referred to it, Tom answered respectfully, "Well, I had thought I would. Mr. Brannigan thinks I should." After a hesitation, Tom asked, "Why? What do you think?"

With a half-laugh Bailey offered, "Aw, Tom Roy, I don't want to confuse you or make your life any harder. You got enough weighing on your mind as it is. I'll just say, God's not making any more of it, and this here's one of the prettiest patches of Land in East Texas. Plus," he added with reverence, "over the years your daddy put a whole lot of himself into this Land." After a hesitation, he concluded, "And if you're ever looking for him, you can find him here."

Taking a slow, sweeping look around him at the pasture sloping gently across the road to the overgrown woods where he and Mark had played "Jungle", Tom replied quietly, "Thanks, Bailey. I appreciate your ... Well, anyway, thanks."

"Hope I haven't said too much. I'll be going along now." He waved again with his hat and boarded his pick-up.

After Bailey left, Tom walked slowly upmeadow to his neighbor's fence line at the highest point of the front pasture. He glanced east at the top of the lakehouse's roof barely visible above the pine-covered hillock that shielded the lake and the house from view from the farm-to-market road that ran in front of the farm. Tom had not been inside the lakehouse since Easter. He did not know when he would again, but he felt that he could.

Turning west, the setting sun was a glossy red-orange ball penetrating the twilight's haze with fields of peach and violet emanating from it. As he stood alone on the breeze-brushed front pasture watching the sun tuck behind distant green hills, for the first time Tom began to consider keeping the farm.

*   *   *

Having completed a circuit of White Rock Lake on the three-speed Schwinns she had rented for them for the day, Siobhan and Brandeis emptied the bicycles' baskets of the picnic she had prepared earlier this Saturday morning at the White Rock Lake cottage. Spreading a quilt on a grassy expanse sloping gently toward the lake, the lovers sprawled on it below the midday sun while their bikes grazed nearby. They nuzzled and necked between courses, eliciting occasional honks and whoops from passersby on Lawther Drive, which encircled the lake.

After lunch they lay beside each other - her head on his arm, and their faces turned away from the sun. They rested silently for several minutes before Brandeis asked, "Now tell me your schedule again for the next few weeks? It wears me out every time I hear it, but I like to know where you are."

"Leaving here for San Francisco tomorrow morning," Siobhan reiterated. "Spend the week working in the Kennedy campaign headquarters and doing some canvassing, I think in Marin County. Then back home for a week. Then back down here to register for summer school, and then I'll just try to get a feel for whether I could go back out to California for Primary Day - or if I need to stay here and jump hot 'n' heavy into my classes. You know how concentrated those six-week courses are." The gleam that appeared in her eyes told Brandeis she had shifted gears, as she decreed, "Bobby's just got to win California. If he can do that, he can take it all. He could really get the nomination." After a solemn moment, she went on, "And he could *really* change things - bring out the best in us." Her face falling, she added, "And if he didn't - but he will - but if he didn't ... I just don't think there's any way they would nominate Clean Gene. And you know what that would mean. 'Same-song-second-verse' Hubert," she sang derisively. "More of the same old 'defending-failed-policies' Hubert. Good ol' Hubert 'surrogate-L-B-J' Humphrey." Brandeis rolled over and kissed her on the mouth, terminating her rhetoric.

"Oooo, I liked that. Anyway, after that I'll be here for the duration. Five weeks of just me, Commercial Banking, and Wolfgang Amadeus Mozart." Twisting a coil of hair at the base of his neck, Siobhan asked hopefully, "And you *are* going to be able to come down one weekend in June? For sure?"

After a hesitation, Brandeis answered, "Yeah," with a tentative hitch in his voice. "Yeah, I'm pretty sure I can."

Siobhan's expression betrayed her upset over the uncertainty of his answer, but she forged ahead nonetheless. "You've just got to come. I just ... I don't think I could bear not seeing you for ... months. And if you can, I could come by Memphis around the middle of July. I'm going to be driving home at the end of summer school." His expression remained distant. "What is it? Don't you want me to?"

"Of course, I want to see you, Siobhan. You just don't know my mother."

"Bran, we've talked about getting married. Someday I'm going to have to know your mother."

"I know. I want you to know her," he said. "But you just don't understand what she's like. I'm sorry I haven't talked to you more about her before. But I've told you some of the stuff she said about this summer. I'm just lucky I'm going to be clerking in my father's office and that I'm not going to be off raising cabbage on the Golan Heights with a tommy gun slung over my shoulder. Listen, however this summer works out, everything'll be fine in September. We'll be back together, and I'll be all yours."

"Do you really want to marry me someday?" Siobhan asked as, with a shake of her head, the breeze off the lake blew her hair clear of her face.

"Of course, I do. That's what I want - more than anything."

"Well, Bran, when we get married, I'm going to want you for twelve months a year, and not just nine."

"That's what I want, too," he said, shaking his head. "You just don't understand."

"Bran, I need you. Do you need me at all?"

"I do, Baby," he said, pulling her to him and pressing her softness against him. "God, I'm going miss this."

After a kiss she asked, "Are you going to miss *me*, too? You could probably find someone else who could give you *this*."

Pulling away, he replied, "I'm going to miss *you*. That's what I mean. I'm going to miss *you*." Holding her tightly again, he asked gently, "But aren't you going to miss this, too?"

"Hell, yes I am," she whispered, burying her face in his neck. "I want to marry you so much. It's so hard to wait. I can just see the reception now. After the priest gives you the glass to stomp and the rabbi crosses himself, Paddy'll walk in and see us dancing in a circle, and I can just hear him yelling in his Irish brogue, 'Aye and Begorrah, they're dancin' the Horah!'" Again reflective, though, Siobhan added, "But it's not going to be easy ... getting to that wedding day, is it?"

Shaking his head, Brandeis asked, "How much do your parents know about me? And about us?"

"A lot. And enough."

"And how do they feel?"

"It really caught them off guard," she sighed. "But, they want me to be happy. And they can tell, you make me very happy. How about yours?" she asked carefully.

"Mine - well, my mother, hasn't come around that far." Tightening his jaw and looking away, he added, "She may be a little less interested in me being happy."

With her voice again filled with emotion, Siobhan cried, "Bran, what's going to happen to us?"

"We'll just see each other when we can, if we can, and we'll talk on the phone when we can, and we'll write."

Holding herself tightly to his side and pressing her face into his neck and his hair, Siobhan said, "Hold me, Bran. I'm really scared for us. For the first time, I'm really scared."

*   *   *

The roommates of 332 McCartney met there one last time to clean out their belongings before turning it over to a series of pep squad, cheerleader and sports camps that would occupy it for the summer.

"So how'd your appointment go with the brain man?" Brandeis asked.

"Just as you've always suspected. The E-E-G came back negative. No brainwave activity whatsoever," Tom laughed. "No, he didn't find anything. He just said, 'yep, you got a lot of heavy stuff on your mind. Just your basic tension and stress. It can come out as a headache, as a backache, as a stiff neck, as a stomach ulcer, or," Tom added, grinning sardonically, "you can take a high-powered rifle to the top of a tall building and start picking people off. It can manifest itself in a lot of ways. Mine just happens to bang me over the head. He ... did suggest maybe I go talk to a ... psychiatrist".

Brandeis buckled his lip and nodded. "Are you going to?"

"It's just real hard for me to bring myself to the idea of doing that. Mark talked to one a couple of times. Didn't seem to help *him* any. Does yours help you?"

Brandeis thought for a moment before replying, "He hasn't changed that much in my life. I guess he's probably just helped me deal with some things that aren't going to change - some things I don't have any control over."

"Well, there you are," Tom said smugly. "I got control over everything in my life. Boy, do I."

"Do you have control over everything that shoots through your mind?"

Tom looked out the window. After a long lapse, he looked back at Brandeis and said, "Really sorry I missed Siobhan this morning. I got away a little later to come back over here than I thought I would. I'm supposed to go out and see Ward this evening."

"She was sorry she missed you, too."

"How are y'all going to be able to go all summer without seeing each other?"

"Ohhh, I told her I was going to ... try to come down here once next month. And she mentioned something about stopping through Memphis on her way back to Chicago in July."

"Are you going to be able to get those past your mother?"

"No," Brandeis answered as he took his turn to look out the window in thought. "I don't know. Maybe. I really don't know. Please check on her when you come over here, will you?"

"Sure," Tom nodded. "You know I will."

"No, we'll just have to see how the summer plays itself out. I know it's going to be hell for you."

Pulling out a thick wad of currency from one pocket and a green-tinted medicine bottle from another, Tom said with a twinkle in his eyes, "Well, at least I've got a pocket full o' miracles. And ... if they can't make me happy, at least they can make me laugh a lot about how sad I am."

"What's in the bottle?" Brandeis asked.

"Darvon."

Wonderful," Brandeis laughed. "Money and drugs. The American Dream." His smile fading, he asked, "Does it help?"

"I don't know. I just got it filled. It seemed to have knocked one out, but it came back. We'll see. The doctor said there were some others we could try if this one doesn't work."

"Good. So, you're enjoying seeing Lizza?"

"Yeah. She's a lot of fun, and her parents are just incredibly nice to me."

"So where does that leave Clair?" Brandeis asked.

"Probably leaves her right where she chose to be - with Gene Ray Driggers. Although I did get a nice letter from her. You know, about Mom and Dad."

"You think you'll see her this summer?"

"It's a small county," he began, and shaking his head, he said, "and who knows. I've given up on being surprised. So, how'd your grades come out?"

"I think I pulled a three-point-eight. How about you?"

"Wow," Tom exhaled. "Looks like I'll get a three-point-o. I think I'll get a 'C' in Biology, but looks like I pulled an 'A' in Briggs' class. The rest 'B's'."

"That's great, Tom. What with everything ..."

Nodding restlessly, Tom said, "Yeah, well, you think the little Sprite's going to make it back up to Memphis?"

Crossing his fingers, Brandeis answered, "Good point. Why don't you follow me out to the interstate, just in case. I think if I can get it out to I-30, it'll probably roll all the way. Especially on the downhill sections." As they rose to walk toward the door, though, Brandeis pulled a crumpled envelope from his back pocket. "Oh, yeah," he laughed. "Almost forgot. A going away message for you from The Cowboy."

"Joe Joe?" Tom asked. "He writes?" He opened it quickly and read:

Tomcat - How's it hanging? I've gone rodeoing. See you in Sept. But don't you come back here without a notch on your dick and a beaver pelt hanging off your belt.

Destroy this note,

JJ

With Tom's car packed and Brandeis' trunk already on a bus to Memphis, the roommates walked out. Brandeis paused after letting Tom out the door. He looked back in and said, "So long, 332," and he glanced at the plyboard above him.

Descending the steps, they ran into Rodg Messing on his way up. "Are you two guys finally checking out?"

"Yeah," Brandeis answered. "We left the key on the dresser, bellhop, and we stole all the towels. I guess you're hanging around for your tip."

"Hey, you're the last ones out of here. I can shut it down now."

"It's been a trip," Brandeis said, offering his hand.

Nodding, Rodg shook his hand and said, "Wouldn't have missed it for anything. Especially enjoyed having 'the little fat boy ' over now and then." As Brandeis' and Tom's eyes bugged out, Rodg burst into laughter which was quickly joined by theirs. As the laughter slowed, Rodg said to Brandeis, "Hey, I need to talk with Tom for a minute, okay?"

Nervously shaking his hand again, Brandeis said, "Sure. See you down at the car, Roomie," and continued down the stairs.

Remembering and appreciating that Rodg's expression of sympathy had been brief and subtle, Tom was reluctant to hear what might be coming. But he found that he still could be surprised as Rodg turned to him and said, "Tom, I read your 'letter to the editor'. It was in the last issue of *Cat Tracks*." Touching his shoulder and reaching out his hand, Rodg declared, "I was very proud of you."

Embarrassed, but in awe of receiving Rodg's blessing, Tom replied only, "Thanks," as they shook hands. Tom looked into the intelligent, clear blue eyes of this one whom he had selected as his example of the perfect blending of idealism and intellect. Tom was almost overcome as he accepted this valedictory plaudit from Rodg Messing. Searching for words, Tom finally asked, "Well, off to the Peace Corps?"

Through the thick glasses that Tom had heard won him a 1-Y deferment, Tom saw the missionary's peace cloaked in determination, as Rodg replied, "No, the Medic Corps."

Chapter 31

Late May

Tom sat on the toilet flipping playing cards toward the upturned fedora a few feet from him on the floor. He had picked up the hat at his house during a trip to gather some of his clothes to bring back to the Carters' where he was now occupying Chet's old room. He could barely remember his father in this style hat. More present in his memory were the narrow brimmed hats of the Fifties and early Sixties that Johnny had liked and had worn until John Kennedy's bare-headed good looks followed immediately by the Beatles' "mop tops" had mortally wounded that fashion for men.

Sitting there in Chet's old bathroom Tom rolled over in his mind the ground he and Ward Brannigan had covered in the past few weeks, but he also reviewed the much lengthier mental list of "to do's" facing him. In a brief, awkward courtroom ceremony in which testimony was given by several of his father's Swan Cafe cronies, Tom's minority status had been waived and an Affadavit of Heirship was authorized by the court, his parents having died intestate and Tom being their sole heir. He had received his insurance checks and immediately paid his father's bank loans. Depositing sufficient amounts in his student account, he had paid all the bills he received. At Ward's suggestion he had put most of the remainder in short-term certificates of deposit while they decided what to do next. Credit life insurance had paid the car loans, and Tom had left his parents' cars in the garage at his house, occasionally using the

Ranchero for hauling and for trips to the farm. The overawing problem was the disposition of the title business. Helen Meisel was grudgingly handling the day-to-day operation and performing the title work, but she continued to make clear that her performance of those roles was a stopgap measure. The need for a permanent solution was a cloud that shadowed Tom constantly. And beyond that, there was the matter of the sale of the house and the farm. Regarding the house, there was no question. Tom was going to sell it. He knew there were no circumstances under which he would ever even spend another night in it, much less live in it again. But the farm was a different matter, as his meeting with Bailey Harper had told him.

Bowman routinely deferred to Ward's judgment and business acumen in all such matters. Drawing from a void of business experience, Tom took Ward's advice - despite his perfunctory but oft-stated disclaimer that it was Tom's property and, therefore, Tom's decision - as the financially correct and economically sound course to take. Consequently, the burden of justifying decisions adverse to Ward's counsel was entirely on Tom. As he toured Dallas with the Brannigans – dining out with them, going to Ward's office, going to the bank - aboard his gargantuan powder blue Lincoln-Continental, Ward told Tom tales of his most successful coups as a stockbroker. And given Ward's background, he had scant patience for real estate's illiquidity and for the headaches of milking enough revenue from it to cover its carrying costs during its typically lengthy holding period. His idea for Tom was to get as liquid as possible by selling his farm and his house. With the funds generated from the sales, along with the life insurance proceeds and the anticipated airline settlement, Ward offered to let Tom in on some of his "most sure-fire" stock deals while investing a portion of the remainder in blue chip stocks and holding the rest in a safety net of conservative interest-earning securities. Dazzled by the litany of high-profit, short-term stock transactions that Ward recounted proudly, Tom entertained visions of wealth untold in his future. Replaying the spiel to an intimidated Uncle Bowman and a wary Aunt Nela, Tom parroted Ward's prescription for "making money while you sleep".

Finally, there was the decision regarding legal action against Global Airlines. Ward had led Tom on a brief tour through the scenario of "threaten, file, bluff, and settle". It all sounded very cynical to the college student. Ward had early dispelled any notion Tom might have had of inflicting financial pain on the airline. He explained that the airline's insurers would pay the settlement. The insurance carriers might then raise the premiums on the airlines. But the airlines would then pass the increases back to their customers in the form of higher ticket prices. Since the settlement would not, therefore, have the punitive effect Tom wished, Ward had counseled that he needed to remove himself from the attitude of trying to right a personal wrong and think more in terms of simply gouging the insurance carrier for as large a settlement as they could obtain. Tom gratefully accepted his offer to contact an attorney with the law firm he used to handle the negotiations.

The missing link in the picture of his parents' financial situation that Tom had thus far been unable to fill in, though, was their tax situation. Neither Tom nor Ward nor Bowman had found any tax returns in the office safe. Thus, starting two weeks prior, Tom had tried without success to contact Keith Ross, his father's CPA, in Springfield. Ross had failed to return his first call, and when Tom called back, he learned that the accountant was out of town for a week. It was, therefore, with anticipation tinged with apprehension that Tom looked forward to this afternoon's meeting with Ross, who had finally returned to town and, a few days later, returned Tom's call.

* * *

Entering the accountant's tacky office in one of Springfield's oldest office buildings, Tom was shown to a metal-framed orange vinyl chair in the waiting room. Twenty minutes after the appointed time of their meeting - with Tom reduced to scanning *Business Week* - the pudgy, white-faced, balding CPA came out into the waiting room and offered a weak handshake to the young, inexperienced client he had inherited. The serious, unsmiling accountant showed him down a narrow hall to his equally tacky office and offered Tom a chair across from his. Looking out his third story window at the blank back of Springfield's new bank tower, Keith Ross, who had introduced himself to Tom with a scant, obligatory offering of condolences, asked, "So, Tom, what can I do for you today?"

Surprised that he had to ask, Tom replied, "Well, as you know, I'm working on my parents' estate, and I need to find out something about my tax situation." Taking out the questionnaire that he had prepared with generous help from Ward, Tom said, "Mr. Ross, if you don't mind, just let me go down this list of questions, and you can fill me in.

"First, I need to know if Dad had filed his 1967 individual income tax return or if it was on extension." Without noting Keith Ross's grimace, Tom continued, "Number two, we haven't been able to find copies of the old returns. I was wondering if you could provide us with copies for the last three years. Third, regarding the estate tax return -"

"Let me stop you for a minute, Tom," Keith interjected with contained distress. "I've been dreading having to tell you about this, but, no, we haven't filed their '67 return ... but ..." he said slowly and with tangible reluctance, "we haven't filed the '65 or '66 either." Having said it, he steeled himself against what he feared would be Tom's reaction. But Ward Brannigan, who had weathered his share of financial surprises, had coached Tom well - both that there would be some, and that Tom would have the resources to deal with them.

After a moment's hesitation to absorb the information, Tom asked, "Do you have any idea what I may owe on those?"

Still awaiting Tom's hysterical reaction, Ross reluctantly replied, "Could be several thousand. Johnny wasn't the best about making quarterly estimate payments."

"What do you think?" Tom asked. "Five, eight, ten thousand?"

"Could be that much," Ross replied with a discomfited wariness.

Considering the information for a moment, Tom squinted his eyes and came back, "Will that be deductible against the estate tax?"

With unguarded relief that the young man across from him had not only absorbed the blow he had been reluctant to deliver since hearing of the death of his beloved though trouble-prone client, but that he had actually come back with a savvy, no-nonsense response, Ross came close to smiling as he answered, "Yes, it will be."

Tom nodded and said, "Good. What do we need to do to get the returns done? And also, I'm going to need for you to help me with the estate tax return." Scanning his notes quickly, he added, "The seven-o-six."

"Well, we've got all the '65 information in house. So you're going to need to get together the '66 and '67 data. I think if you can get hold of the bank statements -" Tom nodded to indicate that he had them "- and some records from Mrs. Meisel, I can show you what you need to do to do the rest."

"Okay," Tom replied, his resolve starting to fade under the recognition that accumulating information for the tax returns was another step out into the dark for him. But as his natural optimism bled through, he joked in a manner that he assumed the accountant would appreciate, "Guess all those practice sets in Principles of Accounting might come in handy after all."

Chapter 32

Early June

Horrified and wide-eyed, Tom fell uncontrollably downward. As he plunged deeper and deeper into the large craggy pit, the vultures he saw circling above the opening grew smaller, as did the opening itself. Freefalling backward, his limbs outstretched, Tom looked left and right and saw openings in the pit walls leading to blue skies and freedom, but he was plummeting straight down at such a high rate of speed he could do nothing to save himself. He realized that he was falling down a shaft through the middle of a mountain or down into a volcano. Frozen in his backward fall, he had no idea how far he was from the bottom, but he almost wished for the answer. The uncertainty of the fall seemed more agonizing than the finality of landing.

He awoke with a jerk, soaked in sweat, short of the bottom.

He lay carefully still, flat on his back and staring into the early morning darkness of Chet's old room. The sensation of falling persisted, and he jerked again, grabbing the sides of the bed with his outstretched hands. He closed his eyes and the sensation was only heightened. Finally, he rolled from the bed and stood beside it. He held his head carefully for fear that a headache would accompany such an awakening, but he was relieved to be free of that pain. He tiptoed quietly to the den and sat in the dark awaiting the arousal of his similarly early-rising aunt and uncle.

Knowing that the day held for him a quick trip to Dallas to meet with Ward and a return the next day for a date with Lizza, Tom made efforts to distract himself from the upsetting way the day had begun. He read the newspaper, watched *The Today Show*, and visited with his aunt and uncle over breakfast. After packing and just before departing, he called Siobhan, who was back for summer school, to make arrangements to take her out for dinner that night. Bidding farewell to Bowman and Nela, he pointed the Le Mans west.

But he kept the nightmare to himself.

* * *

"Siobhan?" Brandeis asked quietly into the receiver.

"Bran?! Bran, is that you?!"

"Yeah, baby -"

"Where have you been? Where are you? I've tried and tried to reach you."

"I'm home. I'm back in Memphis. We went to visit my aunt and uncle in New York City right after I got home from school," he explained unenthusiastically.

"Why haven't you called?"

"I'm sorry," he said haltingly. "I just ... wasn't -"

"No, I'm sorry," she interjected. "I don't mean to grill you." Changing tones as she realized how she sounded, she said, "I love you, Bran. I just love you. And I've missed you so much."

"And I love you."

"But you didn't say anything about going to New York," she said, still trying to rein in her upset.

"I didn't know I was when I left you at the airport. As soon as I got back to town - well, the day after - Mother whisked me and Teddie away to New York. Supposedly for a one-week visit that turned into more than two. I just… wasn't able to call you."

"The whole time you were there, you didn't have a chance to call me once?" she asked, her upset tinged with anger.

"Siobhan, my mother told me not to call you."

"Oh. It's that bad, huh?" she asked quietly.

"Yeah, I'm afraid it is."

"Did you tell her how you feel about me?"

After a long moment he answered, "Yes."

"When can you come down?"

"I can't."

"I'm not going to see you?"

"I love you so much," he declared, his voice breaking, "but I ... she's not going to let me come to Dallas."

Siobhan sighed and replied, "So I guess she's not very interested in having me as a house guest either." To his non-reply, she continued, "So it's the whole summer?"

"Baby, I'll be back in September ... at the end of August. Nothing's changed between us."

"Nothing except your mother holds all the cards."

"Well, she holds the purse strings. She pays the tuition. She pays the room and board," he reasoned.

"Oh, I see," she said coolly. "Bran, does she know that you're calling me right now?"

"Yes."

"Then let's go at it another way. Is this the call she told you to make?"

He hesitated before moaning, "I love you, Siobhan. You've got to know that."

"I know you love me," she said, weak with emotion. "I do know that. But Bran -"

"I am sorry," he interjected. "I've tried to stand up to her. You just don't understand. You don't know her."

"And she doesn't know me. And I don't know how she can do this. Is it because I'm Catholic? Or is it just because I'm the girl you love?" To his silent reply, Siobhan broke into tears. "I'm just so afraid I'm losing you," she sobbed. "That I've lost you."

"No, no, you haven't. You really haven't."

"Can you talk to your father about us?"

"It just doesn't work that way up here," he replied. "She runs the show."

"So that's it? That's it for the summer? I should wait by this phone until those times she's out of the house and you can sneak in a call for a few stolen moments?"

"If you could come up here," he said slowly, "maybe I could get away during the day and see you."

"Oh, Bran. I sneaked into your dorm this semester to see you because I knew we were breaking the rules. But it shouldn't be against the rules for me to see you this summer. And we shouldn't have to sneak around."

"I'm sorry. It was just an idea. I know you're upset."

"I ... don't know what I am," she replied. "I don't know what we are. I just know what I thought I meant to you, and I don't think you fought hard enough for me. Bran, for the two of us to make it, it's going to take ... Courage. And I'm afraid you don't have enough. I love you with all my heart, but I really don't know what's going to happen to us."

Nothing has changed," he said shakily. "I'll -. Damn, she's back. I've got to get off the phone. I'll-"

Click.

*   *   *

As Tom settled into the room Peggy Brannigan had told him to treat as his own for the summer, he was surprised after hearing the phone ring once for Peggy to announce down the hall that the call was for him.

"It's a girl," she whispered.

Assuming it to be Lizza, Tom answered lightly, "Hello."

"Tom? I need for you to come over here ... now ...please."

"Siobhan? What's wrong?"

"Just please come over."

"I'll be right there. Are you at the dorm?"

"Yes."

With a dark apprehension Tom drove the fifteen minutes from Ward's house to Boyd Hall, Siobhan's summer school home. He saw her sitting on the steps in dark glasses, jeans and a faded workshirt. She rose and met him beside his car. Her sniffling, red nose told him that she had been crying.

"Siobhan, what's happened?"

"Tom, can we just get in the car and drive somewhere?" she asked, her voice breaking.

His random crossing of north and northeast Dallas led him to the north end of White Rock Lake. He turned off onto the lakeside road at the north end and started south along the west side of the lake. "I love driving around this lake," he confessed. "It's so peaceful - so removed from the city."

"Yeah," she agreed quietly with pain in her voice.

They drove on silently halfway down the lake. Tom was uncertain whether to probe, to humor, or to maintain silence. Knowing that his goal was to give comfort to this friend whom he loved, but who was obviously hurting deeply, he opted first for small talk to try to bring her out. Glancing across the lake, he saw what he thought to be a diverting place-dropping opportunity. "That church spire over there," he said, pointing across the lake. "In the distance like that, doesn't it remind you of the steeple of Holy Trinity Church at Stratford?"

For the first time she took off her sunglasses as she peered across the lake. Only then, seeing her puffy red eyes and the injury in them that had replaced their normal zest and vibrancy, did Tom see the extent of Siobhan's pain. "No, Tom," she replied, as new tears began to well and to trickle down her cheeks. "It reminds me of a beautiful sunrise ... on a cold morning ... wrapped in a warm blanket ... in Bran's arms." She squinted her eyes closed and bowed her head. "Oh, Tom, I love him so much," she cried out, as her body began to heave uncontrollably, "and ... I'm losing him."

Tom quickly pulled into a parking area and stopped. They leaned toward each other and she buried her face in his shoulder sobbing inconsolably.

"What's happened?" Tom asked.

"Oh," she began, a sad, ironic smile playing on her lips, "I've just put myself in a spot I never thought I would. I'm just so in love with him," she stopped, choking back tears. Taking a breath she exhaled and went on, "I'm sold on him - head-over-heels - addicted to him. Pick your cliché. They all work. I can't get over him. I can't do without him, and I can't do a *damn thing* about how I feel." As the tears began to flow again, she cried, "Tom, if I can't have him, I'm lost." Tom held her again as she sobbed until, spent with emotion, she eased back and curled up in her seat. As she moaned spasmodically with her eyes closed, Tom leaned against her seat and stroked her hair. They sat in the car by the lake for a long time.

As they drove back toward campus, she recounted to Tom their conversation and her fear that Brandeis would never be able to free himself from his mother's control. Trying to place what he was hearing with what he knew of his roommate, Tom remained silent and let Siobhan empty her feelings. Slowing as he approached Boyd Hall, he asked, "Are you going to be alright?"

After a long moment's silence as she continued to stare forward, she replied, "I know you have to leave."

"Chevy, I really don't want to leave you like this," he said, as he stopped in front of the door. "I can call Ward and move some things around. We can probably put off our work until tomorrow. Hey, I was planning on taking you out to eat tonight anyway, right?"

"I'm sorry I'm being such a baby, Tom. I just dread going in there and being alone."

"Let me make a call, okay?"

Turning to him with a weak smile, she nodded, "Please do. You were so sweet to come over here when I called, but I ... I just still need to be with someone who loves me. I hope you don't -"

"It's alright, really," he interjected. "I'll be right back."

Returning to the car, he said, "It's fine with them. Where do you want to go?"

"We don't need to drive anywhere else. We can just - "

With her voice trailing off into indecision Tom offered, "You just want to go over to the SUB-Rosa and get a drink and some fries or something?"

"Let's just sit in the lounge there. You can get a drink. I don't feel like having anything anyway."

Returning toward the couch facing the floor-to-ceiling glass that looked out on the Common and on Old Wesley, Tom stopped short and looked at his beautiful friend as she sat lost in a pensive stare, her hands palm-to-palm in front of her like a child in prayer. Rolling the situation over in his mind, Tom did not worry about taking sides. He was on Brandeis and Siobhan's side. He knew how much they loved each other. He knew they should be together. He did not know, and this concerned him most, what kind of pressure or threat or punishment was being heaped on his friend in Memphis. But he did know that for it to result in Brandeis pulling away from Siobhan, it must be horrific. Until he could talk to him - and like Siobhan, Tom had called Memphis several times over the prior two weeks without result - his goal was to comfort this friend gazing red-eyed in thought or in prayer out on the Common.

Joining her in silent observation of the sparse foot traffic outside,

Tom eased down on the sofa and leaned his head back. "I'm going to call him when I get back to -"

"Tom," she interrupted.

"- the Brannigan's and find out just -"

"Tom, please. You don't have to do that, and I really *don't* want to talk about him. Really."

"Well, I could at least - "

"Tom, please just talk to me about anything else. Tell me about..." She squinted her eyes in contemplation. "I asked you a long time ago to tell me about Mark someday. Do you feel like talking about him? I'd really like to hear about what he was like."

Tom did not move his head but cast his eyes down in reflection. "He was the best big brother a kid could have," Tom answered. Looking back at Siobhan, though, he frowned and offered, "Are you sure you want to talk about this now? I don't mind. I like to get a chance to, really - with someone who's not just asking for the gruesome details. And I know you're not. But I don't want to bring you farther down."

"Don't worry," she replied through misty eyes. "The times you've mentioned him, and from what ...Bran told me, I've just always gotten an impression that there was such a strong love and a special attachment between you and Mark that I'd just like to hear more about him. Like, he's gone, but what you had between you is still alive." As Tom nodded through a thoughtful smile, Siobhan went on, "I don't think hearing more about a relationship like that should make anyone sad."

Tom's smile broke slightly wider as he observed, "We did have a lot of fun together - especially considering our age difference. It was mostly from about the time I was four or five till I was nine or ten that he *played* with me most, but even after that - after he discovered girls - he never quit talking to me and trying to teach me things and get me interested in things.

"But when we played together, it was any little boy's dream because he could re-create any period or place and the people of the time or the place that I wanted to play in. Sure, he had a few personal favorites, so we usually were playing 'Civil War', which we eventually shortened to just 'Civ', or we were playing 'Africa', or we played our Old West game. But we could do American Revolution or World War Two or -. Ha, we even took down the *Encyclopedia Brittanica* one time and went through the entire Battle of Waterloo together. Mark just had such vast general knowledge - but especially of history - because he read all the time." Sighing and shaking his head, Tom continued, "But anyway, I would be the main character, and he would be everyone else. In 'Civ' I would always be a Confederate soldier." To her snorted laugh, he added with a smile, "of course. Usually I would start off as a general, but sometimes I would have to work my way up through the ranks. And he was so patient," Tom laughed at a fresh memory. "While he was busy filling me in on where our first battle would be, who I would be fighting alongside, who was commanding the Union forces, and all the other details, I remember my principal concern at the start of each game of 'Civ' was ... what color my horse was!" Siobhan laughed lightly along with him as he went on, "He just had this complete knowledge of everything about that war - well, especially the war in Virginia - so he could sift me in as this fictional character and then have the actual battle going on exactly as it happened all around me. And he would carry on conversations between the Confederate generals and include me. I can remember how he would steer me toward the field decisions and battle tactics that the battle actually involved."

"How?" Siobhan asked in wonderment.

"Because he would always be my aide-de-camp, too," Tom explained. "And I knew to seek his advice because he would have reports coming in from the battlefield all the time. Of course, I can see now how elaborate it all was. At the time I was quite willing to take for granted my good luck in having him to do all this with.

"We *started* games of 'Civ' so many times that we eventually got to where we had fought the first few battles of the war so often - you know, First and Second Manassas, the Peninsula Campaign, Sharpsburg - that we decided to start passing those up and go straight to Fredericksburg in late '62. Occasionally, we'd even make it to the end of the war. Of course, I never wanted to give up after Appomattox, but ...

"And I was such a morbid little kid. I always wanted the details on all the gory parts. Like, did you know that the bullet that killed A.P. Hill on the breastworks at Petersburg near the end of the war took his thumb off before it hit him in the chest?"

"Tom, I can honestly say that I didn't," Siobhan deadpanned.

"Yeah, oh, and he even had a scary part for me. After Stonewall

Jackson died of the three wounds he received when he was accidentally shot by his own sentries during Chancellorsville, I would be one of the close friends and fellow generals who would have to sit up with the body overnight before the funeral. There he'd be," Tom motioned by spreading his arms before him, "laid out in his casket with only the light of a single candle illuminating the ghostly proceedings. And there I'd be sitting reverently and respectfully beside him - about to pee in my pants for fear that he'd sit up or start talking to me or doing some of that ghost stuff. From a purist's standpoint, that would bother Mark because it would be like I was mixing my fantasies, and ghost fantasies had no sound basis in history."

After a laugh she asked more seriously, "Tom, with all that knowledge and interest, did he ever think about writing about the war or anything."

Frowning, Tom replied, "Oh, yeah. During his teens - through high school - he loved to do research about the Civil War. He had stacks and stacks of notes he had made, and he talked to me a lot about writing books about his favorite battles and generals ... but ... "

"What?" Siobhan asked.

"That summer he came home from his second year at The University," Tom said, turning to stare out onto The Common, "I asked him once if he was ready to write his great Civil War book. And he just looked at me with the saddest, most disillusioned expression, and he said, 'Tom, that was the wrong war'."

"Oh, Tom, I'm so sorry."

"This isn't helping, is it?" Tom asked.

"Yes, it really is," Siobhan protested. "Please don't stop. I really do love hearing about you and Mark. You had so much and you gave each other so much. I'm just amazed that he gave you all that time."

"He liked me," Tom said. "And he knew I'd go along with anything he wanted to do. Like I said, he was the most ravenous reader I've ever known. Read absolutely everything he could get his hands on. And he always wanted me to be an avid reader, too. Well, long about when I got into school - when Mom and Dad quit reading to me - Mark took it upon himself to. He'd read short stories to me, and poems. But he'd read novels to me sometimes, too. Usually a chapter a day. I remember him reading *The Hound of the Baskervilles* to me. And he would put wonderful story-telling flourishes into it. That book scared the crap out of me.

"And when he was reading, he'd always say, 'If there's any word or anything else you don't understand, just stop me and ask. I'll explain it'. Of course, I hardly ever did. He'd never have been able to finish anything. I mean, Lord, he read *The Rime of the Ancient Mariner* to me when I was like nine or ten. Can you imagine?"

"From my two lunk-headed, girl-crazy older brothers? Hardly."

"I had just started driving ... when he died. But I remember in the weeks before, he would let me take him for rides in the country while he read to me. I especially remember him reading from a book of short stories by J.D. Salinger. My favorite - he read it to me while we were riding around once, and then I went back and read it on my own - was 'The Laughing Man'." He looked at Siobhan to gauge if she recognized it. After the negative shake of her head, he continued, "Well, I won't tell you about it. I'll just say that it worked on several levels. Great fantasy and adventure on the surface for an often jolly little empty-headed fourteen-year-old. But on another plane, probably a fair portion of loss, desperation, and fatalism to a lost, desperate, fatalistic twenty-year-old."

Reaching to hug him, Siobhan commiserated, "Oh, Tom. My loss is so small compared to what you had taken away from you. I'm sorry I've been so selfish."

"Chevy, I'm ashamed of myself for getting so maudlin. Here I was, trying to cheer you up and ... "

"Shhh. Don't say that. You've been just what I needed. Tom, I need to ask you something."

"Okay."

Hesitating to think through her question, she finally said, "I'm not going to ask you why he did what he did. But I guess my question is, do *you* know why he did it?"

After a long moment's thought as he stared out into The Common, Tom answered softly, "No."

Taking his hand and squeezing it, she moaned, "Oh, Tom. For you to have loved him like you did, and for him to have meant all that he did to you ..." she said through the tears that again stained her reddened face, "and for you not to know ... why." As she gave him a comforting hug, she whispered, "It's just so scary to trust anybody with your love, isn't it?"

Walking back across campus toward Boyd with Siobhan's arm swagged lazily across Tom's back, he asked, "You sure you're not hungry?"

"No, I guess I might as well face the music and hit these books."

"Well, okay." After a moment's silent conjecture, Tom asked, "Chevy, do you want me to call him?"

Shaking her head, she said, "Just ... do what you want to do. Don't call him on my account." Lifting her tone she asked, "How long are you going to be around?"

"Chevy, I've got to go back to Noofer tomorrow, but I'm sure I'll be back over here in the next few days," he said. "I'll give you a call to tell you when I'm coming. Okay?"

"Sounds good." With a last hug he walked away from the steps of Boyd, but she called out after him, "Hey, Tom."

Turning he watched as she worked her fingers momentarily before flashing him the Sign of the Wild Goose Moon. He returned the sign with a wistful smile and continued walking toward his car. Detouring by the SUB, though, he bought another Dr. Pepper to swig down the two Darvon capsules he had pulled from his pocket to ward off the headache he anticipated.

Chapter 33

Tom awakened with a jerk as his dream world again plunged him downward. Looking up as angry, swirling grey clouds crossed the opening of the shaft down which he was plummeting, he opened his eyes in a start before hitting bottom. The smoky aroma of Crawl Space, the dance club he had taken Lizza to the previous night, revisited him. Sneering at the smell and at the upset that the nightmare caused him, Tom climbed out of bed and slogged toward the bathroom and its cleansing shower.

Leaving the bathroom showered and shaved and in a much better mood, he followed the breakfast aromas down the hall to the kitchen where he hugged Nela as she fried bacon and then to the den where Bowman in his pajamas was performing the morning exercise regimen about which his coronary seven years earlier had given him religion. Greeting his uncle with a wave so as not to make him lose count, Tom flipped on the "Today Show" to a black-and-white still of Robert F. Kennedy lying motionless on a floor - his eyes open, but devoid of life - in the harsh glare of television cameras, a darkened liquid pool below his head.

Tom backed up from the screen in horror. "Oh, God. Oh, God, no," he moaned as he strapped his arms around his waist. Bowman heard him and rose from the floor. He held Tom's shoulders as they listened in stunned silence to the report of the Los Angeles shooting, of the three hours of brain surgery he had undergone, and of the senator's tenuous hold to life.

"I need to go back to my room," Tom told Bowman weakly.

"Do you need me?" Bowman called after him as Nela entered, having not heard the report.

"No, thanks," he waved as he walked quickly to his bathroom while Bowman told Nela what had happened. Moments later as he heaved without result over the toilet, she was at his side. She held his shoulder with her small warm hand while rubbing comfort into his back with the other. She cried softly as she stood beside him, and Tom was reminded of the upset his mother had experienced on November 22, 1963, when, home from high school for lunch and watching a few minutes of a *Father Knows Best* rerun, Tom had learned of the events in Dallas and had reported them to Nancy. He remembered how she and Mark had argued over Kennedy and his "dangerous" Catholicism. As a consequence, Tom had initially wondered at the intensity of his mother's grief over the death of this politician whom she had vigorously opposed during his life. But Tom later had made the connection between the felling by gun of this vibrant, handsome young man long before his time and the similarly violent and untimely end that her son had chosen just more than a year earlier, and he had understood.

"Aunt Nela, when are we going to stop dying?" Tom asked through heaving breaths. "And when is the shooting going to stop?"

"Oh, Son ... oh, Tom," she corrected herself. "There are some crazy people out there. You just have to trust in God and put your faith in Him, and be as careful as you can. That poor family. Lordy, the things they've been through. And all those poor children."

"Siobhan!" Tom suddenly moaned in horror.

*　　　*　　　*

"Woz?" Tom asked tentatively into the phone. "It's Tom." The roommates had not spoken since the day they closed the door of 332. After his talk with Siobhan, Tom had planned to call him, but he had subconsciously been putting it off.

"Tom," Brandeis answered with intensity. "Can you believe this thing about Kennedy?"

"No, I can't. It's horrible. I haven't called Chevy yet. Have you?"

"No."

"Well, it's eight in the morning. I imagine her parents have already called her about it, or she's heard it on the radio, or down the hall. But I wanted to talk to you before I talked to her. Are you about to call her?"

"I've got to leave for the office in five minutes," Brandeis answered testily.

"Are you getting to clerk for your father?"

"Yeah."

"So, are you about to call her?" To the silence that followed, Tom asked, "What's wrong up there, Brandeis?"

"I just don't know when I'm going to be able to call her."

"Well, how about as soon as we get off the phone?"

"That's easier said than done," Brandeis replied.

"No, it's done real easy," Tom retorted. "You pick up the phone and you dial the number of the girl you love. I know you know the number. You've talked to her at least once lately." To his renewed silence, Tom said, "Brandeis, I can't imagine what bad shape she's in right now. And there's nobody she needs to hear from more than you. I don't know about the 'why or wherefore' of anything else that's gone on between you two, but I do know that between the conversation y'all had the other day and what happened last night in California, that's one devastated girl over there by herself in Dallas. She needs to hear from you. Why can't you call her?"

"I'm just not supposed to," he answered, defeat in his voice.

"What have they done to you up there? How can you *not* call her? I mean, with what y'all have had between you. Didn't last semester mean anything?"

"Of course it did. It does. But if I call from here or if I call from the office, it'll be on the phone bill," he said with desperation.

"So wasn't the one the other day?"

"Yeah," Brandeis answered reluctantly.

"Oh," Tom conjectured caustically, "but that was the one you were 'allowed'. So you could break up with her, huh?"

"I didn't break up with her," Brandeis said. "I just told her we had to cool it till September."

"You call it what you want to," Tom said, "but that girl who cried her eyes out on my shoulder a couple of days ago felt like she'd been broken up with. Call her," Tom demanded.

"I can't."

"I can't believe what I'm hearing. I'm so disappointed in you."

"Yeah. Me, too," Brandeis sighed.

"Well, I'll talk to you later," Tom said brusquely. "I've got a friend who needs me, and I need to give her a call."

*   *   *

"I met Bobby," Siobhan said through the tears that had been flowing since her mother's call had awakened her. "I shook his hand. I talked with him, Tom. He's such a wonderful, loving, caring man. That poor family ... and poor us - poor all of us - poor America." She continued shakily, "I think we've lost it, Tom. I'm afraid we've lost our chance."

"Well, he hasn't died. Maybe he can pull out of -"

"He's gone, Tom. Mother told me there was no way he could ... " and the tears took over again.

"Then I guess the torch passes to Teddie?" Tom stated solemnly, grasping for any thought of comfort to salve her pain.

"In this crazy country?" she replied in anger. "If he has any sense, he'll go up to Hyannisport and hide in that compound for the rest of his days. It'd just take one more 'crazy' - and it looks like there's one born every minute - and he'd be gone, too. Oh, Tom," she moaned before bursting again into uncontrollable crying.

Tom listened and spoke quietly and soothingly until she settled down again. "Why don't I come over and see you? I can be there in about three hours," he offered.

"No, no," she protested. "It's alright. My mother's coming down today. You're so sweet to offer, though. Tom, you're just the best friend. I love you."

"I love you, too, Siobhan. And I just hate for you to hurt like this and -"

"Have you talked to Bran?" she asked.

After a moment's hesitation, Tom replied, "No. I guess they must have gone out of town again."

"Yeah," she said dejectedly. "Maybe."

"Are you sure you don't want me to come?"

"No, Tom. You really don't need to." Gathering herself, she added, "But Tom ... I may go home with Mother."

"Oh."

"My heart's just not in being down here. My heart's not ... anywhere."

By the time the mid-afternoon call from a Memphis phone booth finally reached Siobhan's empty dorm room, she was curled up next to her mother in a first class seat winging northward.

*   *   *

Tom, Chet, and the Carters joined the country in vigil before the pale blue light of the television screen. Tom switched from channel to channel seeking clips of the man himself. Seeing the vibrant young senator in the reels of campaign film and family footage somehow gave Tom hope in spite of the grave medical reports. He especially enjoyed the references to Kennedy's self-deprecating humor, laughing as he joked about his "ruthless" image. And Tom watched as Roger Mudd provided voiceover to clips of his interview with Kennedy in which the senator scolded him teasingly for referring to certain prospective convention delegates as being "squeezable". As Mudd additionally pointed out, when being interviewed for television, the senator tended to speak directly into the camera. Tom left the den for bed with that image the last he saw - Robert F. Kennedy speaking from beneath the burdened eyelids of his care for the poor, the downtrodden, the alienated of America and of his hope for their future.

In the early morning as the soul of a third Kennedy brother found Eternity, Tom plummeted once more down the darkened mouth of the mountain. But on this passage the walls began to close in on him as the shaft narrowed. He cried out in pain as sharp rocks jutting from the walls of the opening nicked and cut him during his descent. Finally turning himself in the air to see the bottom as it raced up toward him, he faced the smooth marble tombstone - the Old English engraving of "Windham" carved into its face - that was the floor of the shaft. Suddenly, the moment before hitting the marble floor, the plummeting object was no longer Tom. In his place was a glistening silver sphere. As it struck the tombstone, it exploded into a thousand drops of mercury - like so many silver shotgun pellets.

Chapter 34

Mid-June

The aging Venetian blinds, loose from their bottom stay, flapped and clattered against the glass insert of the oak-framed door as Tom swung it closed behind him. Having entered with his head down in thought, Tom looked up with an apologetic expression toward the receptionist that he assumed he had surprised with the loudness of his entry. He was correct that the noise had surprised her, but he froze in place - apologetic countenance and all - when he saw that the surprise was on Clair's face. Flecks of steel blue glittered in her large, expressive eyes opened wide by hearing the noise and then wider by seeing its source. To prove to himself that he was not totally paralyzed by the encounter, he awkwardly said, "Hi ... Clair."

"Hi, Tom," she replied gently and evenly, as if she had been awaiting his arrival - as if no time had passed since their last meeting.

Continuing to regain his composure and managing to add, "I didn't know you were working here," he was nonetheless stunned by how beautiful she was; by how suddenly and strongly attracted he was to her; by how purely good it felt to see her again. "I didn't talk to you on the phone yesterday, did I?" he asked.

"No," she answered. "You must have talked to Laura. I would have known ..." and her voice trailed off.

As he noted her hair to be lightened from its normally dark blonde hue, Tom remembered how naturally that phenomenon came about from her helping Gramma with the springtime chores. Her skin was likewise tanned and glowing. With his defenses still aslumber from his surprise discovery, Tom gushed, "Clair, you look wonderful. Gosh, it's good to see you."

Looking him up and down in his crisp, new Dreyfuss & Son tan tropical wool suit, starched light blue oxford cloth shirt, chocolate brown and dark blue geometric-patterned tie, and cordovan wingtips, Clair noted Tom's leaner face, his broadened shoulders, and an inch or two more height. Equally defenseless, she replied, "Yeah, it's good to see you, too."

Embarrassment seeped in as control started to push aside Tom's spontaneity. He repeated, "I didn't know you were working here."

"I'm working here for the summer in the afternoons. Typing and answering the phone."

Her tailored white cotton blouse supported an impression of maturity and responsibility, but her hair and the youthfulness of her face betrayed her. Still staring at her, Tom said, "What a surprise to find you here." But he finally felt constrained to tell her why he was there. And as soon as he remembered, he said, "Well, I'm here to see Mr. Quinn. Is he in?"

"Oh," Clair responded, all but shaking her head to clear it. Realizing that they had suddenly switched to a business conversation, she changed voices and answered, "Yes, let me ring him."

As she reached for the phone, though, Lygon Quinn came strolling down the bookcase-lined hallway. "Tom," he boomed in introduction as he extended his hand, "glad you could come over. Come on back and let's talk about what you want done."

Shaking his hand, Tom said stiffly, "How do you do, Mr. Quinn. I'm glad you could see me." As they started down the hall, though, Tom stopped and said apologetically, "Excuse me, sir. I'll be right down there." Leaning back around the corner and catching Clair looking after him, he asked, "Clair, are you going to be here when we get through?"

Without stopping to ask if their conference would last fifteen minutes or fifteen hours, Clair looked directly into his eyes and said, "Yes."

Pointing out to Tom the "mess" they would all be in if anything happened to *him,* Ward and Bowman had urged Tom to have a will drawn up. Ward had suggested he use a Stover County attorney, and at George Collum's recommendation Tom had contacted Lygon Quinn.

Given his void of immediate family and paucity of peripheral kin, the majority of Tom's interview with the cigar-chewing, six-foot-five cowboy barrister was spent selecting secondary beneficiaries. Tom had put off thought of such matters until the start of the fifteen-minute cross-county drive to Bethany. He immediately named Chet as the primary beneficiary. Musing at its similarity to the Miss America Contest's first runner-up declaration - "if for any reason she is unable to carry out the duties ..." - Tom was stumped as to whom he should designate as secondary beneficiary. Though Quinn took care to point out that the will could easily be changed later and that the possibility of triggering that clause of the will was quite remote, Tom gave considerable thought to it anyway - having had more experience than most with the "quite remote".

Realizing that to break up his estate among his aunts and uncle and other cousins could only offer opportunities for hurt feelings, harsh remembrances and unseemly intra-family squabbles, Tom left Lygon Quinn in bemusement and surprise as the attorney scribbled barely legibly on his lined yellow pad his client's instruction that - should Chester Carter predecease him - his estate be sold off and the proceeds split between the Baptist Foundation of Texas and the Boy Scouts of America. His father had more than once voiced to Tom his feeling that his achievement of Eagle Scout was one of the most important accomplishments of his youth. And in Mark's early teens he had served tirelessly as the Scout Master of his Post.

And though Tom was uncertain exactly where he stood with his God, he saw no reason to make his church suffer for it.

"That's pretty unusual," Quinn observed with bemusement, "comin' from a -. How old are you?"

"Twenty."

"- twenty-year-old young man. But we can put it in there. I'll have to contact the two organizations to get the language right. Both of them are used to this kind of bequest, of course. So, there shouldn't be any problem drawing this up. Anything else?" he asked.

"That should cover it," Tom replied.

As they walked down the hall, Quinn took the opportunity to

reiterate his expressions of respect and senses both of community and of personal loss at the passing of Johnny and Nancy Windham. Awkwardly accepting his condolences as they approached the front office, Tom excused himself to speak to Clair.

Walking in on her by surprise as he had earlier, Tom had been caught off guard. He had felt none of the discomfort about seeing her that he had anticipated - considering the way they had ended their relationship three years prior. In stolen moments since, as his mind had occasionally strayed from his discussions with Lygon Quinn, he had entertained a more appropriate level of self-consciousness and guilt about how he had broken up with Clair and about how negatively she must - or at least, should - or perchance, could - feel about him now. And yet, he had noted none of that when he had walked in on her. Her welcome had reminded him of how good it felt to be near her - of how unconditional her enjoyment of being in his presence had always seemed, and seemed now. And, he thought, 'there was the letter.' But perhaps that was it. The letter, the friendliness. Were they pity?

With Clair studiedly looking forward as she heard him approach, Tom stole a gaze at her posed beauty from her back and side as he came around the corner to her desk. "Clair."

"Oh, Tom. Got everything taken care of?" she asked as he stopped at her side.

"Yeah," he answered, soaking in that familiar feeling of attractiveness, of importance, of specialness that being in Clair's presence conveyed to him. "Listen, I want to thank you for your letter last month. It was really nice of you."

"Oh, you're - " she began uncomfortably. "Well, it wasn't much, but ... "

"No, I really appreciated it. Tell me, how is Gramma doing?"

"Oh," she smiled in relief both at the continuation and at the continued safety of their interchange, "just as ornery as ever. But you know she loves this time of year. What with all the fresh fruits and vegetables that the garden's yielding, and with the peaches almost ripe."

"So y'all still have the peach orchard?" he asked, nodding.

"Sure. But, anyway, Gramma's health is good. She says, all she ever needs is just another Spring."

"She loves that land, doesn't she?" Tom said, thinking of his own.

"We both do," Clair stated. With the conversation seeming to lapse, Clair made the leap. "I'm sure she'd love to see you."

"I'd love to see her."

With all the casualness she could muster, she offered, "Well, why don't you come out this afternoon and say 'hi'. It'd really do her heart good to see you."

With obvious regret, he said, "I've got a ... something to do tonight."

"A date with Lizza?" Clair asked.

Shaking his head, Tom allowed, "Boy, I forget how small these towns are."

"Yeah," Clair laughed, "and Bethany's even smaller than New Fredonia." As Tom sloughed off an uncomfortable laugh, Clair added, "Anyway, Gramma would really like to see you if you'd just like to stop by sometime."

"Timing," Tom whispered, shaking his head.

"What?"

"Oh, nothing. Clair, it's really been good seeing you again. You look great."

"Thanks, Tom. It's been good seeing you, too."

As he shuffled reluctantly toward the door, though, he stopped and turned to see that she was watching him as he left. "Clair," he said, and he took two halting steps back toward her.

"Yes."

"Clair, I'm sorry about the way we left things between us - before. I'm really sorry about ... those things I said."

Nodding with shiny eyes as she succeeded in holding herself together, she replied, "Thanks, Tom. I've wanted to hear that for ..."

"Well, it's just something I've wanted to tell you," he said, as he backed toward the door. "I'll see you," he said, waving.

"See you, Tom," she said evenly, returning his wave.

*   *   *

As she picked up on the first ring, Tom ventured haltingly, "Lizza?"

"Oh, hi, Tom!"

"Hi. Listen, I've got one of those killer headaches -"

"Oh, I'm sorry. Have you taken your Darvon?"

"Yeah, but it's still hurting."

"Well, we don't have to go anywhere tonight if you don't feel like it. Would you just like to come over here and watch T-V or something? I could fix us something to eat."

"I think I'd probably better just stay here. I'll call you later."

"Oh," she moaned with disappointment. "Well, I don't want you coming out if you -. Was it going to see the lawyer about the will?"

"What?" Tom asked.

"That brought on the headache?"

"Oh. I don't know. Maybe so."

"Did that go okay?"

"Yeah, it went fine."

"Well," she said with concern, "I know your Aunt Nela'll take good care of you. Call me later if you feel like it."

"Okay," Tom replied, the mendacity of the moment gnawing at him less than he had feared.

*   *   *

Driving toward Promise, Tom felt an unbridled elation both at the way Clair had treated him at the attorney's office and at the way she made him feel about himself. The latter was the familiar sense of value and of pure affection that seemed unchanged from their teens and before. He had feared that the way they had fallen out with each other, the things he had said then, and the three-year lapse in contact since would have soured and forever changed the way she felt about him. The attitude she had displayed earlier in the afternoon had suddenly seemed to clear all those obstacles away. And the pure, basic attraction that he felt for her was likewise undiminished - and it was like nothing Meredith or Lizza or any girl he had dated since Clair had ever come close to igniting in him.

But as he turned off 222 toward Promise - Scatter Mountain looming in the west - the all-too-familiar tightness of undesignated anxiety seized his chest. His inarticulate but forceful dark side whispered to him, 'This is wrong. Don't do it. You have no right.' Madly, he looked up at the canopy of tall trees shading the narrow farm-to-market road, and he reflexively let off the gas fearing that one of the giant pines might topple in his path in order to prevent his visiting Clair. 'Go no further. Turn back,' demanded the voices into his mind. He shook his head from side to side trying both to free their grip and to protest their hateful message.

"Yes, yes, yes," he finally said aloud, nodding emphatically as if trying to convince himself of his worthiness for happiness or at least for a chance at it. He turned on KLIF to the Union Gap's "Willpower" and upped the volume. The voices of darkness receded, but he arrived at the familiar open gate of the Redfearn farm with his chest still pounding.

Tom rolled slowly over the tapering end of the ridge that set the farm off from the farm-to-market road that continued on through Promise toward Piney. Cresting the brow, Tom saw the familiar setting laid out before him. The small white frame farmhouse stood on a knoll at the northwest end of a verdant valley meadow. Its garage was detached by a wide breezeway, which caught the summer's southerly winds after they had been funneled up the vale. Tom had spent many a summer's eve at the picnic table under the giant red oak on the other side of the breezeway watching Clair's silky blonde mane being blown across her neck and face by the cooling puffs of wind off the valley until, with the whip of her head and the toss of her hand, she would lay its shimmering strands across one shoulder and let it cascade down until it draped luxuriantly across her heart. In the near distance behind the house rose Scatter Mountain, vibrant in its summer coat of many greens. Below it was the wood that bounded the farm on the west and guarded within it the pond of Tom's memory. Between the house and the woods was a hay pasture and the large freshly worked produce garden that yielded up most of the two women's food staples for the entire year.

Clair was trundling up a grassy path from the far side of the garden astride the venerable Ford 8N, which her grandfather had bought new the year she was born. Wearing dusty worn jeans, a faded sleeveless workshirt, and a red bandana tied loosely at her neck, she flashed a bright smile as she doffed a crumpled straw hat that looked like it had been handed down to her by Bailey Harper. She hoisted it above her head ready to wave a welcome at the company come to call, but her arm and the hat froze in place when she realized the company was Tom.

Parking beside the house, Tom dismounted the Le Mans and walked toward the shed off the side of the aging, cavernous red barn where he knew she would leave the tractor. Untying the bandana to wipe the perspiration from her glowing face, Clair shook her head with a happy but embarrassed grin as she laughed and scolded him, "How *could* you come out here without giving me any warning? I must look like a field hand."

Observing strands of her thick, honey-hued hair falling on either side of her tanned face from the loose bun she had worn, her sweat V-ing the open, wrinkled collar of her washed-out chambray shirt and circling below her open armpits, her frayed Levis betraying a dusty tan hue, and the spring's mud caked on her work boots, Tom lowered his gaze and declared with quiet profundity, "No. You don't."

Laughing him off with a shake of her head, she replied, "Well, I feel like one. Go sit under the tree," she said, motioning with her head as she started to walk away from the barn. "I'll bring you some lemonade while I clean up."

"Sorry," Tom offered. "I should have called. It was sort of a spur of the moment thing."

"Still doing those, huh?" Clair asked, slinging an ironic and historically informed smile over her shoulder as he followed. He did not reply as they caught the familiar soft gust at their backs while passing through the breezeway.

Glancing up into the aged oak above the picnic table, Tom observed, "The fan's a nice touch. Who'd you get to put it up there for you?" he asked as he traced the conduit from the fan to the armpit of the thick branch supporting it and to the ground.

"What makes you think *I* didn't?" Clair asked - now cleaned up and dressed comfortably in a sleeveless knit top and shorts.

"Did you?"

"No," she laughed. After a hesitation during which the smile eased from her face, she admitted, "Gene Ray did."

With forced nonchalance Tom threw off, "Oh, yeah. I saw you two together in Springfield, oh, a couple of months ago, I guess."

"At Paco's."

"Yeah, that's right. So, are y'all dating?"

Nodding her head while watching Tom's reaction, she replied, "We date some, when he's in town."

"Oh. He doesn't live here anymore?"

"No, he's in Houston right now - training for the fire department ... avoiding the draft."

Reminded of the Hewitt brothers, Tom observed, "Isn't it amazing how half the draftable guys in East Texas have cleared out to Houston to join the H-F-D?"

"Yeah, they've got to be measuring their response time down there in seconds."

"Yeah, right," Tom said. But after nodding an amused smile of agreement, he added, "Can't blame them, though. Not quite fair to think you might have to die just because you can't stay in college - or can't afford to go."

"What's this I'm hearing? Has Tom Windham gone off to college and come back with a social conscience?"

"Come on. Cut me some slack."

Narrowing her eyes, she replied, " I'm just kidding. I like the sound of it."

"So, is he nice to you?"

Looking away, Clair replied, "Yeah, he treats me nice, if not gentlemanly."

"Uh-huh. Remembering him from high school, I would think he would have trouble with 'gentlemanly'."

"But he's real nice to Gramma, and he helps us out around here some."

"Good." With a laugh, he added, "I know I never was much help to you. You knew all this farming stuff, and I was this inept 'townie'. But that wasn't the worst part. What really hurt was that you were even ... stronger." Clair dropped her head in laughter but looked up with a smile that said she had forgotten nothing. "So, what are *you* going to do in September to avoid the draft?" he asked.

"Huh?"

"Didn't you just get through with Stover County J-C?"

"Oh, yeah." She shook her head while answering, "No, I don't know what I'm going to do next. I may lay out a semester - or a year."

"You're kidding. You might not go to college next year?"

"It's not totally unheard of, you know."

"No," Tom replied, suddenly ashamed of the attitude he betrayed. "You're just so smart. I -"

"Tom, Gramma's old, and I don't want to leave her and go away somewhere for two years or more. She'd have a hard time making it without me. And the money's -. Well, college is expensive."

"What about Springfield?" he asked.

"Like I said, college is expensive. And Springfield College is ridiculously expensive."

"Well," Tom offered, "there are scholarships and student loans and things, aren't there?"

"Tom, I tried for those at Springfield. And I still came up way short. And it's the only four-year school around here ... where I could live at home."

"And Gramma won't let you go away somewhere?"

With exasperation she stated, "Of course she would, if I were to say that I wanted to."

"You mean -"

"I mean," she said evenly, "that Gramma has been like a mother to me. She's worked and sacrificed for me, and now she's old. And I owe her something."

"But don't you think she wouldn't want you to miss out on that -"

"Tom, I have a commitment to her," Clair stated while tapping her chest with her knuckles, "that's in here. Right now, this is more important."

Thinking of the financial morass in which he had found his father's affairs and of the additional burden that Johnny had taken on without Tom's knowledge to keep him at WSU, Tom looked away and nodded silently.

Fearing that she had shamed him, Clair quickly asked, "How did you like W-S-U this year?"

"Loved it."

"So what are you majoring in?"

"I haven't had to declare yet, but ... History, I think." He surprised himself with his answer.

"How wonderful."

Her approval made the idea of History as a major immediately more real and more possible. "Yeah, I don't know what I'll do with it. I guess all I could do is teach, but I just enjoy it so much. Maybe later I'll go back and get something ...worthwhile."

"Since when is teaching not 'worthwhile'? You'd be a great one. So, which way are you going? American or European?"

"European."

"Hmmm, what have you had so far?"

"Only the second half of the European history survey course, but I think I'm going to sign up for three in September: the first half of the survey course, possibly a Russian history course, and definitely the first half of English history." The nearness of Clair in a knit shirt and shorts momentarily distracted him, but he continued because it also felt so good to be able to talk so openly with someone. "It's really funny, Clair. During the second half of European, when we were studying the aftermath of the Napoleonic Wars and then the ascendancy of the British 'Empah' - those good ol' Victorian days - I started feeling this strange sense of identification with the British. It was like I had been there - like I had been one of them. I guess it was just this strong wish or something that I had been alive then. Because it was such an incredible time."

"Maybe you were," Clair offered.

"What?"

"Maybe you had a life as an Englishman back then." To Tom's dumbfounded gaze she continued, "I've done some reading about reincarnation and past lives. There are a lot of people who believe in it. A lot have recalled things that happened to them in earlier lives - either in hypnosis or after some trauma." To Tom's continued glare of skepticism, she said, "Hey, it's a possibility. And it may explain feelings like what you've had. I've had a few of those feelings myself."

"I don't know," Tom said with a mix of wariness and bemusement. "That sounds ... un-Christian."

"No, not really. Many who believe in it see it simply as an ongoing communion of a soul with God."

Finally squinting his eyes and frowning, Tom stated, "No, that would really run afoul of established - and clearly proven, I might add - Southern Baptist dogma. I mean, the Bible tells us that we go to Heaven and stay - that is, if you get to go at all. It's not just a holding station."

"Well," Clair countered, "there are those who say that once you get everything worked out down here and get your soul right, you stay there - in communion with God. It really ties in to resurrection."

"How many round trips do you get?"

"Aghh," she replied with a mix of exasperation and amusement, "you're still impossible."

Looking down the valley behind Clair and up into the oaken canopy, Tom allowed, "Well, maybe I was born around 1815 or 1820. Into English nobility, of course."

"Of course."

"Landed gentry would have been fine." The topic milked, though, Tom continued to look up into the tree. Then looking back down and into Clair's eyes, he realized how much he did not want this to end, how much he just wanted to be with her. "Now, what's the story on this tree?" he asked.

"Don't you remember?" she asked with slight disappointment.

"Most of it. But I just like to hear you tell it."

"When my great-grandfather Ezekiel Redfearn came here in the 1840's from Tennessee, he brought this young red oak, the roots balled up in Tennessee soil, so he'd always have a piece of land from his home with him. One afternoon he sighted Scatter Mountain - was struck by it as a landmark - and stopped to camp right here. The next morning he climbed a tree on top of Scatter for a good view of the area, and, of course, this valley was mostly overgrown with native hardwood," she said, motioning through the breezeway. "But he could tell by the lay of the land, and then as he walked it, by the soil and the spring-fed creek, that it would be good farmland. So he planted the tree here on this bluff and -"

"What about the name 'Promise'?" Tom asked vaguely. "Wasn't there something about -"

She grinned and answered, "Yeah. He later named the settlement that grew up around here 'Promise'." With a deprecating laugh she continued, "Because that was what he thought it was going to be 'The Land of'."

"And what else was there about this tree?"

"Well, his first wife, the one who came down here from Tennessee with him, died in childbirth, and so did the baby," she said sadly. "So he was here by himself for a number of years. But then he met my great-grandmother, and, I suppose after some proper period of courtin', he proposed to her under this tree."

"Yeah," Tom allowed, nodding. But with a sly grin he cracked, "But if your great-granddaddy was the first one here, where'd she come from? 'Another creation over in the next county'?"

Clair smiled and closed her eyes in thought. "Just a minute. I know that one." Placing her hand over her mouth and then jerking it away, she pointed across the table and blurted out, "*Inherit The Wind!*"

Tom winked, "You got it."

"And as part of our family tradition, my grandfather proposed to Gramma under this tree, too."

As the screen door groaned open and banged shut, they looked around to see Gramma using the handrail to walk down the back steps. In her faded floral day dress and light blue checked apron Tom could see little difference in her appearance, but as she carefully walked toward them, Tom observed that the past three years had slowed her. As they rose from the table, Clair said loudly, "Gramma, it's Tom ... come to see us."

Approaching with her hair penned close to her head for the bonnet she commonly wore, Tom could see that her skin, while weathered, retained the healthy color that she had always attributed to a combination of eating homegrown vegetables and fruit, working outdoors, and having deep Southern roots. Looking closely to focus on him, she rustled nervously in one of the front pockets of the apron and pulled out a wadded handkerchief with which she quickly dabbed her eyes. Tom walked to meet her and as they embraced, she shakily moaned, "Oh, Tom Roy ... your momma and daddy ... that Johnny ... and that sweet Nancy ... oh, my boy, my poor boy."

Tom at first did not reply but gently patted her back. "It's so good to see you," he finally offered. "You look as pretty as ever."

"Pshaw," the old woman said, pulling away with a nervously twitching smile and liquid eyes. Patting his chest softly, she said, "We've missed you around here, Son."

"The place looks beautiful," Tom said, scanning the valley before looking over Gramma's shoulder and catching Clair watching him. "Your garden, the hay meadow, everything. What about the peach orchard?" Moving back to the picnic table where he sat again across from Clair, he asked, knowing the answer, "Do you still have it?"

"'Course we do," Gramma snapped, almost taking offense.

"So you girls are still sellin' your peaches on the side of the road?" Tom teased.

"You betcha," Gramma answered.

"Well, how's your crop this year?"

Smiling at Tom's expression of interest, Clair turned the floor over to her grandmother to elucidate on one of the old woman's favorite subjects. "It was mighty close this spring. Miiighty close. Almost didn't have a crop," Gramma stated dramatically before waiting to be urged to explain.

"Why?" Tom queried with appropriate timing. "What happened?"

"Liiiight, light freeze - right at the start of the growin' season," she explained. "Had me plenty a'sceared. Right up till I first saw the fruit start to come out. Then, wouldn'cha know it, not enough rain after that." Shaking her head, she continued, "Don't know how it made it, but it persevered. Had the will to grow in spite of a lack of encouragement. Real 'stick-to-it-edness'. Hung in there and turned out right purty, if I do say so myself. An' I do," she laughed, slapping her apron.

Tom turned momentarily from Gramma and caught Clair staring across the picnic table at him - her expression a mix of appraisal and appreciation. Neither flinched. A wispy breeze caught her hair and started to blow it in front of her face, but she reflexively whipped her head up and to the side. As it draped over her bare tanned shoulder and tumbled down her blouse, Tom caught his breath.

"Reminded me o' that peach crop back - oh, Clairy, when was it?" To her granddaughter's confused shake of her head, she said, "Well, I s'pose it was when you were a little bitty girl - before you moved out here. Anyhow, there was a late freeze. Killed the crop. Broke my heart. The trees came out green and purty, but no fruit. The townsfolk would driiive real slow-like past the stand jist awaitin' for that 'Closed' sign to come down. Lordy, I hated to disappoint 'em like that. Finally, they jis' quit drivin' by at all. We had a big beautiful crop the next year, but hardly sold any."

Clair turned back toward Tom. She fought the urge to put her arms around him and make the dullness in his green eyes vanish. He finally looked up and offered her a sweet, sad smile that did nothing to stop her from wanting to hold him.

"Don't know why the folks quit comin' by. Jis' got outta the habit,

I s'pose. The peaches that next season were better'n ever. Big and juicy. Goldy-orangey colored. Purtier'n a picture."

Clair gave up reason as she slowly reached one hand across the table and moved it gently up Tom's fingers to rest on his hand. But as he returned her gaze, the brutal negative that had insinuated itself into his psyche on his way to Promise stabbed deeply into his heart. So strong was the paralyzing pang of malevolence that he had to mentally restrain himself from grabbing his chest. His mind was a battlefield as he answered the crushing anxiety, 'but I love her'. 'But you'd be bad for her,' came the dark reply. 'But I love her and she could make me happy,' he pleaded within himself. 'And you would destroy her, too,' was the response. 'But I need her,' he cried. '*If* you love her, get away from her. Leave her alone. Don't take her down with you,' the voice commanded, as he sighed sadly aloud.

"Tom, what's wrong?" Clair asked gently.

Looking around at them, Gramma interrupted her discourse to ask, "Hun, didja git a splinter in your hand?"

Looking down and then back up quickly while shaking his head clear, Tom answered, "No, I'm fine. Just thought of something I had to do." But while looking at Gramma with a thin smile, he slowly pulled his hand away from Clair's. In his peripheral vision he saw Clair lean back, pulling in her arms as well.

"Well, you young'ns go ahead and palaver. I got to go in and check on my chicken." Turning toward the screen porch on the back of the house, Gramma began to walk away, but she stopped and asked, "Tom Roy, you staying for supper?"

Finally turning toward Clair and suffering the new pain of seeing her withdraw from him as she stared into the picnic table, Tom answered, "I'd better not. I think Aunt Nela is waiting supper for me. I'd probably better go on."

Clair subtly shook her head clear and offered through a transparently forced smile, "So. Lizza's a cute girl, and I'll bet she's a lot of fun." To Tom's silence she continued, "Of course, I knew Karen better, but I remember when Lizza was a sophomore cheerleader. Really had the energy."

"Clair -" he began, but he fell silent, the struggle lost.

"What?" she asked, exhibiting the control of her feelings that she found so necessary in her relationship with Tom.

"Nothing. Yeah, Lizza's nice. And the Collums have been a lot of help and comfort to me." After a moment he added, "And I'm glad Gene Ray has been nice to you and Gramma."

After saying what they thought they should say, they sat in silence looking away from each other for a long moment. But when Tom started to rise from the table, Clair caught her breath and looked quickly at him. "Are you leaving?" she asked, catching herself before she added "again" to her question.

"I guess I'd better go on," he said, backing away from the table. She did not rise but nodded with resignation. "It's been good seeing you, Clair." He replayed the sound of her name in his mind. He had said it to himself many times over the last few years, but it was different this time because he was saying it aloud to her - although he feared that it might be for the last time.

"Still living it out inside yourself, huh, Tom?"

"It's ...the only way I know how."

Rising and waving weakly as he looked back from beside his car, a wind out of the south rippled through her hair. She again shook it clear of her face. Turning the Le Mans toward the gate, he could not keep himself from whipping his arm out the window and making the sign of the Wild Goose Moon. He drove away without looking to see if she had seen it.

She had, but she replied only with tears - and with anger at herself for hoping again.

He returned home, his head throbbing, and sat by himself in the Carter's small den watching television and waiting for the Darvon to relieve the pain. Its effect, as always, was to further dull his senses and slow his reactions, but his second tablet failed to lessen the immobilizing pressure and pounding against the walls of his skull. So he took another.

Chapter 35

Mid-July

"So you feel pretty comfortable with this fellow running the office?" Chet asked as he and Tom rolled south toward Springfield for lunch. "I mean, I remember your expressing the fear that someone you might hire could come in and steal the business out from under you. Copy your records and get in good with the attorneys in town and just go next door and open up a competing title office."

Tom considered his question carefully before regurgitating the reasoning that had led him in discussions with Ward and George to accept the offer of Neil Forster to come to work for him managing the title office. "Yeah, I feel pretty good about it. He was retired from the title business after working all over East Texas for the last thirty years, and he was someone Dad had known. And the way he presented it, he was just tired of sitting home and wanted to go back into title work because he loved it. He said he wasn't interested in having all the responsibility of running the office, so he was glad Helen was already in place to do that and would stay on in that capacity. He said he just wanted to be able to hunker down and do the work.

"If it all works out as well it looks like it will, the two of them can operate the business for me for the next two or three years till I get out of school, by which time I ought to have a better idea of what I want to do with it. But I'll probably sell it." Tom glanced at Chet for his reaction.

"Sounds like a good set-up and a good plan," Chet said, not noticing the relief with which his approval had blessed his cousin.

"Thanks. I'm trying not to feel guilty about thinking about selling it. You know, it's been in the family for sixty years."

"Well," Chet asked evenly, "would you be happy operating it and making your life's work out of it?"

"No," Tom answered too quickly. "Well, I don't think I would. I mean, I've never learned the business, and I just don't know how much I'd enjoy it. But I might. But I'm not even sure I want to live in Noofer when I grow- when I get out of school."

"Don't let yourself be too tied to the past - just out of respect for it," Chet offered. "If you do, that's where you end up living. Believe me. I mean, you didn't seem to have had that kind of problem selling the house, did you?"

"No," Tom noted. Shaking his head, he said, "Strange how that's somehow different, isn't it? But I knew there was no way I could live in that house again. On the other hand, the decision to keep the farm was because I realized how much I love that place, and I can really see myself going there and enjoying it. The business? Well -"

"Then you're doing the right thing with it. You're holding on to it till you decide, and if you decide you do want to run it, you've got someone there who can teach you how to do the work. Sounds like the best of both worlds."

"Yeah, you know, you're right. Thanks for helping me feel okay about that. And speaking of the house, thanks again for helping me get it ready for the movers." Focusing down the road, Tom added, "I'm sorry about that time I got all ... upset."

"Don't worry about that for a minute," Chet said. "My Lord, all the stuff you've had to get past, and all the memories in that house. Hey, I don't know how you do it. And closing's next what?"

"Next Friday."

"Well, you're really getting the list pared down, aren't you?"

Tom kept to himself the additional relief he was feeling at having recently filed and paid the tax on the three income tax returns Johnny had left for a tomorrow that never came. With this on top of the numerous past due loans and accounts that his father had left unpaid, Tom had come to understand the desperate financial straits from which his father had accidentally and finally escaped. With each revelation of his father's problems Tom had become increasingly protective of his image among those in New Fredonia whom he had loved and who had loved and respected him. Only Ward Brannigan - and then only because Tom so needed his help - had been made privy to all of the details of the situation his father had left.

"Yep," Tom answered, rubbing his chin nervously, "and Monday I'm supposed to meet with Ward and the attorney who's dealing with Global about the settlement."

"Wow! Tom Windham, Boy Businessman!" Chet observed with a laugh.

"That's me," Tom replied - without a laugh.

Noting the edge in Tom's tone, Chet shifted gears asking, "You have a date with Lizza tonight, don't you? What're you two doing?"

Appreciative of the diversion Tom answered, "We're going to see *The Thomas Crown Affair*. The previews look real good. Looks like McQueen gets to play 'dress-up'."

After a hesitation, Chet asked, "So, how are things going between you and Lizza?"

"They're going okay, I guess. I think she's about over me going to see Clair."

Shaking his head, Chet observed, "Yeah, I guess I'm still kind of amazed you told her about that."

"Oh, I figured I might as well. I mean, I was feeling guilty about it. Plus, I just know this county too well. Gramma would have mentioned seeing me to some old biddy, and that old biddy would have told another old biddy - in the teller line at the bank and a teller would have overheard it and mentioned it to Mister Collum - or to her hairdresser at the Henhouse, who also did Mrs. Collum's hair, and so on and so on. You know how efficient the grapevine is around here. God really troubled himself overmuch churning out sixty-six books. Should have just dropped the word at the Henhouse in Bethany on a Thursday. The weekend comb-out set would have spread it to every corner of the world before the Sunday evening service."

* * *

The richly maned brunette with an accent put down the phone, smiled vivaciously, and sprang from bed wearing only a pair of white silk bikini panties. Tom was stunned by the momentary image as she rounded a corner and was out of sight. The rich, tanned skin of her back below the thick, dark brown hair, the marked indenture of her waist, and the sensuous sprawl of her *derriere* captivated his attention and his imagination. Although she was in only two other brief scenes - and then fully clothed - Tom left the theatre desirous of Thomas Crown's chess table, of his grey suit with lavender shirt and tie, but, most especially, of his girlfriend. While Faye Dunaway had worn a style show full of great outfits and had sported a set of false eyelashes long and thick enough that her merely fluttering them could have provided sufficient updraft to keep her lover/prey's glider aloft, it was Astrid Heeren whose next appearance Tom had awaited lustily throughout the remainder of the movie and whose name he had sought out in the movie's credits.

And it was Miss Heeren's posterior view in silk panties that Tom had in mind when he grasped Lizza's buttocks and rubbed down her brief minidress to her smooth bare thigh as they necked on the front porch swing at the Collums' house late that evening.

"Tom," Lizza pulled away and moaned, somehow making of the three-letter name a question, a warning, and a dalliance.

"Wha-a-at?" he replied, mimicking her tone.

"Be careful - right here on the porch."

"You want to go to the car?" he whispered as he leaned into her neck and began to nibble it.

"Well, I think it's a little bit late to do that tonight," she responded.

"Sorry," he murmured. "You just feel real good."

Well, thanks, but let's not get all hot 'n' bothered right here on the porch."

Tom pulled away emitting a frustrated sigh. It was not his first sexually frustrated sigh of the summer. In the three weeks since they had started dating again after an angry one-week hiatus with which Lizza had tried to punish him for having visited Clair, they had been parking several times and had necked enthusiastically, but within limits efficiently telegraphed to him both by her body language and by the timing of her breaks for conversation or thirsty requests for tours of the Dairy Queen. Tom had always complied. He appreciated her tight, gamine figure, and she seemed to enjoy him, but there was no all-consuming, uncontrollable lust from either camp. Occasionally, though, his breathing or his movements betrayed an arousal that tended to make her suddenly thirsty.

"So let's drive somewhere where we *can* get all hot 'n' bothered," he suggested.

"It's too late to do that tonight," she repeated.

"Then tomorrow night?" he urged.

Pulling away from him again and with a troubled smile, Lizza asked, "Tom, what's up? What's come over you?"

Smirking his frustration, he answered, "Hey, you turn me on, okay."

Breaking into an appreciative grin, she replied, "I do?"

"Hey, I've told you. You've got a cute butt."

"Yeah," she nodded, "but I didn't know I -"

"So you want to go somewhere?"

"Where?"

Thinking only for a second but answering more seriously, he looked into her eyes and replied, "The lakehouse?"

With surprise she responded, "You've been there?"

"No. But I've had it cleaned up, and I have the key." As she started to answer, he cut her off adding, "I've wanted to go back there. I just didn't want to go in alone."

"Oh, Tom. I'll go in with you. But we shouldn't tonight. We can go out tomorrow afternoon if you'd like. I'd like to help you through that."

"Forget it," he said in near anger, rising from the swing.

"Tom," she cried, reaching for his hand. "I want to help you. I'll go with you tomorrow."

Catching himself and putting aside his love nest fantasy, he smiled and said, "Okay. Thanks. We can do it tomorrow after church."

"Are you still coming over here for church and for lunch?"

"Sure," he sighed. "I'm just a little pooped." As she rose to give him a kiss, he concluded, "Let's call it a night."

Upon returning to the Carters' Tom tossed restlessly in bed for some time before opting for a long, hot shower with Astrid Heeren.

Chapter 36

"Turn your eyes upon Jesus.

Look full in His wonderful face,

And the things of Earth will grow strangely dim

In the light of His Glory and Grace."

The dozen-member adult choir of Bethany Baptist Church and its electric organ massaged the old hymn deftly as Tom sat reverently beside Lizza in the Collum family pew - unmarked but by tradition. The aging sanctuary had barely a quarter the seating capacity of Tom's church. Large fans, open windows along either wall, and the shade of hovering oaks and elms kept the interior temperature in the low eighties even in midsummer. Tom had been relieved, though, to see the men of the church remove their jackets before sitting, and he had followed suit.

Out the northside windows of the auditorium the faithful could observe the progress of construction of the new red brick sanctuary with its soaring steeple - the simple white wooden cross from the original structure already fixed atop it. In his position as boyfriend of the younger daughter of the chairman of the Board of Deacons, Tom had enjoyed being privy to, while remaining distanced from, the controversy that swept through the church body regarding the fate of the graceful old frame building in which they sat. While the traditionalists in the congregation called for its maintenance as a chapel and meeting room for Bible studies and other large groups, many of the younger families of the church under the charismatic leadership of Shelby Feller called for its demolition and replacement with a structural steel gymnasium.

Well-spoken, borderline-demagogic, formerly alcoholic, and recently born-again, Feller was the volatile repository of that brand of Protestant fanaticism - grating to many, magnetic to many others - particularly available to those whose rebirths were radical one-eighties well into adulthood. Like others of his life experience, his rabidity - in his quest for perfection as a new Christian, in the certainty and inflexibility of his new answers, and in the expectation that all others would fall into line lock-step behind him - was in direct proportion to the sordid depths of his pre-baptismal sinfulness.

Tom had listened in sincere appreciation and support of Anna Collum's argument that the mixing of the new red brick sanctuary and the attached white frame Sunday School classroom buildings - themselves added in clearly recognizable stages - with a gargantuan structure sided with such an ecclesiastically inappropriate building material would be an incongruous mess. She further argued eloquently that the symmetry designed into the complex by the architect of the new sanctuary in confluence with the existing buildings would be destroyed.

During this special music presented by the choir, Tom, knowing that the calliope-like cycle of standing and sitting through the first half of the standard Southern Baptist worship service was over and that the purely sedentary portion of the service had begun, took Lizza's hand in his, and they dropped their two-fisted clinch onto the pew against each others thighs. Doing so, he looked down the row and returned the sweet smile of Anna Collum, who had noted the hand-holding out of the corner of her eye. As he considered whether the previous night's standoff had defined the limits of his physical relationship with Lizza, Tom realized that emotionally he had drawn as much motherly nurturing and approval from Anna as he had affection and intimacy from her daughter. And while George Collum had exhibited a discomfort and an awkwardness when observing Lizza's outward expressions of affection for Tom and Tom's for her, his wife seemed to revel in them. With a warm smile of his own Tom returned her wink.

At the conclusion of the music Brother Bobby Lee Peck took the pulpit of Bethany Baptist. Youthfully fortyish, his cup running over with self-assurance - if not self-awareness - he sported a thick head of brassily dark blonde hair with wide sideburns trailing down from his temples. Attired in navy suit, white shirt and white tie contrasted against an oversized bright red carnation, he brusquely took hold of the raised sides of the lectern and with penetrating blue eyes above a gummy grin confidently scanned the congregation from wall to aisle to wall. In the theatrically evangelical style of the veteran itinerant revivalist, the preacher softened up his audience with a couple of jokes whose locale and characters he had transmuted onto Bethany Baptist and certain prominent members of its congregation - including a reference to Alf Slater which caused Tom to crane his neck around in search of Fred/Freddie's father. The veteran of a young lifetime of observing preaching styles, Tom instinctively recognized the urgency of his delivery as being unique to these one-week-wonders. Quickly building his argument in favor of the current and future advantages of turning one's life over to the Lord and accepting his Saving Grace, the rhythm, the modulation, and the volume of Peck's delivery were perfectly paced to draw in the congregation and to carry them along with him toward the high-pitched frenzied warnings of Eternal Damnation to which forbearance from pursuing his recommended course would inevitably lead. But approaching his concluding crescendo, he made a statement on which Tom hung.

Peck proclaimed, "He was here before The Beginning, and He will be here after The End. He has seen what has gone before, and He knows what is to come. God is never surprised."

Those final four words caught Tom unaware and left him stunned. The more he rolled their implications over in his mind, the more troubled he became. He drifted through the remainder of the sermon oblivious to its content. During the invitation hymn at the conclusion of Peck's message, in which all the verses of "Just As I Am" were repeated in honor of the revival preacher's presence and during which three young souls publicly professed their faith in Jesus Christ as their Personal Lord and Saviour along with the predictable spate of rededications, Tom reflexively mouthed the words of the familiar worship service-ending song even through the dramatic *a capella* rendering of the repeat of its final verse. But he was troubled. Lizza glanced at him twice noting the strange distance in his eyes. Taking the pulpit both to congratulate Brother Bobby Lee Peck for his sermon and for the souls he had won to Christ and to close the service was Harleton Hill, Bethany's grey-faced, balding pastor. He called on Shelby Feller to offer up the benediction.

"Lord, we just come to You as the Lowest of the Low - the First among Sinners," began the deep, doleful voice front and right from Tom. "And we just pray, Lord, Your forgiveness and Your tender mercies on our worthless mortal souls. Christ Jesus, we just ... "

Tom finally became diverted from his quandary as he began to count the number of cloyingly humbler-than-thou "justs" inserted into the prayer of the new deacon. 'Nine', he toted. 'And not once', he additionally noted, 'did Feller ask God to '*just* bless the missionaries on home and foreign fields'. What's this denomination coming to?' Tom thought.

With Feller's 'Amen', though, Tom came back with the question to his God, 'Were You surprised to hear that?'

Though polite, if distracted, through Sunday lunch, Tom's distance gave the Collum women pause. Ascribing his moodiness to an attack of grief, as she was wont to do, Anna rewarded his distraction with care and attentiveness. Assuming it to be related to their porch swing contretemps the prior night, Lizza answered distance with distance. When, after lunch, he begged off on their proposed trip to the farm and the lakehouse, though, in favor of going to the office to gather materials for his trip the next day to Dallas, Lizza transmitted her concern into a lingering good-bye kiss on the front porch.

Returning to the Carters' instead, Tom called Browning Lee and requested an immediate audience.

*   *   *

The musty aroma and the fading white plaster walls above wainscoting betrayed the age of the parsonage and this, its study, but the dark-stained wood trim along with the muted strains of Vivaldi's violins gave the room an easy, welcoming comfort as the shepherd and one of his troubled flock seated themselves in facing burgundy leather wingback chairs.

"What's on your mind, Tom?" Browning Lee asked. The gentle smile and the consoling eyes below the laden eyelids and brows told Tom, as they had since the preacher's arrival almost ten years prior, that he really did want to know what was on Tom's mind, and that whatever it was, it was alright to voice it.

"Doctor Lee," Tom began, in deference to the honorary Doctor of Divinity degree bestowed by Browning Lee's alma mater shortly before his acceptance of the call to First Church New Fredonia, "the evangelist over at Bethany today ... "

"Brothah' Bobby Lee Peck?" Lee asked with interest, his signature silver-white crop of hair slightly askew from his interrupted Sunday afternoon nap.

"Yes sir. I was attending their worship service with the Collums." Winning Doctor Lee's smile of approval, Tom continued, "Anyway, he made a statement that really troubled me, and I wanted to talk with you about it."

"Okay, Tom."

"He said a lot of other things, but one thing he said was, 'God is never surprised'." As Browning Lee nodded silently, Tom tried to read his expression before going forward. "Is that what we believe? I mean, is that what *you* believe? What I'm supposed to believe?"

"Yes, Tom, it is what *I* believe," Lee answered forthrightly. "God is omniscient, all-knowing. He sees the sparrow fall – "

Tom broke in, "And he knows it's about to fall?"

"Yes."

"So it's all fixed?" Tom asked, betraying frustration. "We don't have any choice in the matter? There's no ... chance?"

"We, each of us, exercise our own free will," Lee countered calmly. "We make our own decisions."

"Just a minute," Tom said. "*We* make our own decisions? *We* exercise our free will?" After a hesitation, he asked with a confused frown, "But God knows what it's going to be?"

"God knows what has gone before, and He knows what is to come," the pastor answered.

"Well, then, where's the sport in it for Him? I mean, if He created it, set it in motion, has watched it all this time but has always known everything that was going to happen next – "

"Tom, God is not in it for the sport," Browning Lee countered with muted consternation.

"Okay, but what I'm saying is, 'What's the point? Why are we trying to do anything? Why did God put us here?' The implications of 'God is never surprised' are pretty depressing to me. I mean, it just seems so fatalistic."

"He put us here to exercise our free will as individuals and to obey Him and to choose to be Christians. And then to advance His cause on this Earth - to help win others to Christ, to guarantee their salvation as well as our own."

"But he knows which ones of us are going to do that," Tom asked with frustration, "and which ones aren't?"

"Tom, it's our choice."

"So, he knew that plane was going to fall out of the sky? He knew that shotgun was going to go off?"

"He didn't cause those things to happen, Tom."

"He didn't spin off a world and give it natural laws? Created Man and gave him a mind to think? What about Mark Windham in 1962, who blew a hole in his heart? Did God know about that? He didn't set in motion weather systems and define metal tolerances that wound up littering a farm outside Butler Mills with the wreckage of a prop-jet and sixty-seven bodies? He started all that," Tom continued bitterly, "and always knew how it was going to come out?"

"Tom," Browning Lee replied with a tolerant and mournful sigh, "God loves you. And He has a purpose for your life - "

"Yes," Tom agreed with a wary frown, "that's what I'm afraid of. What could possibly be the purpose that He has in mind for me that would first require violently wiping out my entire family before I'm twenty-one?"

Tom," Doctor Lee said with quiet patience, "you just have to believe in Him, and -"

"Oh, I believe," Tom confirmed. "That I've never questioned. All of this didn't come from nowhere - from no one. Don't worry. I *believe* in God." His voice trailing away in anguish, he concluded, "I just don't like Him. And ... I don't think He likes me."

Chapter 37

Driving away from the Monday morning sunrise toward Dallas, Tom again scanned the letter he had found among his father's papers while preparing his income tax returns:

Dear Johnny,

Thanks for your note on the due date. I certainly understand your inability to pay anything at this time. I've put a couple of kids through school, too, so I know what you're talking about. But please do send me something on this as soon as you can.

Johnny, you know I love you like a brother and am always willing to do anything I can to help you out. I don't know if this is the right time to say this, but I hope you will soon take me up on my offer to talk over your financial situation with you. You are already past the point when you needed to start working toward a stable retirement situation, and I know Social Security will not give you and Nancy the kind of financial freedom that you would want.

Anyway, I just want you to know that I'm available to discuss it with.

Hook'em Horns!!

Ward

Crossing to the windows of Ward Brannigan's sumptuous corner office high in the Southland Life Tower, Tom looked northeast locating White Rock Lake. As he awaited Brannigan's return from a conference with another broker, Tom was reminded of his roommate by the shimmering waters cloaked in the dense green of the surrounding Lakewood neighborhood. He had talked to Brandeis twice over the past few weeks - both times at his father's law office. They had spoken of Siobhan only to compare notes. Each had tried to call her in June and neither had found anyone at home - not even a maid. Tom was glad to hear, though, that Brandeis had taken the additional step - pouring heaps of change into a pay phone during a lunch hour - to call her father's construction company office. Introducing himself as a school friend of Siobhan but having apparently been recognized by Padraic McKenna's secretary as the boy who had done her boss's daughter wrong, he was curtly told that the family was traveling - extensively. The date of their return - indefinite.

"Sorry about that," Ward said as he hurried to his desk waving a disorganized sheaf of paper in one hand and motioning Tom to retake his seat with the other. "Now, where were we?" he asked in the rapid-fire delivery that Tom had discovered he reserved for office use. "Oh yeah, we've got the two-thirty appointment this afternoon with the attorney. So I'll see you there," Ward said, offering a conference-closing handshake.

Taking a breath to fortify himself before going forward, Tom said, "Ward, thanks so much for your help with that and with everything else this morning, but there's one more thing I need to discuss with you." Reaching into the monogrammed briefcase that the Brannigans had surprised him with on a recent stay, Tom pulled out Ward's letter to Johnny. "I ran across this among Dad's papers while I was gathering the information for the tax returns." He handed it to Ward, who scanned it quickly and returned a sad glance as Tom asked, "How much did Dad owe you? I want to pay you today."

Ward missed only a half-beat in replying, "It's clear. He had paid it all back before the ... before the end of April."

With a sad smile Tom said, "Ward, I looked through all his bank statements. There wasn't a check to you." Sloughing off a sigh, Tom added, "I figured you'd say that. Listen, I want to clear this up, so please tell me how much he owed you."

"Tom, you don't have to do this. Please just consider it closed - a closed matter."

"There have just been so many things that have ... come to light this summer. So many things Dad didn't do right. I just want to clear them all up. Clear his name. So please just tell me how much I owe you."

Ward placed the papers on his desk and silently joined Tom by the window. Cupping in his hand the shoulder of his good friend's son, Ward said, "Tom, your dad was a good, good man. Don't ever let anyone tell you different. No one gets through this life without problems. But a lot of folks get through it without sharing themselves with others. Your dad wasn't one of those folks. He was a fine man. A giving and loving man."

"I know he was. It's just that ... I just don't want his memory to have a cloud over it - for me or for you or for anyone." Pulling away from Ward, Tom said, "So I really want you to tell me how much he owed you - so I can pay you."

"Tom, tell you what. I don't want this money. I am simply not going to take money from you. But your dad had paid it down to thirty-five hundred dollars. And if you need to pay it - to make you feel okay about it - what I'd like for you to do is to pick out someone or some cause that Johnny would have wanted you to help and use the money to help them. Will you do that?" As Tom considered the proposal, Ward added, "Believe me, it'll make me feel good; it'll make you feel good; and I know Johnny's up there watching us right now; and it'll make him feel good, too."

Staring into White Rock Lake, a smile of resolution eased across Tom's face as he nodded his assent.

*   *   *

Driving down the tollway toward downtown in the early afternoon, Tom felt apprehensive about the coming meeting with the attorney. He knew that Ward would be at his side and that his experience with legal matters would more than cover for Tom's novice status. But the feeling of being in over his head, of being a child playing grownups' games by rules foreign to him was terrifying. He had survived the recent weeks' challenges of completing the three years' tax returns, of selling his house, and of hiring the new manager, but he had also paid the emotional cost of maintaining the control that he had sought and then guarded so carefully since that nightmarish afternoon in late April. Popping two Darvon to calm himself for the meeting, Tom glanced in the mirror at the nervous tick above his eye that had become a fellow traveler. The tightness of his starched collar and knotted tie and the heat of the new navy suit coat that he had forgotten to remove before entering the tollway completed his matched set of discomforts.

Tom tossed a quarter into the basket at the downtown toll station and followed the road south to its merger into Harry Hines Boulevard. Glancing anxiously beside him at the briefcase chock-full of the disorganized documentation of his summer's work, Tom found the directions to the attorney's office. Jerking his eyes back up to appraise the traffic situation, he saw Nopalito's. It was unchanged. The neon sign, the plate glass window, the lean of the siding - it was all there, all the same.

Seeing the approaching signal light turn green, Tom gunned the Le Mans and shot past the restaurant at fifty-five, but the words of "Bob Dylan's Dream" drifted over him:

'I wish ... I wish, I wish in vain
That we could sit simply in that room again.
Ten thousand dollars at the drop of a hat -
I'd give it all gladly,
If our lives could be like that.'

Chapter 38

Early August

After his aunt handed him the phone wearing an 'I have no idea' expression, Tom was surprised by the response to his 'hello'.

"Tom, this is Margaret McKenna," she said in a friendly tone, "calling from Chicago."

Tom banked as a sign of his maturity the fact that he did not immediately inquire of Mrs. McKenna, 'How's the weather up there?' But realizing that the call could only be about Siobhan, he answered, "Good morning, Mrs. McKenna. How is Chev- Siobhan doing?"

After a pause the sweet voice, its lilting brogue the stuff of movies to the East Texas boy, replied with concern, "I'm calling because Siobhan - I think you kids call her 'Chevy', and that's fine - anyway, Siobhan is ... having a hard time of it -"

"I know, Mrs. McKenna," Tom broke in to confirm. "Brandeis is a good friend of mine, too, and -"

"No, Tom. Well, yes, of course, that boy hurt her so. But, Tom, Siobhan had an accident on her bicycle five weeks ago and broke her arm and damaged her shoulder -"

"Oh, no!" he replied. "I'm so sorry. Well, is she okay?"

"Yes, finally. But she's been in a lot of pain."

Pangs of guilt suddenly catching up with him, Tom stated, "Well, I tried to call Chevy several times after you came down and got her in

June. But no one was ever home. I just figured y'all had gone somewhere for the summer."

"Yes, we left on a motor tour of New England and the East Coast soon after we got back from Dallas, and we were out for a couple of weeks. The accident happened the day after we got home. The poor dear has had such a bad time of it."

"May I talk to her?"

"She's asleep right now. She's sleeping a lot - still on her pain medication, you know. But I'll try to get her to call you when she awakens."

Catching on the tentativeness in the concerned mother's voice, Tom asked, "Mrs. McKenna, is there anything I can do to help her?"

With a painful sigh she replied, "Tom, my little girl has been real ... down. She just hasn't been herself since - well, since some time before the accident. We've just returned from a week in London. We went as soon as her doctors gave us the go-ahead. Well, we rented a flat right in the middle of things - near Piccadilly - and we shopped and saw shows ... but ..."

"What can I do to help?" Tom asked.

"I'm really at my wit's end. I'm sure this will sound strange, but I was wondering if I bought you a plane ticket, if you would come up here and spend some time with her. You could stay with us. We have plenty of room. I just feel it would really lift her spirits."

Tom's mind raced through the crosscurrents of conflict Mrs. McKenna's request had triggered. He knew that Brandeis was who Siobhan really needed. But the Brandeis she needed was the one who had been free to love her in Dallas, and not the one locked in his mother's grip in Memphis. Tom quickly realized that to hold out the possibility of Brandeis going to see her and then having it dashed by his mother's almost certain refusal could only deepen his friend's depression. But this brought Tom back to himself and to a completely different problem. Tom had not flown since April. He had flown by himself as a teenager to Paris and to Mexico City; therefore, he had no fear of the logistics of commercial flight. But since April he had blocked out the question of when or if he would fly again. Now it was suddenly before him. And he realized he was simply not ready to face it. Not wishing to admit his fear or superstition or whatever wall there was that he was unprepared to scale, but most eager to help his friend, Tom reached a compromise in his mind that put off the question of when or whether.

"Mrs. McKenna, I had been thinking of taking a road trip before school starts back. I need to swing by Dallas tomorrow, but I'll just leave from there ... and drive to Chicago."

Surprised by his reply, she said, "Oh, well, don't you need to check with -" and then catching herself, she fumbled and said, "someone?"

Tom, too, had thought briefly about asking his aunt, but he realized it to be one of those matters in the no-man's-land of parental authority about which he and the Carters would all feel awkward. After committing himself to the course, he glanced back at Tom Windham, twenty-year-old kid, and granted that perhaps another barrier protecting him from adulthood had fallen. "No, ma'am," he answered with resolve. After scribbling down the directions from the outskirts of Chicago to their house, he asked, "How long should the drive take?"

"About two or three days," she answered warily. "Tom, are you sure -"

"Then I'll see you in three or four. By the way," he finally asked, "how's the weather up there?"

* * *

Lizza broke away from his kiss and groaned, "Stop, Tom," as he rubbed his hand up her thigh under her culottes.

In frustration Tom rolled away from her onto his back on the quilt he had pulled from one of the beds in the lakehouse and had spread on the lawn that ran down to the lake. Propping himself on his elbows he stared into the semi-darkness of the hot evening.

"Tom, I'm sorry, but - " Lizza began. "No, I'm really not sorry," she half-laughed. "I'm just not ready to do that." Looking around, she went on, "Especially not here."

"Well, then let's go inside," he said coyly as he looked at her with a smile.

"Aahhh. Maybe it was better when you *didn't* want to go in the lakehouse. So glad I helped you get past that."

"Hey, I'm leaving town tomorrow on a dangerous sojourn into the unknown - alone. Won't be back for - well, who knows if I'll ever get back. Can't you just grant me this one last request?" he begged as he rolled back toward her.

"You're *not* about to start singing 'White Cliffs of Dover', are you? I mean, it's not like you're heading for 'Nam or anything."

"Yet," he whimpered.

"Oh, you rat," she laughed as she bussed him quickly. "Come on. You're off on a lark to Chicago to visit *in the home of* this gorgeous blonde that you've always told me about. Pardon me if I'm not awash in sympathy."

"So upon my return," he asked, borrowing his roommate's David Niven accent, "having proved my devotion to you - and only you - then, my dearest, can we…get it on?!"

"Tom, Tom, Tom. What am I going to do with you? No, don't answer," she said, clipping his reply with a long kiss. Pulling away, she said, "Well, I guess, since it seems foremost on your mind tonight, we might as well talk about … doing it."

"What?!" he grimaced. "Let's don't talk. Let's just do it," he said leaning into her.

Ignoring his call to action, she stated, "I either want to do it before I go off to Stephens or … I want to wait till I get married."

"Ahh," Tom nodded, biting his lip and feigning understanding. "If you go with pre-Stephens," and he shot his hand in the air, "can I help?"

"Sure," she answered. "Who else would it be? Plus, I'd want it to be with a 'virgil' - "

"A what?!"

"A virgin male. A virgil. Anyway, I'd want it to be with a virgil, so I wouldn't feel so inept."

Shaking his head with a huff, Tom asked indignantly, "So just what the devil makes you think I'm a virgin, er, a virgil?"

"Well, you are, aren't you?"

"Is there some animal-like scent of innocence and sexual ineptitude I give off or something?"

"Well, *aren't* you?"

"Well, yes. But I don't like for you to assume it. I'd prefer your being amazed and agog at my admission of virgility. It hasn't been my idea. I think God's been saving me for something … for someone. Maybe it's you."

Shaking her head, Lizza replied, "No. Oh no, I'm not the one he's been saving you for. If he's been saving you for someone, it's probably either Clair or someone you haven't even met. It's not me."

"Well, thanks."

"No, Tom, understand. I love you. But I'm not in love with you. I hope we're close for the rest of our lives, but we're not going to get married. Don't worry. There's someone else around the county who can do this for me if I decide to get it done?"

"Who?!"

"I'm not sure yet, but I'll figure it out."

"Lizza, that's pretty slutty talk. No, if you need to do this, I would only let you do it with me."

Laughing, she replied, "Uhn-uhn. You're not getting me to go against God's will and de-flower you just for my sordid purposes."

"Hey, you're already talking about breaking Southern Baptist Sub-Commandment Seven-A, 'Don't even fornicate'. You might as well take me down with you."

"You're really warming to this idea, aren't you?"

"Welll -"

"Well, don't. I'm probably not even going to do anything. I mean, I really don't know if I could do it and not tell Mom and Pops."

"Then, for goodness sake, don't do it," Tom said. "'Cause I'm sure you'd have to tell them who you did it with."

"You really *like* being 'Mister Nice Guy' to them, don't you?"

"No, I just like them a lot, and, sure, I like for them to think well of me. But I'm not trying to fool them about me. I mean, don't you think I'm nice - really?"

"Sure," she nodded in agreement. "In fact, probably much too nice to be the one to pop *my* cherry."

"Now, I didn't say that."

"Oh, no, I could never ask you to do that now."

"Hey, you don't have to ask. I'm offering."

"So now we're up to incurring the wrath of God and of George and Anna Collum just for some meaningless dalliance? Something that might mean nothing more to us than 'just shaking hands'?"

"You're right," Tom said thoughtfully. "You probably should wait. I'm glad we talked this out. You could have made a serious mistake."

"I still may - just not with you," she teased.

"If this conversation were taking place in *Peanuts*," Tom pointed out, "this would be when Charlie Brown would throw up his hands and yell, 'Aaagghhhhh!'"

*   *   *

Cruising northeast from Oklahoma City toward Tulsa, Tom was feeling proud of himself. Though his aunt and uncle and Peggy Brannigan had voiced trepidations about his setting off on his own - and each of the women had independently offered to accompany him - he had just successfully maneuvered himself through his first major city. And at the recommendation of Ward, who alone had expressed confidence in Tom's ability to accomplish the solo sojourn, he had even found and enjoyed the Mexican food at the cavernous Casa Bonita Restaurant.

Enjoying the 'coolness' of the expensive ground-glass wraparound tortoise-shell *Graduate*-esque sunglasses he had had made at an optical shop in NorthPark, he approached a large highway sign placed in the median. He removed the glasses to be sure that he read it right.

DO NOT
DRIVE
INTO
SMOKE

The message of the six-foot-tall sandwich board sign stunned Tom as he passed it and noted in his rearview mirror that it was being visited upon the oncoming traffic as well. "Do Not Drive Into Smoke", he repeated aloud. 'Heavy', he thought, as he attempted to interpret the psychological and metaphysical implications of the cryptic message. A few miles down the road he encountered an identical sign, and the message jumped out at him again. Finally determining it to be a modern-day example of God reaching down and guiding the hand of a mortal - in this case, an Oklahoma Highway Department supervisor - to deliver one of His obscure tomes to Mankind in general and, with His "no surprises" advance knowledge that Tom would be on that road that day, to Tom Windham in particular, Tom glanced heavenward through his tinted windshield and replied, "Hey, Big Guy, it sure wasn't my idea to.

If You remember - and of course, You do - I wasn't given any choice in the matter."

Spending his first night under the familiar Holiday Inn sign in Springfield, Missouri, Tom steeled himself against the coming challenge of making his way through St. Louis. Responding to his lifelong fascination with maps, it was with special relish that he went about deciphering the cartographic logistics of his journey the following day and, beyond that, on to Chicago. Having filled the backseat of the Le Mans with a plethora of road atlases and state and regional road maps containing sufficient built-in redundancies and fail-safe back-up systems to satisfy the most meticulous NASA engineer, Tom scanned his foldout treasury.

After spending the next morning traversing the fertile expanse of Missouri, Tom stopped for a late lunch short of St. Louis and reviewed his maps once more. Over-prepared as he was and making his passage through the city in the early afternoon, the actual crossing was anti-climactic - until he reached the bridge over the Mississippi. Here as at Memphis, his usual crossing point, the breadth and majesty of the river again amazed him.

Across the river he chose U.S. 40, south of the direct route through Springfield, so that he could stay overnight at Urbana rather than arriving in Chicago in darkness. After checking in at the local Holiday Inn, he drove to the University of Illinois campus and blended into the summer school student body. Seized by an acute lapse into thoughtfulness, he found a campus bookstore and bought Lizza a 'Fighting Illini' sweatshirt before retiring to his room with his maps and his take-out pizza.

Arriving at his destination late the following morning, Tom was silently ushered into a plant-filled sunroom by Mrs. McKenna. Thus given a moment to look at Siobhan before she saw him, he was reminded of the first time he had seen her and how he had ogled her up and down while she stared at their amphibian friend, Jeremiah. Attired in a loose-fitting caftan and stretched out on a lounge chair carefully couching her right arm in her left at her waist, she stared out into the backyard as the late morning sun bounced off the shimmering blue of the backyard swimming pool through a wall of windows. Tom was struck first by her paleness, which was emphasized by the reflective glow of the sun off the water. Never before had he seen one square inch of her body surface that was not tan. It took away little from her natural beauty, but along with the inch of dark roots visible at her hairline, it heralded an apathy and joylessness anathema to the girl who had loved life and his roommate so well through the spring.

Glancing around at him, a dead-eyed smile tracked across her face as she rose with wobbly care favoring her cradled arm. "Tom," she announced with a tired sigh. "I can't believe Meg asked you to do this, and I can't believe you did it."

Stunned by her weakened appearance, Tom still managed a smile. He gave her an affectionate if careful hug, patting her back as he held her. Finally pulling away he scanned her natural rose-hued lips, her unlined, unshaded, un-mascara'd eyes, and her smooth, pearlescent skin and asked, "Why do you even wear make-up?"

Pulling sprouts of hair straight up from her head, she laughed weakly and asked, "And how do you like this hair? Going *au naturel*."

"Not a natural blonde? Is there no Santa Claus?"

"I still can't believe you're here," she said. But Tom detected in her voice a trace of grogginess. "Well, here. Sit down," she urged, and he joined her in a chair beside her chaise lounge. "Did Mom offer you anything?"

"I think she's getting me a Coke."

"Sorry," she said. "No D-P's up here in Yankee-land."

"So how are your arm and your shoulder feeling?"

Holding her upper arm softly, she replied, "Oh, there's still some pain."

"Well, what happened?"

"It was really stupid of me. I was riding my bike through a park that I had ridden through a hundred times before - a thousand times before - but it had rained and then dried up while we were out of town. And I wasn't looking where I was going, rode off the road - which I've done before - but I rode down into a dry tire groove and instead of easing out of it, idiot that I am, I jerked the handlebar back to the left, and it just flipped me over on my side. I landed hard on my arm on some tree branches that had been stacked on the ground there - and, Snap!"

"Ouch," Tom grimaced. In response to the noticeable slurring that Tom observed as she spoke, he asked, "Are you still in a lot of pain?"

"Yeah, it comes and goes."

"So are you still taking something for it," he asked.

She looked away and nodded.

Staring into the gently jostling waters of the pool and the manicured lawn and shrubs beyond as they blended into a forested tract in the distance, Tom finally said the name. "Has Brandeis ever been able to get hold of you?" Continuing to gaze at the mesmerizing movement of the pool's water, Siobhan replied with a slow, expressionless shake of her head. "Well, I know he's tried to call you - several times. From what your mother said on the phone, I guess you must have been out of town." Winning only continued silence, a thought dawned and he said with animation, "So you went to London?" Siobhan converted the slow shake of her head to a slow nod. "From what she said, it sounds like you had a great time. Tell me about it."

Slowly turning her head toward Tom and drawing in the focus in her dispirited eyes, she replied weakly, "Tom, I'm tired of London." And she began to weep softly.

Tom moved to join her on the lounge and, while taking care to favor her right arm, he cradled and consoled her as she cried. "I'm so sorry I've been out of touch with you all this time. I can only imagine how tough this summer's been for you."

With resignation bordering on defeat, she stated sadly, "Oh, you haven't missed much. Mostly this. Just crying ... and masturbating, masturbating and crying." With a feeble laugh she added, "I take a lot of baths."

Managing a feeble laugh of his own - and losing only a second to the mental picture his imagination quickly dashed off - Tom asked, "Well, wouldn't you like to get up and get out of here and do something?"

"Yeah, that sounds good," she answered with blunted interest. But following with a sigh, she added, "But first, let me take a little nap. I'm just so tired."

Putting together the behavior he had observed and comparing it with his own sensation-numbing vice, Tom dipped his eyes and glanced up at his sad friend asking, "Chevy, are you on something?"

Pulling a green-tinted container from the pocket of her caftan, she giggled with muted glee and rattled the contents, "Fiorinal Three. You want one? Can you handle codeine?"

Pulling a folded tissue from his pocket, he opened it to reveal four red tablets and replied with a laugh, "No thanks, I brought my own stuff. Darvon. For my migraines. No codeine, though."

A drunken laugh rippled through her as she replied, "We're a fine pair, aren't we? But really, I can't recommend the codeine *high*-ly enough. Two or three of these and within minutes you start getting tingly all over. But it's a good soft tingly. First your nose goes, then your lips. You can feel it in your fingers and toes. And then," she said softly, waving her open palm before her eyes and closing them as it passed, "Sleep. No thought, no dreams, no troubles. Just ... sleep."

Shaking his head with a frown, Tom admitted, "No, I sure don't get that with the Darvon. I just get this flat dullness. Like my brain is swelled to about three times its normal size, but it's all lopsided off one way or the other, and the swelling kind of pushes out my thoughts and my emotions. And if I'm lucky, the headache I *usually* have when I take it." But looking into the once vibrant, now vacant, eyes of his friend, Tom felt a sudden fear for both of them. Glancing behind him at a canvas tuxedo sofa, Tom said, "I'm pooped, too. Let's both conk out. We can do something later. Come on over here."

She assented and followed him to the couch where he sat upright at one end and motioned for her to place her head in his lap. Having done so, he softly caressed her hair until she was fast asleep. Leaning his head back, he soon joined her. A half hour later he awakened to find her still sleeping soundly, her head on his thigh and a circle of drool on his slacks from her open mouth. Her body was coiled into a cozy tuck inside her caftan.

As he watched the line of the early afternoon sun give way to the shade of the house, he let Siobhan continue to sleep while his mind wandered among a smorgasbord of cartography, theology, history, and Clair Kennerly. But mostly he wondered what he could do to help his somnolent friend and to help himself.

Once, after his slumber, Siobhan's mother quietly looked in on them. Tom shushed her, pointing down with a wink to her daughter at rest in his lap, and she disappeared wearing a relieved smile. When later Siobhan stirred, rubbing her head on his thigh, he became fearful of an involuntary erection. After dismissing with a stifled jest the image of his hard penis thumping the back of her head until she awakened, he successfully warded it off only by meticulously recounting in his mind the scores, the significant plays, and the individual Longhorn heroes of the halcyon '61 and '63 seasons.

Chapter 39

"I don't know why," Tom said in anguish. "I really don't know why, but when she reached over and touched my hand like that, something deep inside me said, 'Leave Clair out of this. Don't draw her into whatever you're going through'."

Perched beside him, her right arm wrapped in her lap, on a grassy lawn in Lakeshore Park and gazing out into the deep hazy blue-green of Lake Michigan, Siobhan sighed and asked, "What *are* you going through?"

Testing his new sunshades as he scanned high in the summer sky for a reply, he finally allowed, "Oh, just so much turmoil. Both within and all around me. I've gotten a lot of business stuff settled since then, but ... inside ..."

Taking his hand, she said, "Tom, you *deserve* to be happy. Whether it's with Clair or with Lizza - don't ever think you don't deserve it."

Holding onto her hand, Tom replied, "And I'm telling you never to think you don't deserve it either. When you get back to school, give the guy a chance. He can be yours again."

With the afternoon sun behind them and a warm breeze blowing off the lake into their faces, Siobhan removed her sunglasses and squinted her clear blue eyes as she peered across the water. "You've given me so much strength these last few days. I was pretty far gone. Way *down*," she said, lowering her voice. "But I'm not ready to go back into that - to go back there. Yeah, we could be together again - there - away from Memphis.

And I'm sure there would be times I could fool myself into thinking he was really mine. But, anyway," she said with a shake of her hair and turning back to face Tom, "I've decided to stay up here. I may sign up for some classes at University of Chicago or Loyola. I'm not sure."

Nodding as he cloaked his disappointment, Tom said softly, "I don't guess I blame you. You've got to do what's best for yourself. And I sure can't give you any guarantees about what my roommate might do. He really surprised me - and disappointed me. I never had any idea what kind of hold -"

"I know. I should have picked up some of the signs, but I guess I didn't want to."

Glancing at his watch, Tom said, "Come on. I think we can stuff down one more of those Gino's pizzas. Godawmighty, that's good pizza." But before they walked away from the lake, Tom looked back into the park, and Siobhan lingered beside him.

"Tom, what is it?"

"I was just wondering. What are you going to do around here? I mean, besides taking a few classes? What's going to keep you from going down again?" As she stood beside him pensively, he continued seriously, "This is not meant irreverently, but, do you know what R-F-K would tell you to do?" To her furrowed brow in response, he said, "He'd tell you to use what you've got ... and get involved."

"And just what do I have?" she asked. "Paddy already gives boocoodles of money to all the 'worthy' causes."

Pointing at a nearby playground, he offered, "You don't think it could change one of those kids' lives to learn how to play the piano? What about five of them? Or fifteen? Go down on the south side somewhere and offer them what you have - Music. I think you and the kids would both be the better for it."

With a winsome smile, she asked, "Poor Tom, have we turned you into a Liberal Democrat? Can Catholicism be far behind?" But fearing that she had belittled his suggestion, she hugged him and whispered, "Thanks, that's a good idea. And thanks for caring."

After their raid on Gino's they walked south along crowded Michigan Avenue. The couple stopped on the bridge over the Chicago River and looked up- and downstream at the bordering buildings.

"Don't you want to stay a few more days?" she begged, her arm looped through his.

"I'd probably better head on back. I've got to get a few more things tied down before school starts."

"Too bad. You're going to miss Groesbeck, you know?"

"What?"

"Yeah, he phoned me a week or so ago. Well, he talked to Mom actually. But he said he was coming up here for the convention as a correspondent from a Waco paper."

"That's great. I don't guess you're planning -"

"I think Meg and I are going up to the Door County house during the convention. I don't really want to be in town."

"I don't blame you."

"So," she said brightly, "what did you like best about our big-shouldered city? Besides the pizza and the prime rib at Lawry's, of course."

"Cultural-ally speaking," he replied, "I guess it would have to be that giant red metal sculpture."

"The Picasso?"

"Yeah, it reminded me of Snoopy doing his vulture." As they stood laughing while leaning on the rail of the bridge, Tom turned to Siobhan and said, "Chevy, do you have your Fiorinal on you?"

"Always. Curiously, I just haven't been in as much pain the last couple of days."

"Let me see them."

As she fished the container out of her purse, Tom drew his bottle of Darvon from his pocket. Handing the bottle to him, she watched in confusion as he twisted off both caps. Keeping his eyes on hers, he emptied the bottles into the river. Helplessly lunging after them with her right arm, she moaned and looked back at him with a momentary flash of anger.

"I think your arm's better," he observed with a sly smile.

She hugged him tightly for a long moment before pulling away and saying, "I've got two big lunk-headed, rough-housing brothers. And I love 'em both. But you're the other brother I wish I'd had."

He finally drew from her the full-bodied belly laugh that he remembered, when he replied, "And you're the sister I wish I'd had ... incest with."

*   *   *

Tom was made to feel at home at Ray's Diner by the waitress's emptying of his ice water into a fresh glass and the pouring of the sweet milk he had ordered to accompany his apple pie from the carton into his chilled ice water glass. He had seen her counterparts at the Swan in New Fredonia perform the same small ceremony countless times. The long, narrow diner in the Indianapolis suburb of Speedway boasted counter service plus a few booths, and the familiar banter along the bar line told Tom it catered mostly to regulars.

Keeping his ears open, he noted references both to the Republicans tapping of Nixon as the standard bearer at their convention the night before and to the seeming inevitability of Humphrey being his foe. Tom's informal earshot poll garnered the prevalent supposition being that the Republican would have a freer hand to end The War. Though there was still expressed support for Blackjack's point of view that the only thing standing between deadlock and victory was the restrictions placed on the military, the obvious message was that what the election was about was The War - the punishment of those who had gotten America into it and the anointing of he who could deliver the country out of it, the latter preferably with some modicum of 'American Honor' still intact.

'Would any of these men and women,' Tom wondered bitterly, 'truly come forward and offer up *their* sons and grandsons on the altar of 'American Honor'? Much less, God forbid, themselves?'

Since Tom took the view that the two Establishment candidates were essentially different sides of the same coin and that events would probably sweep them along rather than vice versa, he found more interesting the voice who mentioned the stunning events in Czechoslovakia. Having been out of touch the past five days, it was at the diner that Tom heard of the withdrawal of the Russian troops and tanks from Prague. This suggestion of a backing down and backing away of the monolithic Soviet Menace was a monumental event to this child of the Cold War. It suggested a response to reason and to humanity from this dark force that had led America into Space, had forced his grandfather to consider shooting neighbors who sought entrance into the fallout shelter he never got around to building, and had sent Tom out into the hallway of New Fredonia Junior High to crouch against his locker while his teachers talked fatalistically of the uselessness of the Civil Defense exercise and of the millions who would die anyway. 'If I survive The War,' Tom thought, 'maybe there's a chance we can all survive The Peace.'

But political considerations aside, Tom had come to Speedway to tour the town's *raison d'etre*: The Indianapolis Motor Speedway. Though oval track racing was generally neither within his field of interest nor his area of racing expertise, Indy was Indy. After viewing the museum and Gasoline Alley, it was with chills that Tom, aboard the tour bus, took a lap of the race course.

At the start-finish line Tom saw the three-foot-wide strip of bricks, which - with a certain Hoosier tongue-in-cheek - had been retained from the original brick-paved track to keep alive the track's nickname, The Brickyard. From there Tom scanned the grandstands, imagining himself among the crowd that had filled them for race day, with the red wedge-shaped STP-Lotus Turbine of Jimmy Clark on the pole. But as he swung the camera in his mind around toward the empty, wind-whipped pit lane, he acknowledged to whichever god ruled racing that he had not been there in May and neither had Clark - and the turbines, which were, had died out there on the track short of Glory.

*   *   *

"That river is hypnotic," Tom observed, as he and Brandeis watched the barge traffic on the Mississippi creep along in front of them far below their bluff view.

"Yeah, I come over here a lot at lunch."

"I'll bet. I'm glad you were able to take the afternoon off."

"What Father and I know and Mother doesn't won't kill her," Brandeis stated. "Even though we'd both like it to sometimes," he half-laughed. "I'm just sorry you missed my Uncle Bob. He's a great guy. Funny as hell. The office clown."

"Bob?" Tom asked. "So what was his problem already that he got such an un-Kosher name?"

"Well, until about 1939, it was Adolph," Brandeis said seriously. "He and a whole lot more changed theirs." Lightening his visage, though,

Brandeis added, "Oh yeah, you'd also like him, because he's a member of 'Jews for Jesus'."

"'Jews for Jesus', huh? Gee, I didn't even know He was running."

"Smart ass. I'm really glad you came down through here and called. I've missed you - of all people."

Having skirted the subject through their initial discussions of their summer's activities - including Tom's mixed feelings about his encounter with Clair - he finally stated, "Chevy's not coming back to Wazoo for the Fall."

Brandeis looked across the river at the overcast sky hanging above Arkansas before slowly closing his eyes in pain. "How is she?"

Tom replied regarding her injury, her travel, and her depression - but not her dependency - before he finally blurted out, "I'll never understand how you could let what y'all had go."

"Oh, Tom," Brandeis moaned. "We were happy. We were ecstatic when it was just the two of us - there in Dallas - with nothing else to consider. But my mother may be right. Our kind should probably stay with our own. And her with hers."

"*Your* kind?! *Her* kind?! I can't believe I'm hearing this. I thought the *kind* you two were were the kind who love each other. The best kind. If that was how it was for you in Dallas, you never should have left there. I don't know what the hold that wo- your mother has over you, but Memphis seems to be an unhealthy place for your heart to be."

Brandeis did not reply, and the two friends looked down into the water as the swirling eddies carved constantly shifting designs onto the surface. Brandeis finally spoke. "Did I ever tell you that in high school ... I had ... attempted suicide ... twice?"

Recoiling from him coldly, Tom asked, "How?"

"Sleeping pills," Brandeis answered. "At friend's houses both times. They found me in time. Walked me around. Poured coffee down me -"

Tom broke in, "Next time check with me. I'll get you a twelve-gauge. When they find you, all your friends'll have to do is wipe you off the wall."

"Tom," Brandeis replied with shock.

"Sorry," Tom snarled. "I just don't have a lot of respect for anybody who tries suicide - and doesn't succeed." It took Tom a long moment to return to the present and to regain his focus on Brandeis. "I am sorry. That was just the wrong thing to say to me. I can't build up too much sympathy."

"I didn't want sympathy," Brandeis replied. "I wanted understanding."

"I understand that your mother's got you real messed up - that you've got a chance for happiness," Tom said, his tone increasingly strident, "and that you refuse to reach out and take it."

Brandeis sucked in a breath while staring Tom down, and replied, "*Listen* to yourself."

Chapter 40

Late August

Clair was luminous in her peach-hued princess-style bridesmaid's dress and its matching wide-brimmed hat. The dress's scooped neck showcased her tan, and her luxuriant honey blonde tresses pulled back from her face revealed her regal neck adorned by her mother's tiny antique cameo. As Clair occupied her position at the front of Bethany Baptist's new sanctuary as bridesmaid to her friend Jennie Corrigan, Tom relished the opportunity to stare at her - legally - for minutes at a time even as he stood beside his teenage girlfriend. While he enjoyed the full frontal view of Clair as she and the congregation awaited the bride, he enjoyed as much the classic profile that she offered during the exchanging of the vows.

Tom felt only nominal guilt for having accepted the Collums' invitation to join them for this wedding - with the full knowledge that Clair would figure prominently in the ceremony. A study in intersecting loyalties, it featured the daughter of one of George Collum's fellow deacons and one of Anna Collum's best friends as bride and the Collum's older daughter Karen, who had spent the summer in Austin at The University, joining Clair as a bridesmaid.

As "The Wedding March" ripped briskly off the keys of the church's new pipe organ and the bride and groom trotted gaily up the aisle - their entourage in close pursuit - Tom anxiously examined the glowing faces of the female attendants. Clair did seek him out as he stood near the aisle on the bride's side, but when she caught his eye, the icy glare she rendered unto him gave him a start. Both expressions were duly noted by Lizza, who nodded high and away with a blithe smile.

As Tom and Lizza stood at the window of the old sanctuary, its pews removed but its fate still in limbo, looking out at the new building while balancing crystal cups of punch on matching salad plates, Clair, looking like a Breck Girl stepping off a magazine page, walked deliberately across the room to them. Her expression of seriousness verging on anger was one Tom had never seen her aim at him.

"Lizza, excuse me, I need to borrow your boyfriend for a few minutes," she said courteously but firmly.

"Sure," Lizza said, unruffled. "Just hose him down before you bring him back."

Turning to Tom, she directed, "Tom, come with me. We need to talk."

In the vacant Beginners' Sunday School classroom to which she had led him, its squat furnishings left askew by the Wednesday night nursery crowd, Clair turned to Tom and barked, "Well, Mister John Beresford Tipton, do you have Michael Anthony out scouting the countryside for the next surprise beneficiary of your largesse?"

"What?" Tom asked in confusion. Thinking quickly, though, he asked, "How did you find out? I specifically told the dean at Springfield to keep it absolutely confidential. Did someone at the college tell you?"

"Gramma told me!"

"Gramma?! Who told her?"

"Maydene Slater. And as for who told her, take your pick. She told her while she was having her hair done at the Henhouse. And if it was all over there, it's all over everywhere."

"Well, that sure wasn't what I meant to happen," Tom said. Thinking quickly, he realized that he had told only Chet and Nela - committing both to oaths of silence - and he knew the source was not Chet. "I'm really sorry, Clair. I guess that's embarrassing for you. I was just trying to do -"

She cut him off, "I don't give a damn what Maydene Slater or any of those other old biddies at the Henhouse think about me. But I don't like lies being told or implied about me, and I sure don't like them when they hurt Gramma."

"Was she upset about it?" Tom asked.

"No, not yet, because she's just innocent enough to think it was a purely altruistic act."

"Which it was," Tom declared. "Well, I'm not actually sure what 'altruistic' means, but, judging from the context, it was."

"Well, it sounded like you wanted credit from someone."

"So are you *going*?"

Her jaw firm and her eyes unblinking, she finally answered, "Yes." As they stared one another down, she added more softly, "But Tom, that was such a ... weird thing to do."

"Would you have taken the money from me if I had offered it to you?"

"No."

"Well?"

"But, I mean, why me?" she asked with wonder. "You hadn't seen me in three years. Visited me one afternoon in June. Left abruptly. I haven't heard from you since. Did you pay Lizza's tuition, too?"

"No. George Collum did. He insisted."

Waving an open hand back and forth between them, she asked, "Tom, what do we have? What ... is this?"

"I don't know," Tom answered curtly. "Don't you think if I did, I would've done something about it?"

"Aaahhh," she growled. "Well, this county is too small for you to do something like that and it not suggest something else. I don't want to be gossiped about and I don't want to have my - And I don't want Gramma to be upset. So until you figure yourself out and are ready to talk to me - *talk to me first*," she repeated, "just leave us alone." She turned and began to walk toward the door, but, with no less anger on her face, she whipped around - her silken hair and flowing skirt whirling as she did so. Returning to him, she took his cheeks in her hands and kissed him hard on the lips. Pulling away and dropping his face, she barked, "There. Thanks." And she whirled again and left the room. Stunned, Tom watched wordlessly as she departed, and he leaned down momentarily to gain support from the back of a very short chair.

When Tom returned to Lizza's side, she noted the rattle of the crystal cup against the plate when he lifted it from the windowsill. With a sly smile she queried, "So, was the old girlfriend a little P-O'd about the tuition?"

Dropping his jaw, followed by his head, in amazement, Tom asked, "Did Brinkley announce it on the news last night, and I was the only one who missed it or something?"

With a laugh Lizza replied, "Mom told me about it. Pops had heard it at Rotary."

"When do we get to leave this county and go back to anonymity?" Tom asked in frustration.

"Tomorrow," she answered evenly.

Changing to a conciliatory tone, he asked, "Does that upset you that I did that?"

"Naa. The rulebook says it should, but you know I never play by the rules. Didn't even read the book. Besides I know you're just prone to do quirky stuff like that. Plus," she mused, "Mom assured me that you must have prayed about it."

Tilting his head to the side, Tom thought, 'Yeah, I did.' "Well, Mom and Dad always liked Clair –" Tom began to explain.

"Whoa, it's okay. I don't have a problem with it. I mean, it's not like we're ever getting married or anything. It was a *nice* thing to do. Strange, but nice, and therefore, perfectly in character. Listen, let's hit the exit. I've got to throw some more things in the trunk before we go out tonight."

Tom glanced around the room before they left, but he drew a blank.

* * *

Rising from the Collums' porch swing, Tom allowed, "Well, I guess we'd better call it a night. You've got a long drive tomorrow. What did you say it was? Twelve hours to Stephens?" Nodding, she stood up beside him and kissed him on the cheek before they walked to the door together. After a longer kiss he gently pulled away and said, "Lizza, thanks for a wonderful summer. You really helped me through some ... heavy stuff. You write, and I'll write, and I'll call, and I'll see you at Thanksgiving."

Without agreeing, she said, "Tom, you're a wonderful guy. But I'm afraid you may be ... occupied at Thanksgiving." They kissed again, but as she reached for the door, she turned to him with a coy smile and said, "Tom Roy Windham, I'll always remember you ... as the one that got away."

Dropping her hand, he replied, "Elizabeth Anne Collum, I, on the other hand, will remember you ... merely as the latest in a long and distinguished line of escapees."

* * *

Sitting side by side in weathering grey Adirondack chairs on the railless fishing pier that jutted into the north end of the lake a hundred yards above the boathouse, Chet studiously observed the motionless cork at the end of the line dangling from his cane pole while Tom gazed in appreciation at the red-orange sunset reflected, from among the tall pines on the west shore, in the lake's still waters. Attired in a crumpled straw hat, paint-stained T-shirt, cut-off jeans, three day's growth of beard, and generous layers of mosquito repellent, the older cousin was working his way down through the Lone Star-half of an icy tub of beer and Dr. Peppers. Tom, in a faded navy Izod, khaki shorts and farm-stained sneakers, took a swig of his soft drink and whispered, in reverence both for the fish and for the fisherman, "With everyone knowing, I just feel like I look pretty foolish, having done that."

"No, no, Tom," Chet replied in a matched whisper, his glare unmoved from the cork. "You're mixed up. Life gives you many more opportunities to make a complete ass of yourself than it does to accomplish something worthwhile. I, personally, have far more often been offered and graciously accepted the former course. But what you did falls into the latter. Doing that for Clair was a purely good thing. Period. Don't let anyone try to tell you different. I'm just sorry my mother saw fit to cluck about it to the wrong hen."

Propping his head back against threaded fingers and the chair back, Tom moaned, "Clair."

"Shhh," Chet scolded as his cork started to wobble teasingly in the water.

Tom joined him in watching until it became still again, never having submerged. As his older cousin shrugged in frustration, Tom went on, returning to a whisper, "I'm just afraid I've screwed it up with her forever."

Still concentrating on the cork, Chet offered, "Life is long. A lot can change."

Tom took an imaginary pencil from behind his ear, saying, "Not so fast. I'm writing this down."

Hoisting his pole, the hook that cleared the water revealed the shapeless pink nub of a former worm. "Damn," Chet seethed. "Hook's too big for these piddly-ass bream." He turned to Tom as he reached into the rich, dark soil in the tin can at his side and said, "And don't be in such a hurry for resolution. Enjoy the trip. And even the part that's not enjoyable is part of the experience, and can teach you something. You've crammed so much into this summer, and a lot of it had to be done. But now, go back to school, go see a lot of movies, date a lot of girls, eat a lot of pizza, drink a lot of beer - well, Dr. Pepper. Let the thing with Clair - if there is a thing with Clair - happen or not happen, but don't force it. You've just had so much turmoil and so much grown-up stuff to contend with. Pack away the business suit and the briefcase. Enjoy being a kid for awhile - while you can. It only comes by once."

"Keep going," Tom said. "I'm still writing."

"Laugh if you will," he allowed as he baited his hook, "but the rest will come altogether too soon. And then you'll be trapped in a life that takes some of those options away." Speaking out into the lake, without regard to the fish, Chet continued, "The thing you have right now ... is Time. It's funny. When you're young, you have more than you know what to do with. You spend it frivolously; then you learn to regret its waste. Well, you do if you have the good fortune to live long enough to regret its waste."

"So what's *your* secret?" Tom asked. "As old as you are," he deadpanned, "you still seem to be able to enjoy your life, and you don't seem too serious about it or too - what's the word? constrained - by a bunch of obligations and responsibilities. How do you get by with it?"

A chorus of cicadas suddenly launched into their rhythmic rattle through the nearby trees and the reeds at the water's edge. "Whooo, listen to those 'katy-dids'," Chet noted. "No, you were asking, 'how do I get by with it?' Simple. My secret is that I continue to cling, and will continue to cling - tenaciously - to my right, for at least one side of me - all my life - to remain superficial, shallow, and immature. I think that's what keeps me young," he declared, extending his pole out over the water and dropping his freshly baited line into it up to the cork. "Arrested development ... has really taken a bad rap."

"Sounds good to me."

"Hey, life is too short to give in to those obligations and responsibilities at the expense of your soul."

"Whoa. A minute ago you said life was 'long'. Now you're saying it's 'too short'. Which is it?"

"It's both. It's long, and within it there's time for change and healing. Everything doesn't have to be decided or figured out right now and then carved in stone and hoisted into place for all time to come. But it's too short to waste any of it on doing a lot of crap we don't want to do out of obligation to some false set of standards that saps our energy and our feelings and makes us put off enjoying and loving each other.

"I have some acquaintances and former classmates, and I've observed some people around town, who seem bound and determined to live their lives for everyone else but themselves. My ex-wife was one of them -"

"Was that why y'all split up?" Tom asked. Chet's head lunged barely forward on hearing Tom's question, as if his monologue had bumped into a barrier. "Sorry," Tom said as Chet considered his response while pulling his cleanly picked hook out of the water and laying his pole on the pier.

"No, that's alright. Yeah, I guess that aspect of her was part of our problem."

"I remember Vicki, but not well. Y'all weren't married for very long, were you?"

"Four years," Chet answered, as he pried the top off another Lone Star. "But we lived in Austin part of that time. It was when we came back here that things started to unravel."

"What happened?" Tom asked. But immediately he started shaking his head and waving his open palms in front of him, saying, "I'm sorry. That's none of my business."

"It's okay," Chet said, as he pulled his Coleman lantern from behind his chair and began pumping air into it. Lighting it and eking out a zone of pale yellow illumination against the approaching darkness, he continued, "We had a problem with - let's see, what did the counselor call it? Intimacy. I think that's often their euphemism for 'sex', which we certainly had problems with. Although … it may have been my problem, too, for confusing the two." As his sixth beer reddened his face and loosened his tongue, Chet rose from his chair and walked to the edge of the deck. Unzipping his frayed shorts and relieving himself into the lake as he slowly scanned the evening sky, he continued, "Anyway, that sure wasn't all of it. It was just the clearest and most often tripped-over problem we had.

"I guess I had built up some expectations while we were dating that we obviously should have talked a lot more about. Like, at all. What it got down to," he sighed, as he shook off and zipped up, "was that, once we got married, I wanted to make love a lot. One or more times a day for the first twenty or so years would've been fine with me. But to her, once or twice a week, stretching out later to two or three times a month pretty much fulfilled her obligation under the marriage contract. And that wasn't 'making love', let me hasten to add; that was 'having sex'. There's a vast difference."

With a reflective sigh, Chet squatted on the pier in front of Tom. As a warm southerly breeze up the lake brought timid waves lapping lightly against the pier, he looked up at Tom - his young cousin's smooth, round face aglow in the yellow-white light of the lantern - and he recalled, "She had this thing she did with her thigh that always told me when we were through. It was just this slightest ... nudge ... of whichever of her thighs was closest to the edge of the bed. It usually came real soon after I popped. And it told me she was through. Her commitment was fulfilled. She was ready for me to get off her and for her to get out of bed and get down the hall to the bathroom where she'd deposit my gift in the toilet and clean herself up. This was not a sexy woman," he declared. "I've had 'sexy' since then. Very different."

"So," Tom wondered, relishing both their closeness and the topic, "why aren't you with 'Sexy' now?"

"Because," Chet cautioned, "let me hasten to add, that's far from all there is to it. There's talking and laughing and having things in common. And, Tom, there's being *nice* to each other - consistently. Over the years that last one counts for a hell of a lot. Vicki and I never had it on a consistent basis. But I've watched it between my parents, and you just can't beat it.

"It's funny," Chet continued with a half-laugh, "or really sad, I suppose. But at the end of our marriage things flip-flopped. Sex was all we had left. During those last months when we were both pulling away from each other, the only time we touched, the only time we kissed, was when we were in bed. Sex became a solitary, stand-alone act. Very awkward." Staring into the bottomless darkness of the lake, he concluded, "Devoid of love; devoid of feeling. Oddly, the last strand that held our marriage together - until we both finally admitted it was a farce."

After a moment's silence Chet slapped himself playfully, "Mmm, the way I do go on when I'm into the brew. Been hittin' it way too heavy the last couple of years. You know, still trying to get over the disappointment of Pink Air not coming in 1966. But now, listen, little cousin. If you tell your aunt about any of this, she'll have my balls. And subsequently, I yours."

"No problem," Tom replied, grinning broadly. "Thanks for the advice."

Frowning in sudden reflection, Chet wondered, "Oh Lord, was that advice I just dispensed? Well, what did you get out of it?"

"Find someone nice 'n' sexy," Tom retorted.

"No, no," Chet insisted, dog-paddling his hands apart. "More separation. Nice ... and sexy." After a laugh he glanced at his watch and said, "Guess we'd better clear out of here. I've got to get a earrr-ly start tomorrow."

"Lord, I hate to see you go."

"I'll be back Thanksgiving and Christmas. And then you're coming up for Spring Break, right?"

"Sure, but -"

"Hey, why don't you just drive up with me tomorrow?" Chet asked. "You could turn around and fly back in a day or so."

Tom thought quickly and answered, "That's a great idea, but I better not. I've still got some things to do before I head back to school. Plus, I'm just not sure about the flying thing yet."

Nodding, Chet responded, "Yeah, I can understand that. You haven't flown anywhere since then, have you?"

"No. It's strange. It's like, either the law of averages is so heavily weighted in my favor that I could fly a million miles a year for the next hundred years and never even hit an air pocket. *Or,* there's a curse on the House of Windham and the first plane I get on's going to drop out of the sky like a rock. But flying's such a convenience; I know I'll get back to it sometime. I just don't know when. But I need to get some stuff ready for school anyway."

As they rose to gather their gear, Chet slung an arm around Tom's shoulder and said, "Cousin, be happy."

Chapter 41

"Hey, Joe Joe, how's it hangin'?"

"Long, wrinkled, and purple from overuse," Joe Joe replied as he joined Tom in the line at SUB-Rosa's counter.

"Or misuse," Tom said. Dr. Peppers and fries in hand, the two juniors scouted out a booth in the SUB-Rosa - filled as it was with fellow returning upperclassmen.

"Pus-saay!" Joe Joe exclaimed to Tom with an earnest, if prurient, profundity just out of earshot of Justine Lecataret as she swished by their booth with two Mu Nu's and a Sigma Sig obediently in tow.

"Quiet down, Bartlow," Tom said. "Sounds like it was a long, hot summer up in the Panhandle, huh?"

"Aw, I'd say I got my share - and somebody else's, too."

After hearing a few inflated tales of Joe Joe's summer on the ranch and on the local rodeo circuit, Tom asked, "Don't guess you saw any of Thia, did you?"

"Matter of fact, I did. I swung down through here once to pick up a horse for my daddy, and I took her out," Joe Joe said with diminished enthusiasm.

"So, did another one bite the dust?"

"That girl's got a mind of her own," Joe Joe said with a negative shake of his head.

"Happening to more and more of them," Tom observed.

"S'nothin' ten inches o' whalebone wouldn't cure, though."

"Maybe," Tom quipped, "but it sounds like she'd rather keep dating *you*."

As he started to retort, his attention was diverted and he announced, "Semen alert! Semen alert!" As Tom considered ducking under the table, his friend continued in an announcer's monotone, "Experiencing dangerously high levels of jockey juice build-up."

"Shut up, you idiot," Tom protested with a laugh.

"Didn't you see that girl, Windham?"

Turning to catch the attractive rear view of a co-ed's thick brunette hair falling to the belt of her skintight faded jeans, Tom nodded as Joe Joe recalled, "If the back of her belt had said 'Snake Bit' on it, I'd'a swore it was La Juana Jilly, a barrel rider from Thalia. Last time I saw her, we were slappin' bellies in the back o' my pick-up on a high mesa outside o' Clayton, New Mexico. It was a month or so back - after a rodeo dance, and we'd both been *deeply* into the 'hooch'. Lord, the night was clear and starry, and I'd swear I could see the lights o' Santa Fe. Anyhow, she was drunker'n a skunk and I wasn't far behind, and she wanted to do it - wearin' nothin' but our hats and our boots. So I obliged. But she insisted on bein' on top, and that was fine, too. We'd th'owed a coupla saddle blankets in the back, but we got real active. I'm still pullin' feed pellets outta my crack! Anyways, she was good ... *daaamn* good ... 'cept she kept wavin' her hat in the air and slappin' me on the flanks with it - first one side and then the other - and yellin' 'Diablo! Diablo!' Damn, I'm glad I made her take off those spurs."

* * *

Sitting in the window of their new room in Postlethwaite, Tom had been trying unsuccessfully to play an honest game of Solitaire Chess on his pegboard travel set when he saw Brandeis pull into a three-quarter length parking space across the street in the freshly black-topped Sprite. Unfolding out of the tiny sports car, he stretched and scanned the broad red brick Georgian facade of the four-story upperclassmen's dorm. He stopped and returned a wary gaze at the tentative wave from his once and future roommate. The severity of his working haircut that Tom had first noticed in Memphis left him with a series of low kinky waves. But for the powder blue Sprite, Tom wondered if he would have recognized him.

The nervousness Tom felt was uncomfortably akin to what he had experienced so long ago after his birthday night confessional. Brandeis entered carrying only an overnight bag. Tom decided to put to an early test the serious demeanor that his friend wore into the room. Glancing down at his bag, Tom asked, "You planning on getting this semester wrapped up in the next couple of days?"

Dipping his head without a smile, Brandeis replied, "My trunk's coming in at the bus station this afternoon. Would you mind driving me down to pick it up? I could probably get someone else."

"I'll take you. How'd the Sprite make the trip?"

"Not very well, really. I fed it oil all the way down here, and it's missing pretty bad."

With a mournful frown Tom asked, "Well, now that you're here, don't you need to take it somewhere to get it worked on? I'd be glad to take you and drive you around or let you use the Le Mans till it's fixed."

"Thanks, but now that I'm here, I probably won't need it much. And they said there wasn't anything in the college budget to get major work done on it -"

"Oh, well, okay. Like I said, I'll be glad to drive you anywhere."

As they toured the floor, they lamented the absence of the McCartney gang. Glancing in on the common bathroom and noting with disappointment its lack of a private shower, Tom was reminded and mentioned, "Hey, did you know Harvey was up in Chicago covering the convention?"

Wincing at the mention of the city, Brandeis replied, "No. You haven't seen him on T-V, have you?"

"No, but knowing him, he's in the thick of it - going for the story. I wonder if he's been arrested," Tom said as they clopped down three flights of stairs to the lobby.

"I'm sure we'll get his firsthand eyewitness report as soon as he gets back. News, pictures, and commentary," Brandeis said before falling silent. Boarding the car, though, he finally asked quietly, "Did she come back?"

Pulling out of his parking space, Tom did not look at his roommate but shook his head. "I talked to her last week, and she said she still wasn't in any shape to go back to school ... anywhere. But when she can, she's not coming back down here." Finally glancing at his roommate's joyless visage, he added with pride, "She said she might take my advice and look into teaching piano to some underprivileged kids."

Jerking his head back in surprise, Brandeis nodded and asked, "Hmmm. That was your idea?"

"Yeah, I guess all you knee-jerk liberals shouting in my ear last year didn't leave me totally unmoved."

Upon return to their room, as Brandeis made reference to the paucity of his social life over the summer, the negative feelings Tom was experiencing spawned a random concern. "Did you see any of your *old school chum* this summer?" Winning only a perplexed glare from Brandeis, Tom reiterated, "You know, *that* old school chum? The one you saw last Christ- "

"Oh," Brandeis replied with displeasure. "No, well, yeah. I mean, I *saw* him at the Diaspora Ball. But I -"

"The what?"

The Diaspora Ball. It's not really a 'ball'. It's a get-together that just sort of happens every August for the Jewish college students in Memphis heading off or heading back to school. He was there, but I didn't - Well, it's really none of -" After a tense moment of silence, Brandeis said, "Anyway, I had a date."

With too much surprise Tom responded, "You did? With who?"

"A girl I went to high school with. Linda Green."

"Linda Green? Sounds pretty Gentile."

"She's not. We're not all named Bernstein or Wasserman," Brandeis snapped.

"You didn't mention her when I was in Memphis."

Brandeis replied, "We had only had one date then. She goes to Southwestern - there in Memphis."

"I'm just surprised. Is it serious?"

Sloughing off a roll of his eyes, Brandeis answered, "Hardly. I don't know why I'm telling you this, but, I kissed her ... once."

"Was that all it took?" Tom asked. Biting his lip, Brandeis nodded his head downward. "Well, I'm sure it came as a great relief to your mother - that you were dating a fellow Chosen One."

Brandeis rose from his desk chair and walked silently to the window. Assessing their new view of the tops of street-shrouding live oaks, of the facing classroom building, and of The Zim in the distance, Brandeis said quietly, "Tom, I'm Jewish."

"You're what?" Tom asked, straining to hear.

Turning to face his roommate, Brandeis stared sternly into Tom's eyes and repeated, "I'm Jewish. And -"

"Never said you weren't," Tom retorted. "But I'm Baptist, and if I was in love with a girl like Chevy and was *God All-Mighty* lucky enough to have her love me back, I'm *damned* if I'd let our religions stand in our way. Wouldn't let them anywhere close. Does being Jewish lock you into this tiny pool of candidates that, by definition, excludes the person you happen to love ... and who loves you desperately ... and who needs you?"

"We've got a responsibility to our heritage that you could never understand."

"What about your responsibility to yourself? To Siobhan?"

"We can't spend our lives thinking only of ourselves. We have - "

"Tradi-*tion*, tradition ... tradi-*tion*!" Tom sang gutterally with Tevye-esque snaps of his fingers before clapping an imaginary tambourine over his head and launching into, "Yadda, dadda, dadda-"

"Hold it!" Brandeis interjected. "Did you read about the murder of that gas station clerk down past the south end of the Drag last week?"

Caught off guard, Tom replied, "Well, yeah, but -"

"And how the victim was set to go to Duke on a full scholarship in pre-med? He'd be up there matriculating right now had not some lunatic blown his head off for a hundred-and-twenty-three dollars out of his cash drawer." As Tom continued to nod solemnly, Brandeis went on, "Perfectly senseless. Maniacal. An intolerable waste of a life - of someone with unlimited potential to do good for mankind. The cure for cancer may have died with that store clerk. Think of the loss to his family, of the broken lives left behind. I don't need to tell *you*, do I?" As Tom shook his head, Brandeis concluded, "Okay, now multiply that by the *millions* of young Jewish men and women, teenagers and children brutally massacred, murdered and wiped from the face of the earth in The Holocaust. Think of the pain of their families, what was left of their families. Think of the love they missed - of their lives left unfulfilled. Think of the loss of all that potential - of the knowledge wasted, of the science undiscovered, of the art not painted, of the literature not written, of the songs not sung ... of all the questions not just left unanswered ... not even asked. I *owe* something to that generation - to their memory. *That* is what *I*, a Jew, can understand ... and *you*, not a Jew, cannot."

*   *   *

As Tom had sat in the Carters' den the prior week mesmerized in horror at the dashing of the dreams of the Czechoslovakian people under the treads of the Russian tanks, so now - as the halls of WSU began to fill again - he found himself standing amid stunned, gawking klatches of fellow students in the lobby of Postlethwaite or at the SUB, watching the crushing of the hope of America's youth under the bludgeoning blows of Chicago police billy clubs. And as the foundation for a safer world that Tom had idealistically envisioned turned to rubble on the streets of Prague, as his optimism for America was tear-gassed and pummeled in Grant Park, and as the cry of the Civil Rights movement after the gunning down of Doctor King rose with a more violent, more urgent tone, the bodies kept stacking up in Vietnam. After the murder of Kennedy and the squelching of McCarthy's crusade, and as the negotiators in Paris squabbled over the shape of the furniture, Tom carried with him a distant foreboding that - on top of everything else he had been through - his fate might yet await him half a world away in a triple-canopy jungle.

Chapter 42

Mid-September

The dark, richly-grained wood paneling of Meriwether Hemple & Meriwether's conference room seemed to close in on Tom as he nursed - sip by awful sip - the muscular black coffee that Braxton Clay had urged on him and which he had been too intimidated either to refuse or to dilute. His only escape was the view through the wall-to-wall windows that showcased the residential neighborhoods and the occasional commercial outcroppings to the north of downtown. Burly, grey clouds boded another thunderstorm rolling in from the southwest as Dallas alternately sweltered, bathed, and toweled off through summer's death throes.

After briefly describing his negotiations with Global's insurance carriers, Clay concluded, "Bottom line: their initial settlement proposal is seventy-five-thousand dollars."

Narrowing his eyes, lacing his fingers, and poking his chin with his forefingers, Tom evinced his practiced expression of quiet contemplation and calculation while, in fact, he awaited a first word from someone better informed than he. In this case he waited either for Ward or for Braxton Clay to brand the stated amount as outrageously low, outrageously high, or about right - for he had no idea.

Obliging Tom, Ward asked Clay, "Well, what do you think of it?"

"Depends on whether you're willing to litigate or not ... or on whether you're at least willing to threaten litigation. If you don't mind taking the time, we might could wring some more out of them - maybe a lot more. But it's up to you," he said, looking first at Ward and then at Tom.

Having confirmed, from discussions over the summer with the Brannigans and the Carters - whom Tom had come to call "The Board of Directors", often playfully, sometimes not - and from deliberations with his own conflict-avoiding soul, that he did not want to take the airline to court, Tom asked, "Without the threat of litigation, do you think we could do any better than this seventy-five thousand?"

"Probably," the attorney nodded. "This is the first number they've thrown out. I'm sure they expect it to go up. What we don't know, of course, is their 'cutoff' number. The number where they'd break off talks and prepare for court. It may be a hundred. It may be more. It's probably something short of one-fifty."

"And what could litigation do for us?" Ward asked.

"Somewhere between 'nothing' and 'a lot'," Clay answered. "A huge amount. Of course, that's a long difficult course to pursue." After a moment's calculation he added, "With Tom already out of the house and almost on his own anyway, that weakens our case for replacement of lost support. Your mother wasn't working, so there's no lost earnings there. And, ironically, since they died together, there's no support that would need to be provided to the widow - either from the estate or from you. They'd do a lot of investigation of the numbers we'd have to give them regarding your father's income." Tom frowned at the prospect but did not address it.

"So what do we need to do?" Tom asked.

"You need to figure out what you think you're entitled to, ask them for it, and go from there," Braxton Clay answered. "But Son, believe me, if your number's too low, they don't hand out mulligans."

Later that evening in Ward's dimly lit, richly furnished study, Tom's mentor drew on a long, fat cigar. Letting the heavy smoke seethe from between his teeth and rise to form a grey foggy wreath around his head, Ward smiled proudly and said, "Havanas."

In reply Tom gurgled his Dr. Pepper before swallowing slowly. Lifting the bottle straight up and scanning its bottom, he mimicked his host's pride, saying, "Mount Pleasant Bottling Plant."

After a laugh Ward asked, the rapidity of his speech signaling to Tom their transition into a business discussion, "So what are you planning on countering with?"

"Well, I've given it a lot of thought. I've gone back and added up Dad's earnings over the last few years and averaged it. And I've tried to project that out to if he had been able to work to retirement at sixty-five." Ward listened intently as Tom continued from that point into a lengthy, obtuse explanation which he knew, but hoped Ward would not recognize, to be a sufficiently reasoned computation to support what was actually his guess at a realistic bargaining number. He knew this number had to fall high enough above the insurer's offer to approach their cutoff number but low enough not to push them away from the table and into court. But chiefly he felt that - to maintain Ward's respect by eschewing the suggestion that he was crudely negotiating the value of his parents' lives - he could not admit to Ward that the number at which he arrived was nothing more than a bargaining point. Even if Ward were thinking the same thing. At the conclusion of his remarks he said, "Therefore, I'm going to ask them for one-hundred-and-twenty-five-thousand dollars."

Ward nodded, blew a huge puff of smoke away from Tom, and observed, "That sounds good ... but I wouldn't go through the explanation of how you arrived at it." Although Ward added, "No reason to give them anything they could use in court," Tom conjectured that Ward did share his view of the proceedings - even if neither could admit it.

*   *   *

The roommates held their ears as the massive hulk of the Boeing 707 filled the starless sky above them passing less than a hundred feet overhead. Having disassembled the Sprite's new top and stowed it behind the seats, they sat gazing skyward from its cockpit as the tail of the airplane disappeared over the catch fence at the north end of Love Field's east runway. They had backed into the turn-in below the fence off of Shoreline Drive, and they had parked facing the dark placid waters of Bachman Lake. As the drone of the 707's engines' reverse thrust moved away from them, Brandeis started to whistle the theme from *The High and the Mighty*.

"How're you doing?" he paused after a chorus to ask.

"No problem," Tom answered. As the smell of jet exhaust drifted down over them, Tom continued, "I can watch 'em, and I can smell 'em, and I can hear 'em. Next step, I guess, is actually getting on one. Which I don't see myself having to do till Spring Break. I ought to have it licked by then. Thanks for bringing me out here tonight, though. This helps."

"Glad to," Brandeis replied. "I come out here ever once in awhile … just to think about things."

"Ever think about getting on a plane and heading for Chicago?"

"More than once. I didn't realize how obsessed I was with her till I got back to Dallas." Looking around outside the car, he observed, "We parked here once."

Tom silently watched him with the same ambivalence he had felt toward his roommate since the tearful call he had received from Siobhan in June. 'So what are you doing *here*?' he thought, 'and what is she doing *there*?' But thinking again, he chided himself, 'Probably the same thing Clair's doing in Promise.'

During a long silence they turned their view back toward Bachman as its waters reflected the lights off Northwest Highway, which bounded the lake on the north. His gaze fixed on an airport light standard perched on a concrete block rising from the lake, Brandeis gave a barely perceptible shake of his head. "I screwed it, Tom. It's gone."

"So what're you going to make of yourself? Going from here?" Tom asked.

"A great, unhappy lawyer," Brandeis declared with a frozen stare.

Dropping his mouth open and looking skyward as the beam of an approaching jet's lights grew before him, Tom asked, "Why don't you pull out of here; head over to Preston Road; hook a left, and don't stop till you hit Chicago? I'm not gettin' diddly done around here either. I'd go with you."

"Too late!" he yelled, slamming awake the high-pitched horn of the Sprite - both screams lost in the roaring whoosh of a descending DC-8.

*   *   *

"One-hundred twenty-five-thousand," Tom said, as evenly as he could. He narrowed his eyes to judge the reaction of John Rivkin, who sat across from Ward and blocked Tom's view of East Dallas out Ward's office window.

With a smirking grin the insurance company's attorney replied, "Curious number. So all we're doing her is just bargaining, huh?" To

Tom's horror, he continued caustically, "Fine. We can do that. So we're at seventy-five and you're at one-twenty-five. So next, I guess I say 'eighty' and you say 'one-twenty' and I say 'ninety' and you say 'one-ten' and I say 'one hundred' and you say 'Deal!' Right?"

Tom looked down at his lap. Then glancing up, he turned to read Ward's angry, clinched jaw.

"Am I right?" Rivkin asked. "Isn't that about the size of it? Shall we say 'a hundred'?"

Coldly, Ward replied, "We'll take it under advisement with our attorneys and contact you."

"That will be fine," Rivkin said with a fixed grin. Closing his briefcase, he rose to leave. Offering his hand to each, he received grudging shakes and walked from the office.

"I'm sorry about that," Ward said. Patting Tom on the back, he continued, "He had no right to ... " and his voice trailed off.

Nodding, Tom focused on White Rock Lake and quietly admitted, "I guess he was right."

"No, he wasn't. We're not bargaining. We're just trying to get for you what you need and what you deserve ... because you lost your parents ... on their airplane. There's nothing wrong with that, and don't think there is."

"I'd rather not talk to him again," Tom said sadly. After a moment, though, he added quietly, "Don't you think we ought to take the ... their offer?"

"Unless you're willing to threaten going to court," Ward replied, "yeah, we probably should. That's about what I figured it would be. I'll call him later and tell him." Examining the downcast stare of his young charge, Ward took his shoulders gently and said, "Tom, don't feel bad about this."

Raising his head skyward and drawing in a deep breath, Tom replied, "I'm trying not to. I just wish I could hurt Global for what they've taken away from me. But like you've said, the insurance company'll cover for the airline; then charge them a higher premium; and the airline'll pass it on to you and John Q. Public - and me, if I ever give them the chance again. I hate Global, and I hate this system." But locking his eyes in focus on the seedy eastern end of downtown far below, Tom finally raised an eyebrow, warped his chin and thought, 'A hundred thousand dollars.'

* * *

Turning from his campus mailbox while sifting through his correspondence, Tom was greeted by a smiling, bespectacled young man who required a double take from Tom to recognize. The rimless eyeglasses and the thick mahogany mane gave Fred Slater the appearance more of the collegians on either coast than of one at a conservative Texas campus. Scanning down at his royal blue sweatshirt, Tom read in red and white, "Wazout en Paree".

After jovial greetings Tom said, "Yeah, I called you once this summer and your mom said you were doing the summer program in France. How was it?"

"*Magnifique*," Fred replied. "Marched in demonstrations every day. Manned the barricades. Learned some great French slang. Hardly cracked a book."

"Wow! The summer of your dreams! One question. Why'd you come back?"

"Dad had me shang-hai'd and brought back."

"Did you get your six hours credit?" Tom asked.

"Three. Let's just say, Alf was a tad P-O'd."

"I'll bet. Tell me, though. Did you really get involved in all those demonstrations?"

"Sure," Fred bragged. "And you know those 'Frogs'. They really know how to throw a revolution."

"Did you learn much French?" Tom asked in wonderment.

"More body language than words," he leered.

"Oh, were there women involved?"

"Tom," Fred said, lowering his voice to an intimate tone, "I met this girl one night - Danielle. I was - get this - standing on a barricade, holding a flaming torch, singing 'La Marseillaise', and she walked up - "

"Did you know the words?"

"Sure. That was the French I learned. Anyway, she walked up to me, and we started talking. And she hardly knew any English. But we talked that whole night - off and on. Well, it was more like playing charades. But we learned a lot about each other. It was just before I had to come back. But we swapped addresses. And I've gotten a letter from her." With an exasperated laugh he admitted, "But I had to take it to Doctor Oliver in the French Department to translate it."

"She sounds incredible. What did she look like?"

"Dark brown hair down to here," he said, cutting his hand across the small of his back. "Huuuuge brown eyes, and just a beautiful small face. Full lips - "

"You going back?"

"Next June," he answered quickly. "Not that Alf and Maydene know that yet."

"Yeah, didn't you just love Paris?" Tom asked. "You know, I was there in - "

With a nod Fred interrupted with a frown, "Say, did you hear about the Z-P-L?"

"No."

"They're closing it."

"What? Why? I mean I heard about the freshman who got run over there during 'Rush'. But, hell, he was drunk and shouldn't have fallen asleep on the ground in the first place. And it only broke one leg."

"Yeah, but his grand-daddy was a trustee," Fred pointed out. "But that's not the reason. They're putting in a new computer science center on the side of it opposite The Zim. And they're going to pave what's left in between. And it'll be patrolled."

"Computers," Tom spat ruefully. "Pulling us – kicking and screaming - into the twentieth century."

"'Fraid so," Fred replied. With a reflective cock of his head he added, "Just give me a bottle of Bordeaux and a table in the sun on a street in Montparnasse with Danielle in her miniskirt. And you can *have* the twentieth century."

"Flaming torch," Tom observed. "Barricades. 'La Marseillaise'. And Danielle Bardot. Shhih."

* * *

Walking into his room after class the next day Tom found Brandeis sprawled on the floor between their beds wearing only his briefs. He was lying on his back on the *tallith* his mother had sent him and which he had converted into a throw rug. His arms extended toward the beds with crooks at the elbows and his legs extended toward the door with his feet overlapping, he cocked his head to the side.

Snapping his fingers and pointing at his roommate, Tom said, "No, let me guess. The crowd turned against you, and Herod sent you back to Pilate."

"Wrong," Brandeis answered.

"Aahhhh, you just ate fifty hard-boiled eggs on a bet."

"You must have seen the eggshells in the trashcan," he replied, and he began singing, *"I don't care if it rains or freezes 'cause I got my dime store 'Judas'*... "

As Tom glanced with a smile at the dark-featured young stranger poised on the side of his bed, Brandeis introduced them, waving his hand back and forth, "Tom Windham, David Weiss. David Weiss, Tom Windham. David and I have 'Poli Sci-International Organizations' together," Brandeis explained as they shook hands.

"Yeah, how's that class going?" Tom asked.

"The first five minutes was about the League of Nations," David answered. "And everything since then's been U-N."

Are you pre-law, too?" Tom asked.

As David nodded, Brandeis offered with interest, "And he's planning on going International Law. He grew up in Mexico City, so he's already bilingual."

His eyes brightening, Tom commented, "Hey, I was in Mexico D-F for the Grand Prix last year." As David nodded, Tom added, "I saw Clark get his penultimate nine there."

"To us of the 'Great Unwashed and Uninformed'," Brandeis retorted caustically, "the pretentious Mister Windham is referring to Jimmy Clark's next-to-last Formula One win before he bought some trees in Deutschland."

"Bought some trees?" Tom countered. "Ah, a fellow traveler in pretense."

David Weiss glanced from his host to his new acquaintance as they stared at each other, and he rose from the bed. "I better shag ass over to the 'libe'," he said. "Nice to meet you, Tom. Think about what I mentioned to you," he directed at Brandeis as he left.

A sullen silence followed Weiss' departure as Tom installed himself at his desk and unloaded his cordovan leather briefcase. Some time later as Brandeis looked up and caught Tom's eye as it circled the room in search of an Intermediate Accounting solution, Brandeis asked, "Why did you stick that letter up there?"

Tom glanced around at the letter from Ward's brokerage firm that he had tacked to the corkboard wall at the back of his desktop and below his built-in bookshelf. "Why?" Tom asked. "Did you look at it?"

"I didn't, but David did, and anyone else who walks in the room and sits down there can. I have company sometimes, you know."

"Well, it's none of their business."

"So why did you put it up there?"

"I need it when I check my stock quotes in the paper to see where I stand."

"You can't remember *four* stocks?" Brandeis asked.

"There are *six*," Tom countered.

"Sor-ree. Six."

"Why? What did they say?"

"Just that it seemed strange that you'd have it there. Like you might be showing off or something."

Yanking the tacks from the wall and letting the letter drop to his desk, Tom said, "Well, maybe next semester I need to live somewhere where I can get some privacy."

"No, maybe I do," Brandeis countered. "David was talking to me about pledging Sigma Alpha Mu. That's 'Sammie' to you Gentiles."

Lowering his ramparts, Tom asked, "Are you really thinking about doing that?"

"I don't know. I may," Brandeis sighed. "I'm so disgusted with ... " but the thought drifted away.

"Hey, I'm sorry," Tom said. "It's just been a bad day for me. Had some bad news."

"What's that?"

"Ah, I got a call yesterday from the office ... in Noofer. The office manager - this older lady - is sick. And I don't know how long she's going to be out. The manager that I hired ... started talking to me about wanting to buy me out."

"I didn't think you were ready to do that," Brandeis said.

"No, I'm really not. I'm not sure I want to. But he's already talked to some attorneys around town about backing him."

"And buying you out? Or opening his own office?"

"Buying me out - *he said* - but the threat is that if I say 'no', he'd just go next door and open up."

"Sorry, Tom. With the stuff you're still having to handle, I know my moods don't help."

Forget it, Woz. I know what you've lost, too."

* * *

As rain peppered against the windows, Tom, Ward, Braxton Clay, and John Rivkin stood around the small conference table in a corner of Ward's office. Glancing quickly at the denominations of the two checks that Rivkin had slid across the desk toward them after Tom had signed off on the settlement agreement, Ward looked puzzled and asked, "Seventy-five thousand and twenty-five thousand?"

"Why the two checks?" Tom asked.

Rivkin thought for only a second before his face brightened and with a smile replied breezily, "Oh, one's for him ... and the other one's for her."

Directing an expression of disgust at the insurer's attorney, Ward reached to steady Tom. Stunned, the young man looked away - his eyes closed, his head down. "*Him* and *her*?" Ward asked slowly with controlled if not contained anger.

Smiling nervously as he noted Ward's expression, Braxton Clay offered, "Mister Rivkin, why don't you let me see you out?"

When they had left, Tom repeated, "Him and her," as he picked up the checks. Dangling each from a forefinger and thumb, he thought, 'Will I ever be able to get the blood off these?'

* * *

As the rainstorm that shrouded downtown made its way across Dallas, Tom's lethargic roommate rose from his desk and turned to the open window. After closing it to the sprinkles of rain that started to peck at the glass, Brandeis stretched his arms above him and leaned against the window casing. From their fourth floor aerie he stared grimly across campus at the turned soil and the grading equipment in the ZPL and whispered, "Rosebud."

Chapter 43

Mid-October

"Poooooorr Okies, Poooooorr Okies," the jubilant Longhorn fans started to wail in patronizing dolefulness above the din of the Texas-O.U. crowd as it departed the Cotton Bowl. The Sooner fans were silent, awestruck. But having had their years of castigating the Texas fans with post-game choruses of "Poor Bevo" and with the knowledge that - like a loyal political opposition - their day would come another year, they were good sports about it. As the crowd ushered Tom and Brandeis down the descending corridors of the Cotton Bowl's ramp system, Tom joined joyfully in the traditional victory lament. Moving slowly among the ebullient orange-clad and despondent scarlett-clad masses, Tom's eyes were still moist from the tears he had shed during the Longhorns' ultimate fourth quarter touchdown drive to pull out a 26-20 victory over the heavily favored Sooners.

"That was the sixteenth Texas-O-U game I've been to in my twenty years," Tom yelled to Brandeis, "and that was the best ever." Brandeis returned the nod and the sad, knowing half-smile that had become so familiar to his roommate.

Like believers emerging from the catacombs, the boys finally escaped the labyrinthine passages into the warm autumn air outside Gate 2, the main entrance to the Cotton Bowl. The crowd continued to surge and to swirl in the plaza in front of the stadium and along the side streets. Tom persuaded Brandeis to join him again in the serpentine line at Fletcher's for one last traditional golden brown corn dog as Tom had done with his father for the prior fifteen second Saturdays in October.

Chomping on them as the football crowd merged into the State Fair crowd and tromped across the lawn next to the Hall of State Building, a flood of emotions and a gush of memories rushed over Tom. He felt physically weak, and as they neared the broad boulevard separating the stadium complex from the Esplanade, Tom grabbed Brandeis' arm. Wheeling to respond, Brandeis was shocked by the pallid face and moist brow of his friend. "Tom! What is it?"

Tom started to speak, but suddenly he choked. Coughing desperately for breath and clearance, his color changed quickly to red, and Brandeis started to pound him on the back. With his knees weakening Tom bent over and braced his hands on them as Brandeis held his shoulder with one hand and beat his back with the other. Finally an obstinate chunk of wiener and corn meal came up, but following it came the rest of the corn dog - and the one before - and the Dr. Pepper in between. Tom longed for the warm soothing hands of his mother - one supporting his brow, the other gently patting his back as she had through many middle-of-the-night childhood sessions over the toilet in the Boys Bathroom. But he was glad to have his friend beside him as Brandeis reached over his back to hold his shoulders while he coughed and spit. With drool and mucus dangling from his mouth and nose, Tom looked around helplessly for a towel. Seeing his dilemma, Brandeis yanked out his shirttail and offered it. But waving him off with an appreciative nod, Tom pulled out his own - swabbing his face and blowing his nose. Finally rising slowly, he became aware of the swirling crowd as it allowed him a wide berth. Too weak to register much embarrassment, though, Tom allowed Brandeis to sit him down on the curb of the boulevard.

"You okay?" Brandeis asked.

Spitting at the gutter and blowing his nose again, Tom nodded before raising his head and inhaling deeply. Running his hand through his hair, he turned slowly and looked back at the broad expanse of the stadium.

Brandeis followed his gaze, but looking back at his friend, he said, "I'm glad you talked me into coming with you. You're right. That was more than a football game." After a hesitation he asked carefully, "What were you about to say ... before you got sick?"

Closing his eyes and inhaling again as if trying to ingest an aura, a sense of place and time, Tom was slow to reply. "I was going to say, 'I wish Dad could have seen the Wishbone T'. I know it's hard for you to understand, but he lived and died every autumn with the fortunes of Texas Longhorn football. I grew up thinking the last words to 'The Star-Spangled Banner' were, 'Beat the Hell out of O-U!' And you're right. 'Texas-O-U' is a lot more than a football game. Of course, I would have gone to U-T, if it hadn't been for Mark. Mom couldn't have handled it. But anyway, all my life this game's been an annual pilgrimage. Both sides have had seasons made and coaches' jobs saved by winning this one, without regard to the rest of the season. And Dad and Mom and Mark and I shared some wonderful times watching that game, coming to the Fair. I appreciate your coming with me. I've got this tradition to uphold, but it sure would have been hard coming alone. Thanks."

Reminded again of the last drive, Tom said, "He would've loved watching James Street work that Triple Option, though. Sorry about the crying."

"Hey, I cry at movies. You cry at football games. We're even," Brandeis allowed.

"Anyway," Tom observed, "that's Texas-O-U."

* * *

The graffiti Tom pointed out to Brandeis read:

GOD IS DEAD

But don't worry. Mary's pregnant again.

As Tom laughed, Brandeis smirked wearily. Having spent most of a quiet Sunday studying in their room, Tom had coaxed Brandeis to 'Quarter of Three' in his latest effort to lift his spirits. As they sat listening to a jazz combo from WSU's music department, Tom asked in his raspy post-game voice, "Are you going to major in moping for the rest of your life?"

"Huh?" Brandeis asked.

"Are you just planning on moping around Wazoo for another couple of years and then sulking through law school somewhere for three and then leading the sad, unsmiling life of Memphis' most anonymous law research mole until one morning you wake up dead?"

"Leave me alone."

"Sorry. Just trying to draw you out a little."

Groaning as he swung his head from side to side, Brandeis said, "I don't know. I guess that's what I thought I could do. Just turn on automatic pilot and live it out."

"Don't you think you're a little young for that?"

"I'm just a coward. Siobhan said to me once that I didn't have the courage to take my life away from my mother, and maybe she was right. I guess I can just keep asking her what she wants me to do next. Won't have to worry about anything."

"You're not serious."

"Naa, I'm just surprised at myself and the way I feel about things. Tom, you and I came here with different attitudes. You came to Wazoo to find out what you wanted to do with your life. I came here knowing exactly what I wanted. The Law. I know I've joked about being directed by my family toward law school, but that was just to hide my embarrassment at being so career-oriented - among all you misguided ne'er-do-wells that I wanted as friends. I've known I was going to be a lawyer - and wanted to be - since the third grade when I first went to watch my father in court. I never knew how anything else in my life would go, but I always figured I had that - the Law - and it would be the framework I could build the rest of my life around. And then along came Siobhan McKenna, and everything turned upside down. All the old rules and the old presumptions went out the window because she suddenly just filled up my life and became more important than everything else -."

"By your choice," Tom said pointedly.

"Yes. Sure, she was my obsession. *Is* my obsession. She forced me into nothing. But then my mother - oh, let's see. What all did the shrink and I figure out? But then my mother started pulling me back. She used the Law, my Judaism, Siobhan's Catholicism, my career, and, of course, basically her position of respect as my mother - really pulled out all the stops to get me headed back to her position of control over me - and one where, coincidentally, I could have the career I had always professed to wanting - best Jew lawyer in Memphis.

"But what she didn't know and what I hid from myself all summer and didn't realize until the last few weeks - these weeks here without Siobhan - was that last year - last spring - I experienced a basic change in my career goals." His eyes grew watery as he smiled a pitiful, ironic smile and said, "I've looked at my skills, my capabilities, my aptitudes, and my interests - just like the career counselors say you should - and I found that loving Siobhan McKenna was the best thing I ever did. I was better at it, got more fulfillment and joy out of it than anything else I had ever had in my life or anything - or anyone - else I can imagine ever coming into it. And I've lost her - by my own doing - by my own weakness and lack of courage. And I'm left with exactly what I deserve. Well, let me tell you. Neither Judaism nor my mother nor the Law nor the Prophets ... can keep me warm."

* * *

At five o'clock the next morning Tom gave up on his attempts to achieve sustained sleep. Showering and dressing quickly, he left a note for Brandeis indicating that he was making a quick trip to New Fredonia and would be back the next day. Too queasy to eat breakfast, he left campus before six and drove to Love Field.

Gritting his teeth as he passed the Global ticket counter, he approached the American Airlines counter warily. "I need a round trip ticket to Chicago, and I need to leave on your next available flight and return tonight."

Glancing at the clock above her, the clerk flashed a perky smile and replied, "If you hurry, we can get you on the seven-thirty flight, non-stop, arriving O'Hare at ten-o-two. And on the return," she said, quickly checking schedules, "we have a five-thirty-seven departure arriving Love at eight-eleven and a seven-eighteen flight arriving at - "

"Do you have space on the five-thirty-seven?" Tom asked quickly.

"Yes."

"For two?"

"Beg pardon."

"I need a one-way ticket, Chicago-to-Love, on the same flight in addition to my roundtrip ticket," he declared.

"Done," she replied with a smile. After quickly assembling the two tickets and limbering up Tom's new American Express card, she said, pointing toward the "To All Flights" sign, "Now, make a run for Gate Twenty-Nine."

Turning from her comforting smile, he looked up at the sign she had identified. He turned back to look at her, though, and he was made painfully aware of the expression of terror that he wore by the marked change on her face. With a stark, questioning frown, she asked, "Sir, is something wrong?"

"Oh, no, nothing," he responded as he turned away from her and started toward the wide mouth of the corridor to which she had directed him.

Walking quickly around the corner to enter the walkway that led to the gates, he hesitated at the foot of the wide, ascending corridor. There on the right, forming part of the hallway, was a black rubber surface bounded by escalator-like banisters. Tom recognized it immediately as Love Field's infamous 'moving sidewalk', and he was reminded of the event in the Fifties that had idled it. It had killed a little girl. He remembered his horror and gory fascination that one of his peers had died in the grasp of a mechanical sidewalk - how at that age his imagining how she had died must have been even more grisly than the event itself. But there it stood, an endless black rubber mat now nothing more than a part of a hallway. A tragic reminder of the price of progress and technology, it had laid idle since the commission of its crime. Its punishment had not been death by removal but life imprisonment by non-use. Tom took the carpeted walkway.

Aboard the plane he found his senses to be disturbingly acute. Food and jet fuel aromas mixed with troubling engine roars and vibrations to bring a sweat to his face and underarms. Strapped in as tightly as his seatbelt would allow, Tom desperately grasped both arms of his aisle seat on his otherwise empty row. The jerk of the craft away from its gate startled him. At the head of the runway he tensed further as the pilot built power in the jet engines. He tried to relieve his nervousness again by noting that his death-grip on the seat arms had indeed turned his knuckles white, but as the accumulated thrust launched the airplane down the runway and skyward, Tom gave up all pretense of unconcern and bowed his head toward his lap until the jet's severe angle of ascent lessened. Refusing breakfast and refreshments, Tom kept to his seat – seatbelt engaged - to the flight's conclusion. Jerking nervously upon touchdown at O'Hare, he tensed again as the pilot applied the loud counter-torque of reverse thrust. Throughout the flight and upon landing, the stewardesses had observed him warily as his lips frequently moved in silent communication with God, his co-pilot.

Upon landing he made quickly for the restroom, where he vomited repeatedly. After twenty minutes and down to the yellow-green bile, Tom walked weakly toward the cabstand. Before departing the airport, though, he was struck by his first non-flight-related pessimistic thought regarding his mission, and he found a pay phone where he confirmed that Siobhan's mother was home.

* * *

As they sat on the couch where he and Siobhan had napped in the summer and looked out on the covered pool and the bare trees beyond, Tom closed his half hour plea to Meg McKenna.

"Please let me take her back down to Texas with me. I'll take good care of her. I think if they could just see each other -"

"I don't know," Mrs. McKenna said. "I probably should talk to her father about it."

"You know he wouldn't let her go."

"No, he probably wouldn't. That boy being Jewish had been a mark against him in Paddy's book from day one. Then when he did what he did to her, well ... "

"I know. That's why it's up to you - right now - to let her go."

"Oh, Tom, it's just so frightening. You know how far down she went this summer. And she's made so much progress since then."

"I know it's scary for you. But how happy is she now? Mrs. McKenna, I would just ask you to leave it up to Siobhan. Let her decide for herself."

"Tawm!" Siobhan yelled as she stepped down into the sunroom and rushed to hug him.

After a long squeeze, he pulled back to look at her. Her hair and face now looked like they had reversed shades since the first time he saw her. The tan had moved to her hair, which was now a rich light brown and hung almost to her shoulders. Her face was pale but her eyes were as beautiful as ever, and - if lacking the vibrancy of before - were clear and alert.

Your hair," he said. "I love it."

"Yeah, I had it reverse-frosted, so I guess this is the real me. Say, why aren't you in class?" she laughed. But looking around at her mother's concerned expression, the smile drained instantly from her face and she pulled back cautiously. "What is it? What's wrong? Bran? What about Bran?"

"No, Brandeis is fine. Well, actually he's a wreck. But he's a healthy wreck."

"Well then - ?" she began, glancing again at her mother.

"Darlin', Tom's come up here to talk with you about something." Turning to face him again, Mrs. McKenna said, "I'll go along with whatever Siobhan decides - and, if need be, I'll take care of things with her father. Now, you two talk," she urged as she hugged each of them and left the room.

"What's going on?" Siobhan asked.

Tom pulled an envelope from the inside pocket of his blazer. "This is a one-way ticket for you to fly back to Dallas with me this evening. Want to come?"

Gasping momentarily in surprise, she finally asked, "Was this Bran's idea?" Narrowing her eyes at Tom's non-response, she asked, "Does he know about it?"

"No. I just realized you were both too hard-headed for either of you to make the first move. And he needs you like I've never seen one human being need another."

"So are you telling me that you and Clair have set a wedding date?" she queried.

"Hey, I've got my own set of demons. God and I are still looking for the right herd of swine to cast them into. Besides, I'm not what this is about. Are you coming with me?"

"Are we going to stop by Memphis to clear this with Shirley on the way down?"

"He can pull away from her," Tom said. "I know he can. And when he sees you again, I know he will. You two just need each other too much for you not to be together."

Drawing herself up, Siobhan replied, "Tom, you were right about what you said back in the summer. There are some things I can give - besides money - that can help. I've been working part-time as a teacher's aide in music at - get this - Our Redeemer, with some of the scholarship kids - mostly black. And it's really fulfilling - for me and for them. It's not a full life. It's sure not what I had - with Bran. Nothing else ever could be. But it's the start of a life, and it's something I could fill a lot of my time with and feel good about."

"Yeah, but - "

"What I'm saying is, my life's not over if I don't get Bran."

"Good, Chevy. That's wonderful," Tom said as his forehead cleared and he smiled softly. "I don't think the same can be said of Woz, though. And I'd just hate for either of you to miss out on what you could have together. Will you come back with me?"

"Tom, you know I love him with all my heart. But again, what about his mother?"

"Trust me," Tom said. "I've got a plan." As she narrowed her eyes and tilted her head in contemplation, Tom repeated, "Trust me."

As he awaited her reply, she made a circular scan of the serious yet boyish face of this best friend there to plead the case of his best friend - this single brother, this seeker after his other. Finally, she lowered her gaze and answered, "Alright."

Leaving the sunroom together, they were greeted by Mrs. McKenna and two packed bags. As the mother and daughter bid an uncertain farewell, Tom made a call.

"Aunt Nela, I'm bringing a girl home tonight. We'll be in late, and I'll need for her to stay with you for a few days," he said, finally laughing. "No, we didn't." "No, we haven't." "No, we don't have to." "Aunt Nela, I'll explain it all when we get there." "She can stay in my room." "Whoa! Like I was about to say, she can stay in my room, and I'll sleep at Chet's." "See you before midnight. And Aunt Nela, I love you, but ... *don't tell anyone about this!*"

As they took their seats for the return flight to Dallas, Tom looked at Siobhan and said, "I've got one request of you."

Returning his smile, she replied, "Name it."

"When we get ready to take off, will you hold my hand - just till we get up in the air?"

Taking his hand in hers, she did not release it until touchdown at Love.

Chapter 44

"You're going to love *Harvest*," Tom said enthusiastically to his roommate as they traversed campus toward the SUB.

"Hey, I did the State Fair with you Saturday. How can this be anything but an anti-climax? Oh, no," Brandeis asked quickly, "they don't sell those corn dogs there, do they?"

"No, wise ass. But you can have every kind of pie or cake or goodie you've ever dreamed of. And Aunt Nela and Uncle Bowman are real eager to have you visit. I've told you, Harvest is kind of his baby, and they'll enjoy showing it off to you. You're going to love going down there. I guarantee it."

"Alright, alright. God, you've been in a chipper mood since you got back from that dash to Noofer. Are you sure you didn't see Clair or something?"

"No," Tom replied, "it just feels good to have worked out that moratorium on the business with Forster."

"What was the deal?"

"Well, you know, he had put some pressure on me to sell the business to him, but apparently when he discussed that or opening a competing office with some of the attorneys and bankers in town, they discouraged him from forcing my hand. 'Least that's what George Collum told me he had heard. Speaks pretty highly of how Dad was regarded around town," Tom said. "Plus, Helen's come back to work, and that took some of the workload off Neil. So, we just agreed to wait until at least the Christmas holidays to do anything about it."

"How are you feeling about the business these days? I mean, are you thinking you'd ever want to operate it yourself? Or ... "

Tom considered the question as they climbed the front steps of the SUB. Slowly shaking his head, he began to speak, but on the expansive tiled landing in front of the door the profile of a curiously familiar figure caught Tom's eye, and he fell silent. The young man bulged against a dingy knee-length army-green trenchcoat from beneath which frayed, faded bell-bottom jeans fanned out. Dark curly locks sprouted from his red bandana headband and rested in oily ringlets on his coat collar, and his wispy ungroomed beard was painfully thin. As he stood distributing a handout at the SUB door, Tom finally recognized him - especially by his prominent horn-rimmed glasses. But he appeared to have exploded from the plump, cherub-faced sprite whom Tom had last seen in May into a sadly overweight derelict.

"Harvey!" Tom shouted as he approached. Turning full-face in response, the figure further shocked Tom less by the red crescent-shaped scar above his right eyebrow than by the vacant scan of the eye and downturn of the lips that brightened only after the long count it took him to recognize his former neighbors.

Tom suddenly felt guilty that he had not done more to locate Harvey since the beginning of the semester. He had remembered that in May Harvey had said he would be living in an off-campus apartment come September. When Tom had missed his byline in *Cat Tracks*, he had assumed that he might have transferred to Baylor to work for the campus paper or for the Waco newspaper Siobhan had told Tom he was covering the Democratic Convention for. He had asked no further.

"Tom, Woz," Harvey said with a wave and with a smile that had aged far too much over the summer. "Good to see you guys."

After handshakes Tom masked his quick glance down at the coin- and currency-filled cap at Harvey's feet and asked, "Where've you been, Groesbeck? I've looked for you in *Cat Tracks*, and ... nothing."

As Brandeis agreed and registered like concern, Harvey stated evenly, "I missed the start of classes by a few weeks, so I'm just up here staying with some friends."

"Well, what was the Convention like?" Brandeis asked.

His eyes narrowing for an instant in a reflexive anger before returning to dull, Harvey pointed at his scar. "Afraid I missed a lot of it - after the lights went out."

"You got that there?!" Tom asked. "From the police?"

"Let's just say, from the riot. I can honestly say, 'I never knew what hit me'. Or who. I just wheeled around once, caught a whiff of tear gas, closed my eyes, and ... Whunk! But I saw plenty of my fellow 'revolutionaries' catch it from the Pigs - idiots just like me who actually thought they could change things."

"So, were you in the hospital up there?" Tom asked.

"Yeah, Tom. For the two days I was unconscious when my parents flew up scared to death they were going to get to raise a vegetable. Yeah, the Pigs let me stay in the hospital."

"You mean they arrested you, even after all that?" Brandeis asked.

"Well, no. They just told my parents, 'Take him home and keep him out of trouble. Or we'll come down dere an' bust his head agin!'" he shouted, raising an imaginary billy club in the air.

"My God," Brandeis said.

"Hey, I'm about six weeks behind, knowing what's going on in the world," Tom said. "You know I always count on you to keep me abreast."

"And he doesn't mean Sophia's," Brandeis cracked, attempting to match Tom's tone.

Ignoring Brandeis, Harvey scoffed, "In the last six weeks - I don't know. I don't keep up anymore. What does it matter? I'm sure a few thousand more of us bit the dust in 'Nam. And I imagine the same group of crazy old men sentenced twice as many more of us to take their places. And next month America'll put on another sham election. And the crazy old men'll play musical chairs and pull out L-B-J's, but the war'll go on - and so will the killing and the dying."

As Brandeis turned away uncomfortably in silence, Tom said, "I can remember when you wanted to go over and cover that war."

Sloughing off a sullen sigh, Harvey said, "I guess you could say the 'B'ys in Blue' knocked some sense into me."

"So what're you handing out?" Brandeis asked.

His face nearly breaking into a smile, Harvey answered, "Oh, yeah, now this has been fun. The guys I'm staying with, we're doing an underground paper. It's - "

"Are they - ?" Tom began.

"College dropouts and bums?" Harvey countered. "Some of them. Some of them are still in class."

"What is it?" Brandeis asked. "Anti-War? Anti-Establishment?"

His angry frustration reappearing, Harvey replied, "Don't you guys get it? Haven't you been listening? None of that matters. Nothing's going to change, and we can't make it. Naa, this is just for the fun of it. Here," he said, handing each of them several copies of the legal size sheet.

"*The Mangled Claw*," Tom noted as he dropped a dollar in the cap. "Catchy."

"Thanks," Harvey replied as Brandeis followed suit with a quarter. "Have fun with it. Say, where's Chevy?"

As Brandeis answered, "Chicago," and gave a brief, awkward reply, Tom smiled.

*   *   *

Siobhan scooted out of the red vinyl seat and stood beside the booth when she saw the young woman she assumed to be Clair push open the door of the Dairy Queen. A scan by Clair of the spotty mid-afternoon crowd in the dining area quickly brought her to Siobhan. The young women sized one another up as they walked toward the middle of the room. Clair received from Siobhan an open smile of discovery as she noted the model's face, the outstanding figure, and the tailored outfit of the stranger who had called her and whose presence in the tired red-brick- and tinted-glass-walled interior of the New Fredonia Dairy Queen was not unlike dropping a Neiman-Marcus store into a Panhandle wheat field. Dressed in a Stewart-tartan plaid mini-kilt, a starched white buttondown collar blouse, a pale yellow cashmere V-neck sweater vest, and penny loafers, Siobhan was greeted by a wary smile of estimation from Clair, who had come straight from school in her faded navy cotton skirt, light blue blouse, and campus-worn Weejuns. Siobhan acknowledged that Clair was as beautiful as Tom had described in detail to her on the flight to Dallas two nights earlier.

Extending a welcoming hand, Siobhan said, "I can't tell you how glad I am to meet you. Thanks for coming."

"Well, thanks for your call. Any friend of Tom's is a friend of mine," she replied, but Siobhan noted a subtle edge in Clair's delivery of the cliché.

"In honor of our friend Windham, let's have a Dr. Pepper," Siobhan said with a laugh.

"A D-P's fine."

Gathering their drinks, they returned to the booth by the window. The bright afternoon sky filtering through the smoked glass had warmed over the course of the day from the morning's chilly hint of cooler autumn weather.

"I can't believe all I brought down here was this heavy stuff," Siobhan said.

"So ... how long are you planning on ... being here?" Clair asked, as evenly as she could.

Siobhan smiled and replied, "I'll bet you're wondering who the hell I am and what the hell I'm doing here."

Drawn in by Siobhan's infectious laugh, Clair chuckled and replied, "How the hell did you guess?" She was beginning to like this Yankee girl in spite of the knot in her stomach.

"Well, let me allay any fears you're much too beautiful to have," Siobhan began, and she related to Clair the gist of Tom's mission to Chicago. Wrapping her arms around her waist, she concluded, " ... and this hare-brained plan of his is to bring Bran down here Friday - supposedly to go to Harvest with him. And, we'll just see what happens then. Right now, I just wish these giant monarchs would clear out of my stomach. But, no, I assure you. I'm not a problem for you."

"So I have nothing to fear but Tom himself, huh?" Clair mused.

"What?"

"Nothing," Clair said, waving dismissively. "So how do you like East Texas?"

"I love it. It's really beautiful, and the people are so friendly. And the Carters are so nice to me - even though they're not quite sure what to do with me." With a laugh, she reported, "I've hung out at the truck stop some. Uncle Bowman's a riot. And Aunt Nela's so sweet. And feeds me. Holy Father, every time I look up, she's shoveling a new pie down my throat." Puffing out her cheeks, she laughed, "Bran and Tom had better get down here quick or I'm not going to be able to get through the door."

"So how is Tom?" Clair asked.

Her smile fading slowly, Siobhan replied, "Well, I haven't seen that much of him really. Just when he came up back during the summer - and the summer's kind of a blur to me - and then Monday when he just showed up out of nowhere." Seeing Clair to be unsatisfied with anything less than details, she went on, "I don't know; he seems to be behind some kind of a mask as far as his own feelings are concerned. I mean, he talked to me about you most of the way down here on the plane the other night, but I never could get him to explain why he isn't talking to you. He told me about the kiss at the wedding reception. He said you *really* surprised him, and it was a great kiss - but it almost felt like being slapped with your lips."

"Pretty fair assessment," Clair said.

"Like with the tuition, though," she observed more seriously, "he's very interested in helping others - those that he loves - like you and Bran and ... me, but - "

"He told *you* about paying my tuition?"

"I'm so sorry I mentioned that," Siobhan said quickly. "You have to understand, though. Monday was the first time he had flown anywhere since his parents' ... since the crash, and he was unbelievably nervous. We talked and talked just to fill the flight time." Shaking her head at herself, she pleaded, "He *told* me about how upset you were about that, and there I go bringing it up. I'm very sorry I said that. Please don't hold it against him." After a hesitation, she added, "But it really was such a sweet thing to do. Anyway, as I was saying, he gets something out of helping those he loves, but he just holds so much inside."

"So what else is new?" Clair said caustically.

"What do you mean?"

"When I was dating Tom in high school, he was always capable of surprises - good ... and bad. It seemed like he rolled everything through his mind, talked it out with himself, came to his own conclusions, and then sprang it on the world. And especially on me. His last surprise for me was a bad one. We broke up…quit dating…for reasons known only to Tom. But," Clair sighed, "the world's given him some surprises, too. Maybe he just thinks that's the way it works."

"I knew him before his parents died," Siobhan observed, "and I've known him since, and he is different, of course. It seems like he's just trying to avoid dealing with anything about himself, so he gets involved helping the people he loves. And I know you're at the top of that list. He's talked about you on and off ever since I've known him. I don't know if you still care, but he always leaves the door open when he speaks of you. There's just something holding him back," she said, shaking her head.

"I saw him once this summer - before the wedding reception. We had a really nice visit. He came out to the house and saw my grandmother and me. And I just … touched his hand," Clair said, "and he pulled away - physically pulled away … and emotionally, too. And then I didn't hear anymore from him. He was dating another girl at the time. I don't know; maybe they're-"

"No," Siobhan said firmly. "They're not."

Shaking her head clear, Clair said in a controlled tone, "Yeah, well, thanks. I just wondered … where he was now. I'll always care about him. Thanks for being so easy to talk to."

"Thanks, yourself." Patting her hand, Siobhan said, "And someday I hope you two care from somewhere other than afar. I've had some of that the last few months, and I know what hell it is to go through. Now I'm on pins and needles. Tom tells me Bran's distraught - can't do without me. Well, he's done without me these last months. And I don't know if he can ever get away from his mother. I'm sorry it has to be either her or me, but it looks like it does."

Gazing out the window at the traffic on 199 and at the circling high school kids, Siobhan said, "And in a couple of days, I'll see him again - be with him. I hope it doesn't blow up in our faces. I hope it doesn't turn out to be one of those bad surprises."

* * *

Having stuffed his copy in a pocket of his notebook, Tom came across it late in the evening while studying. He unfolded it and read:

THE MANGLED CLAW

A.M.F. Holds Dylan

On this the thirty-seventh day of Bob Dylan's captivity, his captors, the August 3, 1923 Cell, a radical militant arm of the Anti-Metaphorical Front, issued a cryptic message indicating that Mr. Dylan was near the completion of his explanation of every symbolic reference in "Like a Rolling Stone", and his release was imminent. The Cell, so named for the date their spiritual leader, Calvin Coolidge, assumed the presidency, had previously admitted responsibility for the harrowing fifty-four-day captivity of Procol Harum. In other developments it has been reported by their publicists that Kenny Rogers and the First Edition are considering the removal of "Just Dropped In To See What Condition My Condition Was In" from record store shelves.

Movie Review

In a word, we found the new Franco-Italian production, Papillon Farfallo, to be: Flighty.

Christ the Kid

In boxing news Christ the Kid lost on a split decision to the Italian fighter, Punchus (Clean Hands) Pilate. The Nazarene Machine stayed with the more experienced fighter until the seventh round when Pilate nailed him with a right cross. The Kid took a three count before springing back to life, but the judges gave him the thumbs down while the crowd was crying for blood. A possible rematch is still up in the air.

1968: Year of the Hoax

Theodore H. White has confirmed through his publisher, Atheneum, *with corroboration from news executives at the three television networks the widespread rumor that all of the events reported thus far as having happened in 1968 were actually staged for the network cameras to boost sales of his upcoming book, <u>The Making of the President: 1968</u>. Mr. White, the publisher, and the networks offer their apologies and suggest that we all go back to doing whatever we were doing at the end of 1967 as if none of this had happened.*

<u>*GOD MESS AMERIKA*</u>

Chapter 45

Late October

As the Le Mans hurtled east on I-20 amid hardwood forests flaunting their autumn colors, Brandeis said, "This is beautiful country. I'm glad you harassed me into coming. Now, what's going on in Noofer? Some kind of fruits and vegetables show with rides for the kids?"

"It's called 'Harvest'," Tom replied. "And it's a lot more than that. Yeah, there are produce judgings and cooking contests - best pie, best turnip dish, stuff like that - and a livestock auction. But 'Harvest' is really like a great big homecoming for the whole town, the whole county. It's this one long weekend every year when New Fredonia natives who've moved away know to drop whatever they're doing and come home and see old friends. It goes back to the time just after W-W-Two when so many of the county's people had gone off to war or moved off to work in defense factories, and once gone, a lot of them didn't move back. But they wanted to set a time outside the regular holidays, when all of them that could would come back and visit. So Uncle Bowman and Dad and a lot of townsfolk organized it, and it just kind of grew.

"And they have a Harvest Pageant. Well, we missed it. They had it last night. And they'll have the Harvest Ball tomorrow night."

"Should I have brought my tux?" Brandeis asked with a laugh.

Still seriously, Tom answered, "No, it's for older types. And there's the carnival around the Square, too. You'll enjoy it," he concluded. But smiling into himself, he added, "No, don't worry. You won't be bored."

Topping the hill that overlooked the lake and the lakehouse, Tom registered a momentary concern when his car lights revealed the "Lou Carter's Truck Stop" pick-up beside the house.

"Who's here?" Brandeis asked.

"Don't know," Tom replied. "Maybe Uncle Bowman. They're both so busy with Harvest, I told them we'd just stay out here and come in for breakfast. But maybe he dropped by."

Dismounting from the Le Mans next to the truck, Brandeis yelled after Tom, "You forgot your bag."

"I'll unlock the house and come back for it," Tom answered as he followed him up the steps on the north side of the grey-brown cedar-sided lakehouse to the wraparound redwood deck.

Finding the key unnecessary, Tom entered the house and broke into a smile as he looked up. Brandeis followed, and he was surprised when Tom reached to take his luggage.

The centerpiece of the lakehouse was a great-room running its length. Its high gabled ceiling was distinguished by a thick center beam and exposed rough-hewn rafters. The room V-ed forward toward the lake with a massive rock fireplace at the V's apex and floor-to-ceiling glass on either side of it comprising the east wall of the room and looking out on the lake. To the right of the fireplace was the baby grand piano that had belonged to Johnny's mother. Before the fireplace was a sunken open area with a thick multicolored rug and stacks of large throw pillows.

And standing by the piano was Siobhan.

Displaying a placid, even smile, her hands knitted together in front of her, she wore a navy cashmere V-neck sweater and jeans. She loosed one hand to anchor herself against the piano as Brandeis took no time to recognize her in spite of her pale skin and the darker hair touching her shoulders.

"Siobhan!" he called, as he started toward her, almost falling into the conversation pit as Tom barked to warn him. "Siobhan!" he repeated. He stopped when he saw she was not moving toward him reciprocally, "I'm sorry, baby. I'm so sorry," he said as tears welled in their eyes.

As the smile left her face, the battle raged within her over how she had envisioned this moment and the reserve she had rehearsed during the past several days against what she wanted to do now that the moment had finally arrived. As the pleading, quivering, open-armed young man stood helpless and distraught before her - awaiting any signal to advance - she slowly released herself from the support of the piano and dropped her hands to her side. Opening her palms and raising them slightly toward him, she said, "Bran."

Leaving his roommate's luggage by the door, Tom stepped out on the deck as Brandeis reached Siobhan in a bound. He held her fiercely as he covered her with kisses. She gave in silently to his professions of love and remorse and passionately kissed him back.

When she pulled away from him and looked intensely and questioningly into his eyes, he reached with his sleeve to dry his face.

"Bran," she began, slowly and painfully, "I know you love me. But do you love me enough?" As he nodded too quickly, she shook him and asked tearfully, "But can I trust you? Can I trust you ... to love me ... and to put me first in your life?"

"Yes, Siobhan, yes. I'll never hurt you again, and I'll never let go of you," he pledged.

Shaking him again, she asked desperately, "But Bran, do you have the Courage? Do you have the *Courage* ... to love me and stand beside me ... and never leave me? Never let go of me again?"

"Yes," he answered, again quickly. But as he looked down and into himself, Siobhan saw him search his heart for the assurance that he could back up his words. She saw the summing of the costs of loving her ripple across his brow, flash through his eyes. Finally, returning his gaze to hers, he confirmed more quietly and with a passionate determination, "Yes. You're a part of me. You run through my veins." Shaking his head reflectively, he declared, "If I lost you, I'd lose everything. I will *never* let go of you again. I *have* the Courage."

Reading the passion and longing in her eyes to match his, he whisked her up in his arms and carried her through the door behind the piano. Amid a desperate surge of hungry kisses and fierce embraces, they quickly found themselves naked in each others arms sinking into the goose-down mattress on the antique brass double bed that almost filled the tiny bedroom. Enjoying the bliss of sharing their bodies, their hands and lips ran rampant with the delight of rediscovery.

But pulling her lips back from his and pushing him up from her with her hands on his chest, she panted, "Stop! Stop, Bran."

Drunk with desire, he heaved, "Why? What? What's wrong?"

As tears began to glisten in her eyes, she said, "Bran, I'm so scared."

Shaking his head, he moaned, "No, baby, don't - "

Bran," she interjected. "*Brandeis.*"

"I'm so sorry I hurt you, Siobhan," he allowed more soberly. "I love you. I'll make it - "

"Bran," she said, cutting him off again. Gathering her strength and her resolve with deep breaths, she finally said, "Bran ... don't come back ... unless you're coming back to stay."

"I'm back to stay. I'll never leave you again."

* * *

Balancing himself on a joint of the deck's railing, Tom looked out into the twilight as darkness started to descend upon the lake. He reasoned that the longer both of his friends stayed in the house together the better were the odds that his gamble had paid off. Neither he nor Siobhan had conjectured on Monday what might come of the reunion - or what might follow - and he had diverted his aunt's questions to that effect as well. Now, for the first time he began to consider the possibility that they would want to spend the night at the lakehouse. And this brought him to begin rolling over the logistics of maneuvering such an eventuality past his aunt, who had voiced to him on the telephone the prior day the maternal interest she had developed toward Siobhan. On the positive side Tom knew his aunt and uncle would be involved in Harvest activities until late in the night; therefore, there was scant likelihood of a bed check upon their return from the festivities. On the negative, though, like Tom, they were confirmed early-risers without regard to how late they had gotten to bed the night before.

After a half-hour walk along the lake and to the water's edge on both of the piers on the west side, Tom had wound up perched on the rail of the deck. As he considered the possibilities, he walked quietly into the house for a drink. Without surprise he found the den unoccupied. After pouring himself a Dr. Pepper, he sat on the couch to consider whether he should disturb them. But as he drank, he began to hear occasional muted cries of passion, joy, and consolation escaping through the door and the walls of the small bedroom that looked out on the lake.

Staring into the dying light outside the darkened great-room, Tom tussled with the emotions of relief, uncertainty, envy, and desolation. 'Are We even?' he thought. 'Have I atoned ... yet?' Fighting back the dark thoughts that had plagued him since April, he tried once again to pick up the telephone and make the call to Promise. But as he stared at it, the bedroom door opened and Brandeis emerged joyously disheveled and clad only in his jeans.

Tom quickly turned away, but when he looked back at Brandeis, his friend read him too well. "What is it?" Brandeis asked, his smile vanishing into concern.

"I'm ... just happy for you two," Tom replied.

"Is that it?" Brandeis asked, touching his arm.

"Yeah. Looks like things are going okay for y'all," he said, managing a smile.

After a slow nod Brandeis looked out the window in thought and said, "Listen, we'd- "

"Like to stay out here?"

"Yeah, but Siobhan's worried about the Carters."

"Stay," Tom said. "I'll take care of things with them."

"I love this place," Brandeis said reverently, looking around the room. "You would have never forgiven yourself if you had sold it."

"I may never forgive myself anyway," Tom countered.

"What's wrong?" To Tom's head-shaking non-reply, he offered, "I can never ... ever ... thank you enough for doing this for me - for us. You're the best friend a skinny little Jewish guy and his *shiksa* could ever have. But we want you to be happy, too. You deserve it." Grabbing Tom suddenly by his arms, he repeated emphatically, "*You deserve it.*"

"Don't worry about me. I'm just glad you guys are back together. You *are* back together, aren't you? Or do you look like this 'cause she's been in there beatin' the tar out of you?" As Brandeis joined him in a laugh, he said, "Listen, I'm going to the football game. I'll make things okay with Aunt Nela and Uncle Bowman. Don't worry. I think there's some Chef Boy-Ar-Dee out here you can eat and some bread and drinks. I'll bring you some lunch tomorrow," Tom stated and added awkwardly, "and maybe by then you'd be ready to see some of the town and go to Harvest."

"Sounds great," Brandeis responded. "'Thanks' sure isn't enough to say. But ... thanks."

As Brandeis started toward the bedroom, Tom asked, "Woz, is Chevy happy?"

Brandeis turned and answered with a tight-lipped smile and a slow nod.

*   *   *

McAlister Field was a rusted steel and splintered woodplank dinosaur from the Forties, which, over its aging, stooped shoulders, could watch progress on the construction of its bowl-like concrete successor across a grassy parking lot. After this its last year to host New Fredonia Panther football it was due to be converted ignominiously into an elementary school playground. Tom had not sat with his father at a Panther game since early in his junior high years. But he had always known he was just two sections down from the rowdy student seats, which Tom now scanned from the walkway at the bottom of the stands for a familiar face to join. His father's absence and the uncomfortable feeling of being in-between the adults and the high school kids - fewer of whose faces he recognized - upset him further, and he considered turning and leaving.

"Hey, Windham!" came the yell from high in the stands. Following the sound, Tom saw Rob Carver standing and waving broadly at him. Relieved, he hustled up the stairs and joined his former classmate and Rob's stunning raven-haired, ebony-eyed date - a U.T. co-ed, he quickly learned. While sharing small talk with Rob and the olive-skinned beauty all over him, Tom scanned the familiar scene.

At the east end of the home side of the field the men of New Fredonia clumped and strung themselves out along the elbow-high fence that separated the narrow walkway in front of the stands from the gridiron. Rising from their midst was a mix of the heavy grey smoke of their cigarettes and the wispy white steam of their coffee. Tom realized the scene was actually a mere transposition of the Swan Cafe coffee break crowd. The sidelines of McAlister Field was simply where they moved their colloquy on home game Friday nights.

His scan sweeping the field from end zone to end zone, Tom smiled at the new generation of grade school kids who had taken his place and that of his chums playing a rag-tag version of football just beyond the end zone line while the game was in progress. When the real game moved toward their realm, they would silently slip back toward the retaining fence or out of the area altogether. After the approaching team's drive was decided and the action moved back upfield, they would seep quickly back into their play area. And at halftime, assuming neither band was especially large or adventurous, they would extend their games into the end zones.

Tom hoped for the men and for the boys of New Fredonia that the new stadium would be as accommodating.

As halftime approached, Tom saw Gene Ray Driggers descend two steps at a time from the bleachers to his right. After pausing to enjoy the discovery that Driggers' pompadour was thinning noticeably both in front and in back, he spun to look for Clair. Searching the stands, Tom saw her just as she looked away from him. He watched for a moment as she began talking animatedly with Jennie Corrigan Fowler and her new husband. Feeling her eyes on him for the rest of the game, Tom watched in distraction as the Panthers eked out a fumble-strewn victory, 13-7, over Parkerville's Bulldogs.

Arriving at a darkened Carter house after a swing by the Dairy Queen, Tom was surprised to find his aunt and uncle had already turned in for the night. The following morning Tom explained that he and Brandeis had stayed at Chet's while Siobhan had come home to the Carters' late and undetected by them - as he had apparently been - and that she had left early in the morning through the unused living room front door to join Brandeis for breakfast. His explanation was greeted with a wary frown from his aunt and a roll of the eyes from his uncle.

Chapter 46

Harvest

Siobhan awakened with Brandeis snuggled close to her. She did not open her eyes for fear that it was a dream and one that would vanish in the light. But the joyfully familiar, long-absent dull ache in her upper thighs told her it was real. She was careful not to move lest she should awaken him and lose the moment. Her time in dark cars and dark rooms with him had long ago taught her that what she felt - what she touched - gave her far more sensory pleasure than anything she could see. As she gently stroked his curls, tears welled. She whispered gently, "I love you, Bran. I was afraid I'd never get to feel like this again." She smiled as he nuzzled her breasts and held her. Responding to the warmth of his body, she drifted peacefully back to sleep.

Sometime later the light of dawn brought her to again. Brandeis had rolled onto the pillow beside her, and she carefully left the bed, venturing into the kitchen to make coffee. He was awakened still later by the strains of *Fur Elise*, and coming to - naked in bed with sore, tightened stomach muscles - it took him only an instant to realize where he was - and with whom. He stumbled nude out of the bedroom toward the music and the light and the aroma of strong coffee. Leaning against the doorframe and looking out into the sunroom, he was greeted with the profile of his lover. She was clad only in her glasses as she gracefully swept her fingers across the keys of the baby grand. Her smooth, tapering back and the spread of her buttocks on the piano bench beckoned him, and he approached her silently. She stirred only slightly but continued playing when he placed his hands on her shoulders and leaned into her back. They laughed when she hit a wrong key while rubbing her back from side to side against him. As he swung a leg over the piano bench and straddled it beside her, Siobhan quit playing.

Turning to look him up and down, she smiled broadly and said, "Like you once told me, first hard in the morning -"

"Hardest hard all day," he concluded. As they laughed, he ran his tongue back and forth against the inside of his lower lip.

"Lacerated?" As he nodded happily, she concurred, "So's mine."

"And your chin's as red as a beet from my stubble."

"Let's see the elbows," she demanded. Lifting his fists past his ears, he proudly showed them to her. "Raw meat," she marveled.

"Ahh, the old 'cheap sheet' burn."

Spinning toward him, she rose to place herself in his lap. "God, I've missed you," she said, "and us."

Pushing the bench away and tipping it on the floor in the process, he swung her toward the piano and sat her with an unmelodious crescendo on the piano keys. She held tightly to him as he lost himself in the tuneless collection of notes that followed. Still hungry to touch him, Siobhan strapped one arm across his back to hold him close while running her free hand through his hair. As he chewed ravenously on her nipples, she panted, "Thanks again, Shirley, for bottle-feeding this boy!"

*   *   *

Late in the morning as the Le Mans crested the hill and swung down the drive toward the lakehouse, Tom saw his friends side by side propped on their elbows on a patchwork quilt spread on the grassy terrace next to the lake. Seeing them together and happy Tom felt a momentary swell of pride in his handiwork, but the aftertaste of vicariousness sparked a similarly fleeting melancholy. As he parked and approached them, they jumped up from the quilt and ran toward him waving and begging, "Food! Food! Did you bring food!?"

Tom spun and sprinted back to the car for the two sacks of Dairy Queen burgers and fries and the six-pack of Cokes. Returning to the picnic table, Tom asked, "Didn't y'all find the canned spaghetti and the bread and the drinks in the house?"

"Yes," she answered desperately. "Gone."

"All gone," Brandeis confirmed.

As the trio spread the impromptu feast and began quickly to devour it, they spoke between bites of the beauty of the setting and of the lakehouse. Gazing out across the lake at the maples and yellowing oaks that dappled the pines and cedars on the facing bank and at their shimmering reflection in the water, Tom offered, "Yeah, Dad was lucky to get it. Back in the early Fifties while he was having an especially good year in the title business, the owner of this farm went bankrupt, and Dad got a real good deal on it. I'm just lucky to have Araberry to look after it for me and clean up around here." Looking out at the St. Augustine lawn where wheat-colored sprigs were beginning to muscle aside the green, Tom continued, "He keeps this lawn and mows the pastures."

Narrowing his eyes, Brandeis asked, "Where does he live?"

"Just over that hill," Tom said, pointing across the lake. "It's an old sharecropper's house that was on the property. Dad let him use it in return for helping out around here, and I cut the same deal with him." Looking back and forth between his friends at the surprised grins that suddenly appeared, he asked, "Why?" And joining them as they began to giggle, "What did y'all do?"

"Right over that hill?" Brandeis asked with a chuckle.

"Yeah," Tom motioned again, "where you see that smoke rising - from his cooking stove, I guess. Why?"

"Well," Siobhan admitted, "let's just say, we thought we were alone out here, and we took advantage of that sunny deck to try to return a little color to these bodies - all over. And while we were sunning, well, we got a bit carried away once. But I don't *think* we made enough noise to disturb him."

"Although we did scare a flock of ducks off the lake. But that may have been from the vibrations," Brandeis crowed.

"Bran," Siobhan scolded, slapping his arm.

"So, I take it you two are getting along okay," Tom observed. To coy nods as they touched and kissed - lingering overlong on each others lips, he cleared his throat and asked, "So, are y'all going to be ready to come back to Dallas with me tomorrow?" To the glances that shot between them, Tom continued, "I mean, I barely cleared last night with my aunt and uncle this morning, and tonight's going to be even more of a hurdle. Besides, Woz, we have school Monday - and, if you remember, I missed last Monday."

Siobhan glowed as Brandeis answered, "I know, Tom. And we don't want you to get in trouble with the Carters. But we need tonight. And we're ... not sure about tomorrow. We may do - something else."

"What?"

"We're not sure," Siobhan reiterated. "Let's talk about it tomorrow. Listen, I've been hearing about Harvest all week. Why don't we go see it?"

Absorbing the uncertainty with which they viewed their future, Tom swung his eyes back toward the stand of trees across the lake as he absent-mindedly nodded assent to Siobhan's suggestion. The pale grey smoke that continued to rise above the trees suddenly caught his attention, and he smiled broadly. "That's not Araberry's cook stove," he declared. "That's ribbon cane syrup."

"That's what?" Siobhan asked.

"It's ribbon cane syrup season. Araberry and his cronies are over there boiling down sugar cane to make ribbon cane syrup," Tom said with delight. Ignoring the possibility that the Yankee among them had ever heard of it, Tom asked Brandeis, "Have you ever tasted it?"

"No, but is it anything like maple syrup? My uncle in New York used to have a farm in Vermont where they made it, and they'd send us a can every year."

"No, this is a lot thicker. More like molasses. You want to go over and watch them make it?"

"Sure," Siobhan answered.

"I wonder if he'll recognize you with your clothes on," Tom teased.

After stuffing down the last of their lunch, the threesome walked to the south end of the lake, crossed the dam, and followed the narrow tree-canopied road through the woods toward Araberry's. As a crisp autumn breeze out of the east cooled them, the high late morning sun played hide-and-seek, darting in and out among the tall, spindly pine trunks and the broad yellow-green-leafed scrub oaks.

Arriving at Araberry's clearing, Tom yelled and waved broadly so as not to startle the clutch of old men huddled under the tin lean-to roof of Araberry's shed talking and laughing as they performed the annual ceremony of ribbon cane syrup-making.

"Mister Tom, that you?" Araberry asked with a friendly wave and a bright-eyed smile, motioning them toward the shed.

Tom winced mentally this time at the title he had a few months earlier enjoyed – the novelty having passed and the history now dawning on him. "Good morning, Araberry. And it's just 'Tom'."

After making introductions Araberry led them through the syrup-making process. From its beginning, with his mule tethered to a 15-foot length of tree-limb attached in turn to the sugar cane grinder, to its terminus at a faucet, the wizened old man explained each step with flourish. There, leaning down to demonstrate, he took a clean quart-sized can from a shelf and placed it on the wooden base below the spigot. Opening it, the thick, rich dark brown product of their labor started to fill the can. Switching off the spigot and collecting the residual flow, Araberry offered it to the trio. "Stick your finger in there and git yourself a taste," he urged. Each did, withdrawing slick golden brown coatings over their forefingers. Twisting his back and forth to break the thin string of syrup that hung from it, Tom thrust his forefinger into his mouth - sucking and licking every drop of the thick warm concoction from it. As he moaned in delight, Brandeis and Siobhan followed suit.

"Whoa," she said with a surprised grin. "So sweet. Almost a smoky sweet."

"Yeah," Brandeis agreed. "I thought it might be like maple syrup, but it's not like anything I ever tasted. I used to love getting that maple syrup every year. We went up to Vermont one summer and stayed on the farm. I just couldn't quite grasp how the syrup I was putting on my pancakes came out of a tree."

"Would it bother her if I gave her a pat?" Siobhan asked, nodding toward the mule. "I don't want to disturb her or throw her off her pace."

"Aw, that's alright," Araberry answered. "She's about due for a rest." Patting its firm shoulders and its thick neck, she cooed baby-talk as the mule slowed to a halt.

As Brandeis scanned the clearing, Tom took note and suggested, "Come on up here. There's a good view of the house and the lake from this rise." Climbing a gradual, well-worn footpath to a knoll, they turned to look at the scene they had left. As Araberry held the mule's harness while Siobhan made friends with her, Brandeis noted the tiny grey-brown shack where the old man lived and, behind it, the rich, fudge-colored rows of Araberry's produce garden - bordered on one side by withered corn stalks. He gazed left to the combination storage shed and syrup factory junked around its perimeter with ancient rusting hand tools and farm implements. And beyond the shed, the masticated husks of the sugar cane stalks produced more smoke than flame as they burned. Sunlight captured the billowing grey-white clouds arising from the pyre as they filtered through the trees emphasizing the angular shadows cast by the forest. Swirling slowly in the indecisive northwesterly breeze, the smoke briefly obscured the shed and the mule-path before again revealing Siobhan, Araberry and his friends as they conversed with animation and delight.

"Never let this place go," Brandeis said quietly.

"Not to worry," Tom replied as he too surveyed the view. "Are you ready for Harvest?"

*   *   *

Tom slyly positioned Brandeis on the outside of their seat in the Scrambler and placed himself in the middle and Siobhan on the inside, with the explanation that, "I'm afraid you two have been seeing too much of each other." He then treated himself to the fun both of squashing his roommate against the side of their seat and of being squashed on the other side by an uncontrollably giggling Siobhan, as the centrifugal force of the Scrambler sandwiched the three tighter with every rotation.

Leaving the ride, Brandeis complained of foul play - even suggesting a conspiracy involving the complicity of his girlfriend - at Tom's having taken advantage of his ignorance by manipulating the seating arrangement to his own scurrilous and lecherous ends. After the threesome rode the Tilt-A-Whirl, the Octopus, and the Ferris Wheel together, Tom and Brandeis watched a few rotations of the Hammer as they waited in line for it, and begged off. Momentarily disappointed and freely tossing off dispersions against their manhood, Siobhan remembered having seen Bowman from atop the Octopus. Yanking Brandeis along behind her with Tom in tow, she found him surveying the proceedings from a lawn chair on the courthouse terrace. Running up behind him and loosing herself from Brandeis, she swung an arm around him and plopped in his lap.

"Well, good afternoon, sweetheart," he greeted her with surprise.

"Whatcha up to, Uncle Bowman?" she asked.

"Aw, just sittin' here with m'teeth in m'mouth," he replied.

"Well, it appears I came up here with a couple of scaredy-cats." Tickling his chin persuasively, she whined, "Will you ride the Hammer with me?"

"Sure thing, darlin'."

As they rotated on the Hammer, Siobhan's shamed escorts watched meekly from below. After the harrowing ride she released an admittedly weakened Bowman to return to his throne, and the trio raided the food booths set up below the store awnings on the west side of the square. After sampling the pumpkin cake and the apple pie at the Full Gospel End Times Ministry booth, they moved to the Piney Volunteer Fire Department entry next door. Tom recognized Herm Heber working behind the red-checked tablecloth-covered folding table and reintroduced himself, reminding him of their mutual acquaintance with George Collum.

"Oh, sure, you're Johnny's boy. Well, what can I do ya' for, son?" he laughed.

What do y'all want?" Tom asked.

"Give us a couple of Cokes, please," Brandeis replied to Herm.

As he pried the lids from two wet bottles and handed them across the table, Brandeis asked, "Are they cold?"

The farmer answered seriously and with assurance, "Colder'n a maiden's heart."

Brandeis turned to make certain Siobhan had heard the guarantee, and they shared warm smiles in mutual appreciation of a time past and a place apart.

The threesome retired to a park bench on the courthouse lawn next to the kiddie rides. Watching the innocent, unbridled enthusiasm of the children as they ran from ride to ride and shouted in joy at the movement and the sounds, and noting their harried but happy parents and their coddling grandparents Brandeis observed, "This town really reminds me of that little village in Vermont near my uncle's farm. We went there a few summers when I was a kid. And while holding themselves apart from us in some ways - just because our family didn't date back to Ethan Allen - they were so friendly and uncomplicated, which is not to say, simple. More like, they had pared life down to what mattered, and knew what it was, and didn't waste a lot of time with what didn't. And having plain, simple fun was a big part of it."

Tom missed the look that passed between Brandeis and Siobhan, but when his roommate gently tapped him with his elbow and indicated their readiness to return to the lakehouse, he assumed a look had been passed.

* * *

Thinking his luck had held for two nights running, Tom tiptoed past his aunt and uncle's bedroom door toward his room. But as he heard their door creak open, he spun to see a scowl of disapproval like none she had ever given him clouding his aunt's visage.

"Aunt Nela!" he exclaimed with a distorted grimace of surprise.

Uncharacteristically unsympathetic, the frown frozen on her face, she demanded, "Where's Siobhan?"

As Bowman emerged sleepy-eyed behind her, Tom managed to reply, "Well, I guess she and Woz are still out taking in the carnival."

"Why are all her clothes gone?" she queried angrily.

Shaking his head in bug-eyed confusion and opening his hands to her as he searched for an appropriate lie, he finally responded truthfully, "I don't know. I didn't know they were." But he realized Siobhan and Brandeis must have come by and collected them from the empty house in the truck stop's pick-up during the early evening after he had returned them to the lakehouse.

"Then we'll just have to wait up for them tonight, won't we?" she declared.

"Aunt Nela ... Uncle Bowman," he said pleadingly.

"Yes, Tom," she demanded, as Bowman frowned with a droopy-eyed irritation behind her.

"Uuhhhh," he sighed in frustration as she awaited his explanation.

"I just think we'd better make certain everyone's accounted for tonight and in their proper beds at 'lights out'," she stated. "And none of that sneaking out for an early breakfast again. I mean, I feel like I have a responsibility to that young lady's mother to make sure-"

"That young lady's twenty-one," Tom rejoindered, gathering his senses. "She's an adult, and she and Woz can - "

"Can what? Where are they?!"

Tom responded slowly and with forced clarity, but without anger, "They are at the lakehouse."

"Alone?" she gasped.

"Yes."

"And when will they be home?" she asked with a wide-eyed glare.

"I don't know."

Breaking off her stare, she turned to Bowman and said, "Well, I think we'd better go out there and bring her back."

Gathering a frustrated breath, Bowman moaned, "Aww, Nela."

Pushing past her husband in the narrow hallway, she said, "Well then I'll just go - "

"No," Tom said forcefully.

Spinning to confront him with a blend of pain and anger scarring her face, she breathlessly asked, "Whahh? What?"

"I'm sorry, Aunt Nela, but please don't go out there."

"Well, I'm sorry, too, young man," she huffed. "But when you brought that girl here, you placed her in our hands, and we have a responsibility for her well-being and to see that no harm comes to her."

"I thank you for letting me bring her here, and she thanks you. She thinks the world of both of you," Tom said. "But it's time for you to let go and let them ... be together."

"In sin?!" To Tom's open-mouthed non-reply, she said, "Tom, I cannot begin to tell you how disappointed I am that you would *arrange* this ... rendezvous. But I'm going to put an end to it," she said, turning again toward her bedroom door.

"No, Aunt Nela, don't," Tom said, shakily summoning his resolve. "They are *my* guests at *my* house. And I know I'm a guest here... and I -"

"Tom!" she cried, aghast. Turning to her husband, she asked, "Bowman?"

Looking first at his nephew and then at his wife, Bowman scratched his head and wearily replied, "Nela, the man's got a point."

* * *

Gripping the brass footboard of the bed in the small bedroom facing the lake, Siobhan could see out the picture window - when she occasionally lifted her head and opened her eyes - the brilliant moon on the rise above the ridge across the lake. As she braced herself on her knees in the bed, she was mesmerized both by the blue-white light of the moon reflecting across the soft ripples in the lake water and by the rhythmic motion of her lover behind her. Brandeis alternately hooked his hands around her hips and ran them up her sides to caress her breasts. Her back warming from his overheated body when he came to her, it cooled to goosebumps from the perspiration he left when he pulled away. His final surge brought her eyes open wide as a 'V' of Canada geese flew south across the face of the moon.

Collapsing back into bed, their love confirmed, their passion fulfilled, and their decision made, they slept securely in each other's arms through the night.

Chapter 47

"You're going to do *what*?!" Tom asked as he faced the happy, moon-eyed couple across the picnic table from him.

"We're going away together," Brandeis repeated evenly. "We're not going back to Dallas."

"Well, where're you going?"

"We're not sure," Siobhan said.

"And, Tom, we're not going to tell you when we are," Brandeis added carefully. "And then you won't have to lie to my mother - "

"When she interrogates me?" Tom asked, envisioning himself tied in a straight-back chair, a single starkly white light bulb dangling above his bloodied face.

"When she comes looking for us," Brandeis admitted. "Will you help us?"

"I'll do my 'dead levelest'," he replied. Holding up his hands and turning their backs to his friends, he joked, "Let's all just remember what these fingernails looked like before the bamboo shoots." Shaking his head and laughing in amazement at the turn of events, Tom exclaimed, "Ho-lee! So you're not going to tell your parents that you're going or where you're going? Neither of you?"

"We talked about it, Tom," Siobhan replied. "We talked about it a lot. And we figured my mother and Bran's father could handle it. But we wouldn't want to put either of them in the position of having to lie -"

"Or of giving away where we are," Brandeis added.

"We just need to be together without anyone interfering," Siobhan said. "If you want to call it running away, okay, we're running away."

Looking at Brandeis, Tom asked, "What about school? And what about law school?"

"There'll be a time for that. We'll both sign up somewhere in the spring. And the Law'll still be there."

"This is just unbelievable," Tom said, shaking a bemused grin. Considering the logistics, he asked, "Well, are ya'll going to go in the Sprite? Do you need for me to take you back to Dallas to get it?"

"The Sprite's not going to get us anywhere," Brandeis answered. "We're just going to take a bus and head north - or east."

"And you don't know where you're going?" Tom asked incredulously.

"We've got some ideas," Siobhan said. "But it really would be better if you didn't know. We'll call you when we get there."

"How much money do you have between you?"

"I've still got the two hundred dollars left from what Mother gave me before I came down here," Siobhan replied.

Checking his pocket, Brandeis said, "And I've got thirty-seven thirty-nine on me."

"Well, how far do you think two-hundred-and-thirty-seven dollars and thirty-nine cents is going to get you?" Tom asked, "And what are you going to do when you get there, wherever it is?"

"We'll work," Brandeis answered.

"And live on what until you get paid?" Tom asked with concern.

"Luuuv," Siobhan responded with a hug and a kiss for Brandeis.

Shaking his head, Tom mugged, "Yuh crazy kids, yuh." As Siobhan reached out to hug him, he said, "Let me think about this a minute." Tom pondered the situation and finally narrowed his eyes, offering, "I think I've got a deal for you. Let's walk down around the lake and y'all can say goodbye to Araberry, and we can talk about it." As they left the deck, he asked, "Where are you going first?" After Brandeis and Siobhan looked at each other and hesitated, Tom added, "Listen, I can take the heat, and you still don't have to tell me where you're finally going to end up. I just need to know where you're going to be tomorrow."

"Well," Brandeis said, "we need for you to take us to Springfield. I've called and we can catch a bus out of there that'll connect through

Memphis to Union City. We're going to go up and see my grandmother before we go any farther. She's not doing well, and - it could be the last time I get to see her."

"I'm sorry," Tom said. "That's the right thing to do." After a moment's reflection, he continued. "Anyway, let me run this past you. Wouldn't y'all do better with a car?"

"Like I said," Brandeis answered, "the Sprite won't make it."

"But the Le Mans would," Tom said.

"Tom!" Siobhan said.

"Let's just make a swap. You know how much I love that Sprite, and I'll get it running again. Give it the kind of home it needs - and deserves. And, of course, that car's worth a good bit more than my little Pontiac."

"Yeah, right," Siobhan said with a laugh.

"So why don't I give you a thousand dollars to boot. I don't have it on me right now, but I can get it for you tomorrow and wire it to Union City. That'd give you a car and twelve-hundred dollars and change."

"Tom, we couldn't let you do that," Siobhan said. "Listen, I'll call my mother in a few days, and she'll get some money to us."

Brandeis cut a look of concern at her, and Tom noted it. "Let's just do it this way. This way you wouldn't be beholden to anyone - neither your parents or me. And I get the Sprite out of the deal."

"You really don't mind doing that?" Brandeis asked.

"It's all I *can* do, so it's what I want to do. I think you're probably right. I think the two of you need to have a chance to get away on your own." Looking at Siobhan, he continued, "I'd been wondering how it would have worked with you coming back to Dallas and getting an apartment or whatever." Shifting his gaze to Brandeis, he said, "Your mother'd be down here lickety-split driving both of you crazy. She might even pull you out of school. No telling what she'd do."

"Yeah," Brandeis said, "we've got to get out of here. We just want to find some place small and simple - like where we are right now - but there's no staying here either."

"No, I'm afraid your mother'd sniff this place out pretty quick. Have you really got the guts to do this? I mean, do you know what you're getting into? Do you know where you're going?"

Stopping at a rise in the narrow wooded road, Brandeis peered back into the eyes of his good friend. "I will take the Ring," he replied, "although I do not know the way."

Tom shook his head and smiled. He hugged his roommate and whispered, "Frodo, you idiot."

As they pulled away from one another in mild embarrassment, Siobhan glanced at both with a deadly smile and a twinkle in her eyes and said, "Ring? Did I hear you say there was a 'ring' involved?"

As if it were an afterthought, Tom asked, "*Are* you going to get married?"

Looking at one another sheepishly, their faces froze momentarily in smiles before they began simultaneously to nod ever so slightly. Their smiles growing, the nod became more pronounced until they simultaneously yelled, "Yes!" and jumped into each other's arms.

"That's wonderful," Tom said, but as a sudden surge of melancholy struck him, he added, "I can't believe you're both leaving." As Brandeis bowed his head and started to explain, Tom pushed an open palm toward him and said, "No, it's okay. You know how much I want you to be with each other and to be happy. I just didn't realize I'd be losing you by bringing you back together."

"Oh, Tom," Siobhan said as she hugged him and kissed him on the cheek. "Wherever we end up, you can come see us. You could come up at Christmas, and - "

But a frightening thought clouded Tom's brow as he interrupted her and glared at Brandeis, "What about The Draft?"

"Hopefully, by the time they've tracked me down, I'll be re-enrolled somewhere."

"But if you don't notify them, aren't you going to be breaking the law?" Tom asked.

"It's a big country," Brandeis replied. "There're millions of guys in the system. Surely they won't miss me for a couple of months."

"What about that, Bran?" Siobhan asked. "Really, what'll happen?"

"I don't know," Brandeis replied. "I've never run into it, and I don't know anyone who has." Looking at Tom and affecting a blasé demeanor, he said, "I'll just plead ignorance. Write them a letter in January when I'm enrolled wherever we are, and it'll all pass."

Shaking his head once, Tom allowed, "Well, I hope that'll satisfy them. So when are you planning on leaving?"

"Since we don't have a bus to catch," Siobhan answered, "I guess we're off as soon as we've said good-bye."

"I'll just take the truck stop's pick-up back into town," Tom said.

"How are you getting back to Dallas, though?" she asked.

After a moment's thought Tom said, "No sweat. I'll find a ride."

"But it's - "

"Don't worry about it, really," Tom said. "Listen, just call me tomorrow from Union City after you find out where the nearest Western Union is, and I'll wire you the grand."

"You know how to do that?" Brandeis asked.

"Yeah, I had to do it once this summer," Tom replied matter-of-factly.

As they topped the rise in the trail that opened onto Araberry's clearing and they looked down on the simple, pastoral scene, Siobhan asked, "Tom, what are *you* going to do? When are you going to call Clair? She's waiting for you."

"She wasn't waiting Friday night," Tom replied.

"What?"

"She was at the game with Gene Ray Driggers."

"He means nothing to her, Tom. Nothing. You've given her so many mixed signals. You need to just call her ... be straight with her ... tell her how much you care."

"I just want her to be happy. She might be happy with him."

"What would be wrong with her being happy with you?" Siobhan asked.

"I don't think I could make her happy -"

"You don't have to *make* her happy," Siobhan interjected quickly. "You could *let* her be happy ... with you."

Looking back at the scene before them, Tom observed, "I forgot. Nobody's home. Araberry's off preaching somewhere."

"But Tom, you're right. She may not wait forever for what she could have with you. She might settle for Gene Ray Driggers or for someone else who says he wants to be there for her. Just 'settling' would be a mistake for both of you."

Returning along the footpath, the trio stopped on the dam at the south end of the lake. Looking out across the water they absorbed the quiet serenity of the scene. Tom turned to his friends with a smile and, holding up his hand in a Vulcan farewell, said, "Live long and prosper."

Returning his smile, Brandeis responded with a Churchillian "V" and said mockingly, "Peace."

Running her hand down Brandeis' back, Siobhan clutched and squeezed a firm cheek of jeans, whispering, "Of ass."

"I wish we could say good-bye to Uncle Bowman and Aunt Nela," Siobhan said to Tom as they stood beside the Le Mans while Brandeis threw their bags in the trunk.

With a sober expression Tom replied, "Well, they're at church now anyway, but this is going to take some explaining to them, too."

"Sorry to leave all this in your lap."

Waving her off, Tom said, "Don't be. I can handle it."

"But aren't you a little tired of handling things ... for other people?"

"Hey, I'll call her, I'll call her," he said with exasperation.

"Good," Siobhan said, clapping her hands. "Glad I didn't have to goad you."

As they laughed, Brandeis walked around to them and said, "We're packed. I guess this is it."

As the smile left Tom's face, only to be forced back onto it a moment later, he said, "Call me tomorrow morning at the Carters'. I'll be waiting to hear from you."

"Oh, Tom," Siobhan cried as she threw her arms around him and hugged him tightly. "You're the best brother a girl ever had. I love you. I'll see you Christmas."

Tom patted his friend and held her, but he did not speak out of fear that he would cry. When Brandeis touched his shoulder, he included him in their embrace. Finally, Tom managed to say, "I love you two. I love you." Pulling away, he added, "And I'll share with you the advice a Protestant God gave me once when He struck me down on the road to Claremore. *Do not drive into smoke.*"

* * *

Tom spent the afternoon walking the farm in his new Wellingtons. He stopped again to visit with Araberry, who was home from preaching, and who had suspended his syrup-making for the Sabbath. Laughing at himself as he calculated when his friends would be safely through Memphis and past the roadblocks Mrs. Wasserman would have had thrown up around the city as soon as Nela had called her with their plan of escape, he waited until late in the evening to return to the Carters to inform them sketchily of the couple's getaway.

Bowman responded with a slow, head-turning whistle. Speechless, Nela took to her bed. By late Monday morning, after trips to the bank and to his office to handle the funds transfer, when Tom returned to the Carters, she had not risen. Leaving a short note of apology at the house, Tom packed, grabbed his checkbook, and tracked Bowman down at the truck stop.

Exchanging a wordless shake of the head and a smile with his uncle, Tom said, "How about going with me over to the 'Shivalay' house in Springfield?"

* * *

"The Chevrolet Corvette is a beautiful, big-tittied California blonde," Joe Joe declared, "and this here's the purtiest one I ever did see."

"Thanks," Tom said proudly as they stood in the parking lot of Joe Joe's apartment complex ogling Tom's new electric blue T-top coupe. Outrageously curvaceous and with prominent side gills, fat raised-lettered tires, recessed headlights, and a razor-sharp chrome front bumper, the Corvette exuded an organic suggestion of speed and of danger.

"It doesn't look much like you right now, Windham, but I'll bet it'll grow on you," Joe Joe adjudged. "Let's see you in it in the shades again."

Donning his wraparound sunglasses and slipping behind the wheel, Tom looked across to the passenger window as Joe Joe peered in at him. "Oh yeah, you're gonna git some. Maybe a lot."

"Let's get the T-top off and work this baby out," Tom urged.

As he helped his friend remove the passenger side section of the top and stow it behind the seats - leaving the chrome crossmember in place - Joe Joe marveled, "What a pussy wagon! Can we just cruise campus for a hour or so before we get out on the road?" he pleaded. "Drive down Sorority Row. I'll pick up the panties and the keys as they throw 'em out the windows." As Tom fired up the engine and pumped the accelerator, Joe Joe asked above the motor's throaty groan, "Which engine?"

"Four-twenty-seven, four-barrel, three-ninety horse," Tom answered, as he flicked the chrome-balled shift lever up into first. Disengaging the clutch while applying a healthy feed of gas, the tires squealed as the front end rose, the rear dug in, and the delighted occupants tensed their neck muscles against the initial surge of acceleration.

"Eeyyooowwww!" they screamed in unison as the first gaggle of co-eds they passed risked whiplash themselves.

Chapter 48

Halloween

Over the campus low, grey clouds hung thick and heavy like old ladies' arms as Tom traversed The Common toward the administration building. With a crash of thunder the rain that had threatened all afternoon began to empty from the skies as he reached the portico that led to Hartman Hall's main entrance. In answer to the curt summons he had received from Dean Chalmers' office, Tom opened one of the heavy double doors and proceeded into the vaulted rotunda of the building. Arriving after hours the massive foyer was dark but for the grey light of the stormy late afternoon passing through its south windows. The ominous clanging shut of the thick twelve-foot door sent a sepulchral echo down the arcade that Tom followed, his new Weejuns clattering loudly against its terrazzo floor. Rounding the corner into the hall that would take him to the office of the Dean of Men, he saw a dark-featured woman in a plain navy suit at the other end of the long corridor speaking with seething animation to the normally witty and easygoing, but currently intimidated and defensive Dean Chalmers. Noting his approach out of the corner of her eye, she turned and, narrowing her gaze and lowering her head menacingly, visited upon Tom a chilling glare. He knew immediately that she could only be Shirley Wasserman. As he walked slowly toward them, humming "Do Not Forsake Me, Oh My Darlin'" into his soul, her venomous stare watched him in.

At five yards from them Chalmers said with relief, "Ah, Tom. Glad you could make it. This is - "

"He knows who I am. Where is my son? Where is Brandeis?"

From his telephone conversations with her the prior semester and from his roommate's description of her, he had pictured her as looking like Christopher Lee in drag. But she was smaller in person, if no less foreboding. Her salt-and-pepper hair was pulled back tightly against her temples and into a bun as severe as her general demeanor. The scowl she presented to Tom was centered in the dark angry eyes that bored into him as she awaited his answer.

Tom did not reply but looked to the Dean of Men for cover. "Mrs. Wasserman, Tom," he said nervously, "why don't we go in my office." Nodding, Tom walked carefully at Chalmers' side as he ushered them through his reception area to his private office. Pulling up a chair to join Tom as he sat opposite her in one of the two side chairs that fronted his desk, Chalmers said, "Tom, Mrs. Wasserman is very concerned - "

And again she cut him off. "You know where he is," she lashed out virulently, "and I want you to tell me now."

"Mrs. Wasserman," the administrator stated, "I want to help you with this matter, but I would appreciate your letting me handle it."

Drawing in the fangs that shot from her eyes, she turned to respond to Chalmers, and her tone was transformed, "Of course, Dean Chalmers," she said penitently. "I am so sorry, but you must understand my upset and my concern - as a mother."

"Of course, I do," he replied, pleased at the change in her demeanor. "Tom, I understand that Mrs. Wasserman's son, Brandeis - your roommate - has left school." Receiving no sign from Tom as the young man chose the easier path of paralysis, the dean continued, "And he has not contacted his parents as to his whereabouts." As Tom persisted in awaiting a direct question before replying, Chalmers huffed and elaborated, "He visited his grandmother in ...?"

"Union City, Tennessee," Mrs. Wasserman offered evenly.

"Yes, Union City, a few days ago, and left there without saying where he was going next. His parents are understandably very upset about this and are trying to locate him or get in touch with him, and we were wondering what you knew about this." To Tom's wide-eyed silence, he went on, "Or whether you had heard from him and knew where he was or what his plans were."

"I don't know where he is," Tom finally stated with fear bleeding through his delivery.

"Have you heard from him?" Mrs. Wasserman asked in the solicitous voice into which he had once heard her change on the telephone.

"No, ma'am."

"Do you know where he's going or what his plans are, Tom?" Chalmers asked.

"No, sir."

"Is there ... anyone with him?" she asked, limiting her calculated focus to Tom.

Realizing that Siobhan might not have accompanied him to see his grandmother, who had apparently spilled the beans, Tom answered haltingly, "I - I don't know."

"Mrs. Wasserman, please let me ask the questions," the Dean of Men protested as he saw the fear in Tom's eyes.

"Certainly," she replied. "I'm sorry."

"Tom, his mother had talked to Brandeis Thursday, and he said he was going home with you for the weekend. Did he?"

"Yes."

"And did he return to Dallas with you - Well, I see here that you were not in class Monday. Did he return to Dallas with you when - ?"

"He couldn't have," she interjected. "Union City is a day's drive from here, and he was there on Monday."

"Mrs. Wasserman, please!" Chalmers exclaimed. Quieted, she narrowed her eyes and stared malevolently at Tom. "Tom, this is a very serious matter, and I'm just trying to get to the bottom of it. I need for you to tell us what happened this weekend, and I need for you to tell us anything you know about Brandeis's intentions or plans."

To avoid the poison darts issuing from her visage, Tom turned in his seat toward Dean Chalmers. In summoning up a response, he thought first of the childhood advice that Mark had jokingly given him when faced with a hard choice or a tough decision. 'What would Robert E. Lee do?' Mark would have said. And Tom knew that - Southern gentleman with the purest of hearts and gentlest of demeanors that he was - the general would have come clean and would have done so respectfully, honestly, and helpfully. But given the circumstances, Tom chose to disregard his brother's nostrum and asked himself instead, 'What would Ward Brannigan do?'

Clearing his throat, Tom said quietly, "Dean Chalmers, this is something I'd really rather not get involved in."

Caught offguard by the response, the dean jerked his head back slightly in reappraisal and said, "Well, Mr. Windham, I'm afraid you *are* involved. Now I'm asking you for some information, and I would appreciate your cooperating."

"Sir, with all due respect, I guess I need to know what would be the consequences to me of not cooperating?"

"See?!" Mrs. Wasserman shouted. "He knows where Brandeis is, and he's hiding him from me. Please make him tell!" She began to weep and added, "I'm just so worried about my son. Please help me."

"Of course you are, Mrs. Wasserman. We'll get to the bottom of this." Turning back to Tom, the dean huffed, "Young man, before you get yourself into any more trouble than you're already in, I'd suggest you give me a full explanation."

Momentarily wavering at Shirley Wasserman's show of emotion and at the dean's persistence, Tom reached deeply and again found his inner Ward. "What trouble am I already in?" he asked. As Dean Chalmers searched for a reply, Tom continued, "I mean, has there been a crime committed here? I last saw Brandeis on Sunday. As you said, his grandmother saw him on Monday. Does my not answering your questions in any way jeopardize my standing as a student here at Wesleyan Southern, and, if so, how?"

"Young man," the administrator said angrily, "you know something about all this, and I want to get to the bottom of it."

"Sir, the problem here is not between you and me or between me and Mrs. Wasserman." Looking at her, he said, "The problem is between you and your son, and if he doesn't want to talk to you, and if he doesn't want you to know where he is, I'll honor that. I guess if I were you, I'd be - "

"Well, you're not!" she interrupted scathingly. Her tears stanched and her combativeness back in play, she declared, "You're hiding my son from me, and I want to know where he is. Now!"

"I honestly do not know where Brandeis is," Tom said emphatically.

"I'm sure he's fine, and I guess you'll just have to wait to hear from him."

The flustered Dean of Men said, "Mister Windham, this is not the end of this ... but ... I suppose I can't *force* you to reveal anything you don't want to. I'll remember this, though."

His resolve again wavering, Tom said, "As I said, sir, there was no disrespect intended. I am only remaining faithful to a pledge given a friend. Is that all, sir?"

"No, that's not all!" Mrs. Wasserman yelled.

"Madam, there is nothing more to be accomplished with this," Chalmers said curtly. With equal shortness he addressed Tom, "You may go."

Outside the dean's office, Tom raised an emptied forefinger - thumb extended - and he blew the smoke from the barrel of the gun that 'shot Frank Miller dead'.

*   *   *

Pulling his mail from his box in the SUB, Tom's heart leapt as he sifted through it and came to a postcard. Postmarked "Charlottesville, Virginia", it featured an autumnal view of Monticello perched regally on its mountain overlooking the city.

> *Tawm -*
> *No, this isn't the place, but it sure is a beautiful one.*
> *We love you. Thanks again and again for <u>everything</u>. We're <u>happy</u>. Will write again soon.*
> Love,
>
> *Chevy & Bran*

Later in the day as he left his English History class in the basement of Old Wesley, Tom scurried through the poorly lighted walkway under the aging building's broad expanse of front steps. From the shadows of a doorway of one of the storage closets along the walkway Shirley Wasserman stepped, barring his egress. "Where is my son?" she demanded.

Noting the toxicity of her glare to be undiminished from the prior day, Tom entertained a momentary concern for his physical safety as he stopped short of her and said, "I told you, I don't know where he is. Leave me alone." Glancing around for faculty support, he saw none, but he did see his fellow students appraising them curiously in the dim light of the pathway as they passed giving the twosome a wide berth.

"I'm not leaving here and I'm not leaving you alone until you tell me where he is and if that slut is with him!" she exclaimed. Looking at the faces of his classmates in embarrassment as she spoke, Tom started walking away from her toward the grey, overcast light of outdoors. She followed after him jeering, "You sent my son away from me, didn't you? And you sent that Irish whore with him. Didn't you? Didn't you?!"

"Leave me alone!" he yelled, as he reached the door to the outside. "And ask yourself why he left."

"God will punish you for this," she seethed.

Dodging away from her, again fearful that she might try to harm him, he repeated, "Leave me alone. I don't know where Brandeis is, and I wouldn't tell you if I did. But I know he's happy just being away from you."

Lashing out with unfettered anger, she declared, "You are a hateful, lying, disrespectful boy, and you will pay for what you have done. Believe me, you will pay."

As Tom hurriedly walked away from her to blend into a nearby crowd of students, he heard her sobbing until she stopped and bleated her final curse, "I will make you suffer as I have suffered."

Shaking his head as he looked back at her in disgust, he said, "*You* are going to make me suffer? Hah. Take a number."

Chapter 49

Thanksgiving

Chet and Tom, having retired to the den of Chet's house upon Tom's return from a long solo noontime drive in search of fall color and of distraction during the Carters' Thanksgiving lunch, took long draws on their Dairy Queen Dr. Peppers.

"Dad was telling me something about you helping your friends make some kind of cross-country getaway," Chet began with wonderment. "And it seems to have left a sizeable bee in Mother's bonnet. What's the story?"

After synopsizing in sketchy detail the events on and before Harvest weekend, Tom concluded, "And they've settled in this little village in northern Vermont, Craftsbury 'something'. You know, one of those cute little New England-y names. They had just found a place to stay and were looking for jobs last time we talked."

"Wow. I can understand the size of that bee now," Chet said with a wide-eyed grin. "So, have they gotten married?"

"No, they stopped to do it in Virginia, but the J-P asked them for I-D, and they got cold feet. They were afraid he'd contact Memphis. But they may be married by now. Now tell me more about Callie, though," Tom urged. "I mean, I heard the party line you gave Aunt Nela and Uncle Bowman this morning, but give me the straight stuff."

"Gee, Tom, where to start. She works at a bookstore in Boulder.

Right across the street from the campus. And she's wonderful. Writes poetry. Likes to spend entire weekends wrapped up with me on the couch, reading. Loves to cook. Looks great doing it."

"She sounds incredible. I'm happy for you. I guess all you needed was a change of scenery. So, are you going to bring her down here to God's Country for Christmas?"

No, her folks live in Walsenburg, so after I spend a few days here, I'm going to meet her there." With a smile of relish he added, "Then we're just going to sock it in for the winter in front of the fire at my apartment. That'd put us both within walking distance of my building and her store. Just lay low till the thaw."

Tom caught himself and decided to wait for Chet to mention Spring Break rather than bringing it up himself.

* * *

Returning from Springfield the following day aboard the Corvette, Chet patted his stomach and reveled, "Lahwsy, how I have missed Paco's. It was funny - during my first month at Boulder, I asked one of my colleagues if there was any decent Mexican food in town. Well, the guy was from the Midwest, but he had been at C-U for two or three years, so I figured he might know. And he assured me, 'yes, there is'. But then he said, 'And don't worry. It's very *mild*'. Yankees," Chet mugged.

Motoring swiftly up 199 toward home, the cousins caught up on each other with a desperation that reflected both the brevity of Chet's holiday visit and the likelihood that his Christmas homecoming might be as short.

"Do you remember Bruce Hewitt?" Tom asked. "You probably taught him when you were teaching at Noofer High. He's my age."

"Yeah," Chet said foggily. "Oh yeah, I remember him now."

"Well, he was in 'Nam for the last year, and I saw him the other day. He made it out alive," Tom said with relief.

"Is he okay?"

"Yeah, physically, at least. But I don't know. I never saw him crack a smile in the time we talked, and he was real jittery."

Nodding, Chet said, "Yeah, I can't tell you how many times I've seen that on the faces of the 'vets' at C-U. They show you a blank face, but there's obviously so much going on behind it. And it seems to milk their personalities and their basic sense of humor. They're really serious about way too much, and when they make a joke or find something to laugh about, there's almost always a caustic or sarcastic cast to it. I don't mean they're all like that. Some have come back and put it right behind them, but others ... "

"Yeah, I know what you mean, though," Tom said. "That's how Bruce was. He just didn't seem to be - all the way home." After a moment's silence, he asked, "So, do you think Nixon'll be able to get us out?"

"Ah, who knows? Yeah, I guess he will. I just wish we hadn't given him four years to do it. I think we should've suspended the rules just for this one presidential election and given the winner a two-year term - or, better yet, eighteen months. Tell him we'd renew his lease only if he ended The War."

"Mind if I ask who you voted for?"

"Not if you don't mind my telling you that after careful consideration and after weighing both parties' stands on the issues, I didn't," Chet responded.

"You didn't vote?"

"Nope." As they pulled up in front of Chet's house, he turned to Tom and stated, "By November fifth, we'd been able to shoot or stab in the back just about anyone in this country who could make a real difference. And we were left with the same old 'business-as-usual', 'peace-with-honor', 'destroy-this-town-to-save-it', 'wrap-me-in-the-flag' gang.

"You know, Tom, I think there was a moment out there in the land ... early this year when it looked like we - like America - had a chance to change things. A chance to move back to that youth and optimism and sense of fairness, though probably not innocence, that we had before John F. Kennedy was assassinated. There was McCarthy and R-F-K and Martin Luther King out there drawing huge followings of people who cared about their fellow man and about ending an unjust war and about healing destructive, festering divisions and about having a strong national purpose based on an unshakable morality. And then it was all gone. Blown away. And I'm afraid we've missed a chance that may not come around again ... for a long, long time. And the *ancien* regime - whether they call themselves Republicans or Democrats, what they are is The Establishment - is still in the saddle. And nothing'll really change. When it's politically expedient to bring the boys home, they won't be able to fill the transports fast enough. Until then, which by my count is a little less than four years away, God help us all."

*   *   *

Approaching the gate of November Ridge Farm, the slowing Corvette ran parallel to a flock of blackbirds feeding in the bright green winter grass with which George Collum had seeded his front pastures. The swell of birds climbed briefly and descended and repeated the move and again in an undulating ripple along the fence line next to Springfield Road. Against the brilliant hue of the grass the picture reminded Tom of a speckled quilt being shaken out.

"I'm sorry she's not in, Tom, but I'm so glad you came out anyway," Anna Collum said with the warm, comforting smile, which Tom had missed as much as he had missed her daughter. Ushering him through the foyer, she explained, "No, she went home with her roommate from Michigan. I guess if we want to see that little 'mess', we're just going to have to go up to Stephens ourselves."

Entering the den on the back of the house, the heat from the fireplace reached out and drew him to it as an early cold snap had caused Stover County to bundle up for the holidays. "Come on in this house," came the booming voice of George Collum as he left the comfort of his easy chair and crossed the room to his young friend. Pulling back after shaking hands, he noted the fuller head of hair, the thicker sideburns, and the hint of leanness in Tom's cheeks. "Look like you've grown up a year or two since the last time I saw you," George offered.

"He's growing up into a fine looking young man, isn't he?" Anna added adoringly. Knowing that not to be an observation communicated between men, George barely nodded once in agreement.

"Well, y'all both look great," Tom responded, though he noted that George's hair was continuing to thin. Walking across to the window, he looked out toward November Ridge. "The trees still look pretty," he observed as he viewed below the greying afternoon sky the fading autumnal flares of color clinging yet to the oaks and maples on the ridge.

"Yeah," George agreed as the Collums joined Tom at the window, "but you should've been here about two or three weeks ago. Reds and oranges and yellows and purples -"

"It was truly glorious," Anna stated, before adding, "If we do say so ourselves." Walking toward the kitchen, Anna asked over her shoulder, "You won't make George eat his pie alone, will you, Tom?"

"Well, since you put it that way …"

"Looks like all those leaves'll be gone by Monday, though," George noted, "if this 'Norther' that blew in last night keeps huffin' and puffin'."

Tom nodded as he looked at the row of thinning maples on the backyard's fence line. Their tops leaned with the wind as the breeze pulled off a scattering of leaves and threw them against the dark red wall of the nearby barn. There they gathered and swirled around the corner, dispersing into the front pasture - itself bright green from the rye seeding.

Hearing a high-pitched yelp behind them, both men turned to see Anna chasing a chocolate-and-white pup into the den. Waving in feigned aggravation, she said, "Just opened the back door a crack and this little varmint scooted right in."

The puppy crossed quickly to George's feet and flipped on his back, urine dripping from it onto the area rug where they stood. "Runt!" George yelled in disgust.

"Here," Anna said with a laugh, offering him the hand towel she had draped over her shoulder. "I'll let you tend to your next champion pointer."

Tom was already on his knees rubbing the smooth short hair of the dog, and it licked him enthusiastically as he sought to calm it. "There, there, boy. Boy?" Tom wondered as he took a quick look. "Yeah, boy. There, there. When did you get him?"

"Yesterday," George said as he joined Tom on the floor with the dog, toweling the carpet and pulling on the pup's smooth, broad ears. "All feet 'n' head 'n' ears right now," George allowed.

"And tummy," Tom said as he rubbed its tight, swollen belly. "What's his name?"

"Haven't named him yet," George grunted. "You want to?"

"Can I?" Tom asked excitedly, drawing more honor from the privilege than the donor saw in its giving.

"Sure."

Taking the becalmed pup's face in his hands and playing with its excess jowl, Tom narrowed his eyes in consideration and finally adjudged, "You look like a 'Theodore' to me."

"Uhn-uhn," George said quickly. "This is a huntin' dog. The name's gotta be - "

"Monosyllabic?" Tom asked.

"No, short," George replied with a wink.

"Ahh," Tom acknowledged with a reciprocal nod.

"So you think 'Ted'?" George asked.

"Naahhw," Tom replied as he continued to examine the droopy-eyed face. "He could be a Theodore, but I just don't see him as Ted. A rough-and-tumble huntin' dog, huh?" The light dawning in his eyes, Tom proclaimed, "Spike! He's definitely a 'Spike'."

George considered only momentarily before slapping Tom's back and lifting the dog up over their heads holding it with one hand under its chest and his other balancing its behind. "All hail Prince Spike, future grand champion!" he announced as a yellow trickle dampened the cuff of his shirt.

As the men discussed the Longhorns' eight-game winning streak concluding with a romp over the Aggies and their impending Cotton Bowl date with a respectable Tennessee team, Anna poured coffee and a glass of milk and cut slices of apple pie in the kitchen. Playing with the puppy in front of the fire, Tom and George heard the phone ring, but George motioned that Anna would get it. Momentarily, she entered the room with a look of concern, and said, "Tom, that was Bowman. There's a brush fire at the McAlister place. He said it was a big one."

Rising and looking out the window, Tom saw no smoke beyond November Ridge, the McAlister farm being at least seven miles from the Collums'. George and Tom glared in understanding and apprehension, though, as the wind from the north continued to push the tops of the fencerow maples unrelentingly.

"That brush is as dry as it was in August. It's a tinderbox. And in this wind ..." George warned, shaking his head.

"Did Bowman say if the fire department was out there?" Tom asked of Anna.

"He said they were already fighting fires all over the county, so they could only send one truck and a few men. He said you - "

"I'd better get over there," Tom said.

"I'll get together some men around here and head on over," George said. "You think you ought to go start hosing down the roof of the cabin?"

Shaking his head as he thought of the canopy of pines overhanging the lakehouse, he said, "If it gets that far, there's no saving it."

As Tom bolted for the door, Anna Collum intercepted him. "Tom, have you ever even fought a fire before?" she asked in near panic.

"No. But I've watched."

Chapter 50

Barton McAlister had coached the fabled Panther football teams of the Thirties and early Forties with legendary skill and success. "Coach Mac" had retired from teaching shortly before Tom reached high school, and Tom had felt deprived at his departure having heard second-hand from Mark dozens of the football anecdotes with which Coach Mac had regularly peppered the biology class that the venerable ex-coach had taught him. As Tom drove the Ranchero toward his own farm - having made a fast stop at the Carters' to don workshirt, jeans, Wellingtons and Johnny's wool-lined corduroy coat - he remembered the November during Mark's junior year in high school. Under similar circumstances, Coach Mac had, with the principal's acquiesence - the principal being a former quarterback of his - accepted volunteers of any able-bodied boy in high school to leave class and to join him to fight just such a fire at his farm. The classrooms had emptied, and Tom remembered how his mother had finally had to throw away Mark's "fire-fighting" jeans and shirt after giving up on ever getting the smoky smell out. But Coach Mac's new ranch house and his livestock had been saved, and the acreage burned had been limited.

And Johnny Windham, who had fought the fire alongside his older son, had breathed a deep sigh of relief - because the McAlister place bordered his on the north.

Coach Mac had died in 1966 some months before the school board had voted to de-commission and mothball the football field that bore his name. Tom had regretfully made it through high school without being called out of class to fight a fire. As he approached the fence line between the McAlister place and his own, Tom took solace that no fire was in sight. But looking over the trees in a forested patch of his neighbor's land, he saw the heavy pall of smoke moving south, and he shuddered. The McAlister farm was four times the size of his, and it included pastures and several small woods, but it had very little water and it was comprised mostly of unworked, scruffy undergrowth - a dry veldt which could offer only a suicidal welcome to a wind-borne blaze.

Tom turned the Ranchero onto the oil road that led to the Widow McAlister's house. A foggy shroud hung over the blacktop as the adrenalin coursing through him made him fidget with the new buckskin work gloves he had remembered to fish out from behind the seat. He came upon a brace of pick-ups parked askew on either side of the road, and he wheeled in quickly. He could not see the house, which he knew should be in front of him, because of an impenetrable wall of smoke tracking from what he perceived to be north by northeast. He smiled at himself momentarily as his fear for the safety of the vehicles from a possible fire coming from behind him was instantly abated by the observation that the ground on both sides of the road was already scorched. 'Don't guess it'll burn again,' he reasoned. The same observation, though, made him fearful for the fate of the widow's house. Stepping out of his truck, he was struck simultaneously by the choking oxygen-starved smoke that enveloped him, by the incongruous cold that accompanied it, and by the disorienting effect of hearing both the distant barking of unseen voices and the crackling of unseen flames.

Making his way quickly down the road by foot, he was relieved to find the ranch house undisturbed. Walking past the unattended Piney V.F.D. fire truck he came upon a trio of soot-stained teenagers being instructed by Brendan Reynolds, a service station operator and a deacon at First Baptist whom Tom had known since infancy. "Tom Roy!" he yelled excitedly, his wide eyes flashing brightly from the black stains of the wrinkles that trailed away toward his temples. "Son, this sucker's headin' your way!" he exclaimed, waving broadly toward the southeast. Momentarily stunned, Tom took a step back and sucked for breath but drew in smoke. Racing into his lungs, it caused him to cough convulsively for several seconds. His former Sunday School teacher moved quickly, leaning into his truck bed for a red shop towel. Soaking it with water from a tall thermos, he offered it to Tom. "Here. Breathe through this, and carry it with you."

Regaining his breath and his senses, Tom asked, "Where can I go to help?"

"Jump in the truck with me, and I'll carry you down there. You boys get in the back," he urged. Following one-lane dirt trails through untouched stretches of forest and pasture as well as through scorched and smoldering clumps of scrub oaks, pine, and underbrush, Reynolds informed him that the fire was being fought principally by hand-to-hand combat between a long line of battle-weary volunteers and an unrelenting wind that urged the fire - hopscotching along the ground and through the trees - southward.

"Your front pasture's not in any danger," he explained loudly over the rattle of the old company truck along the rutted road. "There's just scrub brush between here and there, and there's enough men workin' along there to contain it. They're probably beatin' it out now. But the problem's those big woods on the backside of here," he said, waving in an easterly direction. "You know, they merge right into the woods on the north end of your lake, and that fire could work its way right down both sides ... and to the lakehouse."

"What can we do about it?" Tom asked.

"Well, they got a dozer and a tractor with a tiller out there cuttin' a firebreak north to south well in front of the woods and then turnin' back west a hundred yards or so above your fence line and going across. They wanted to set a backfire on the fire side of the break to burn up the brush before the main fire gets to it, but they ran out of time. So we're just going to have to fight it when it comes and keep it from leapin' over the break and gittin' to the woods." As Reynolds suddenly stopped the truck after driving over a low grassfire, Tom made out through the smoke and late afternoon darkness lines of men stretching north and west as the flames sparkled and exploded through the underbrush. Dismounting the truck as a tongue of flame leapt from one sparsely leafed small oak to another, Tom chased after Reynolds as he started to roll slowly away. Slapping on the window, Tom opened the door when the pick-up jerked to a halt.

"Where are you going?" Tom asked.

"Driving on down there across the firebreak," he yelled back.

"Well, what do I fight the fire with?"

Dropping his face into his hands with his first smile, the deacon said, "Whoops, well that'd help, wouldn't it?"

"Yeah!" Tom yelled without humor.

"Reach in the back and get a hatchet. Then go down there," he said, pointing to a mixed clump of trees, "and chop yourself down about a five- or six-foot-tall pine sapling, and just start beatin' the tar out of anything you see that's orange and hot. Get one of those guys along here to give you a sector to work. But this here outfit ain't sufferin' from over-organization, so just watch out for yourself and go ahead and do whatever you think'll help. And, Tom, keep lookin' around you. Don't get caught in it. And use that towel I give you if you get choked." With a wave and "Good luck," he waited momentarily for Tom to find the hatchet before gunning the truck east to deliver his teenage cargo.

After quickly selecting a thickly foliaged young sapling and hacking at it for too long with the dull hatchet, Tom pushed it to the ground, stepped on it to break its trunk, and twisted it vigorously before chopping away the final shreds of yellow meat that kept it earthbound. Stowing the hatchet in his belt and approaching the disorganized line of volunteers and the uneven line of the fire, Tom heard a disembodied voice shout from the smoke, "Hey! Go on over to your left there and work that sector!" Through a break in the smoke, Tom saw that the grizzled stranger was talking to him as he waved animatedly to the west.

"Okay!"

"Bowden was overcome by the smoke," the stranger shouted. "Be careful. This wind's crazy out here."

Tom began to walk away, but he stopped for a moment to orient himself. Turning toward the oncoming blaze, he held the damp cloth over his nose and mouth and confirmed the truth of the stranger's words. The wind was no longer gusting consistently to the south. Looking toward a section of fence, he saw the shapes of the terrain made odd from this unfamiliar angle - but part of his farm nonetheless. Turning back north, Tom staked out the line he would defend. He set out toward the flame, beating it back energetically and effectively - his back to his Land.

Blowing thick, blackened mucus into his moist, filthy towel, Tom viewed with pride the fire line he and his anonymous cohorts had fought to a standstill over the past hours. The smoke from other parts of the fire and from the grey, smoldering vegetation around him continued to burn his eyes as he searched his shirttail for one last clean spot with which to rub them. Determining through nods and waves and shouts of victory up and down the line that the fire had been halted along the firebreak running west to east parallel with his own northern fence line, Tom began to slog wearily eastward toward the elbow of the firebreak to assure himself of the salvation of the forest. Dragging his darkened sapling behind him, he turned northward at the bend in the lane of graded earth, and he was engulfed anew in heavy smoke.

"Hey, get that!" came a frantic shout through the grey shroud as the underbrush across the break ignited before him from an air-borne spark. Wielding his trusty pine sapling, he reflexively swatted the flames dead as he had done countless times in his previous sector when gusts of wind had urged the fire to leapfrog the earthen moat. "Thanks," said the disembodied voice of Tom's ally.

"How's it going up here?" Tom asked.

"Just about got it out, I think," the stranger replied as Tom began to make him out through the thinning smoke.

Impatiently, Tom asked, "Well, do you or don't you?"

"Better check with one of the firemen up there for the final word," the stranger replied coldly.

"Sorry," Tom mumbled. "I guess I'm a little bushed." Hoisting a thumb southward, he said, "That's *my* place next door, and I was just –"

"Your place is safe. It's not getting there," the grizzled young man declared with an assuring smile.

Coughing again, he waved a farewell to his fellow defender and staggered north up the line. Eventually he found Brendan Reynolds beside his pick-up holding forth to his soot-stained young charges.

"We beat this dragon to a draw?" Tom asked as he approached.

"Sure 'nough," Brendan replied with curiosity as to who was addressing him. "Oh, Tom Roy, that's you. Son, you look like one of the End Men at the Firemen's Minstrel," he added with a broad laugh.

Tom returned a respectful smile, and he held the sting within. The reference to the Minstrel, which the volunteer firemen of New Fredonia had until recently performed in blackface, took Tom aback. It was the first time he had thought of the show since well before the past spring, and it caused a moment of ambivalence. The sadness triggered was both for the loss of his right to enjoy the show from a child's point of view and for the bigotry evident in his having enjoyed it for the years that he had. He now knew, and he could not go back.

Leaving his charred weapon on the field of battle, Tom accepted Reynolds' plaudits and his offer of a ride back to the Ranchero. Finally alone, Tom walked slowly around the truck and lifted himself onto its extended tailgate, his feet dangling to the ground. It was then that the pain-numbing adrenalin on which Tom had been operating seemed to evaporate into the evening air. The soreness from flailing his fire-swatter began to cry out from the muscles in his arms and shoulders and back. Along with general body fatigue came a sudden chill. Leaning back first on his elbows on the truck bed, Tom soon lay down on the work-scarred, rusted surface.

Lying there looking up silently into the starry quilt of the evening sky, Tom observed a surprising phenomenon. He listened closely before hoisting his right arm heavenward. Using the loose, grimy sleeve of his workshirt as a windsock, he observed a stillness mindful to him of the limp, motionless American flag at the east end of McAlister Field on a windless first home-game early September night. The silence, save for the occasional crackle of embers from the charred remains of a tree, and the motionless shirtsleeve, which he finally let drop beside him, told him that the wind had beaten a retreat from the field of battle. As he smiled wryly considering whether the conflagration's defeat had been a Victory of Men or a Gift of God, Tom heard the soft crunching of gravel and debris in the road of one whom he assumed to be a fellow warrior.

Propping first on his elbows and then rising on the support of his hands to look over the side of the truck, he saw someone approaching. Like an apparition emerging from the smoke that now hung over the landscape, the unidentified figure caused Tom to squint his burning eyes as he peered through the foggy veil.

It was Clair.

With competing emotions of joy, welcome, and relief much stronger than the body they occupied, he was able to manage a weak smile and a nod as she approached the truck and, clasping her hands, leaned her elbows on the sidewalls. Her hair draped silken and straight down either side of her face and over the embroidered workshirt inside her open navy pea coat. Her clean, soft face was illuminated by the flicker of a stubborn yellow flame in the burned out trunk of a scrub oak next to the road. Not lost on Tom was the incongruity of her fresh, vibrant beauty against this scene of desolation and destruction.

With an easy smile and without surprise, she asked, "What brings you to this neck o' the woods?"

"Weiner roast," Tom replied. "It got outta' hand. What about you?"

"Just came back to pick up some boys I had brought over from Promise for the festivities."

"About to take them home?"

"Seems they've already gotten a ride."

Leaning forward and dropping himself to the ground, he looked at her wearily and said, "I'm going to the lakehouse to clean up. Would you like to come along?" She walked around from the side of the truck and confronted him. Looking earnestly into his eyes, she reached out and gripped his upper arms. "Careful," he said, "I'm filthy."

Disregarding his warning, she pulled his arms toward her, and he wrapped them around her. Leaning into his soot-stained shirt and face, she kissed him, and he kissed her back.

Chapter 51

Tom emerged from the shower in the lakehouse's master bath. Sniffing his shoulder, he still registered a smoky scent, but at least his body and his hair were clean. Donning the fresh jeans and the "Wazoo" sweatshirt he had recently deposited in the dresser in the master bedroom, he ran a comb through his wet hair and walked into the den. Clair was seated amid the throw pillows in the conversation pit leaning back against the front of the couch before the fire she had built. Her gaze locked onto the dancing flames until she became aware of Tom's presence, she turned to offer him a warm, welcoming smile and a tall, icy glass of Dr. Pepper.

"Does that feel better?" she asked.

"A lot," he said as he joined her on the floor. "But I'm afraid I still smell like I spilled a bottle of 'Essence de Joan of Arc' on me."

Leaning into him, she sniffed his neck saying, "Smell good to me."

Pressing his face into her cheek, he drew encouragement that his senses were returning to normal when he recognized the unforgotten scent of her skin. Brushing his lips up from her chin to her cheek and to the lobe of her ear, he breathed softly into it before she pulled away, lightly touching his chest.

Understanding her hesitancy he moved back from her reciprocally - allowing her space - and time. "Where were you coming from when you saw my truck?" he asked.

"The McAlister house. Mrs. McAlister's such a sweet lady. Reminds me of Gramma. She was so thankful that the house had been saved. She wasn't that worried about the rest of the property. She had this peace about her as far as the acreage was concerned. She told me, 'Things that are natural - like the Land - regenerate themselves.' Said it was just 'God's way'. She said they may not come back just the way they were before, but they'd come back."

Watching her as she spoke, Tom was filled with wonderment at how much he wanted Clair, and he was too weary and too needful to trouble himself overmuch with how little he deserved to be there with her experiencing that wonderment. But the weariness showed through. As she finished speaking, he dropped his head back onto the seat of the couch and rotated it to look at her.

"Tom, are you alright?" she asked as she leaned her head over his.

"I'm so tired, Clair. So tired." Looking up at her, he added weakly, "All I want to do right now is just let go and be with you."

"Oh, Tom. I know you're worn out. What can I get you? Are you hungry? Or do you need some aspirin? Anything. I could go up to Starr's Grocery if there was anything - "

"Clair, I just need *you*. I'm not just tired from fighting that fire. I'm tired of controlling myself and holding myself ... away from you." Running his eyes back and forth across her face, he whispered, "You're so beautiful, and you look at me with such- It's hard work leaving you alone."

Shaking her head slowly from side to side, she cupped his head in her arm leaning her forehead gently into his and asked, "Then why the hell do you do it?" Joining her in shaking his head, he did not reply. Pulling away, she stared at him with his eyes closed and his mouth slightly open. "Tom, say what you want to, but you look weak. Let me fix you something to eat, okay?"

"Sure," Tom responded. Light returning to his eyes, he said, "Hey, Chet and I brought some Paco's hot sauce and tostados out here the other night. You want some?"

"Yeah, but what else is there I could fix for you?"

"Aw, I always keep some cans of Chef Boy-Ar-Dee and some Vienna Sausage out here, and I think there's some bread."

"Pretty continental taste there, Windham."

Manning the tall stools at the bar that looked into the galley kitchen, they crunched voraciously on the hot sauce and chips and guzzled Dr.

Peppers while the canned spaghetti and meatballs heated on the stove. After eating his half of the can and part of hers, Tom suggested they take the remaining appetizers back to the fireside. Clair caught him up on her semester's work at Springfield College. Speaking comfortably and with enthusiasm of her work and of her campus involvement there, neither mentioned his sponsorship, and both were relieved.

But as she spoke of a dance in October, she said, "And after the dance, we -" and she hesitated before concluding, her voice trailing off, "went to a midnight breakfast given by the Chancellor."

After a pregnant silence, Tom finally asked, "So, are you and Gene Ray still going out?"

"Some," she answered blankly. "Are you still seeing Lizza?"

"Aahhh, hard to say. Haven't seen her since August, and she went to Michigan for Thanksgiving, and -"

"It's okay," Clair interjected. "You don't owe me any explanation."

"I wish I did."

After a silent moment Clair turned to look back into the great-room and said, "This house is beautiful."

"Thanks. I've finally started enjoying it."

"Good, Tom. Had many girls out here?" she asked with a laugh.

"Haven't had any. Anywhere. Not Lizza, not anyone."

With an ironic grin and a half-laugh, she said, "Tom, it really is okay. Like I told myself a long time ago, 'If I don't get you this lifetime, I'll get you the next'."

Tom examined her strong, courageous face, filled though it was with an undeniable love - or weakness - for him, and he declared, "I share neither your certainty of a future life nor Aunt Nela's certainty of an after-life. So you'll pardon me if I stuff as much into this one as I can. Just on the off chance that - this is it." Removing the tray from between them, Tom leaned toward Clair as both of them unfolded their legs. Taking her in his arms he kissed her fiercely while lowering her into the pile of throw pillows in the richly carpeted pit between the sizzling, popping fire and the couch. They continued to kiss passionately as their hands joyfully rediscovered the familiar and happily found the new of each other's bodies.

Lifting himself from her, he looked into the eyes that returned his love as he hesitated with his fingers poised on the top button of her blouse. Reading neither reticence nor resistance in her deep blue eyes, he unbuttoned it while kissing her hungrily. After hoisting his sweatshirt over his head, he lay beside her amidst the strewn pillows. She kissed him more slowly as if in a daze. Responding to her rhythm, Tom restrained his movements and concentrated on the pure sensation of her flesh touching his.

Pulling slightly away from her lips, he smiled and whispered, "Finally." As she nodded and shared his smile, he added, "Clair, I just love you. I love you with everything inside me."

"And I love you, Tom. I always have." Reaching for the top button of his jeans, she whispered, "And I'm through not telling you what I want."

"Are you sure this is what you want?"

"*You* are what I want. Now." Kissing him again hungrily, she shook her head slightly and leaned away to say, "I don't care what went before, and I don't care what comes after. Just love me…here…now."

"That was incredible," he whispered to her through a grin that was pure youth and joy as she clung to him. He closed his eyes to feel again the unmatched sensation of every contact point of his body against hers. "I love you, Clair. You've made me so happy."

"And you have me, Tom," she said. "That was great, wasn't it?"

"It was everything. You are everything I want."

"Oh, Tom. It's so right to love you. That's why I could never stop."

As he lifted his body from hers to gaze at the curves and valleys of her exquisite nakedness, she shuddered from the loss of his body heat and from the cold at floor level. Noting the fire to have burned down to orange embers, he said, "Hold on. I'll save us from frostbite." Rising carefully to shield his genitals from her gaze, he turned quickly and unhooked a patchwork quilt from the wall. After turning out the remaining kitchen lights and stoking the fire, he returned to cover her with the quilt.

"Wait," Clair said as he stood over her. Rolling on her back to reveal herself to him, she said, "Let me see you." Hesitantly, he let go the quilt and it dropped to the floor between them. As he stood over her in the orange light of the rejuvenating flames, she said, "Tom, you're beautiful. And we're twin souls. Thank you for loving me tonight. I'll never forget it."

Easing down beside her and tucking the quilt carefully around them, he whispered, "You're beautiful, too. The most beautiful thing I've ever seen. Stay with me tonight."

A moment's concern showed in her face as she considered Gramma, her reputation, and their history. But putting it all behind her, she said, "Let me make a call."

"Jenny, I need for you to call Gramma and tell her I'm spending the night with you tonight. Tell her I'm washing my hair right now." "Yeah." "Yes." "Thanks."

"Chet. I ... won't be coming home tonight. Tell them I'm staying over with you, okay?" "Yeah." "Yep, I sure did." "Thanks."

As they stood naked and swaddled in the quilt, Tom hung up the wall phone in the kitchen and rumbled in his deep voice made gravelly from the smoke, "I just want to wrap you in my arms. Care for you. Keep you safe and warm - if not dry."

Laughing at him as he shrieked a shout of happiness, she said huskily, "Aalllll night."

"Do you want to ... go get in one of the beds?" he asked with the gleeful abandon of a child handed the keys to F.A.O. Schwartz.

"I kind of like it there by the fire," she answered while lacing his neck with kisses.

Without commenting, he unwound from the quilt, whisked her up in his arms and carried her to the scattered mound of pillows. "More hot sauce and chips," he declared. "I'm famished." Laughing at a revelation, he added, "I think I finally understand why Woz and Chevy were *eating* all the time." Yelling again in unbounded joy, Tom grabbed a laughing Clair and rolled himself into the quilt with her.

"I love you, Tom," she declared as both were suddenly struck by the renewed horizontal encounter of their bodies. "I love you so, so much. And if you love me back *half* as much as I love you ... well, I'll just call that a bonus. Although, I'll say this: it would be the smartest thing you could do - because I would make you happy."

It was a night filled with laughter and tears, sounds and silences, restless sleep and passionate awakenings, and words of love and acts of love. And all dark thoughts took a holiday.

Tom awakened to the crowing of Araberry's rooster across the lake as the first hint of grey light peered through the floor-to-ceiling windows of the great-room. He smiled at the warmth and softness of Clair's naked body tucked tightly behind his, both wrapped in the giant antique quilt. He lay still for a long time replaying in his soul the tactile joys and the sensory sensations of the night. But he also reveled in clearing his mind of thought and absorbing the sheer pleasure of Clair snug against him - her lips caressing his back in her semi-sleep and her arms wrapped around him. Without moving he occasionally opened his eyes to observe the progress of the morning light as the foggy dawn receded down toward the lake and made way for a crisp, clear autumn day. Finally he felt her stir behind him and heard her growl in elemental joy at discovering where she was. Immediately squeezing him to her, she placed her open lips against his back and bestowed on him what he smiled to imagine would show itself to him later as a hickey. Thrilled at her awakening, he rolled over to exchange with her unadorned smiles of joyous delight, and he wrapped his arms around her holding her to him tightly.

"Good morning, Clair. I love you," he said before kissing her full and long. After rolling and rubbing one another for several minutes under the quilt and among the pillows, he suggested, "Let's go outside and look at the lake."

Wrapped together in the quilt, they giggled as they shuffled awkwardly out onto the deck like contestants in a tandem tow-sack race. But as she leaned against the rail of the deck and he enveloped her from behind, they fell silent and looked out at the picture before them. A soupy blanket of fog lay over the lake like swirls of angel hair. Only the boathouse's roof was visible above it. Its alternating pattern of rusted and silvered tin panels giving the appearance of the stylized roof of a pagoda, the scene presented to the lovers was like an oriental silkscreen. After a few silent moments absorbing the setting and the circumstance, they were reawakened by the intrusion of the sun through the pines across the lake.

As much as she was enjoying nibbling on Tom, Clair finally admitted, "I am so hungry."

Tom laughed in agreement. "I'm starved."

"What do we have here?"

"Not enough," he stated. "I'll run up to Starr's and get some things."

Sitting at the bar - Clair in a Black Watch tartan plaid viyella robe that had been Johnny's, and Tom in his jeans - over the breakfast of poached eggs, bacon, wheat toast, and orange juice that Clair had prepared for them, each relished the wide-ranging, free-associating conversation reminiscent of so many they had had before. But Clair saw the concern etched on Tom's brow and in his eyes as he discussed the future of his inherited business.

"And it's been such a load," he said with weariness as they rose and returned to the rail of the deck, "carrying fifteen hours of upper level work while running back and forth down here to check on the business and zooming downtown in Dallas to go over investments with Ward Brannigan. And with all this staring me in the face, it's hard to look forward to the Christmas Break. There's just no end to it. And after that, I've still got another year-and-a-half of school. All those people to answer to. The business to take care of," he said, shaking his head under the load.

"What does a year-and-a-half have to do with anything?" Clair asked, feigning confusion.

"Well, I've got to carry the same load for the next three semesters to graduate - to get out of school," he replied, as if stating the obvious.

"Or else what?!" Clair asked.

"What do you mean?"

"Tom, my gift to you is that question. Those three little words. They come in handy to me a lot. 'Or else what?' If you didn't finish college in three semesters, what would be the penalty? If you just let things ride for a while longer, what would be the cost? If you turned more responsibility for your investments over to that guy in Dallas, to do what he's supposed to be doing anyway as far as I can understand, where's the crime? Who says you have to finish in three semesters, and who says you have to do it at W-S-U. Why don't you take off next semester? Why don't you take off next year?" Tom tilted his head quizzically at the introduction of a totally new and radically different concept. "I mean, what are you in such a rush to get out of school to do? Go to *work*?" she laughed with a playful frown. "There's time for that. Plenty. But you're in a unique position - in the people you've lost and what you've had to go through. And - while I'm blowing off all this hot air - if you don't mind my saying so, it sounds like you've also got enough money in the bank to take some time off. You don't seem to have any compelling need to rush off straight to work.

"Look around you, Tom," she said as they scanned the lake and the facing woods. "This is so beautiful and peaceful. Living out here would not be a bad life. And it sounds like you are overly concerned with pleasing some people who sincerely love and care about you, but who may have some ideas about how you should live your life that don't have anything to do with what would make you happy. Well, God bless 'em and help them on their way, but let them live their *own* lives. It may take a little or a lot of subtle explaining and maneuvering or it may take an outright declaration, but you might should get across to them that what you choose to do is alright if it's what *you* want."

"Is that how you live?" Tom asked with a wry smile.

"Heavens, no," she replied with a self-deprecating sigh and a smile. "I make a lot of concessions to Gramma, as you know. But they're really ones I want to make because her happiness right now is very, very important to me. It's a choice that I've made with this part of my life. But it still doesn't hold me back from doing a lot that I want to do. And you shouldn't let these things either. And Tom, never forget that your aunts and uncles and friends and relations will go on with their lives without regard to what you do."

Tuning in to the quiet and peace of the scene before him, Tom smiled and breathed deeply the clean, country air, redolent of the majestic solitude of the place that he had come to love. He spoke slowly and softly, "Clair, if I stayed out here ... for awhile ... would you come see me ... spend some time with me."

"It's against the rules for me to say this, Tom. But if it weren't for Gramma - and if you'd ask me to - I'd move out here. But yes, I'd come out here. I'd come out here *a lot*. Probably about anytime you wanted me to."

Visions of Clair and firesides, blankets and snow, picnics and long walks rolled across his mind in pleasurable waves. "I love you, Clair," Tom said quietly, and holding her to him tightly, he kissed her. But they froze in shock as the telephone rang. Thinking quickly, though, Tom said reassuringly, "Whoever it is, it's okay."

"Tom?"

"Oh, Chet," he said with relief. "Yeah, what's up?"

"Aunt Nela's beginning to express a lot of interest in your whereabouts. And don't forget, I need to ride back with you to catch a plane. I'm not sure where you stand, but you might should either come back in or at least call in. Sorry, buddy."

"Okay, Cuz. Thanks for the help - and for the warning."

As Tom hung up the receiver, Clair nodded her head in understanding and said, "I probably need to get home, too."

After a shower together that extended to the limit imposed by the capacity of the hot water heater, they started to dress. With a prideful laugh, Tom walked toward the kitchen for another glass of orange juice and crowed over his shoulder, "Well, somebody's not going to marry a virgin."

Returning to the bedroom, he found Clair standing before the mirror in her jeans and her bra with the brush in her hand frozen against the side of her head. Wearing an expression of injury, she seemed lost in a stare into the mirror.

"Clair, what is it?"

Turning to him and dropping her hands to her side, she asked, "Was that all this was, Tom? Just a mutual de-flowering?"

As he shook his head and began to say, "No," she continued, "Because, Tom, if that's all you thought we were doing out here, let me correct you. I've already been de-flowered."

Stunned, he backed up to the door and said in a disembodied tone, "No, I was just kidding. I didn't mean - " But a darkness passed across his face as he asked, "Who? Gene Ray?"

"Tom, don't look at me like that," she said as tears began to well in her eyes.

"Was it Gene Ray?" he asked with bitterness.

"No, it was not Gene Ray."

"Then who?"

"You don't know him, and it doesn't matter," she sighed with exasperation. "It was a long time ago. It was ... someone I dated right after we broke up. I don't know why I let it happen," she said hesitantly. But dropping her head, she said, "I do know why. I thought I really loved him, though I knew it wasn't the way I had loved you. But I'd lost you because I wouldn't go all the way, and I wasn't going to lose love again because of that. But we did it one time," she said, breaking down in tears, "and all it told me was how much I loved *you*! I couldn't put you out of my mind. And we quit seeing each other after that."

Fighting to regain her composure, she said, "And I can't take that back, Tom, and I can't do anything about it." Crossing the room to him, she cried, "And now I've given myself to you, and you've made me so happy." Throwing her arms around him, she kissed his neck and cried, "We love each other. You know it."

But he lifted his arms away from her as a stormcloud of anger passed over his eyes and the dark voices in his soul clamored for distance and for rejection. "This ... " he began in confusion. "I don't know."

"Tom, you're not going to do this to me again, are you?" she moaned as she backed away.

"I ... just don't know."

"I can't believe this is happening," she said, sitting slowly on the side of the bed and dropping her face into her hands.

Buttoning his shirt, he said, "We need to go. I'll wait for you outside."

He stood glaring into the rippling lake water as she finished dressing. Wordlessly, they walked to the Ranchero. As they rolled across his cattleguard and made the short trip to the McAlister place, Clair cried silently but did not speak.

"Is this it?" she finally asked as they drove down the blacktop toward her truck. "Is this how it ends again? This time you leave because I *did* make love to you?"

"Clair, let me have some time," he said wearily.

"More time?" she asked, shaking her head. "Tom, I just want to say this. I don't fully understand my crime in your eyes. Maybe you can twist it around and make it come out that I don't love you like I've said I do - like I had thought I'd shown you. Or maybe you were just looking for an excuse to take back what you'd said or done because you couldn't convince yourself that you deserved as much happiness as we could have together. I don't know. I still don't understand how things work in that head of yours."

They pulled up beside her faded blue pick-up. "I don't know what it's going to take to convince you that I'm *always* going to love you and that I'll always be here for you. No matter what you do or where you are or what you decide to make of yourself ... or of us. I'm going to love you just for who you are, and I'm going to love you ... whoever you turn out to be."

As he heard the door of the cab open and felt her start to leave, he turned and said, "Clair ... it's me. It's not you. It's me."

"I know that. Don't you think I know that, you fool! I love you so much. And I could have loved you so well," Bringing her fist to her chest, she said, "I could have made you *so* happy."

As he turned to look forward without replying, she left the cab of the Ranchero. Driving away from her through the barren, burned-out terrain as a cloud of smoke wafted across his windshield, Tom glanced Heavenward, asked bitterly, "Surprised?" and drove into the smoke.

Chapter 52

Early December

Under the cover of snow-filled clouds Tom slipped back into the United States at Champlain, New York. There was a dirty snow in town, but it cleansed itself as he rolled back out into the countryside. The landscape again became the white pallet of farmland and grey-green woods that it had been in his drive down from Montreal where he had de-planed. His stay in the northeastern corner of New York was noteworthy principally for its brevity as he turned left at Champlain and motored the few miles to the bridge spanning the first of the two northern fingers of Lake Champlain, the eastern side of which was Vermont.

 He laughed at himself while driving through the quaintly rural Alburg township as he realized how homogeneous the Quebecois countryside, the New York countryside, and the Vermont countryside were. Unsurprised by the small town charm of the latter, he had anticipated the short Canadian leg of his sojourn to mimic the French terrain he had observed from the bus between Paris and Le Mans, and he had assumed the urban frenzy of New York City would be felt and heard right up to the state's northern border. There had been, however, no such radical changes at the international and state lines. All looked simply Norman Rockwell American.

 Happily, the roads were clear of snow as he trundled through Vermont and quickly across the second finger of Lake Champlain in the behemoth Ford Galaxie that had been the only rolling stock unreserved at the Avis counter in Montreal. Tom shuddered to think of driving this enormous power-power-automatic American juggernaut on icy roads. To avoid such conditions he chose the broadest red lines on his roadmap, and they led him through St. Albans and Johnson and almost to Hardwick before he turned back north onto Highway 14, a thinner red line and one marked forebodingly as "scenic". What amazed Tom, a veteran of years of plodding slowly and ponderously across the vast expanses of Texas roadmaps, was the rapid-fire order in which he reached and put behind him each of the little villages on his Vermont map. The lay of the rolling land, much forested, much cultivated, only the rare patch gone to seed; the prevalence of crisply well-kept white frame in the small communities and of picturesquely weathered red frame on the farms; and the compacted scale of the whole told Tom that he would love Vermont in any season.

At the Craftsbury sign Tom turned onto a narrower, unevenly shouldered stretch of road through Craftsbury township into the village - no, Tom thought, 'hamlet' - of Craftsbury Common. Easily spotting the church spire of which Brandeis had apprised him, Tom homed in on it. Approaching the church he first noticed the familiar ex-Windham Le Mans, its lower half caked with varying degrees of frosted Yankee mud.

And there on the church steps smiling and waving from beneath toboggans, pea coats, gloves, and mufflers were Siobhan and Brandeis. As Tom rolled to a stop, and leapt from the car, they raced to him. The three friends threw themselves into an exuberant tri-cornered embrace.

When Tom finally pulled away and backed up, the grinning host couple stood with their arms across each other's backs. "Just a minute," he said. "Let me look at you two." Tom was almost tearful both from the bracing cold and from the moment. He shifted his eyes from face to face reading the pure, easy joy in each. Finally giving over to the reality of the elements, though, a full body shiver ran through him, and he puffed out a huge white cloud as the cold permeated his uncovered head and hands, his jeans, and his new mouton-collared suede car coat. Brandeis and Siobhan pulled him again to them, sharing their warmth and rubbing his back vigorously.

"Come on," Siobhan said, "let's get you home! I'll ride with you, and we can follow Bran." Loading into their cars, the Le Mans led the

Galaxie through the tiny village of frosty white frame houses, barren trees, and dormant lawns under a soft grey sky. "More snow's coming," Siobhan said with an eager smile.

"Really?" Tom replied with a little boy's grin. His was the look of anticipation of one who had grown up in northeast Texas where a single two- or three-inch snow per year was the norm and where there had been winters in which the region's children had gone altogether without.

Laughing as Tom examined the dark green and ecru print wallpaper in the cozy kitchen of their cedar shake-sided cabin in the woods up from Little Hosmer Pond, Siobhan said, "We were told it depicts a scene of the heroics of Ethan Allen and his Green Mountain Boys."

"Oh, have they played here lately?" Tom asked.

"Right, and I think they hung this wallpaper when they stopped by. These people here are wonderful, though," she continued as she wadded ground beef into meatballs, seasoning them periodically. "One of the first natives I spoke to when we got here was a crotchety old farmer I called to ask about work. I called him, and for some reason I opened by saying something like, 'This is going to be a strange conversation,' or something stupid like that. Well, the old man comes back," she said, breaking into a New England accent, "and says, 'No, t'won't. It's ovah,' and hung up on me." Their laughter reverberated in the tiny kitchen while she stirred tomato sauce, richly aromatic with bay, basil, and oregano. "I'm so glad you decided to come up here *this* weekend," said Siobhan as she licked the sauce-covered spoon.

"Why?" Tom asked, leaning against the opposite counter and looking out the kitchen window into the approaching night.

"Oh," she laughed, "just because it's four weeks before you were planning on coming up here anyway. Though you can come again then, too. I don't know. It's just so wonderful to see you and have you here with us." Carefully she asked, "How are things going... down there?"

"Kind of closing in on me," Tom said with a forced detachment.

"Well, this is a great place to come and hide from your troubles," she said turning to give him a spoon of simmering sauce for his tasting.

"This stuff is terrific. When does Woz get back?"

"He milks from four till about eight in the morning and three to seven in the afternoon. I'm sorry he had to rush right out as soon as you got here."

"No problem," Tom replied as he spooned the jar of apple sauce Siobhan had given him as an appetizer.

"So, does he enjoy...milking cows?"

"Sure," she replied cheerfully. "Of course, I had to slap him when he pointed out that living with me and working at a dairy was a tad redundant. Aahhhh, you *boys*," she laughed.

"Sounds like y'all are real happy up here."

"We are. He goes out early and comes home and wakes me in the most wonderful ways."

"That's still good, too, huh?" Tom asked, embarrassed as the words left his mouth.

"Oh yeah, it's as great as it ever was," she said openly and eagerly. "But, my God, Tom, there's so much more to it now. So much more to us and to loving each other. We talk about things that we never seemed to have time for before. We cook together. Well," she laughed, "I cook, and he roams around the kitchen nibbling on things - including me."

"I'm so happy for you two. And, frankly, envious as hell. But I guess you're both finally just getting what you deserve – time and peace and each other. But what about you? What do you do with your time?"

"Teaching piano again," she replied brightly. "You know the Congregational Church up on the Common where we met? I went to the priest...er, preacher there and asked if I could use the church's piano to give lessons in return for playing when they needed me at the church. And he said, 'We need you!' Their pianist had just retired, so it worked out great."

"They don't have any trouble with the Vatican tie-in?" Tom chuckled.

Shaking her head, she replied, "The folks around here seem surprisingly willing to let other people live their own lives. It's very refreshing. Plus," she added with enthusiasm, "he put the word out to the community that I was giving lessons, and I've already got quite a few kids. They're all so cute. Rosy-cheeked and bundled up like little dolls."

"Well, since neither of you seem interested in telling me, I guess I'll have to ask. Has there been any 'tying of the knot'? I mean, are you Mrs. Wasserman yet?"

She shook her head. "That's just something we didn't do before we got here, and now it's something we need to do *away* from here because, for the purposes of the people around here, I already *am* Mrs. Wasserman."

"I see what you mean," Tom said. "So, why don't you just go over into New York or go somewhere and ... git hitched?"

"We just got kind of scared off in Virginia when they asked for all this information. Although, we've since heard that some of the J-P's around here are pretty lenient. I mean, they don't ask questions. But we're just real antsy about Bran's draft status. We really want to get him back in school before the world finds out where we are."

"I can understand that."

"I just couldn't lose him again, Tom," she said with a desperation that reminded him of her lost summer. "If the draft board were to catch up with him," she declared with a determined glare, "well, it's an easy jump across the border to Canada."

Taken aback, Tom blurted out, "You're kidding! He'd do that?"

"*We* would do it," she stated seriously. "We love America, and if it were really threatened, Bran and I would both fight to defend it. But Tom, *this* ... is the *wrong war*."

* * *

Exhaling a vapor cloud that momentarily shrouded the snow- and ice-encrusted Little Hosmer Pond, which lay before them, Tom narrowed his eyes and smiled in reverie as he said to Brandeis, "I'll never forget those moments, when we were making love, and I just completely lost control. It was wonderful. And with Clair, it was safe to. I've never trusted another person that much. It felt so right to just give myself over to her."

Standing beside him under a cloud-laden mid-afternoon sky on the ice-encased pier above the lake's frozen surface, Brandeis asked, "So explain to me, Tom. Why in hell did you take yourself back?"

Sobered by the question, he shook his head clear of a memory and replied, "I don't know. It just flew all over me when she said that...she'd done it before."

"You know, Windham, you're quite a piece of work. Tell me the truth. Or at least, tell yourself the truth. Wouldn't you have made it with any halfway decent-looking co-ed on campus who gave you the chance? I mean, come on, can you sit there and tell me you would have turned down an advance from...Justine Lecateret? What about Meredith, or Lizza? Or any of those Noofer girls you would've given up your golf game for? No, I'm sure you would have stayed as pure as that snow out there on the pond, wouldn't you?

"So how can you hold Clair to such a completely different set of rules? And how can you give up what you could have had with her because of something that's *done* - on the books - something that can't be changed and doesn't matter a hill o' beans? The only explanation I can think of is that you're trying to punish yourself for something. Well, if that's it, cut it out!"

"Thank you, Doctor Freud, for that astute analysis."

"No, you don't get off that easy. Yeah, I think all those years of analysis *did* teach me a few things. And what I'm saying is that you've got to put as much soul-searching into this - into how you feel about yourself and your worthiness for happiness, and where Clair fits into it - as you've always been willing - eager - to put into where you stand with your God. Listen, God loves you. You love God. You two are doing fine - "

"Actually, my relationship with God is on the rocks," Tom interjected seriously.

"A lovers' spat," Brandeis quickly countered with a dismissive wave of his hand. "Anyway, anything beyond that is just intellectualizing that you use to keep you from thinking about the rest of your life. Hey, God wants you to be happy, and so does Clair, and so do we. And you *do* deserve to be. Listen, I left a yawning void in my shrink's schedule. Why don't you just call him?"

"I've told you before," Tom said with a frown. "Mark went to one, and Dad said Mark told him he was smarter than the psychiatrist."

"Is the psychiatrist still alive?" Brandeis asked.

"Probably," Tom replied with a critical gaze. "Why?"

"Maybe Mark was wrong."

Tom replied quietly, "That was cruel."

"So's the crap you're doing to yourself."

The friends stood silently scanning the shoreline of the lake. With a shiver, Tom finally said, "Glad y'all took me into the village to that general store. These gloves and longjohns and the toboggan really help. Of course, I'm still not sure how I'm going to use the bathroom with them on."

Acquiescing to the course change, Brandeis offered, "It's just too bad there's all this snow on the pond. We could go ice skating."

"Well, how do you ever get to?" Tom asked in wonderment. "I mean, is there a crew that comes out and sweeps it off or something?"

"That'd take quite a crew. No, we just have to wait for nature to take its course. A good sunny thaw can melt some of the snow and glaze the ice, or a rain'll do it. Although sometimes people sweep off small areas."

"Who else lives around here - in those cabins over there?" Tom asked, pointing up the lake.

"Those are little vacation and weekend cabins, but around here they call them 'camps'. That's what our house was until the Carruthers bought it and started renting it out."

"'Camps', huh? I wouldn't mind having a camp up here. I love this place," Tom said reverently. "It reminds me of my lake minus fifty degrees, plus snow, and fifteen hundred miles from the phone. Walden-esque."

"It's a really simple, wonderful life up here. What's the matter, buddy? Are you learning that money can't buy you happiness?" When his friend did not answer, he offered, "You ready to head on back? Siobhan should be back from the church by now."

Walking through the frosted trees, Tom's fire-scarred Wellingtons and Brandeis' manure-coated L.L. Bean boots crunched in the freshly fallen pallet of snow on the lane up to the cabin. "Woz," Tom began seriously, "did it ever bother you about Chevy that - Well, from what you had said before, I ... "

"Did it bother me that she had done it before?" Brandeis asked.

"Yeah."

"Honestly, even though I figured that she had - I mean, it was pretty evident that she had - it was not anything that was ever talked about - confirmed or denied - between us. I'd be lying to say that I never thought about it, but it didn't bother me. That was her business - before me. I just kind of took the attitude that ... I was glad *one* of us had."

*   *   *

"Well, how'd you like our other staple?" Siobhan asked, as they polished off their dinner of breast of chicken in cream of mushroom soup over rice.

"Excellent," Tom replied, blowing a kiss to the chef. "So, what do you do around here of a Saturday night?" he asked as his hosts rose and began to clear off the aging metal dinette table.

Looking at one another with like smiles, Siobhan finally said, "Oh, cards, dominoes, books."

"If worse comes to worse, we may even talk," Brandeis said.

Looking into the small den, Tom said with surprise, "Yeah, y'all don't even have a T-V, do ya'? Gosh, how do you keep up?"

"Oh," Brandeis replied, pulling Siobhan closer to him, "we've kind of left the world to its own devices. But we get the newspaper, and we have a radio."

"Well, the least I can do is give you a paid subscription to Groesbeck's news hotline, *The Mangled Claw*. I think it's selling better than *Cat Tracks*." He let the topic drop, though, as he looked at his friends wrapped in each others arms - oblivious to him as well as to the world. An ache of loneliness and loss began to creep into his heart, but it was quelled as Siobhan turned slowly toward him with a warm glow in her eyes and in her smile. "What is it?" Tom asked with a curious laugh as Brandeis took his position behind her, wrapping his arms around hers and placing his hands at her waist.

"Tom," she said coyly, then hesitated.

"What is it?" he repeated.

"We're going to have a baby," she replied quietly as her radiant smile lit the room.

Tom quickly took a read on Brandeis' smile behind her. The concern Tom first felt was instantly abated by the open, happy expression on his ex-roommate's face. Approaching her, he asked, nodding as if requesting reassurance, "You've been to the doctor, and you're sure?" Mentally, a calendar raced through his mind, and the sum of weeks seemed too few.

"No, but I know."

"Don't question it," Brandeis suggested light-heartedly. "It's one of those 'female' things. One of those 'feelings'."

"Meg's had three, and she's told me in detail that I didn't even ask for what it felt like when she got pregnant."

As Tom hugged her gently, Brandeis added, "Oh, excuse me. It's one of those 'Irish Catholic female' things."

Backing away and smiling at her lovingly, Tom lifted his hand toward her stomach, but he hesitated. She returned his smile and, taking his hand, slowly placed it on the slightest bulge at her waist. "Hah!" he smiled. "I can't ... I just can't believe it."

Brandeis pulled away and said, "And, Tom, we want you to be the godfather. We figured a Southern Baptist godfather should just about split the difference."

As Tom's eyes misted and he had to look away, Siobhan added, "And between us, we've been calling ... 'it' ... Tommy."

"'Of course, if it's a girl," Brandeis said, "I guess we'll have to name it Tomasina."

"Well, when did y'all know? I mean, Harvest was only ... well, not long ago."

"I didn't realize it," Siobhan said, a blush on her cheeks and in her voice, "until my dear sweet fellow here asked me when I was supposed to start - because, as he so delicately put it, he just kept 'gittin' it 'n' gittin' it'."

"Mister Sensitivity," Tom observed, shaking his head and slugging Brandeis gamely on the arm. "Well, looks like your luck finally ran out."

"Oh," Siobhan said warmly, "I don't know. Maybe our luck's just beginning."

With an understanding nod, Tom leaned in to hug her again and said, "Tommy, huh? Wow." Leaning away and supporting himself against the opposite counter, he took a swig of the hot cocoa Siobhan had made him, and he watched as Brandeis whispered in her ear a suggestion that brought stars to her eyes. Looking back and forth at his friends and casting a reflective eye ceilingward, Tom wondered aloud, "If, as I suspect, this is all a Hollywood fantasy, and I'm really just an extra on the set of the remake of *A Farewell To Arms*, can we please do a re-write on the ending?"

*   *   *

Brandeis rang the welcoming chime of the frosted white cottage as he and his two bundled companions filled the compact front porch with the fog of their breaths. Opening the door, the small elderly gentleman of the house faced them arm in arm in arm and offered, "Can I help ya'?"

"Justice Parkins?" Brandeis inquired.

"I'm Simon Parkins," the balding, stooped little figure replied from behind thick glasses that magnified his milky blue eyes.

"We want to get married," Siobhan blurted out with unbridled glee.

"'At'll be fine, missy, but which one o' these fellas gitshuh?" the spritely old man queried.

Tom quickly began pointing his thumb at his chest, attracting the justice's attention. Noticing Parkins' focus shift to Tom, Brandeis glanced across at him and cried, "No, me."

"No, me!" Tom insisted. "I said first."

The amused justice of the peace declared, "Well, missy, looks like it's up to you."

Glancing back and forth at them, she finally cast her eyes toward Brandeis, saying, "It's almost too close to call, but ... I'll take the Jew."

" ... and by the powuh vested in me by the State of Vuhmont, I declare you Man and Wife," Justice Parkins intoned. With a twinkle in his eye toward the newlyweds, he added, "You may ... " and he began rolling his hands toward them. Picking up quickly on his suggestion, the bride and groom kissed.

After the kiss Tom, Brandeis, Justice Parkins and his wife – the resident witness - looked on as Siobhan reflexively gave her belly the gentlest of pats. Looking around at the sweet smiles of her observers, Siobhan began to blush. Taking both of her hands in his, Brandeis narrowed his focus deep into her eyes and said, "I love you with all of me, and I will love you forever. I love what we've had, and I love what we're going to have together." After kissing her hands, he pulled her to him and kissed his wife again.

As they separated and stared into each other's eyes, Mrs. Parkins turned away and then back producing a tray of five bubbling champagne glasses. While Mister Parkins led the toasts, Tom asked enthusiastically, "So, where're we going on our honeymoon?"

Brandeis snapped his fingers, brightened his eyes, and offered, "Hey, I've already reserved a cottage for us on Little Hosmer Pond."

"But that's forty miles away," Tom protested.

Shooting a hand into the air, Siobhan shouted, "Dibs on top bunk!" as Mrs. Parkins reeled in mortification.

*   *   *

Brandeis sat naked on the edge of the bed in their tiny darkened bedroom as ice pellets pecked at the frosted window. "I don't know how you do that," Siobhan sighed with a smile as she peeled down to her long underwear.

"Just looking at you gives me all the heat I need," he said.

"Good line," she replied with laugh.

"Come here."

As he spread his legs, she walked to the edge of the bed and stopped in front of him. After pulling her shirttail out of her bottoms, he pressed his face into her soft waist and began kissing her gently while wrapping his arms around her hips. She sighed deeply as she rippled her fingers through his thick, curly hair. Finally, she pushed him back, and they scrambled giggling under the heavy layers of ancient blankets and quilts they had found in the closet and had bought at tag sales.

Giggling, kissing and working in tandem, they quickly yanked her underwear off, but they left it under the covers with them to keep it warm. As they wrapped themselves tightly around each other, she whispered in his ear, "Good night, Mister Wasserman."

"Good night, Mrs. Wasserman."

He gently patted her warm belly, and they said, "Good night, Tommy."

*   *   *

The ice storm that had greeted the newlyweds and their best man upon their return to the honeymoon cabin passed quickly across the Northeast Kingdom during the night and early morning, and in its wake came a bright blue Sunday whose sun glossed over the residue of the storm with a sterling glaze. With the Galaxie scraped and packed and Brandeis ready to trudge the half-mile to the Carruthers' dairy barn for the afternoon milking, the three stood by the car and gazed up the hill in wonder at a rounded, freestanding ancient oak. Against a brilliant blue-skied backdrop, the barren, ice-coated tree when touched by the sun's rays appeared incandescent, like a giant crystal bouquet.

"Sure you don't want to stay one more night?" Brandeis asked. "They should have most of the roads salted and sanded by now, but it still might be tricky."

"Naah," Tom said, "this gives me plenty of time to get to my hotel tonight, and the flight's at eight in the morning, so I better head on out."

Brandeis glanced at his watch, and Tom understood that his Jerseys and Brown Swiss would wait for no man. "Take care of these two," he said as he gave Siobhan a soft pat on her stomach and approached Brandeis with open arms, "and take care of yourself, too, ya' big lug."

"So long, buddy," Brandeis said as they hugged. "You coming up after Christmas?"

As Tom hesitated, ticking through his list of commitments, Siobhan said, "I hope he's *very* occupied with Clair after Christmas."

"I don't know," Tom said. "But don't worry. I'll be back. As you see, I can do it any weekend."

"Yeah," Brandeis laughed. "Good luck on Finals. I can tell you're real worried about them."

"Hey, this semester was a write-off. My roommate was a pain in the butt."

"Well, I guess all that's left to say is," and Brandeis began singing, *"We'll meet again -"* and Tom joined him, *" - don't know where, don't know when. But I know we'll meet again some sunny day."*

After the final note they swapped the Sign of the Wild Goose Moon and a final fix of their eyes in a mutual and irreverent glance reminiscent of their first - long ago in January - and Brandeis set off on the crunchy footpath along the ridge toward the dairy.

Turning to Siobhan, Tom gazed at the beautiful contrast - as breathtaking as ever - of her pale, unadorned but flawless face and her vibrantly blue eyes made crystalline by the sun, and he said, "You said something really sweet to me this summer about me being like a brother to you. And I guess it cut too close, and I made some stupid reply. But, Chevy, I want to tell you now. You *are* my sister, and I love you."

"And you are my brother, and I love you," she said quietly. Looking back into the round young face that housed the gentle old eyes, she reached out to lightly push an errant shock of his thick dark hair into place, and she left her hand softly touching his cheek. Smiling at him with tears shining in her eyes, she said slowly and lovingly, "Fifty years from now, when we're old and grey, and our grandkids are gathered round asking what these crazy times were like, we'll remember this, and we'll be able to say to them, 'We were young. We were *beautiful*. And we were there'."

Chapter 53

Mid-December

"Hey, Tom-cat," came the familiar call down the wide main hallway of the SUB. "How's it hangin'?"

"To the floor," Tom replied loudly, causing fear and trepidation among a gaggle of Finals-shocked frosh co-eds clumped nearby.

"Guess I always sold Wasserman short," Joe Joe stated as he and Tom met in the corridor. With a single shake of his head, he added, "That's one gutsy muthah. Gives the rest of us tadpoles out here just flagellatin' from day to day hope, doesn't it?"

As Tom nodded his agreement, though, Joe Joe looked over Tom's shoulder and beyond him. Tom watched in amazement as the never-before-seen concentrated glare of resolve beamed from his friend's eyes. Turning slowly as Joe Joe took a step to his left toward the center of the hallway, Tom worshipfully observed the approach of the stunningly pulchritudinous Justine Lecataret.

Cocking her head down and away in estimation of Joe Joe's intent, Justine - her rich honey blonde waist-length tresses cascading all around her magnificent breasts, her shoulders, and her back - stopped a yard from the suddenly courageous young man in jeans and Justins.

Inhaling deeply to draw up his courage, he began profoundly, "Justine, I don't know if you know me, but I'm Joe Joe Bartlow. I'm a cowboy from the Panhandle. I live on a twenty-thousand-acre spread on the Canadian River where we raise fifteen hunerd head of the finest registered White-faced Hereford cattle that God ever saw fit to set hoof on this Earth."

Gathering himself, he continued, "And I'm askin' you to go out with me tonight ... toward the future possible eventuality ... of marriage. I have nothin' to offer you but what you see before you. Well, this an' the purtiest sunsets you ever did see. Sunsets that spread out miles wide across open prairie...from horizon t' horizon. Well, that an' wakin' up ever mornin' with a smile on your face hearin' the chatter o' the Mexican cooks downstairs and smellin' the bacon and the huevos rancheros bein' whipped up for breakfast. An' that'n drivin' around through the breaks o' the Canadian in my pick-up with me gatherin' up strays, an' spreadin' leniment on me after Friday night rodeos. An', o' course, evenins' down under the tall poplars along the riverbank shootin' turtles out on the sandbars. An' ... well, I guess that's about all I got to offer. 'Cept for the ten-thousand dollars a month in 'awl rawalties' my Daddy's signed over to me for when I turn twenty-five.

"So whaddaya say? Have we got a date?"

Justine inhaled deeply thereby dramatically enhancing her already majestic bustline; she narrowed her huge violet eyes to a glacial glare as she scanned him critically up and down and then down and up again; and she finally replied in a black velvet *basso profundo*, "Yes."

*   *   *

" ... and that was the last I saw of Joe Joe Bartlow," Tom said across fifteen hundred miles of telephone lines.

"Amazing," Brandeis replied with an uncharacteristic soberness.

After an awkward silence during which Tom awaited additional comment from his friend, he finally filled with, "Oh yeah, I'm not going to be able to take the Sprite home over the holidays like I had planned. This mechanic I took it to, who's supposed to be the best in town, is also obviously the most leisurely. He said he'd have it ready when I get back, though. I'm having it totally refurbished. He's already got the engine fixed. And now he's going to do the bodywork. I'm having the seats re-upholstered with a saddle leather, and he's putting a new cream-colored canvas top on it, and he's going to paint it 'B-R-G'," Tom crowed proudly.

"What's that?"

"Do we have to keep going over this?" Tom chided, feigning offense. "British Racing Green."

"Oh, yeah," Brandeis replied unenthusiastically. "That'll look great."

"What's going on up there? You sound like you're in a funk." With sudden concern, Tom added, "Chevy's okay, isn't she?"

"Yeah, she is. She just went to the doctor earlier this week. He did tell her to take it easy. She's had to cut back on giving lessons because she's started throwing up every morning. It's kind of perverse, but she's almost happy that she's sick as a dog all the time, because she's so proud to be pregnant. She wears it like this puke-stained badge of courage."

"So, what is it?" Tom asked. "What's wrong?"

"We finally got around to calling the parents - to bring them up to date."

"Oh. How did that go?"

"She had called her mother, and I had called Father awhile back just to let them know we were safe – and, you know, to get him to do the title transfer on the Sprite. But we called back the other night, and Siobhan talked to her father, too, and we were really glad she did. He had missed her so much, I think about anything she said would've been fine with him. Plus, she said, he could tell how happy she was. And she said that, by itself, made him happy. Her mother was elated and excited and wanted to come up here yesterday," Brandeis half-laughed. "But she convinced her to wait until after Christmas - that we still needed some time alone."

"How'd things go in Memphis?"

"When I called the house, I got Mother. And, Tom, I said, 'This is Brandeis.' And she said, 'Who?' And I said, 'This is your son, Brandeis'." A long silence followed before Brandeis sighed and continued shakily, "And she said, 'I have only one son'."

"Ohhhh, Woz," Tom shuddered. "That's crazy talk," he counseled, while clearly envisioning Shirley Wasserman saying it. "That's just crazy."

"I know," Brandeis answered sadly. "It's just ... it's just real hard to hear something like that. She's my mother, and I love her."

"Did you tell her where you were," Tom asked. "Did you get to tell her she was going to be a grandmother, and that she was already a mother-in-law?"

"Tom, that was all she said to me," he answered weakly, "and that was all I said to her."

"Did you call your dad?"

"Yeah, after that I called Father, and he said he wished I had called him first. He could've warned me. He wished us well. Asked me if we needed any money. Told me he wanted to see me the first chance we could. But there's no telling when that might be."

"I am so sorry, Woz. I hope time will change that. And I hope you have time. I wish she could understand ...how bad it is to leave things ... open, like that." Catching himself, he asked, "Are you getting ready for Christmas up there?"

"Yeah," Brandeis reported, "the Common's all decorated. It's beautiful. We're getting a lot of snow. We've even been doing some caroling with the church and the kids Siobhan teaches."

"Caroling with the church," Tom noted. "Sounds like creeping Protestantism."

Finally laughing lightly, Brandeis asked, "What about you? Do you have any plans?"

"Aw, I think I'll just pass on Christmas this year. It was always a real big day for Mom and Dad, and ... I'm just not ready to have it without them. It sounds more like a good day to wind out that 'Vette and see what it's made of. I may call y'all from El Paso - by noon!"

* * *

Tom greeted with excitement the discovery of a Boulder-postmarked letter in the last check of his mailbox before departing W-S-U for semester break. Ripping into it quickly, he read:

> *Dear Tom,*
> *This is one for the ages. Chet Carter writes a letter! Just wanted to tell you how much I enjoyed our Thanksgiving visits. Even the ride back to Dallas with you to catch the plane. Sorry I laid into you about Clair, but I was bound and determined for you to be happy, and I felt like I was the only person in the car who was. Tom, if you're very,*

very lucky, someone like Clair will come into your life maybe once. A lot of folks have never gotten the chance she's given you. Just let me calmly say: <u>Don't blow it, you idiot!</u> Oops, back on my soapbox again.

Looking forward to seeing you after Christmas.

Your Ol' Cuz,

Chet

P.S. - Thanks for the birthday card, but where was the money? Ha! Oh yeah, you can tell your friend Wasserman that I made it past thirty-three without being worshipped and without being crucified.

Having quickly filled the rear storage compartment of the Corvette and with the passenger seat already stacked window high, Tom prepared to leave WSU behind him once more. Propped against his car, he folded his arms in contemplation of the contrast between this Christmas Break and the prior. Having completed his first ever pre-Christmas finals in mid-December 1967, he recalled the perfectly carefree elation that had coursed through him that afternoon. With finals behind him and almost four weeks of unrestricted time - time devoid of responsibility or obligation - before him, and with no books, tests, or papers suspended above him, Tom had responded to a freakish warm spell in Dallas that had brought temperatures into the upper-sixties. He drove home shirtless and unshod wearing only an old pair of Bermuda shorts, so visceral and immediate - so tangible and keen - had been the sensation of freedom that day.

But this was 1968, and everything had changed. And bundled against the cold, he steeled himself for the return to New Fredonia with the knowledge that *never* again would he feel as free.

As he opened the car door, he saw approaching from a distance the bulbous figure of Harvey Groesbeck. "Hey, you hippie freak!" Tom shouted at him good-naturedly as he noted the long greasy locks issuing from beneath his toboggan and dancing on his shoulders as he came near. But at a short distance, Tom looked into his face and was suddenly paralyzed by the ashen, injured expression that Tom had seen on it only once before.

Bracing himself for whatever bad news the messenger brought, Tom leaned against the car, thrust his hands in his pockets, and asked, "Who?"

Wincing his overstuffed face in empathy, Harvey answered, "Rodg."

"No!" Tom shouted. Squeezing his eyes closed, he groaned, "Oh, God, no. Dead?" he asked as he cupped his hands over his eyes to block the answer from entering his consciousness.

"M-I-A," Harvey replied. "His Med-Evac 'copter was hit and went down on the wrong side of a fire-fight in the Delta."

"Did it crash? Did it burn?" Tom asked.

"No. The Marines said it set down intact, but they couldn't get to them."

"And?"

"And that's all they know."

Leaving the parking lot of Postlethwaite with anxiety burning deep in his chest, Tom motored past a group of carefree freshmen tossing luggage into their trunks. The painful envy of their freedom reared itself again, but he quickly suppressed it - scolding himself for his self-pity when the earnest, idealistic, bespectacled image of Rodg Messing was projected in his mind's eye.

Burrowed into the enveloping cockpit of the Corvette and kept company by the retreating hordes of the British Invasion and the progressively harder American rock played on KLIF, Tom rapidly reeled in New Fredonia. Approaching the Springfield exit with a dirty orange light bouncing off the low clouds above the city from the flares of the nearby gasoline plant, Tom realized that for not many more days could he put off the showdown with Neil Forster over the future of the title company. And it was with a chill late the following morning as he rolled through the square toward the Dairy Queen that he saw Forster entering the long-vacant Cooper Hats building accompanied by Arthur Vaughn, a local real estate broker. Returning home immediately to discuss the matter with Bowman, it was Nela instead who greeted him with word that Chet was spending Christmas in Colorado with Callie's family and that he would not be home until the following week.

Excusing himself from the house, Tom sought sanctuary at the farm. He was halfway through water-skipping the collection of flat rocks that he had garnered from the driveway and lined up on the pier's rail when the phone rang in the lakehouse. Running up from the lake, he realized at the door that he was too late. He walked to the deck's rail and, propping his elbows on it, allowed anxious thoughts of Neil Forster, Shirley Wasserman, and Rodg Messing to intrude. And he thought of Clair, and he wondered where she was and what she was doing at that moment. He assumed sadly that by this time, three weeks out from their Thanksgiving encounter, she had reluctantly stowed him once again in that distant compartment of her heart that she kept reserved for him. But as he closed his eyes and let his memory place the two of them standing on the deck together under the quilt as they had, the phone rang again.

"I just got my Draft Notice," Brandeis stated, as if reading his death sentence.

"Oh, my God," Tom sighed. After a moment to absorb the news, he asked, "When are you supposed to report?"

"I'm due for a physical on the twenty-seventh in Burlington," he said coldly.

How'd they find you?"

"I don't know," he answered bitterly. "I really don't even want to think about it."

"Oh, Woz, you don't think - "

"I *don't* know. And I don't want to know."

Understanding the pointlessness of pursuing the culprit, Tom asked, "How's Chevy taking it?"

"Tom," Brandeis said gravely, "she just got back from seeing the doctor."

"What's wrong with her?"

"She had really gotten hysterical, and I was afraid it was going to be bad for the baby."

"So how is she?" he asked anxiously. "And how's the baby?"

"The doctor said they were alright, but he gave her something to settle her down. But she's still as upset as hell, and I'm really worried about her."

"Well, let me talk to her," Tom said.

"Tom," Siobhan began, "I can't let him go. You know I can't. He just can't go."

"Chevy, he may flunk the physical," Tom replied, groping to give solace. "They may not send him there. He may - "

"I can't risk any of that," she cried. "Tom, I'm so afraid for him. I just can't let him go."

"Chevy, it's the law of the land."

"Well, the law of the land's gone crazy. They can't have Bran. I don't give a *damn* about anything else. The politicians, this country, it's on its own. It's lost us. We no longer choose to participate," she said stridently.

"So what are you going to do? You wouldn't really go to Canada, would you?"

"Tom," she said, gathering herself, "we'll do what we have to do."

"Chevy, you're not making sense," Tom said quietly.

"Not making sense! Are you trying to tell me this war does?! Do the body bags make sense?"

*   *   *

Driving back into New Fredonia, Tom aimlessly traversed the residential streets of the town for several minutes trying to settle himself. But he made the mistake of turning onto the street in front of his old house. Glancing at the residence, he immediately noted something about the landscaping to be askew. Looking again, he saw what it was. The three pine trees next to the driveway were gone - cut off at the ground. Feelings of injury and of loss stabbed at him as he realized with an aching regret that he had neither inquired of the buyer as to his intentions regarding them nor told him of the trees' significance. With a second thought, though, he recognized that the club which commemorated their significance had become prohibitively exclusive. He wished fleetingly for a day - a single day - when nothing changed and nothing unpredictable happened.

Returning to the Carters' in shock - both from his telephone conversation at the lakehouse and from the discovery of the felling of the pines - Tom looked up as the screen door banged shut behind him. Standing in the kitchen by the wall phone was Nela, the receiver dangling from her hand. "It's Neil Forster," she said.

Opening his palms as if trying to stop the world from wobbling out of orbit, he said, "I won't ... I can't ... "

"I think you'd best talk to him," she said. "You can't keep hiding from people."

'Or else what?' he thought as he crossed the room to take the phone.

After cursory greetings, Forster said emphatically, "Tom, we have got to talk."

"I'm just not ready to," Tom answered.

Breathing a disgusted sigh, Forster asked, "Exactly when will you be ready to?"

'When the Big Thicket to Balcones Fault shall come,' he thought. But Tom answered, "How about the Friday after Christmas?" He dreaded the deadline as the words left his lips.

"I guess that'll have to do. Say, ten o'clock in the morning?" Forster asked.

"That's fine," Tom conceded.

"Okay. I'll hold off on doing anything else till then," Forster stated before adding, "but not a minute longer."

Tom hung up the receiver only to be greeted by his last caller of the day - a pain that stabbed fiercely and with a grim familiarity into his forehead above his left eye.

Five hours and eight Anacins later, Tom joined Bowman, who was in from his evening shift at the truck stop, in the den. After tossing in bed for an hour with the dull pain and still duller senses left by the medication, Tom had given up on sleep and sat with his uncle watching the late movie.

Tom had seen snatches of *It's A Wonderful Life* over the years, but he had never seen it in its entirety. Even though dissected by commercials, its unfolding helped make clear to Tom why Johnny Windham had always called it his favorite movie. Tom winced in pain at each occasion when George Bailey chose to subrogate his own personal happiness and ambition in favor of his brother or of his father or of his father's memory or of the people of Bedford Falls. He thought of how his father had given up college at his own father's death to carry on the family business and to support his mother. Tom remembered the love his father had for his sister, and he recalled not one word of resentment from Johnny that she had been free to finish college. And he thought sadly of the end of his father's life and of the financial and emotional malaise into which he had sunk - of the ungrateful son unaware and unconcerned about the high cost of keeping him in an expensive private university, of living daily with the shell of the woman who had loved him but who at the end spoke coldly of her hatred of him, of the brilliant son who had flared with promise and then burned himself out so tragically early, of the tightening noose of debt and dishonor closing on him daily.

During the singing of "Auld Lang Syne" at the movie's conclusion and after Bowman had excused himself to bed, Tom sat in the dark den and thought, 'Where was your Clarence, Dad? Where was your Clarence?'

Chapter 54

Christmas Eve

"We're going to cross over into Canada tomorrow," Brandeis said numbly.

Shaking his head in shock as he stood at the hall phone at the Carters', Tom took a second to absorb his friend's words. "Why? What's happened?"

"It's Siobhan, Tom. We just got back from the doctor, and she said he told her that unless she gets some relief from all her anxiety about this thing, she could ... lose the baby."

"Oh, Woz. Oh, no. I'm so sorry. Damn."

"So we've got to go," Brandeis said. "We can't let - I mean, I need her and I love her so much. And I'm afraid of what it would - " After a moment as he coughed and sniffed to clear his speech, he said, "I've got to get hold of myself. She needs me, and it's up to me to do this. And it's the right thing to do for all three of us."

"It is, Woz," Tom said. "People are more important than borders, and damn sure more important than this war." As Brandeis continued to compose himself, Tom observed quietly, "I just can't believe it's come to this."

"Listen, I've got to go. I've got some more things to get together."

"Wait a minute," Tom replied with confusion. "I can't handle this."

"We'll call you from Montreal. It'll be okay."

"Woz," Tom said with caution, "do you realize what you're giving up? You're leaving your *country*."

"We don't need a country. We've got each other." After a silence, Brandeis said, "I love you, Tom. Take care."

"Bye, Woz. My God," he choked. "I love you, too. Let me say goodbye to Chevy. I'll keep it brief."

After an aside to Brandeis to send him off to the dairy, Siobhan said, "Tawm, everything's going to be alright. It really is."

Forcing a smile on his face to strengthen his resolve to comfort her, he said, "You're not going to break into King's 'I've Been to the Mountaintop' speech, are you?"

"No," she laughed nervously. "But tomorrow, we *will* be on the other side. And we'll be happy together there. Just know that, okay?"

"Okay. But listen, let's get off, because I want you to get some rest before tomorrow. I just can't believe that about the baby being in danger," Tom said with concern.

After a moment's hesitation she answered, "Don't."

"What?!"

"Tom, the baby's fine. I told Bran that to get him to go. The draft notice - and the thought that his mother turned him in - has devastated him. His face looks like a death mask, and he's got this fatalistic attitude about it that scares the hell out of me. He's in no shape to do this, and I just can't see him surviving it. Have you seen our losses of American boys this year? He's prime meat for that death mill, and I can't let it happen. I won't."

"Wow," Tom replied in wonderment. "That one came out of left field."

"Tom, there are already so many American kids in Canada, and there'll be so many more. They'll have to let us come back someday. Especially the way the country is turning against The War."

"That's quite a gamble."

"It's one we've *got* to take. Tom, I've got to go now to get things packed and ready to go. But you've got to promise me something first."

"Name it," Tom said.

"Go to Clair. Now."

"Ohh, Chevy. I- I can't even think about that now. You two are - "

"Tom," she began slowly, "it is *all* so much simpler than you make it out to be. In fact, don't even *think* about it. Just put all the complications and the history and the memories and the mistakes behind you, and just…go love her."

"I'll try."

"Don't try," Siobhan scolded. "Do. Call her. Promise me."

"I promise."

"Okay, Tom. And remember. Don't let anything else get in your way. Just go love her."

Chapter 55

Clair was in bed reading when the phone rang. She grabbed the receiver after the first ring to prevent the late night call from awakening Gramma.

"Clair, I need to talk to you," Tom said with a tone of desperation that confirmed his plea.

The crushing pain of their last conversation already an unwelcome nightly visitor, she replied, "Sure you want to talk to such a wayward, wanton woman? A woman with ... a past."

His voice broke nearly to a cry as he replied, "Clair, all I know is, I've got to talk to someone who loves me - with no strings. And I don't know anyone who loves me more - and expects less of me - than you. Everything's falling in on me, and I need you."

Recognizing the uncharacteristic and unsettling desperation in his voice, her resolve vanished. "I'm sorry, Tom. Where are you?"

"I'm ... I don't know. I've been driving around for hours. I'm at some ... pay phone."

Noting the disorientation in his voice, Clair spoke with a desperation of her own, "Tom, where are you? I'll come get you." To his silence, she raised her voice, "I'll come to you, Tom. Where are you?!"

Sobered by her concern, he answered in a more even tone, "No, no, Clair. That's okay. Just let me come out there."

Not trusting his newfound balance and growing more upset herself, she objected, "No, Tom, I don't want you to drive! I'll come to you. Just please tell me where you are."

More settled and regretful that he had upset her, Tom replied clearly, "Clair, if there's anything I can do, it's drive." His slight laugh that followed gave her comfort.

"Are you sure, Tom? I'd come anywhere you were."

I know you would. I'll be out there in ten minutes."

"Tom?"

"It's okay, Clair. Meet me outside so we don't wake up Gramma," he said.

"What is it, Tom? What's happened?"

"I'll be there in ten minutes."

She heard the click of his receiver as she pleaded, "Be careful."

Crossing the cattle guard of the Redfearn farm, Tom homed in on the Christmas lights of Gramma's house. The glowing lights separated the house from the surrounding dark as the moon hid behind clouds. As Tom approached, the cozy warmth of the farmhouse reached out to him. The lights of red, green and blue on the Christmas tree, which Clair had cut on Scatter Mountain, twinkled through the front window that she had spray-frosted. And standing on the porch in Gramma's oversized woolen shawl sweater, her arms crossed against the cold, was Clair. Pulling the Corvette to a stop in front of the house, he focused on her face. Framed as it was by the silken blonde hair tumbling down the front of the sweater to her crossed arms, he flashed back to the love he had seen and felt as she had melted into him before the fireplace at the lakehouse. As she bounced down from the steps toward him, he sighed and closed his eyes momentarily in reverie. Stepping from the car, he stood still beside it, and she stopped short of him trying to read the anxiety in his face.

"Tom?"

He did not speak at first, choosing to inhale the fresh, cold night air and the love and concern in her eyes. Finally he said, "Clair, please hold me," and he opened his arms to her. She went quickly to him and held him tightly, pressing her face into his neck. They closed their eyes and hugged each other - until Tom began to quiver. Barely perceptible at first, his breathing soon became uneven.

Through sudden tears and still holding him to her, Clair cried, "Tom, what is it? What's wrong?"

He could not answer, but he nodded his head toward the house.

The unguarded anguish in his face and his labored breathing terrified Clair, and she held him firmly as they walked to the house. Though Clair had lit logs in the fireplace of the small front sitting room immediately after receiving his call, the otherwise unheated room still retained its late December eve chill. She sat him down on the couch before the fireplace and draped Gramma's knitted wool afghan over his back and shoulders. She sat close beside him rubbing his back and arms without speaking as Tom glared at the fledgling flames. Slowly, his breathing became more even. Clair heard the water gurgling in the tea kettle preliminary to whistling.

"How about some nice hot tea?" she whispered. Without changing expression or diverting his stare, he nodded. Before rising, she held him tightly and asked, "Are you going to be alright?" Again he nodded and she rose to tend to the tea.

Upon her return with two steaming mugs, the grimace of hopelessness on his face brought a burning tightness to her chest. He accepted the mug she offered, but he did not drink. He held it with both hands below his lips and slowly blew its vapor toward the fire. She sat beside him sipping her tea and watching. The fire had caught up, and it began to warm them. As it cracked and sizzled, Tom took a drink of his tea before setting the mug aside. He propped his elbows on his knees, clasped his hands together and began to rub beneath his chin with his thumbs as he broke his silence. Evenly, quietly, as if speaking to the fire on which he continued to focus, he said, "God and I killed my parents."

Perplexed and thinking she must have misunderstood, Clair pulled back and asked, "What?"

"God and I entered into a conspiracy to kill my parents. I told Him I wanted them dead. I told Him how to do it. And He did it."

Confused and horrified, Clair gasped. "Tom, what are you saying? What are you talking about?"

"And what's more - " he began, but he fell silent.

"Tom, I don't know what you mean. I don't know what you think you've done. But I can tell that something is eating you up inside. Talk to me." Both were silent for a time until Clair said, "Please tell me what you mean."

Tom dropped his forehead into his hands and rubbed his hair back before raising his head and turning away from the fire finally to face her. "Oh, Clair, you do love me, don't you?"

"Yes, Tom, yes, with all my heart. And I want to help you. Please talk to me."

Looking into her eyes - filled as they were with concern, compassion and love - Tom drew strength and said, "Clair, that day back in April - the day of the ... the day they died - " His voice broke, but he continued, "That afternoon, when they were flying back to Dallas, I was walking to class. I heard a plane flying overhead. I stopped ... and looked up ... and - " His breath returned to the fast, uneven pace that Clair had heard upon his arrival. She moved in next to him and wrapped her arms around him. Her warmth and presence helped to still his choppy breathing. He subtly moved away from her, though, as if perceiving that she would not want to be close to him when he said what followed.

"Clair, I looked up at that plane far overhead. I imagined my parents in it ... and I shouted to myself, 'Blow up! Blow up!'"

Clair drew a deep breath and held it. Pain replaced concern in the expression on her face.

Tom continued, "And it did. I told God I wanted their plane to blow up, and it did. Broke up in one of God's storms. Blew apart in the sky. And everyone died, and Mom and Dad died. And what's more, as I stood there on the sidewalk telling God to kill my parents —" He broke into an eerie half-smile as he continued, "I looked down at my shoes, and I was standing on a crack in the sidewalk. 'Step on a crack; break your mother's back. Step on a crack; break your mother's back!' And I said it to myself over and —"

"Stop it, Tom! Stop doing that to yourself. Stop it! My God, what a load of guilt you've been carrying around with you." She wrapped her arms around him and held him tightly. His body was limp, spent from his confession. "Please don't do that to yourself. You know you didn't kill them, and neither did God. He just created a universe with physical laws, and that pilot violated them - by flying his plane into that storm. No one did anything on purpose. Oh, Tom, I love you. And I can't believe you've been carrying this burden alone." Tom began to cry softly as he rested his head on her shoulder. "It's okay, honey. It's okay," Clair repeated through her own tears. She leaned him back against the sofa and held him in silence.

Finally she pulled her face away from him and said gently, "Tom, you know what you did that afternoon - with that other plane - didn't have anything to do with your parents' plane crashing. Don't you?" Tom did not reply but stared into the fire. "Okay, so tell me, because I'll bet you have. Have you tried the same thing since?"

The irony in Tom's voice and the narrowed glint in his eyes frightened Clair as he replied slowly, "Yeah, but it only worked that one time."

"Oh, Tom. My God. Why put yourself through this? Of course you have a lot of guilt about how things were between you when they died. Show me anyone our age who doesn't go at it with their parents and have all kinds of unresolved problems with them at any given moment."

"Yeah," Tom replied more evenly, "I know that's part of it. Everything between us was ... " he laughed mirthlessly and shook his head. "I was about to say 'everything was so up in the air.' Poor choice of words."

"But you're right," Clair said. "All of us live like we've got forever to straighten things out. Lord, I leave some things open with Gramma for days, and she's almost eighty. Only a hopelessly pessimistic and death-obsessed person would be so careful as to keep all their relationships tidied up and finalized. But no normal person would live like that. I don't. You don't. And they didn't. Tom, you *know* - in your heart of hearts - you know they knew you loved them. You know how much joy you gave them; how proud they were of you. Isn't that finally all that really matters?"

Tom closed his eyes, and his face went blank. He finally whispered, "I hope so. My God, I can't believe it. What am I having? Pre-Christmas depression? Mom would say I got a jump on the season."

Clair buried her lips in his cheek and kissed him softly. "Sounds like a lot more than that to me," she whispered.

Tom pulled away again and looked at Clair with fear in his eyes. "Yeah, there is more," he said, turning a steely gaze back toward the fire.

"What is it, Tom?"

Clair," he began but hesitated, drawing in a breath. "Clair, this is so horrible to say ... but, it's like, it was time for them to die." Hanging his head low, he looked up at her troubled expression. "And I've come to know that over these past months, yet I couldn't admit it to myself - much less anyone else. Their lives were destroyed, and they were destroying mine. I loved them, but I hated what they were doing to each other, and to me. I've felt subconsciously that they had to die if I was going to live. It was either them or me. So I conspired with God to kill them - to blow them out of the air, and damned if He didn't do it."

"Tom, quit doing this," Clair said with pain but with authority. "I don't know what your parents were doing to destroy your life, and I don't need to know or want to know. Of course, I know they were never the same after Mark died. What parents would be? But, Tom, please quit doing this. You're punishing yourself for a crazy quirk of imagination and bad timing. It sounds like you just had the rotten luck of getting caught imagining a simple solution to what was obviously a much more complicated family problem ... and having that solution - by this horrible coincidence - actually happen. You're hardly the first kid to let your curiosity run away with itself and imagine the unfettered joys of being rid of their parents. Your only crime is that you got caught doing it - in the worst way."

Tom had been listening, but at a distance. "You'd say anything to pull me back from this, wouldn't you?"

"I just love you, Tom, and I see so much more worth and goodness in you than you seem willing to give yourself credit for having. I *want* to help you through this. Please let me."

"Oh," he replied with a resignation betrayed in the tone of his voice and the slump of his body, "it helps a lot just to get it off my chest ... and to know you can still love me ... even after hearing it."

"I do, Tom. I'm here for you." They stared silently into each other's eyes until Clair continued, "I can't believe I'm about to be so crazy - or to take this chance again - but ... you need me to help you get through this. And I can. And I want to. I know I could be so good for you, if you'd just let me. Just let me in, Tom."

"My Clair," he replied through a weak smile. "You're amazing. But what if I didn't have anything to give back." After a hesitation, he added, "I mean, what's in it for you?"

"You, Tom. You give me so much."

Looking down and away, he said, "I don't remember giving you much. Just heartbreak after heartbreak against one wonderful night."

"Tom, you - "

"I just honest-to-God worry ... that I don't have enough real love left in me to give you what you deserve. I worry that all that ... that happened ... that went before ... has dulled my heart and just made me a ... a visitor in my own life."

"That was not a dull heart in the man that laid beside me at Thanksgiving."

Tom responded with a look of happiness and acceptance that gave her momentary hope. But the darkness quickly returned like a pall across his face as he said, "Yeah, and look what I did to you then - again."

Clair stated slowly and deliberately, "Tom, I will *take* my chances." Taking his hand in hers, she said, "Don't blow this. Take what I'm offering. Give back what you can - what you want to. It *will* be enough."

Turning to her and looking warmly into her eyes, he said, "Clair, I do know how much you love me. I know that if I could be happy with anyone under heaven, it would be you. And I know, and I want you to know and to have this forever. I know that I love you more than I could ever love anyone else." Hesitating, with his smile dimming slowly to a frown of despair, he added, "But I just don't know if I have enough love in me. And I don't want to pull you down with me and ruin your life. There's just too much to you."

"Well, there's a hell of a lot to you, too," she cried. "Like I said, I will take my chances." Grabbing the collar of his jacket and pulling him to her, she began kissing him passionately. At first, he responded to her, returning her kisses with equal passion. But soon he pulled away, and she dropped her face into his chest. "Love me, Tom," she said. "Please just love me. It would be the best thing you could do - for both of us."

As she rested quietly in his arms, Tom said deliberately but with compassion, ""I do love you, Clair. I do. I love you so much. But, let's face it. My family tree has borne some pretty unstable, self-destructive, and, yeah, even unlucky, fruit. I just don't think it would be fair or right ... for me to inflict myself on you."

Clair gritted her teeth and with a clinched fist hit Tom squarely in the chest, saying, "*Damn it*. It's not fair for you to make that choice for me. You don't have to come out like any of them. You're different. And damn it again, Tom; they didn't have me. And you do. And I can help you get through anything. I want to. And I'll *fight* that dark side of you *for* you ... *with* you. And we'll both win. Because, Tom, that loving, funny, caring side that was you before everyone started dying on you ... is worth it. It just is."

"Oh, Clair," he began. "It's just that - "

"Tom, let me put it in terms you'll understand. Love beareth all things; believeth all things; hopeth all things; endureth all things. That's the love I'm offering you."

Tom gazed into the open fire while Clair waited. Finally he began to rise from the couch.

"What is it? Where are you going?"

"I need to drive," he answered blankly. "I need to think."

"No, Tom," Clair replied. "Don't leave. It's too late. Stay here on the couch. Don't leave."

"I've got to."

"Why? Where are you going?"

"Oh," he replied wearily, "I started The Course. I guess I'll finish it."

"No, Tom, don't do that. You're in no shape to. Stay with me ... here," she said, rising and taking a step back toward her bedroom.

"I'm fine. I need the time, Clair."

Changing her tone, she stood beside him before the fire and said, "Tom, the love is here. Give us a chance. Please don't go."

Tom did not reply but pulled her to him wrapping her in his arms. He kissed her softly as the fire crackled and the mantle clock ticked past midnight. And they continued to kiss until Tom finally pulled away and said, "I've got to go. I need to drive."

Closing her eyes and turning her face away, Clair asked, "Are you coming back?"

Rubbing her shoulders and her back, he stared into the fire and said quietly, "I've just got to drive."

As he started to walk toward the door, Clair folded her arms across her chest as if to restrain herself. She did not look after him as she heard the door open, but she felt him hesitate there. Finally, she turned and looked across the room at him. Her deep, expressionless stare took him back to Fat City where he had been drawn into the depth of her gaze across the crowded dance floor twelve months before.

She said evenly, "Tom, we're survivors - you and me."

Returning her stare and nodding, he closed the door behind him and walked to his car. She slowly followed him to the door and out onto the front porch. The skies had cleared and the moon hung brightly over Scatter Mountain, bathing the Corvette in an eerie blue light. She stood still with her arms folded against the cold as he fired up the engine. Turning for a last look at her, though, he saw her arm extended as she gave him the Sign of the Wild Goose Moon. He returned the Sign before pulling away and disappearing over the rise toward the gate.

Chapter 56

Tom drove on automatic back toward Texas 222 with his mind awash in images from his visit with Clair. His spoken fears and uncertainty about his capacity to give her the kind of love he knew she deserved nagged at him. He did not question how much he loved Clair. He knew he was right when he told her that he loved her more than he could ever love anyone else.

At the intersection with 222, he contemplated whether to pick up The Course from there or to go back to New Fredonia for a clean start. Noting the late hour, the emptiness of the road, and the perfect weather conditions, he opted to return to town and to go for a record run.

New Fredonia was shut tight and tucked in when Tom U-turned east of the Texas 222-U.S. 199 intersection. He smiled inwardly at his selective obedience to the law as he carefully awaited the green light at the deserted intersection with the full knowledge that he would cross the Holly Creek bottom at more than double the posted speed limit. At the green, Tom glanced at his watch and motored away quickly but not loudly. The Corvette was soon threading smoothly and rapidly through the darkened countryside.

His fear of allowing Clair into his life was that the same destructive forces that had shattered his family might be at work in him and that they might be beyond his control. Such an idea was difficult for him to fathom, but so had been the forces that had unhinged the lives of his parents and of his brother. His mother's emotional instability, his brother's self-destruction, his father's weakness - each of them capable of love, of sensitivity, of humor, of rational thought, but seemingly incapable of controlling those dark sides that finally won out and destroyed their lives. Tom tried to review his attributes and faults - to search his heart, his mind, and his soul for the genetic deficiency, for the inherited malignancy. Hopelessness made inroads as he realized his inadequacy to stand outside of himself and look that deeply back in. He imagined his mother and Mark in their rational moments doing the same thing. And they had obviously been unable to see the roots of their problems or they would have surely done something to change themselves. Clair had correctly branded him along with her as a Survivor. But he feared that while his family had escaped their tragic flaws through death, he might be sentenced to a life of unhappiness, of emotional inertia, and of dulled contact with this world that he loved - while awaiting the self-delusion and self-destructiveness that clearly had manifested themselves in his family to fell him as well.

Clouds had returned and obscured the moon thus making the mountain invisible by the time the Corvette thundered past the turnoff to Promise. When he reached the FM 2132 cutoff short of Bethany, Tom realized that he was well on his way to blasting easily through his current record time for The Course. Past the cutoff he drew the appropriate mental "click" from downshifting to third to take the thirty-mile-per-hour turns at fifty. Rushing up through the "Esses" in the firm, road-hugging 'Vette was a thrill like nothing the Le Mans had ever provided.

Pervading all of the negative doubts and fears with which his emotions kept colliding around the bends and turns of The Course, though, was the warm glow of Clair's love. Tom smiled with unabashed optimism and hope in agreeing that having her in his life could make a difference, could give him the positive, supportive anchor that neither his parents nor Mark had had. But he also saw the opportunity to render an unselfish act by removing himself from Clair's life for her benefit no matter the cost to him - this under the assumption that his life and that of anyone who lived theirs close to his was doomed by the damage done to his psyche by the ways his family had lived and by the ways his family had died. Just before spiraling down into a labyrinth of despair, though, a voice from the side of his soul that wanted him to win whispered, 'Martyrdom, ah martyrdom, how seductive your siren call. Thanks again, Mom.'

Noting the absence of approaching headlights from either direction, Tom gunned the Corvette through the stop sign, flinging it off 2132 and onto Springfield Road. By the time he reached the brow of the hill that marked the start of the Holly Creek bottom straightaway - his *faux* Mulsanne - the speedometer neared one hundred. Diving down the hill, the sports car picked up speed. One hundred ten. One hundred twenty. Its stability at these speeds, to which the pilot was virgin, amazed him.

As he leveled out on the stretch of road across the bottom and began to set up for the narrow bridge and the kink in the straight just beyond it, Tom thought he caught a glimpse of something strange and stationary far down the straight close to the rise of the hill on the other side. He was uncertain as to what he had seen, and the approaching bridge rails obscured whatever it had been. And suddenly he was on the bridge. He glanced at the speedometer quickly enough to see that it was past one hundred thirty. Just as suddenly he was across the bridge and tweaking the steering wheel at the kink in the straight. He smiled as he realized he had made it through without lifting the accelerator.

The realignment of the path of the Corvette's headlights, though, clearly showed the objects that Tom's peripheral vision had hinted at earlier. For there blocking each lane of traffic were two of Old Man Helmsley's prize Jersey cows.

'Is this how it ends?!' the marquee in his mind flashed instantly. For an eternal millisecond he gave himself over to the Shortcut Home, to that Final Disappointment.

But his instinct was for Life. His reflexes took over and sent his right hand to grasp the chrome ball of his shifter and his left foot to hover vigilantly above the clutch pedal while he quickly lifted his right foot from the accelerator. He touched the brake pedal only enough to remind him of the danger of locking the brakes as the rear-end weaved slightly. Easing back down on the brake pedal, he began pumping it as he simultaneously hit the horn in hopes of frightening the cattle away from the road. They did not move but instead turned their heads to stare into the lights. Drawing closer, he considered going between them, but he knew it would mean taking off the head of one and the rump of the other, and a last second move by either could put her through the windshield and into the cockpit. At seventy he frantically geared down to third. The rear-end jerked a bit, but it brought his speed down more rapidly. The cow that was risking her head began to chew her cud as Tom, at forty miles-per-hour jammed the shift lever into second, let off on the clutch, and stood on the brakes. Though still not prodded to take evasive action, the cows' eyes had grown wide as at twenty he downshifted up into first and popped the clutch which, along with squealing tires and searing brakes, brought the car to a halt with a dead engine in the middle of the road ten feet short of the herd of two.

He gripped the steering wheel tightly and leaned his head against it for a moment. He looked up and glanced in his mirror and, noting no approaching traffic, shakily got out of the car. The lead cow mooed at him. After a moment of staring at her, Tom mooed back, and he began to laugh. Soon he was laughing uncontrollably with his arms and head sprawled across the Corvette's top. When he looked up again - still laughing and mooing - he noted that the cattle had moved off the road back toward Helmsley's fence. Glancing back toward the bridge, Tom shuddered at the image of throngs of junior high boys from all over East Texas – their fascination with gore, death and their accoutrements at its pinnacle at their age - combing the bottom for the myriad shards of electric blue fiberglas that would have been littered there. Returning to the Corvette's cockpit, he realized that his record run would have to wait until 1969. It would not be accomplished this night.

*   *   *

Tom parked on the knoll overlooking the lakehouse and the lake. After blowing a kiss to the Jerseys, he had cruised sedately past the Collum farm and through Piney. As he had approached the entrance to his farm, he felt drawn to it in search of an answer. Leaving the car, he observed the surroundings. Looking up from the lake into the heavens, all was quiet but for the song of the grasshoppers. Having cleared again, the sky was full of stars and a few blotchy clouds outlined by the light of the moon. Standing there as if awaiting a sign from God, a memory leapt out and surprised him.

It was of a similar night at least ten years earlier standing with his family at the same spot on the hill overlooking the lake. They had just left the lakehouse and were returning to their car. Suddenly, the night sky was made day as a brilliant yellow-orange flame rent the heavens above the lake cutting a giant fiery swath and turning the dark blue around them to bright purple. The four of them had been left agog and without explanation as no sound and no result had accompanied the fire that had spilled from the heavens as if God's flaming sword had pierced the veil of night, had ripped it in a gash downward, and was then returned to its scabbard. The next day the family had learned that it had been the explosion of an Air Force jet some twenty miles away.

Standing there now, Tom smiled at the remembrance of his disappointment that it had not been a sign from God - apocalyptic, redemptive, or otherwise. He wished for such a sign now - something sudden, stark, and irrefutable to tell him that his life was not hopeless, that his love for Clair was a positive step toward happiness for both of them, and that it was not the destructive delusion that he feared. As he stood on the brow of the hill now recalling the incident, the coincidence that his parents had died in such an explosion came to him moments later. His initial reaction was one of shame that it had taken him several moments and a head full of thoughts before realizing the morbid tie-in. 'Ah, well,' he thought, 'ashamed in front of whom? You'll forgive me, won't you, God? For that and so much more. For all of it. That's what you do. Right?' Looking Heavenward, he added, 'Okay, and while we're having this chat - You *do* love me, don't You? Yeah, well, I love You, too. And I've missed You.'

Looking back down at the lake in the light of the moon that had again freed itself of the clouds, Tom thought first of Clair. By the pond those years ago, by the fire at Thanksgiving, at Fat City, at the picnic table under the giant oak, on the porch at Gramma's. And his mind drifted on to Dallas and to WSU, to thoughts of Brandeis and of Siobhan. The swim meet ... *Wait Until Dark* ... Nopalito's ... on the banks of Lake Michigan and of the Mississippi ... the look on Siobhan's face at the wedding when she gently patted the new life within her ... the two of them by this same lake asprawl on the grass. And glancing at the dock, Tom remembered a perfect summer day when he had fished from the roof of the boathouse while Mark lay beside him on the giant antique quilt reading. Johnny was mowing the lawn, and the fragrance of the freshly mowed St. Augustine wafted over the lake. Nancy, wearing a bright floral sundress, had made lemonade, tuna salad sandwiches, and chocolate chip cookies and had brought them down to the boys ...

As clouds passed in front of the moon, the lake ceased to glisten, and Tom returned from his reverie. Leaning back against the Corvette, he folded his arms and spoke aloud, "I think all of you who have gone before ... love me ... and want me to be happy ... and I love all of you."

Driving carefully the rest of The Course back toward New Fredonia, Tom turned on the radio to still his emotions. Interrupting The Seekers, he listened as they sang:

' ... It's a long, long journey, so stay by my side.
When I walk through the storm, you'll be my guide.
If they gave me a fortune, my treasure would be small.
I could lose it all tomorrow and never mind at all,
But if I should lose your love, dear,
I don't know what I'd do
'Cause I know I'll never find another you ... '

Pulling up slowly to the start-finish line intersection, the Corvette's throaty exhaust panting in anticipation, Tom hesitated momentarily. Finally, his expression cleared and a smile eased across his face - as he cut the wheel toward Promise.

THE END